dave roman
astronaut academy
Zero Gravity

:01

First Second

New York & London

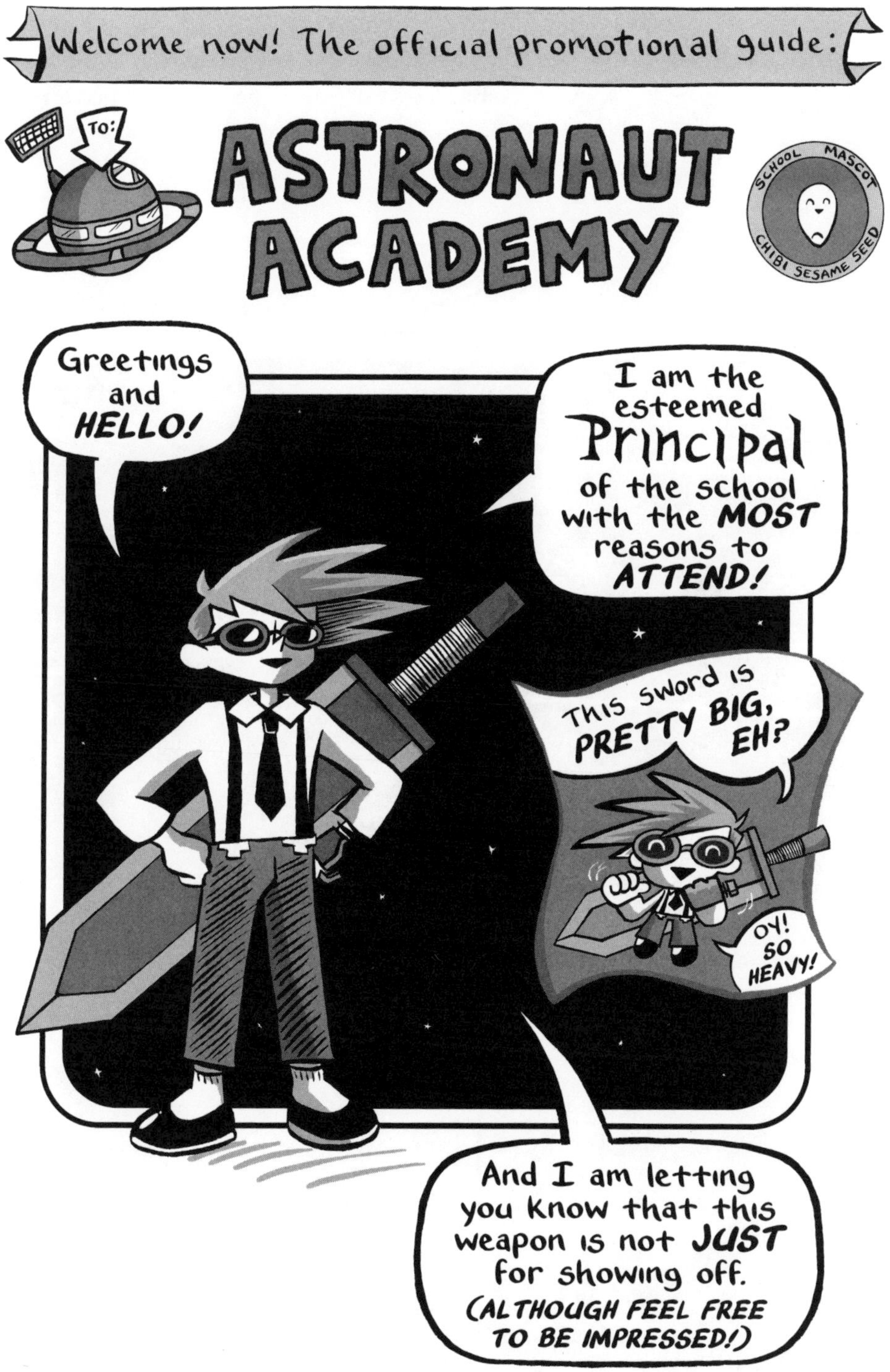
Welcome now! The official promotional guide:
TO:
ASTRONAUT ACADEMY
SCHOOL MASCOT CHIBI SESAME SEED
Greetings and HELLO!
I am the esteemed Principal of the school with the MOST reasons to ATTEND!
This Sword is PRETTY BIG, EH?
OY! SO HEAVY!
And I am letting you know that this weapon is not JUST for showing off.
(ALTHOUGH FEEL FREE TO BE IMPRESSED!)

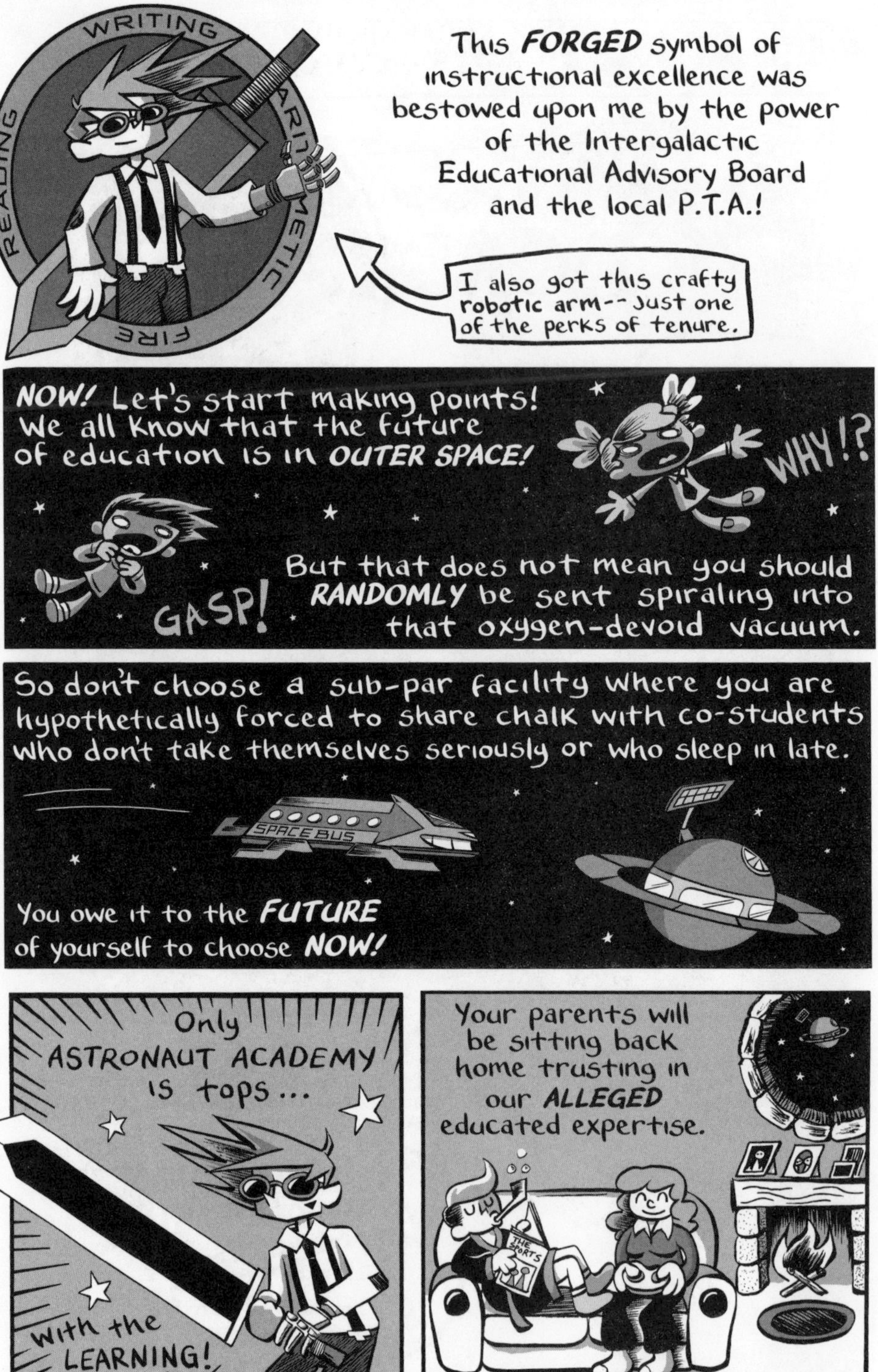
WRITING
ARITHMETIC
FIRE
READING
This **FORGED** symbol of instructional excellence was bestowed upon me by the power of the Intergalactic Educational Advisory Board and the local P.T.A.!
I also got this crafty robotic arm--just one of the perks of tenure.
NOW! Let's start making points! We all know that the future of education is in **OUTER SPACE!**
WHY!?
GASP!
But that does not mean you should **RANDOMLY** be sent spiraling into that oxygen-devoid vacuum.
So don't choose a sub-par facility where you are hypothetically forced to share chalk with co-students who don't take themselves seriously or who sleep in late.
SPACE BUS
You owe it to the **FUTURE** of yourself to choose **NOW!**
Only ASTRONAUT ACADEMY is tops...
with the LEARNING!
Your parents will be sitting back home trusting in our **ALLEGED** educated expertise.
THE SPORTS

A diverse curriculum means

MANY CLASSES TO CHOOSE!

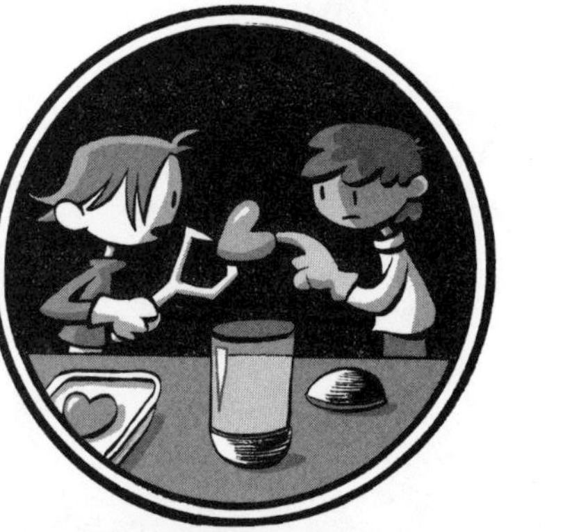

ADVANCED HEART STUDIES!

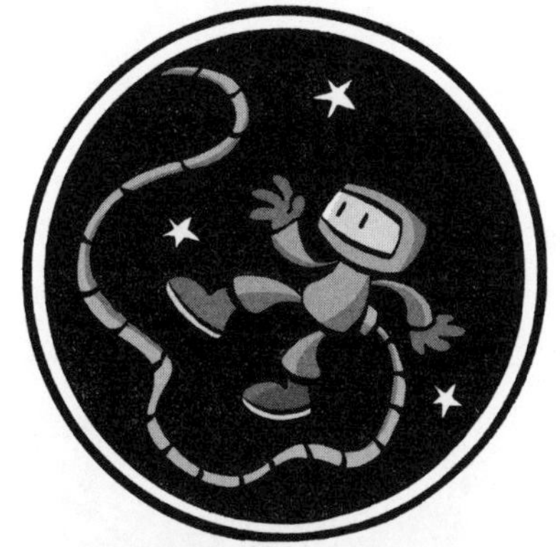

ANTI-GRAVITY GYMNASTICS!

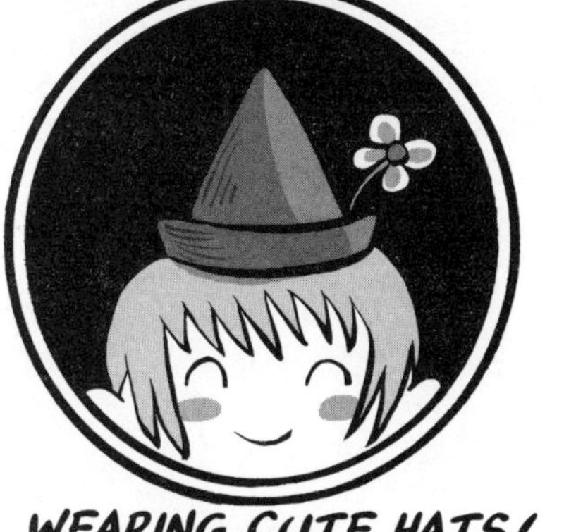

WEARING CUTE HATS!

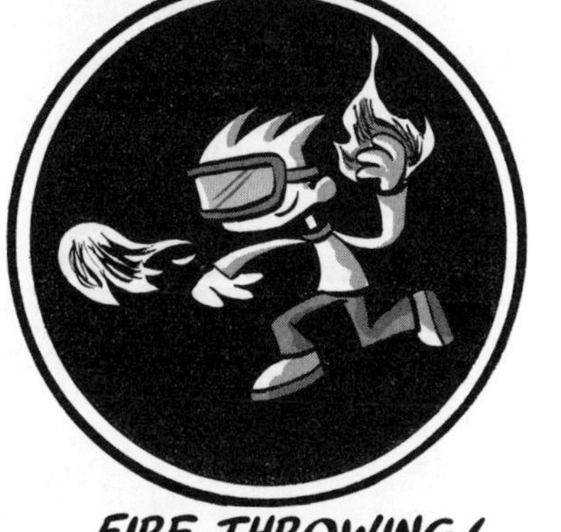

FIRE THROWING!

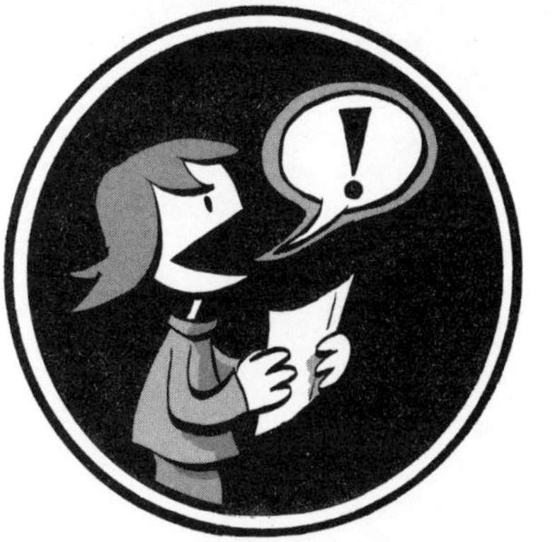
!

RUN-ON SENTENCES!

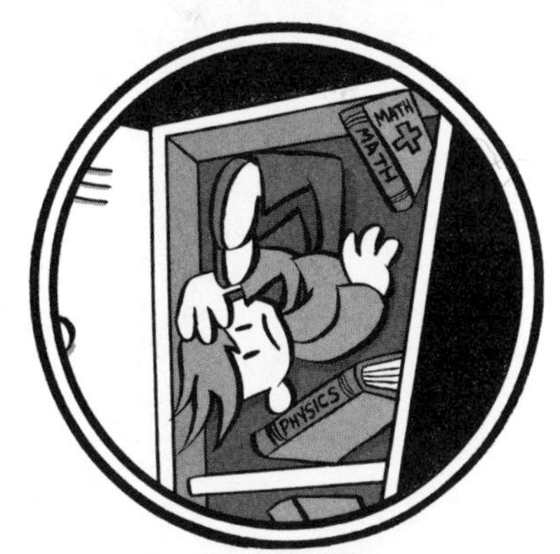
MATH
MATH
PHYSICS

LOCKER!

AND SEVERAL OTHERS!!! (without illustrated examples)

If dominating test scores is as important to ***YOU*** as it is to ***MY SWORD***, then you'll love that our teachers are on ***PAYROLL!***

LIKE: Mrs. Bunn

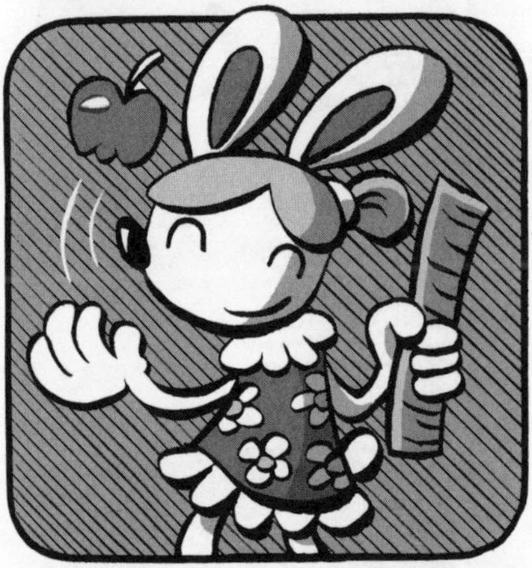

Who is old enough to know so many answers to ***QUESTIONS!***
(YOU MIGHT BE IMPRESSED!)

AND: Mr. Namagucci

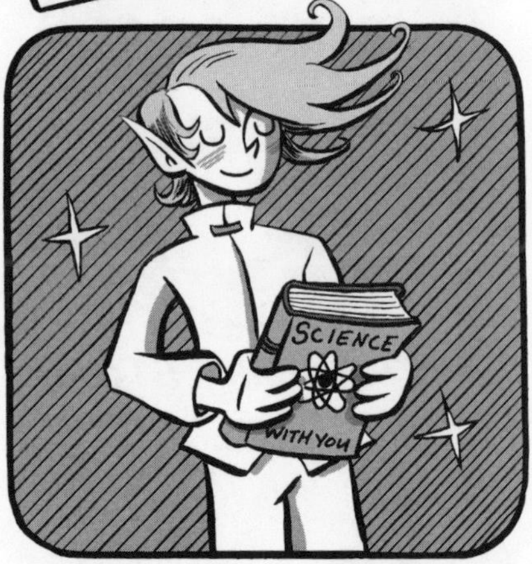
SCIENCE
WITH YOU

Who may or may not have magical powers but is still ***HANDSOME!***
(ASK AROUND!)

AS WELL AS: Señor Panda

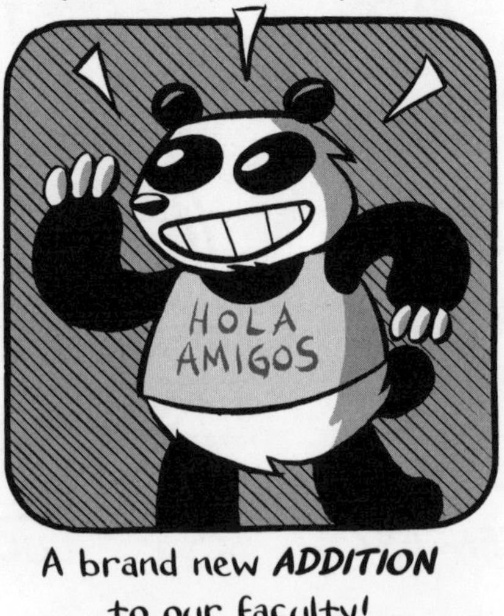
HOLA AMIGOS

A brand new ***ADDITION*** to our faculty!
(STILL NOT EXTINCT!)

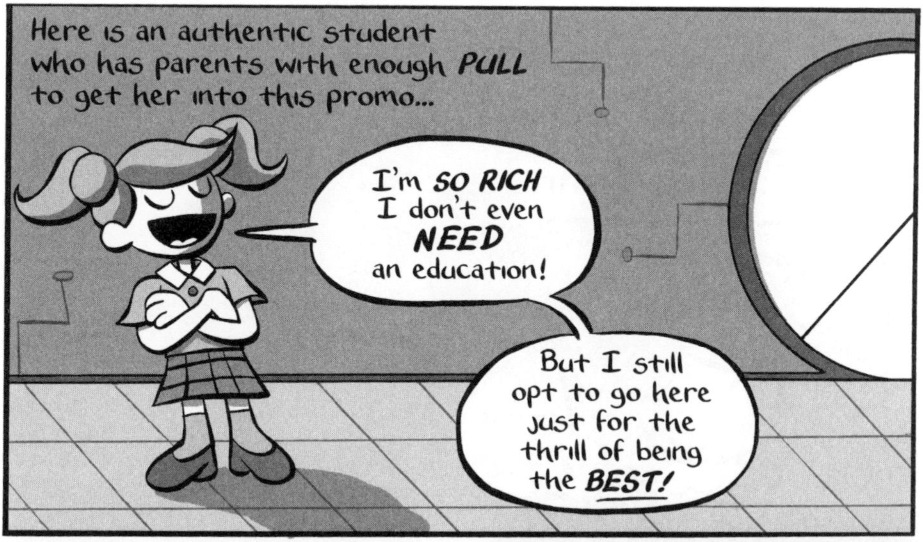
Here is an authentic student who has parents with enough PULL to get her into this promo...
I'm SO RICH I don't even NEED an education!
But I still opt to go here just for the thrill of being the BEST!

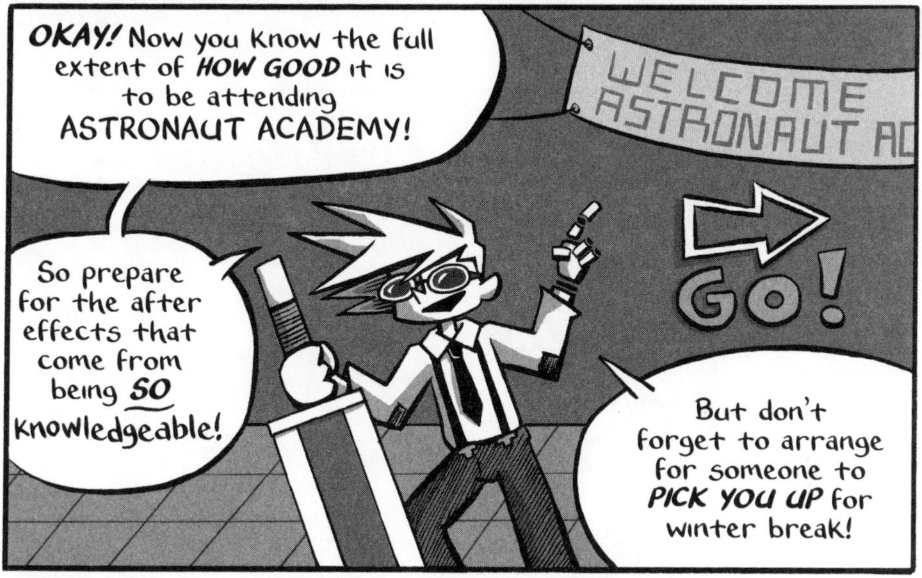
OKAY! Now you know the full extent of HOW GOOD it is to be attending ASTRONAUT ACADEMY!
WELCOME ASTRONAUT AC
So prepare for the after effects that come from being SO knowledgeable!
GO!
But don't forget to arrange for someone to PICK YOU UP for winter break!

FULL TIME SCHOOL APPLICATION

Applicant's Name: Hakata Soy — Alias (if applicable): Wolf Leader

Signal Code: 66212 — Current # of Hearts: 2

Address of Origin: Metador Station, Delta Quad, L3

Completed Schooling: (W) PRE-K K AE — Previous School Attended: N/A

Parent[s] Name: Ananth & Akima — Parent/Guardian's Signal code: 66210

Has your child received anti-gravity training? (Y) N

Does your child have heart conditions? (Y) N

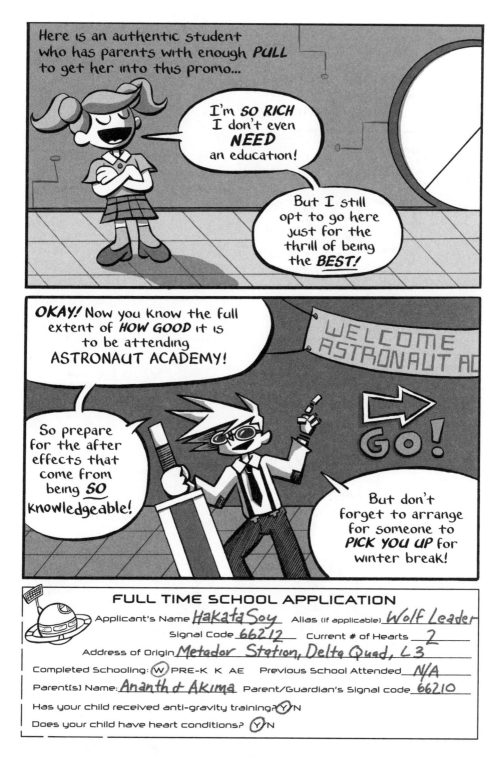

astronaut academy

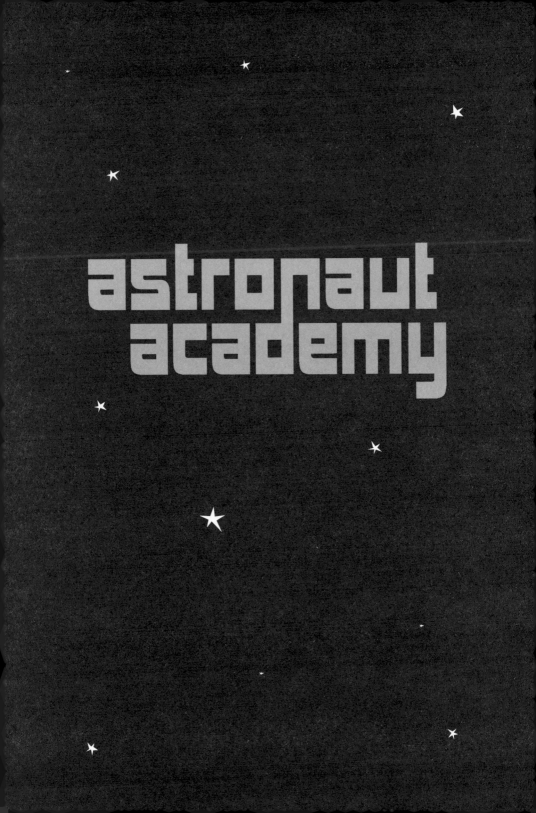

first semester

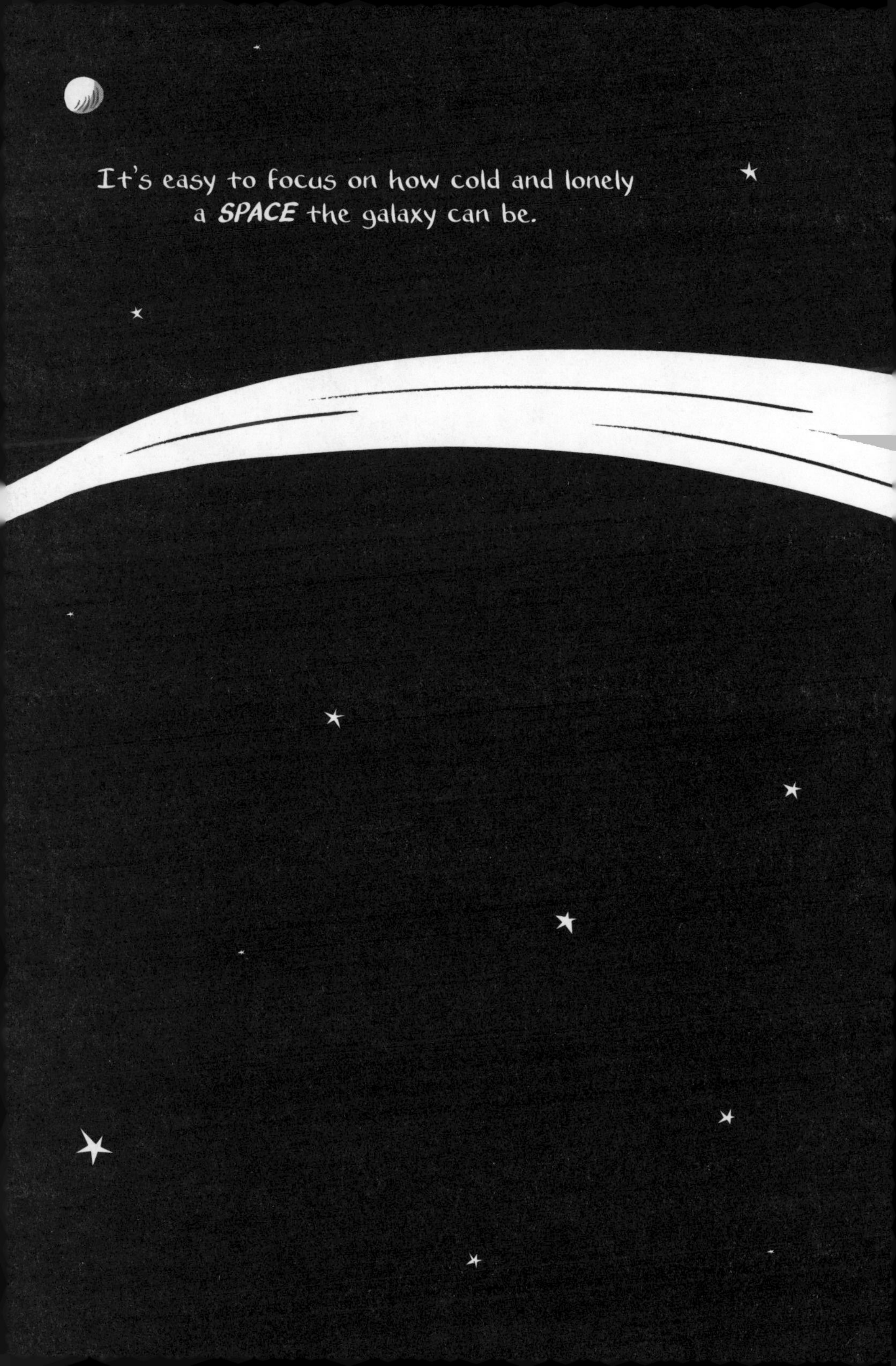
It's easy to focus on how cold and lonely a SPACE the galaxy can be.

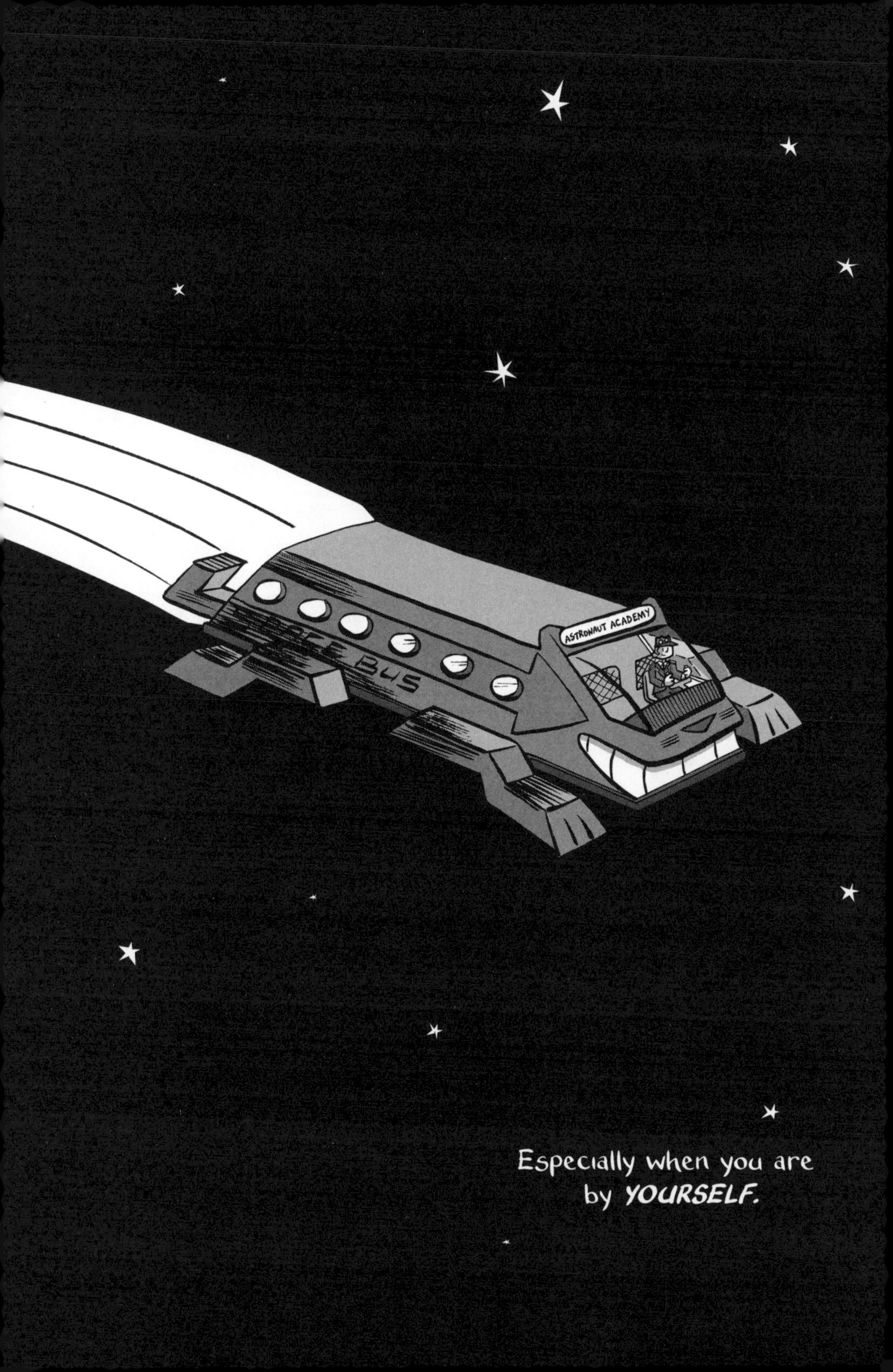
ASTRONAUT ACADEMY
Especially when you are
by YOURSELF.

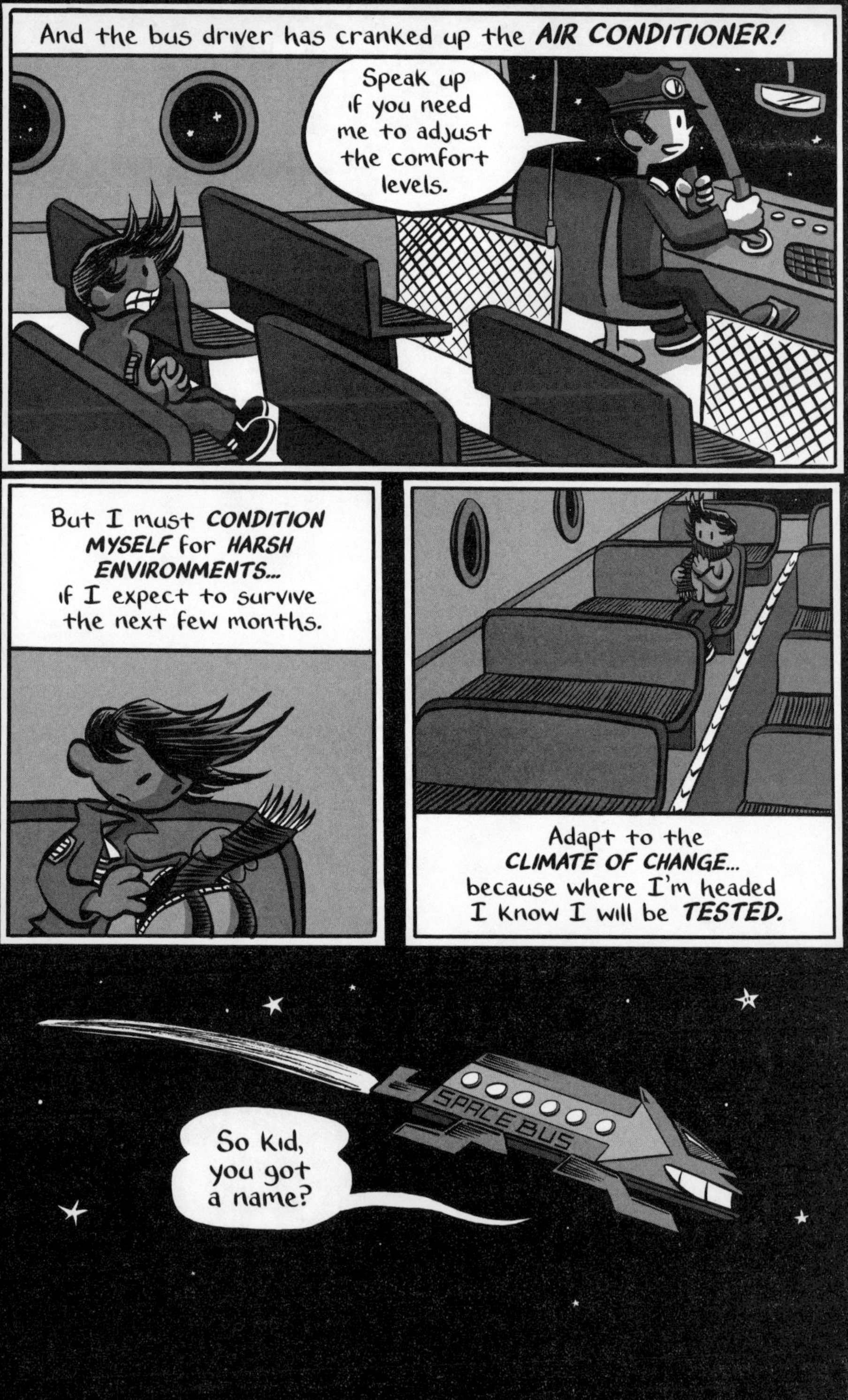

And the bus driver has cranked up the AIR CONDITIONER!
Speak up if you need me to adjust the comfort levels.
But I must CONDITION MYSELF for HARSH ENVIRONMENTS... if I expect to survive the next few months.
Adapt to the CLIMATE OF CHANGE... because where I'm headed I know I will be TESTED.
SPACE BUS
So kid, you got a name?

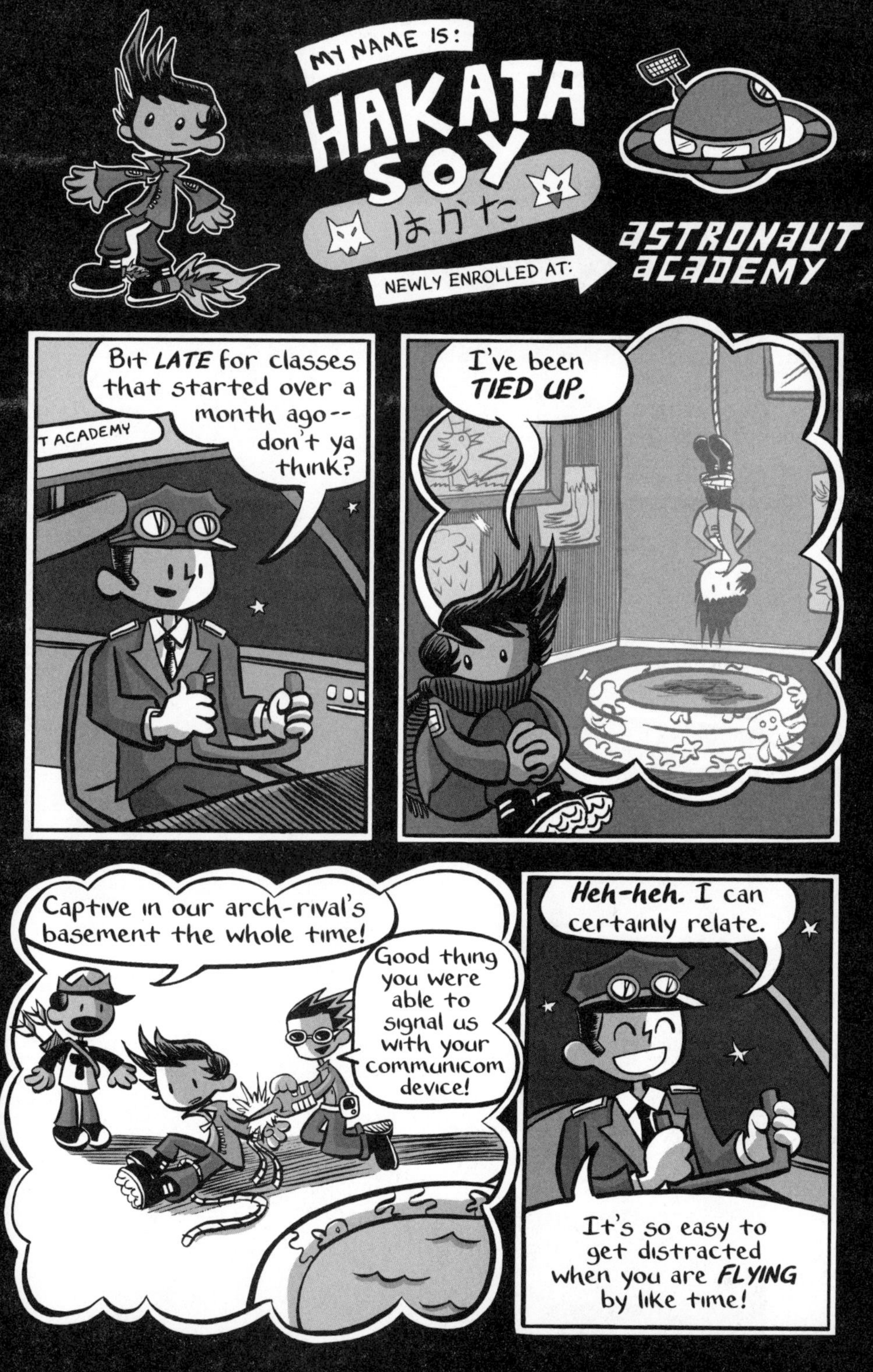
MY NAME IS:
HAKATA SOY
はかた
NEWLY ENROLLED AT:
ASTRONAUT ACADEMY
T ACADEMY
Bit LATE for classes that started over a month ago-- don't ya think?
I've been TIED UP.
Captive in our arch-rival's basement the whole time!
Good thing you were able to signal us with your communicom device!
Heh-heh. I can certainly relate.
It's so easy to get distracted when you are FLYING by like time!

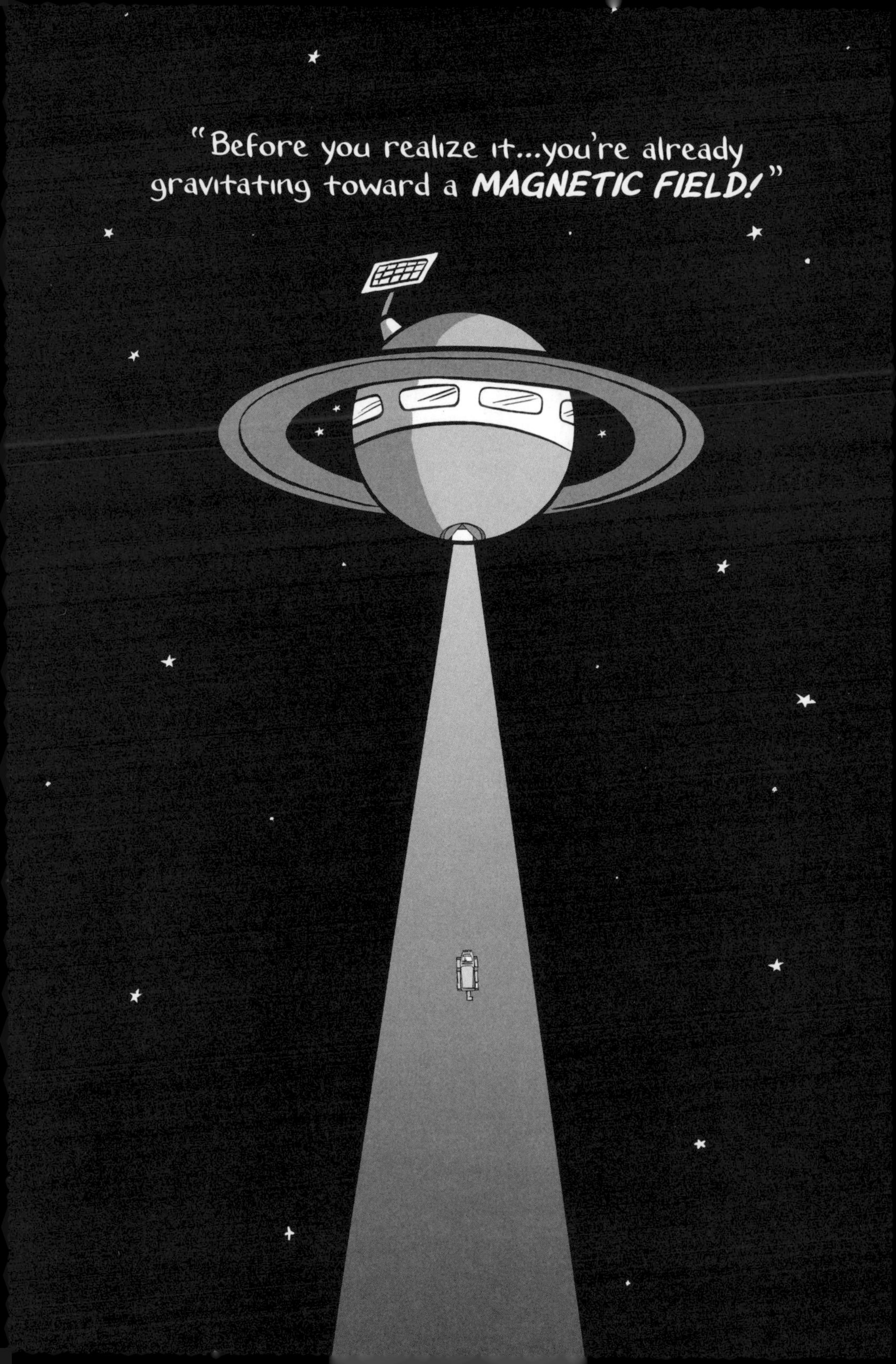
"Before you realize it...you're already gravitating toward a MAGNETIC FIELD!"

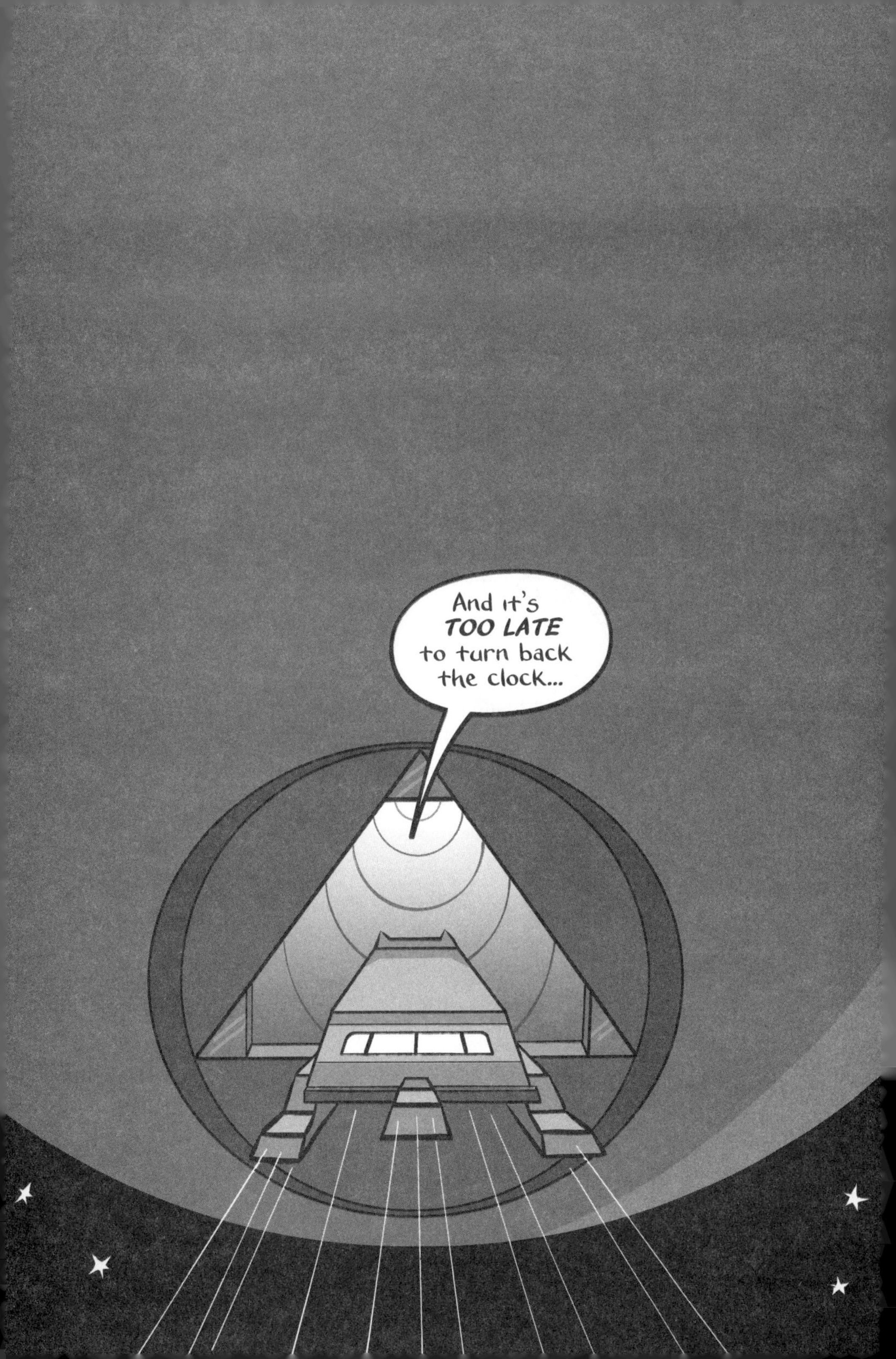
And it's TOO LATE to turn back the clock...

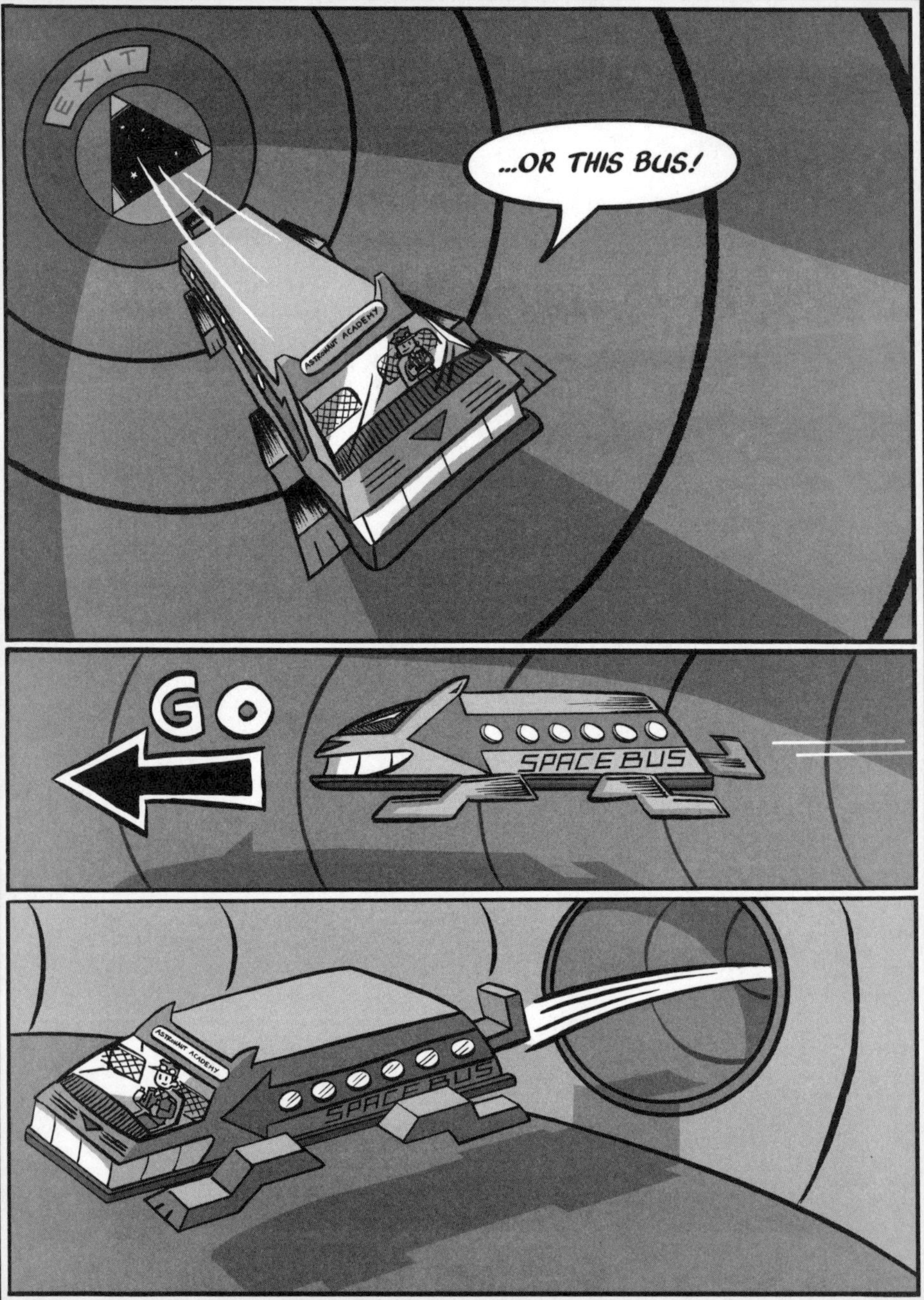
EXIT
...OR THIS BUS!
ASTRONAUT ACADEMY
GO
SPACE BUS
ASTRONAUT ACADEMY
SPACE BUS

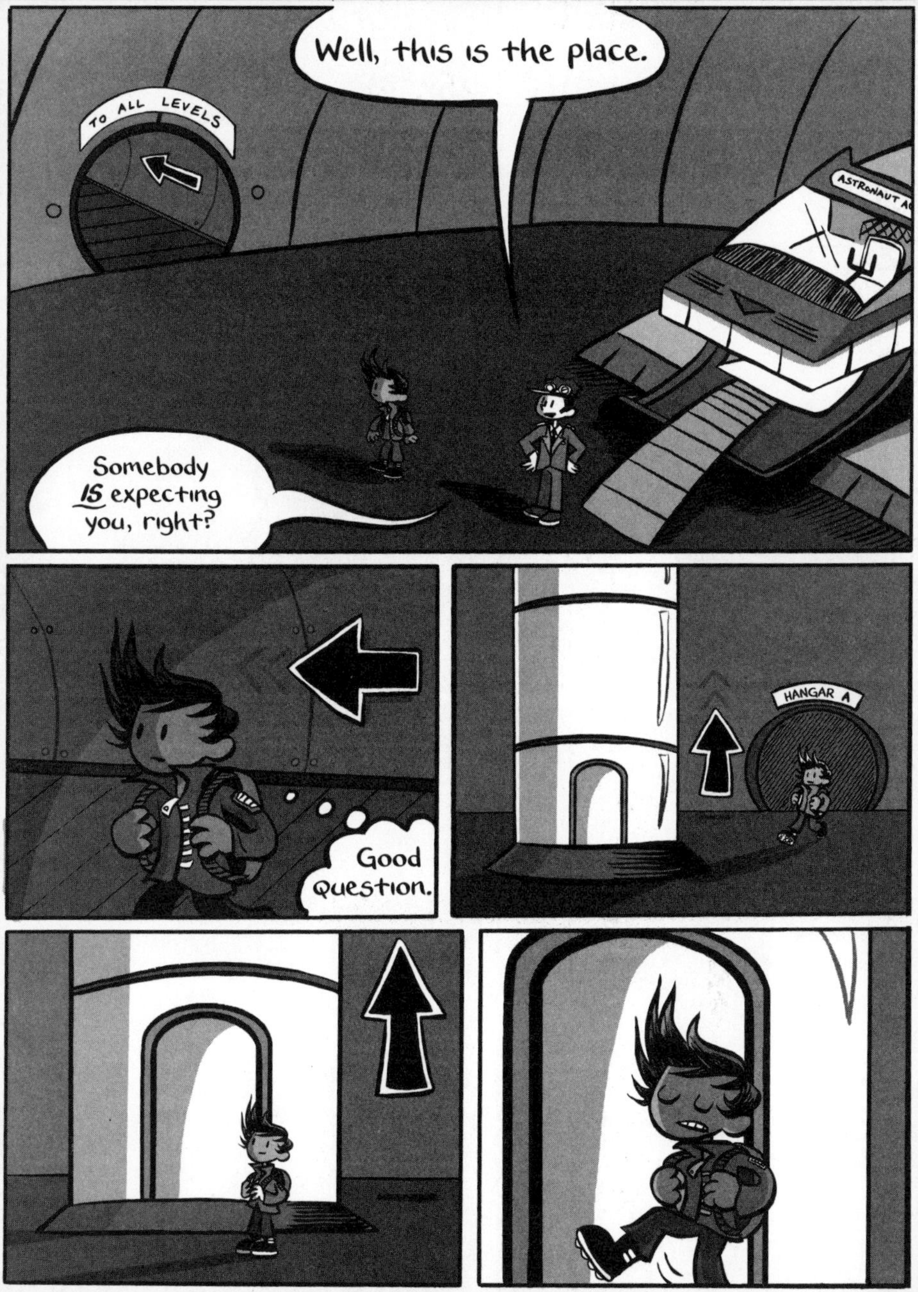
Well, this is the place.
TO ALL LEVELS
ASTRONAUT A
Somebody IS expecting you, right?
Good Question.
HANGAR A

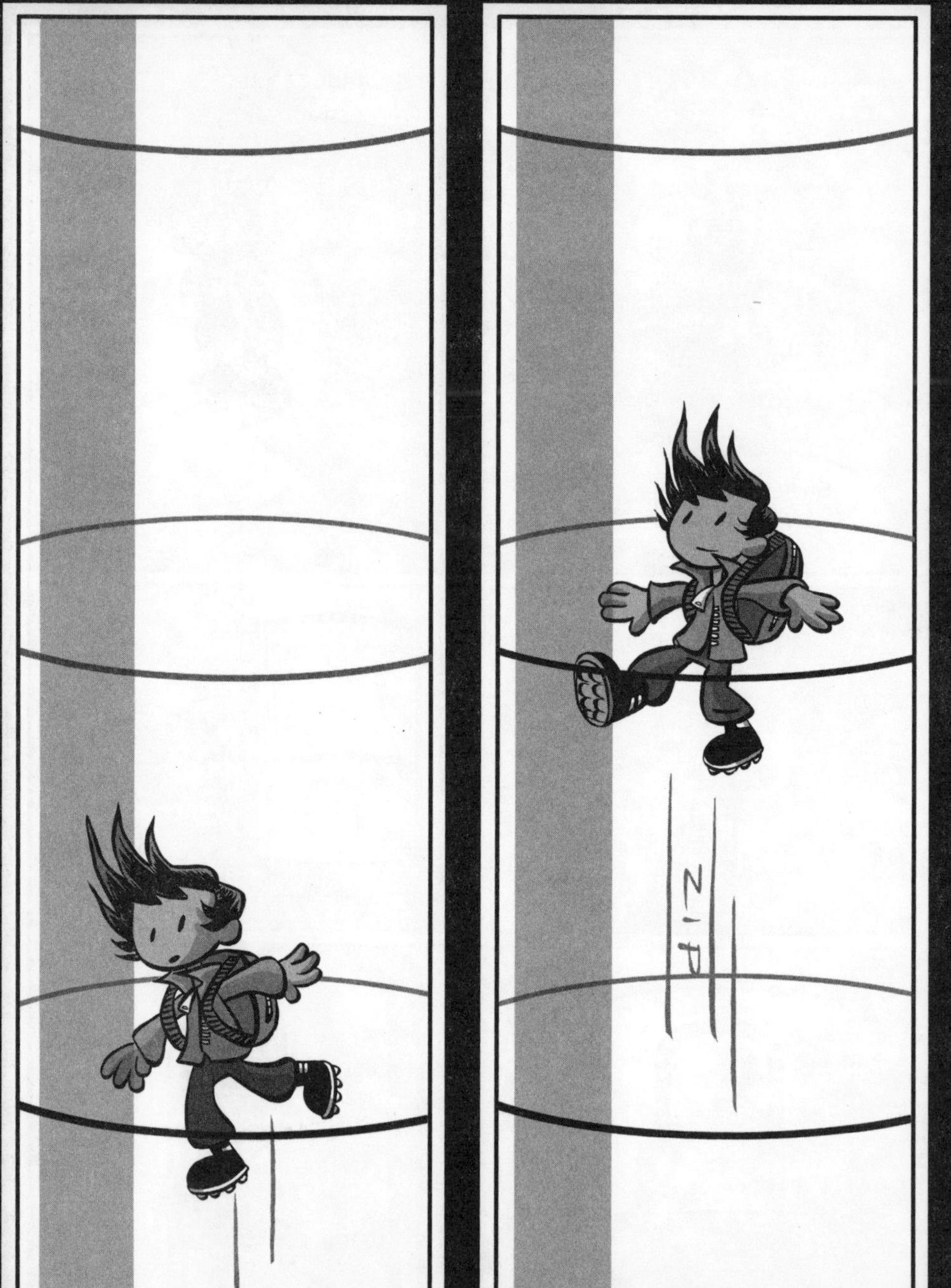
ZIP

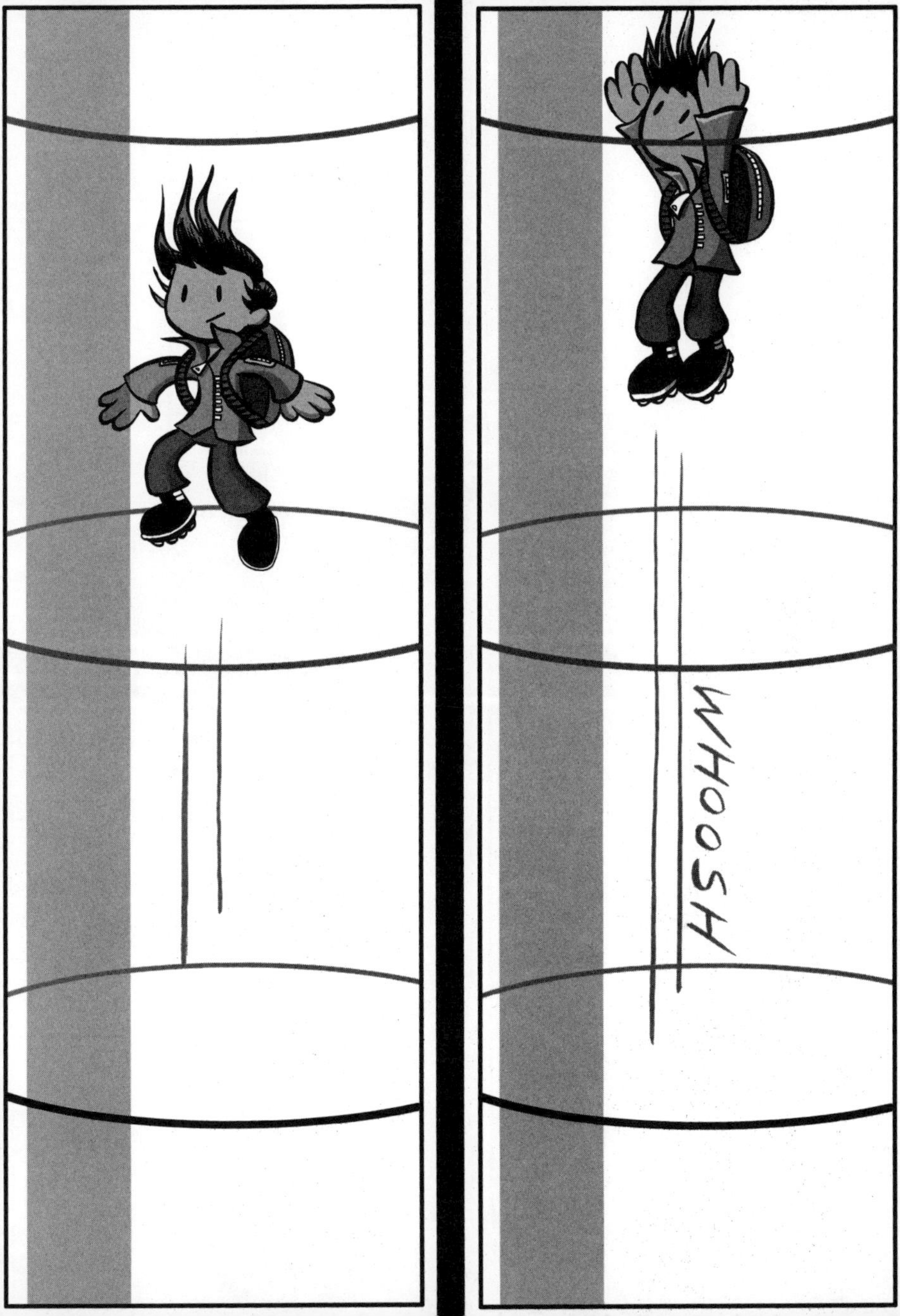
WHOOSH

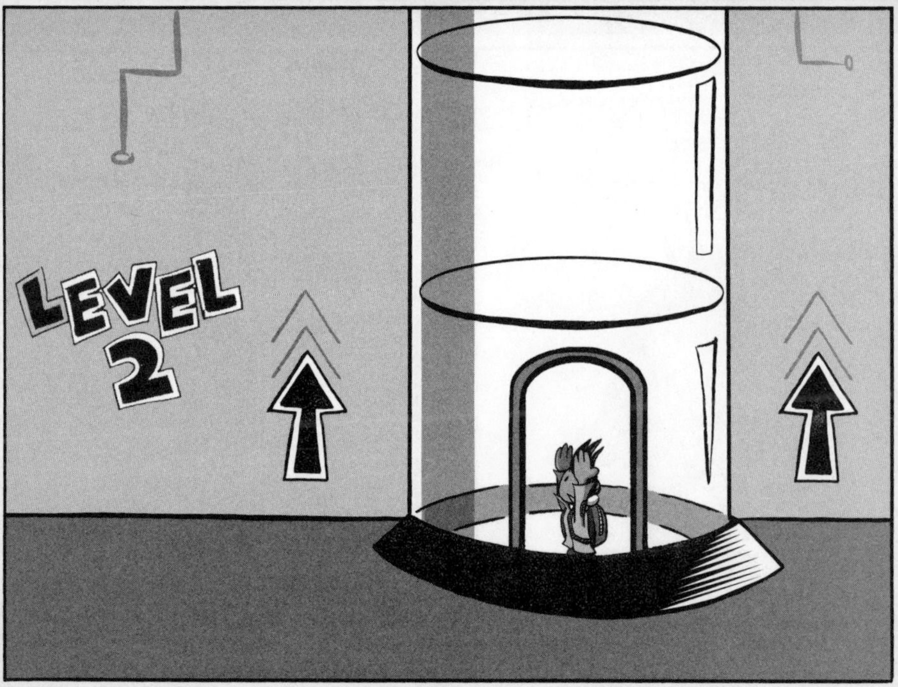
LEVEL
2

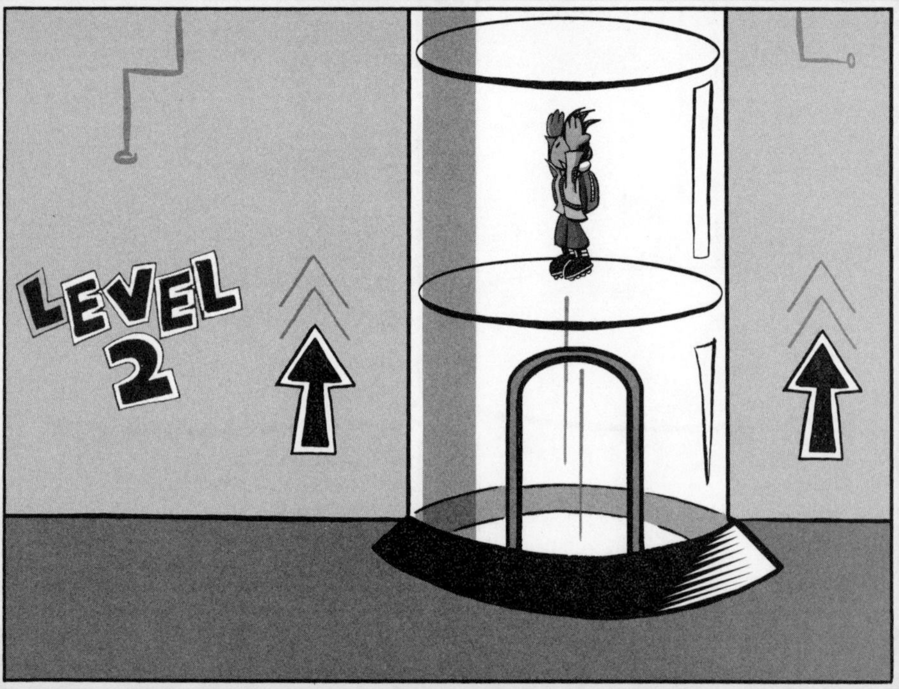
LEVEL
2

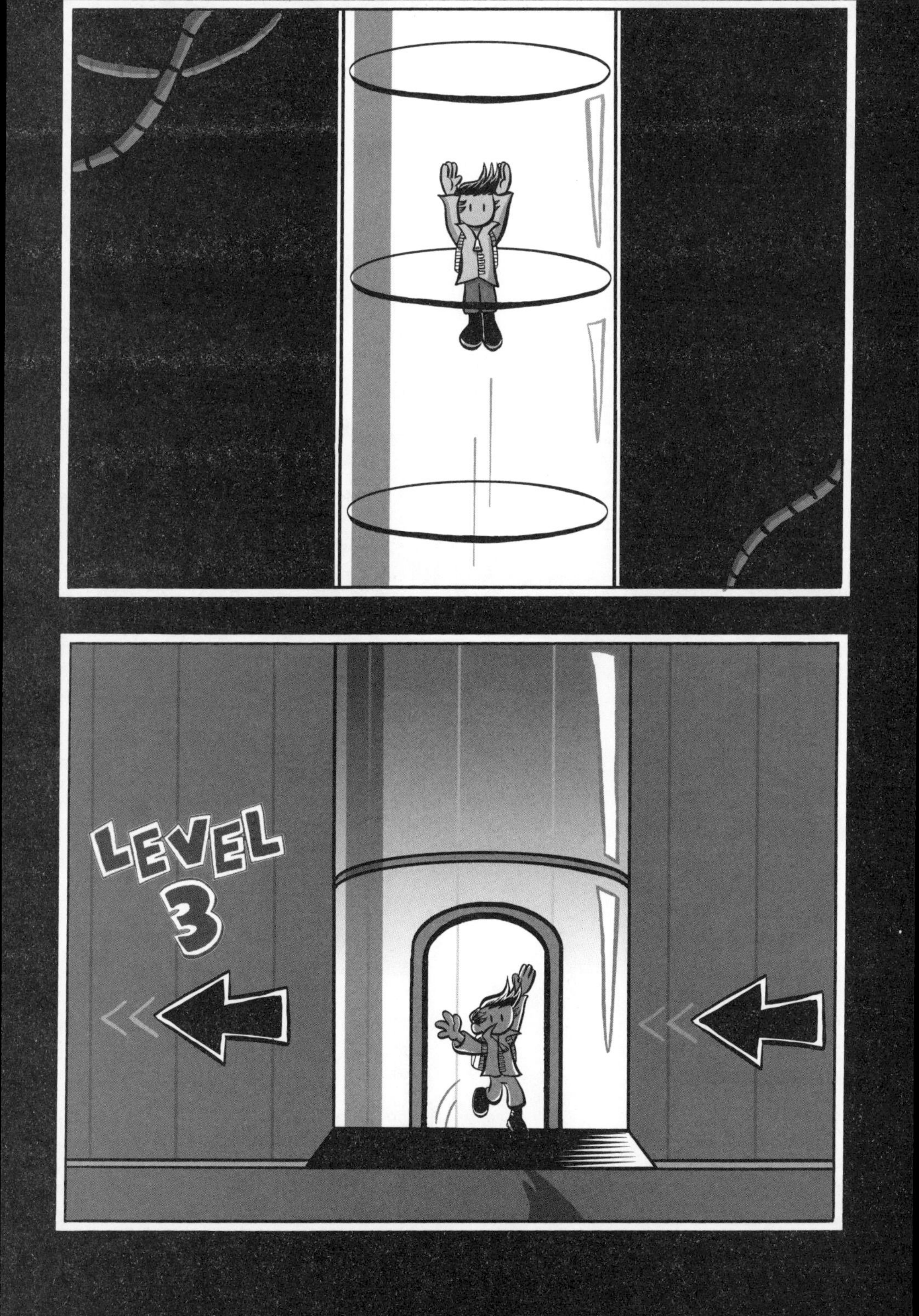
LEVEL
3

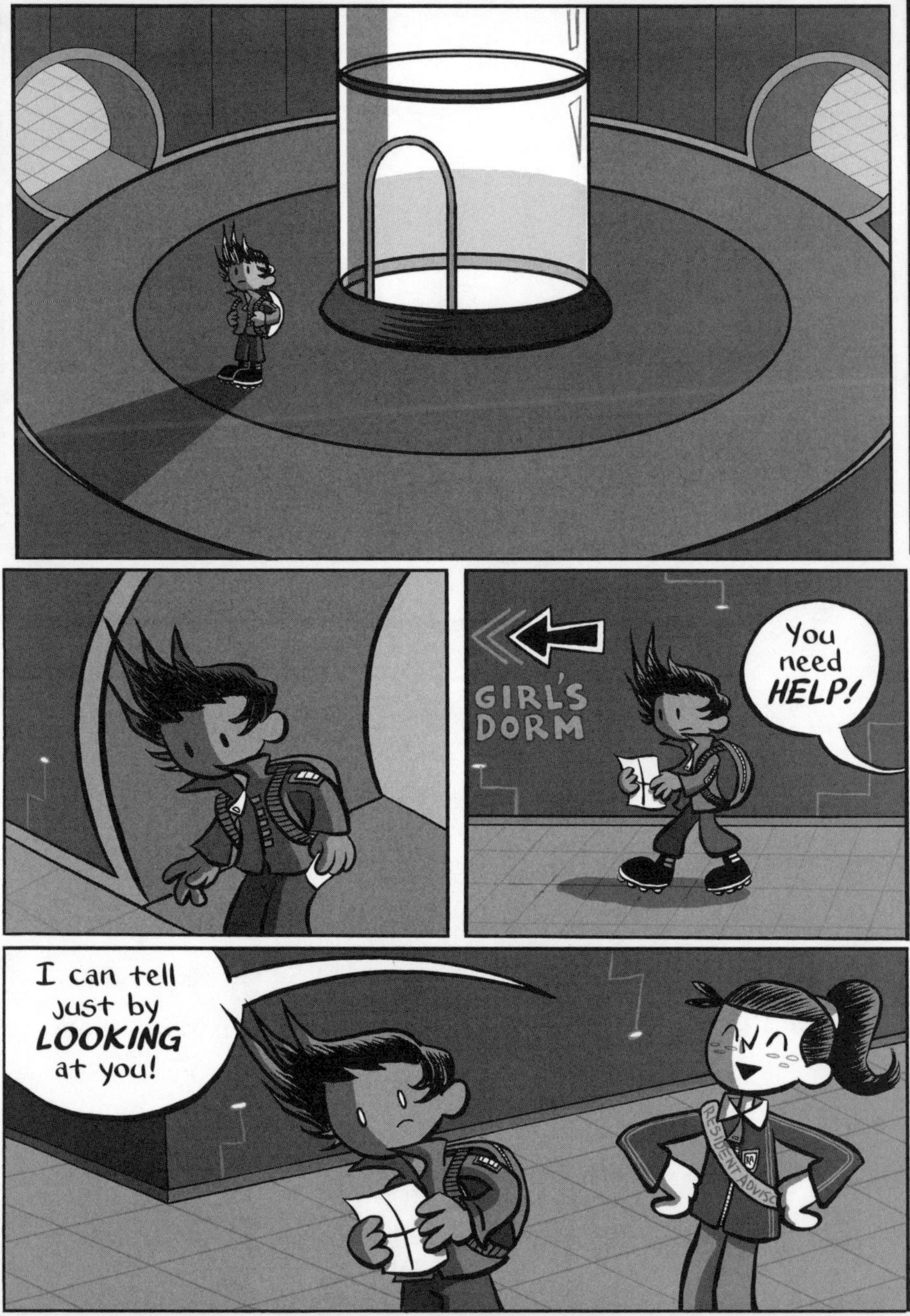
GIRL'S DORM
You need HELP!
I can tell just by LOOKING at you!
RESIDENT ADVISO

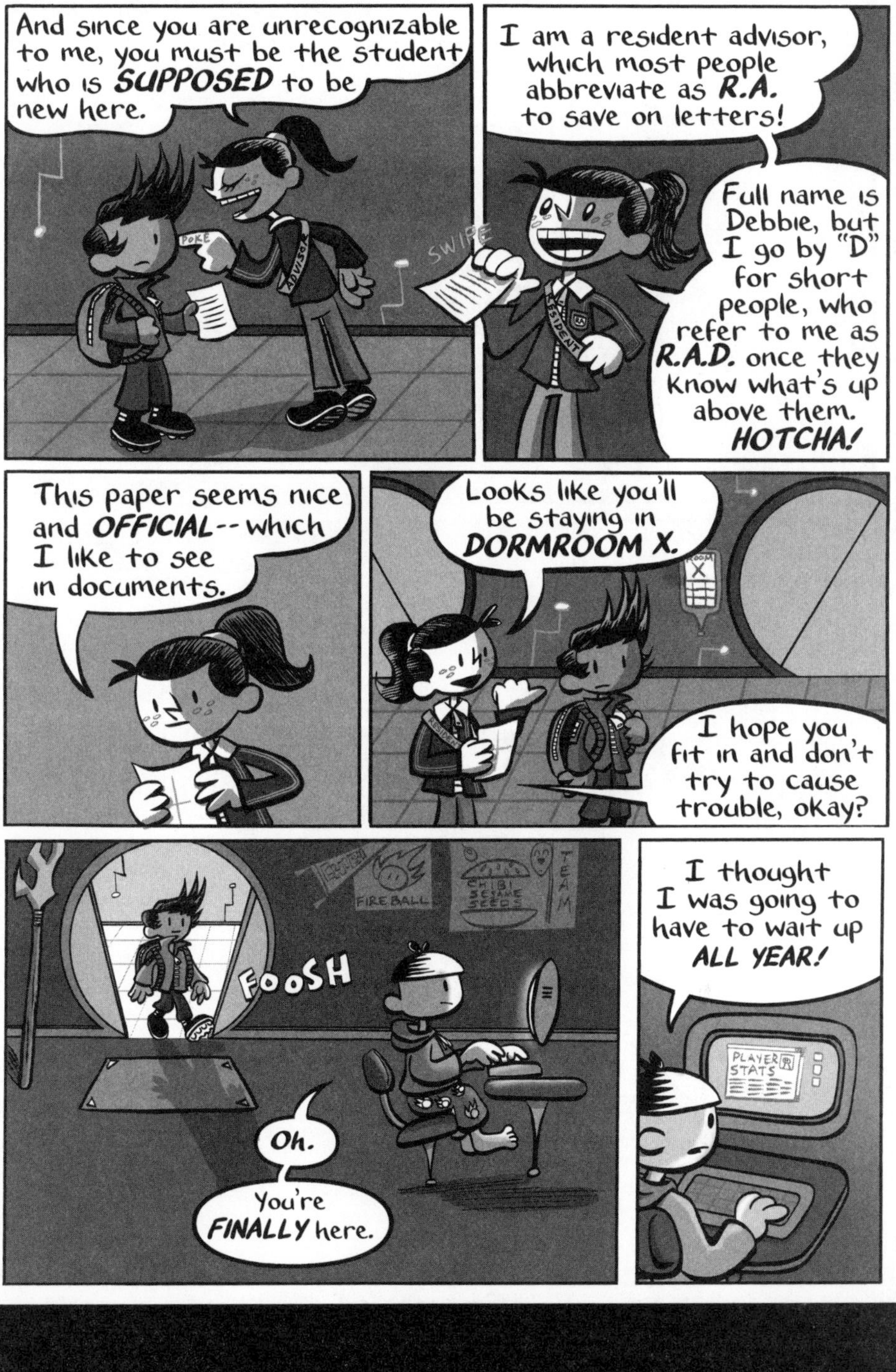
And since you are unrecognizable to me, you must be the student who is SUPPOSED to be new here.
POKE
ADVISOR
I am a resident advisor, which most people abbreviate as R.A. to save on letters!
SWIPE
RESIDENT
Full name is Debbie, but I go by "D" for short people, who refer to me as R.A.D. once they know what's up above them. HOTCHA!
This paper seems nice and OFFICIAL-- which I like to see in documents.
Looks like you'll be staying in DORMROOM X.
ROOM X
I hope you fit in and don't try to cause trouble, okay?
FIREBALL
CHIBI SESAME SEEDS
TEAM
FOOSH
Oh.
You're FINALLY here.
I thought I was going to have to wait up ALL YEAR!
PLAYER STATS

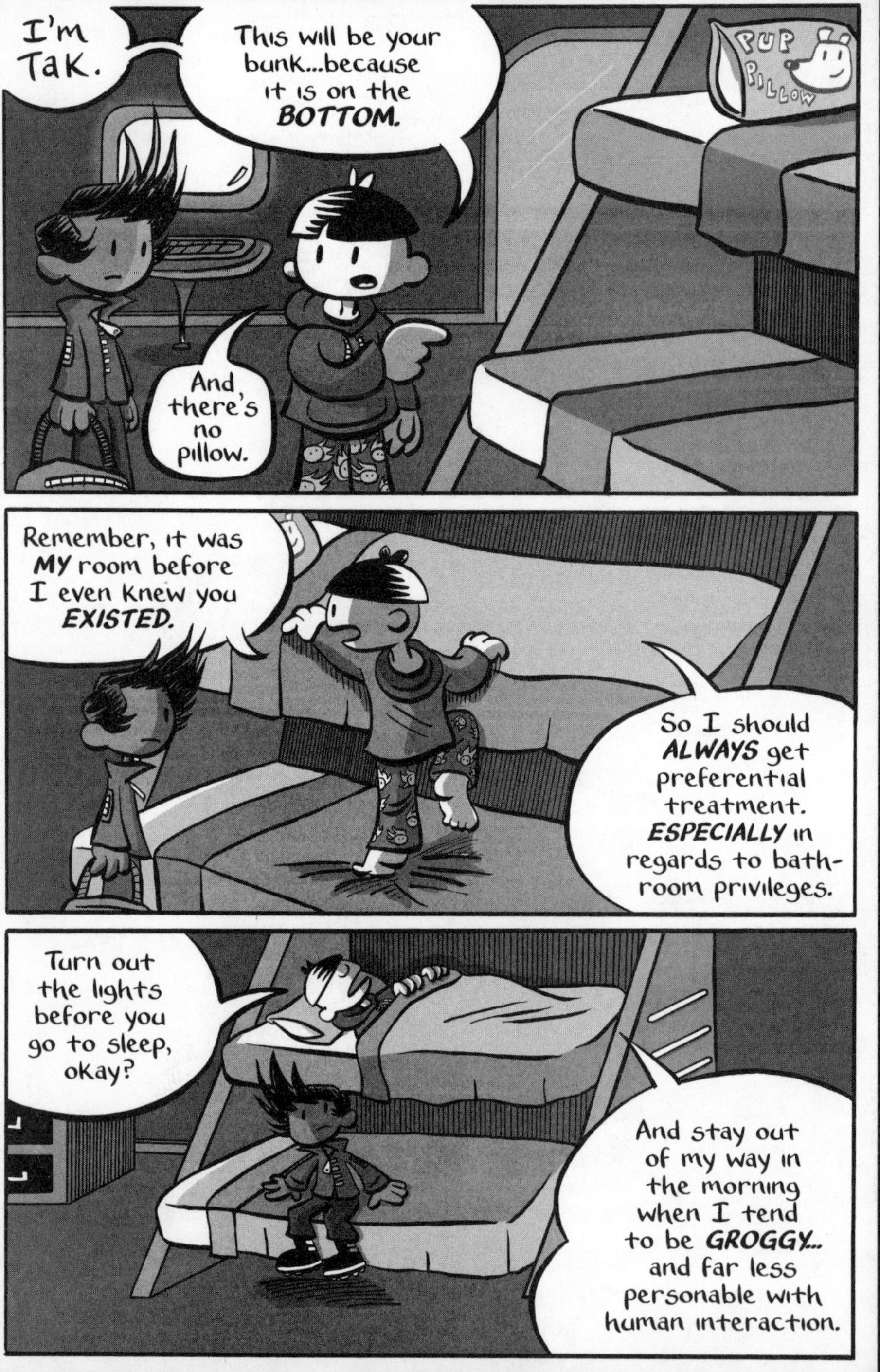

I'm TaK.
This will be your bunk...because it is on the BOTTOM.
PUP PILLOW
And there's no pillow.
Remember, it was MY room before I even knew you EXISTED.
So I should ALWAYS get preferential treatment. ESPECIALLY in regards to bathroom privileges.
Turn out the lights before you go to sleep, okay?
And stay out of my way in the morning when I tend to be GROGGY... and far less personable with human interaction.

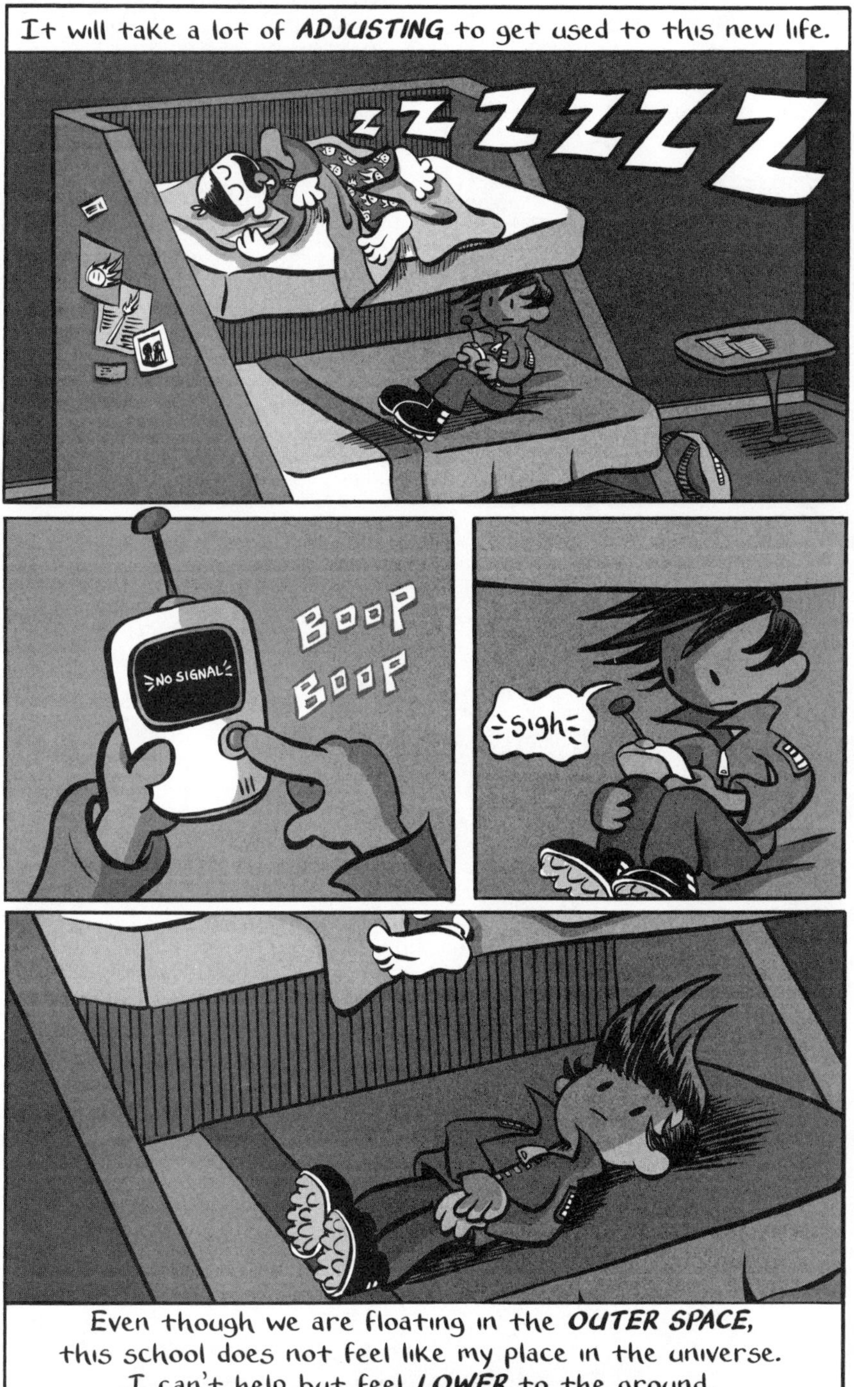
It will take a lot of ADJUSTING to get used to this new life.
ZZZZZZZ
NO SIGNAL
BOOP
BOOP
Sigh
Even though we are floating in the OUTER SPACE,
this school does not feel like my place in the universe.
I can't help but feel LOWER to the ground.

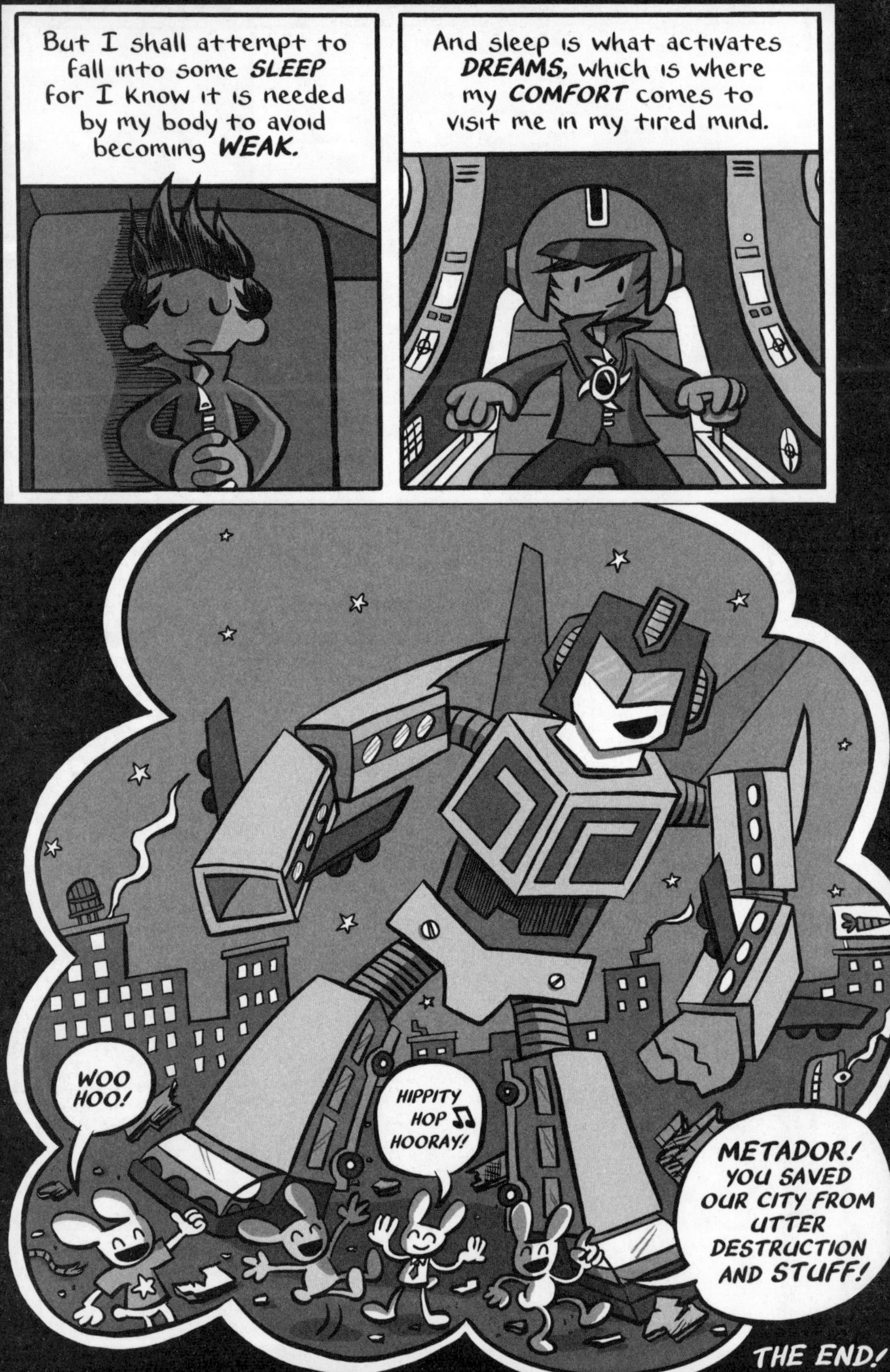
But I shall attempt to fall into some SLEEP for I know it is needed by my body to avoid becoming WEAK.
And sleep is what activates DREAMS, which is where my COMFORT comes to visit me in my tired mind.
WOO HOO!
HIPPITY HOP ♫ HOORAY!
METADOR! YOU SAVED OUR CITY FROM UTTER DESTRUCTION AND STUFF!
THE END!

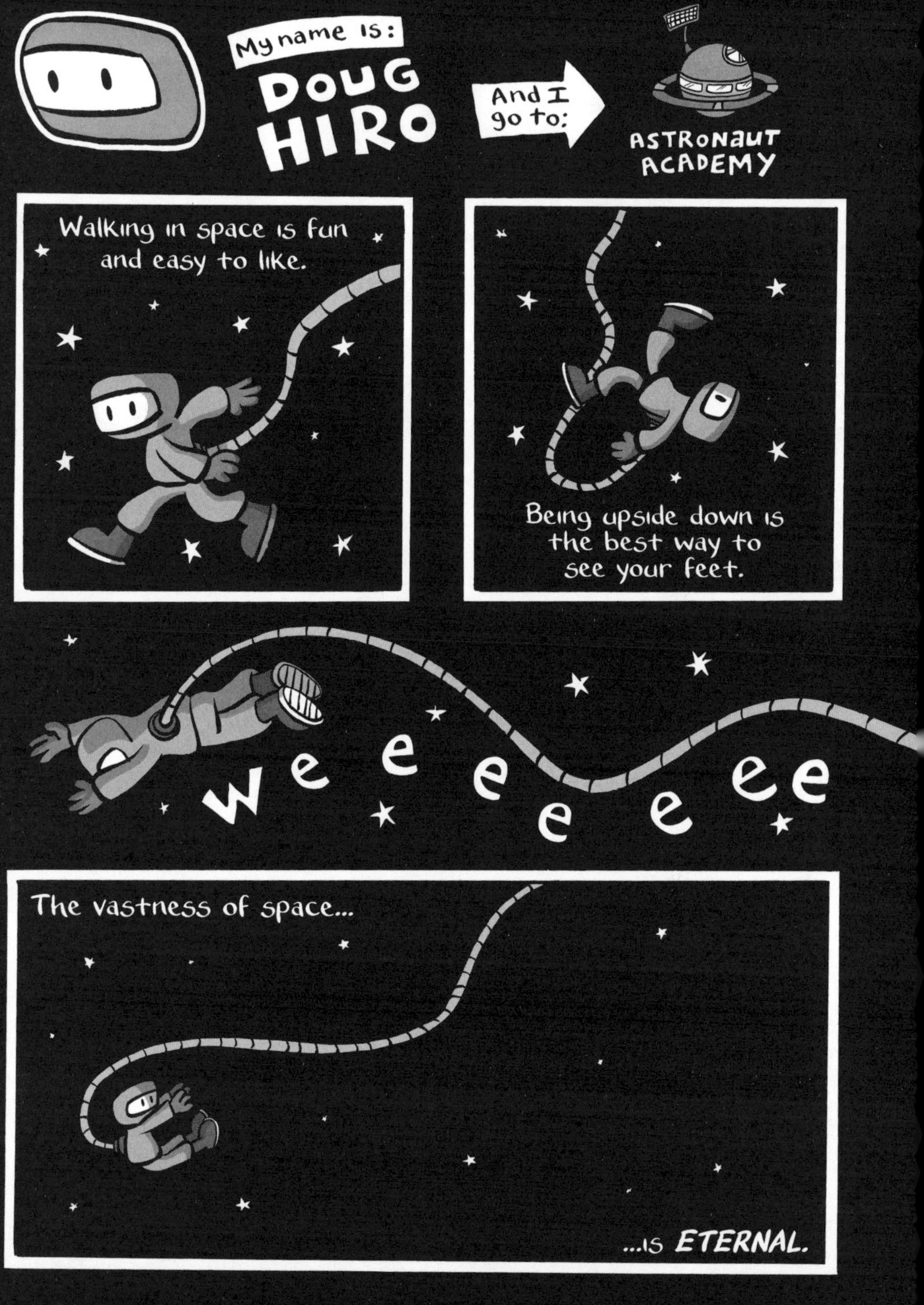

My name is:
DOUG HIRO
And I go to:
ASTRONAUT ACADEMY
Walking in space is fun and easy to like.
Being upside down is the best way to see your feet.
weeeeeeee
The vastness of space...
...is ETERNAL.

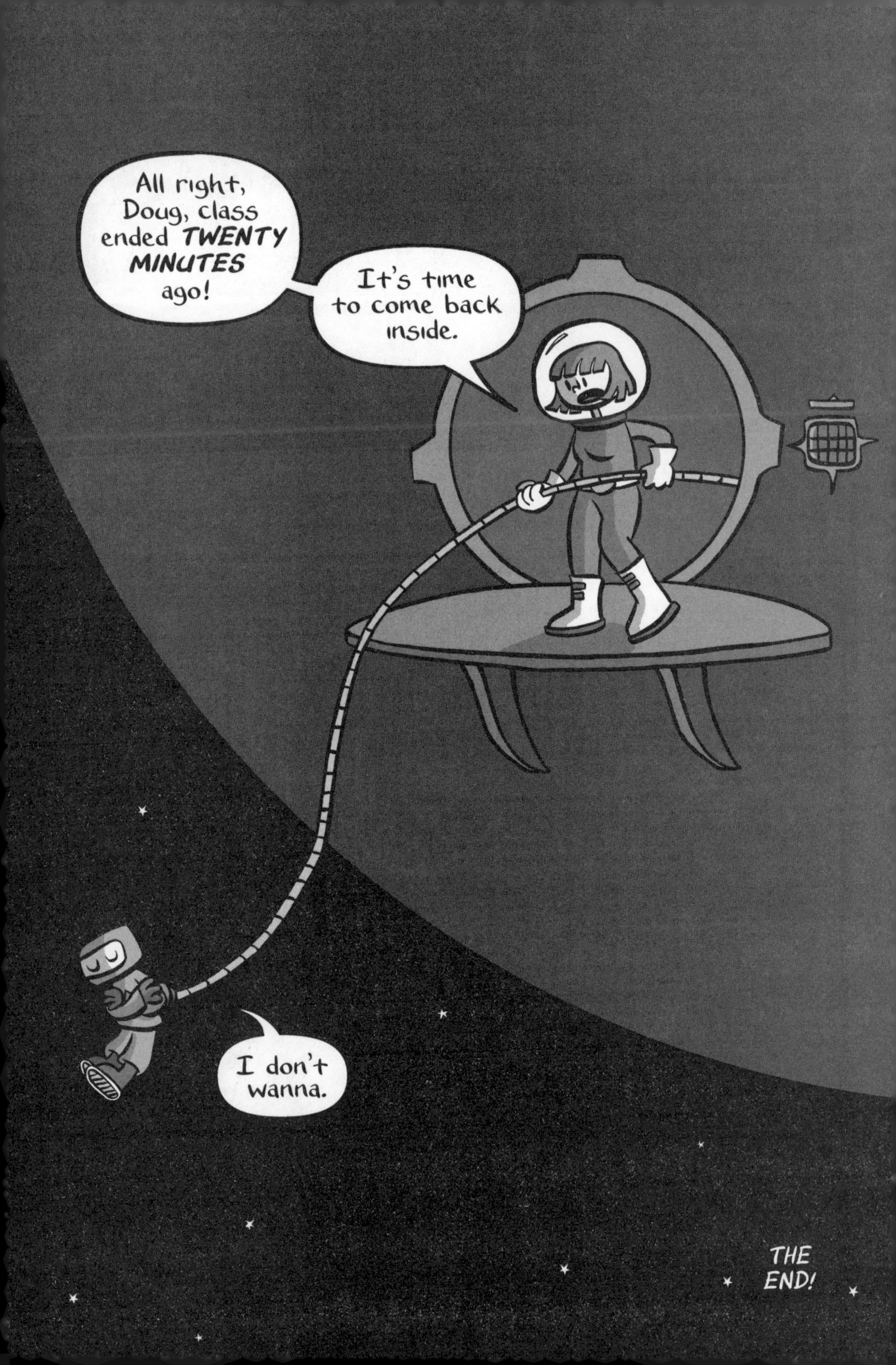
All right, Doug, class ended **TWENTY MINUTES** ago!
It's time to come back inside.
I don't wanna.
THE END!

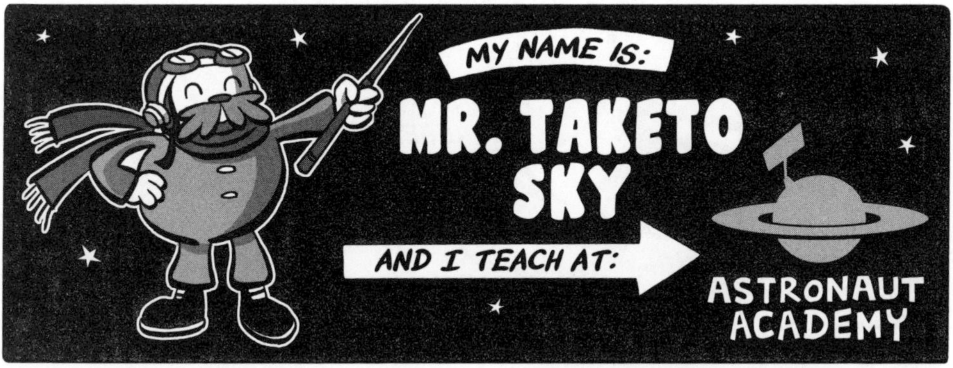
MY NAME IS:
MR. TAKETO SKY
AND I TEACH AT:
ASTRONAUT ACADEMY

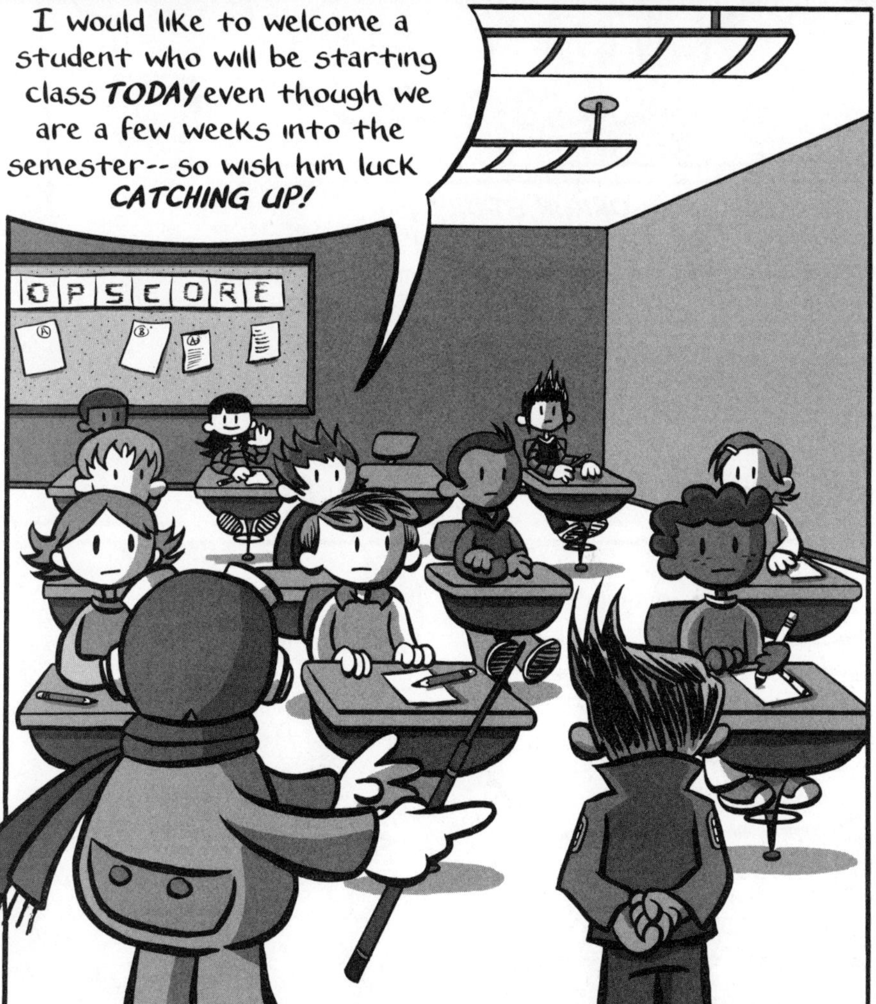
I would like to welcome a student who will be starting class TODAY even though we are a few weeks into the semester-- so wish him luck CATCHING UP!
OPSCORE

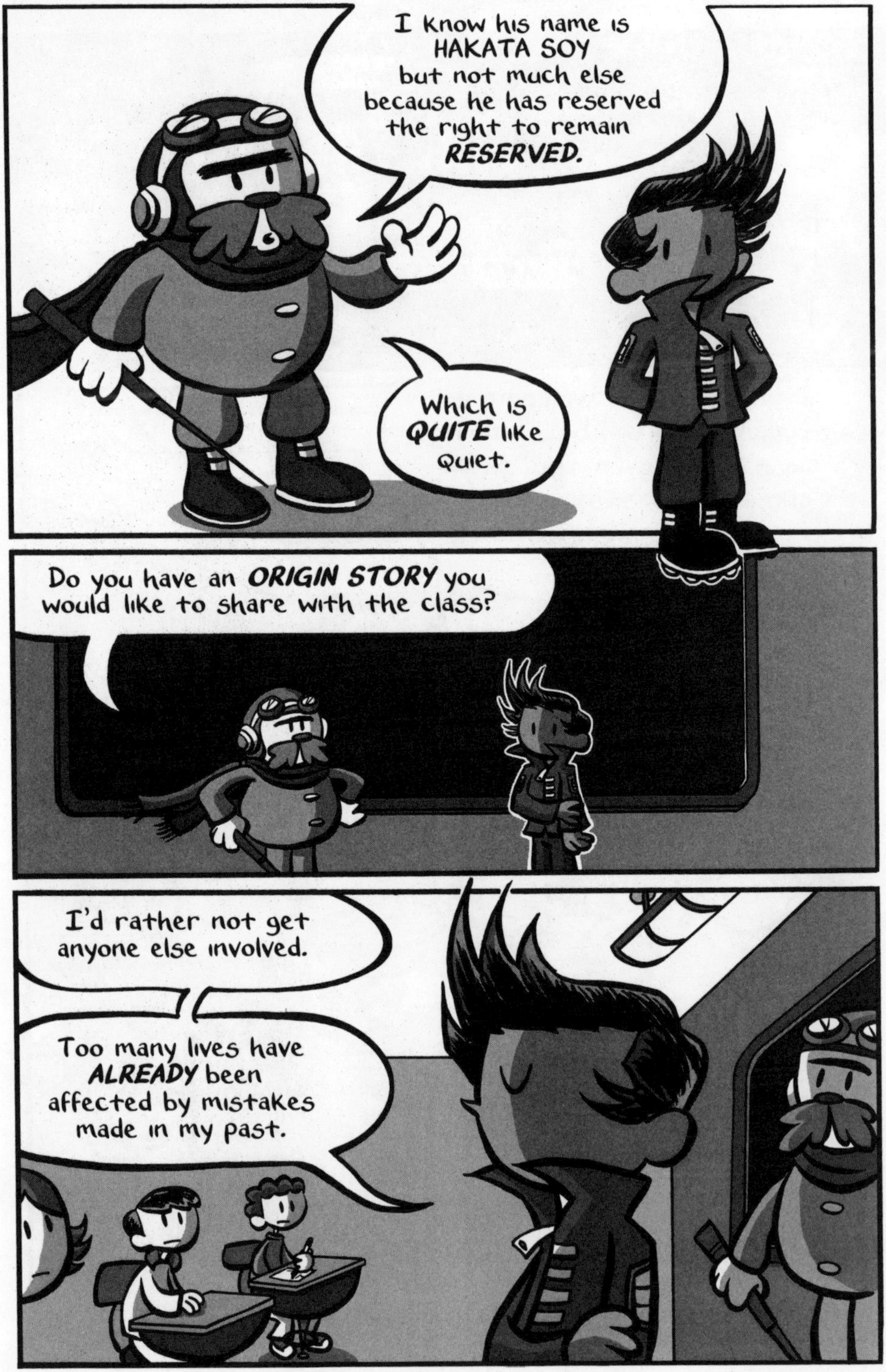
I know his name is HAKATA SOY but not much else because he has reserved the right to remain *RESERVED.*
Which is *QUITE* like quiet.
Do you have an *ORIGIN STORY* you would like to share with the class?
I'd rather not get anyone else involved.
Too many lives have *ALREADY* been affected by mistakes made in my past.

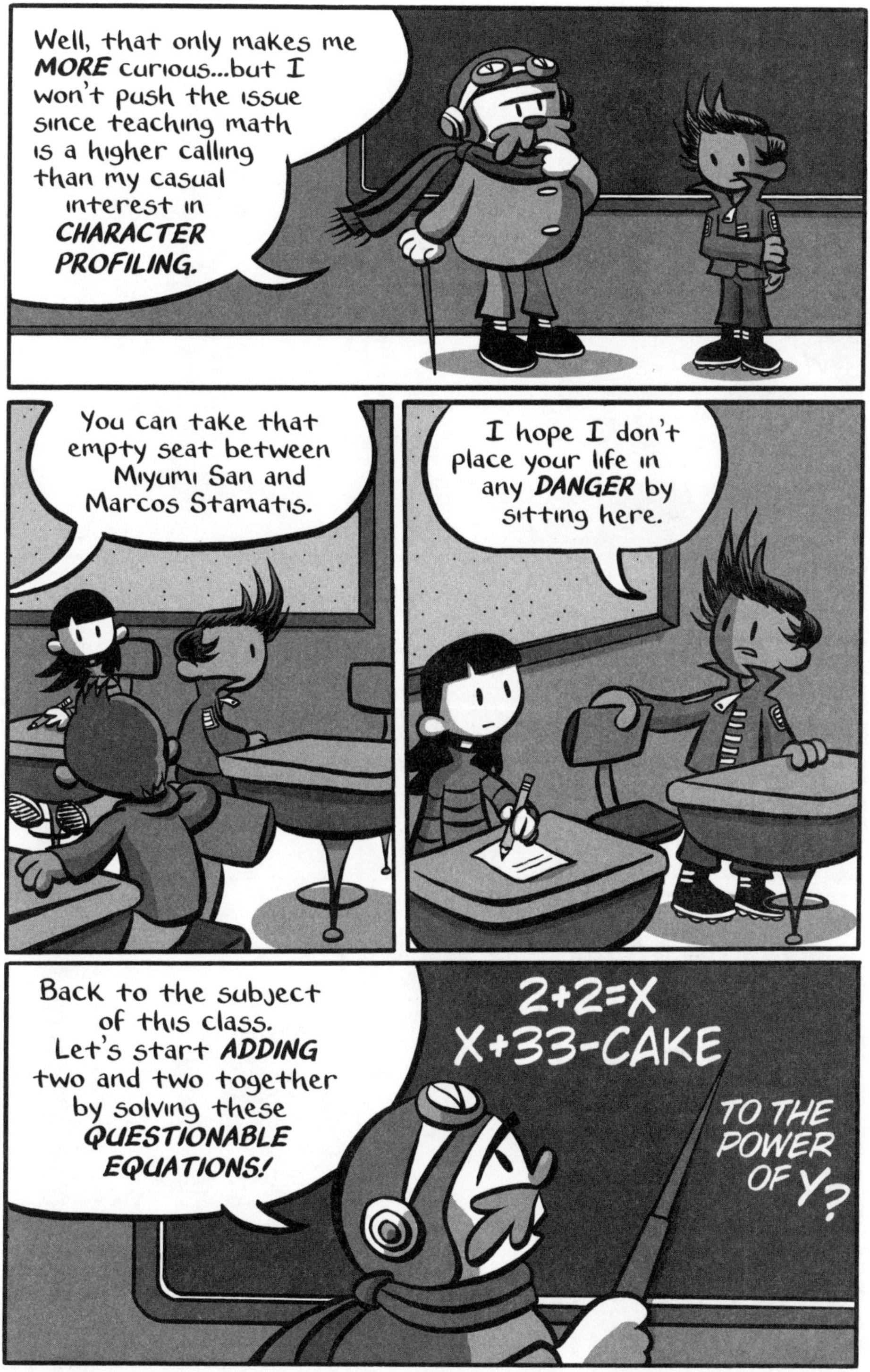
Well, that only makes me MORE curious...but I won't push the issue since teaching math is a higher calling than my casual interest in CHARACTER PROFILING.
You can take that empty seat between Miyumi San and Marcos Stamatis.
I hope I don't place your life in any DANGER by sitting here.
Back to the subject of this class. Let's start ADDING two and two together by solving these QUESTIONABLE EQUATIONS!
2+2=X
X+33-CAKE
TO THE POWER OF Y?

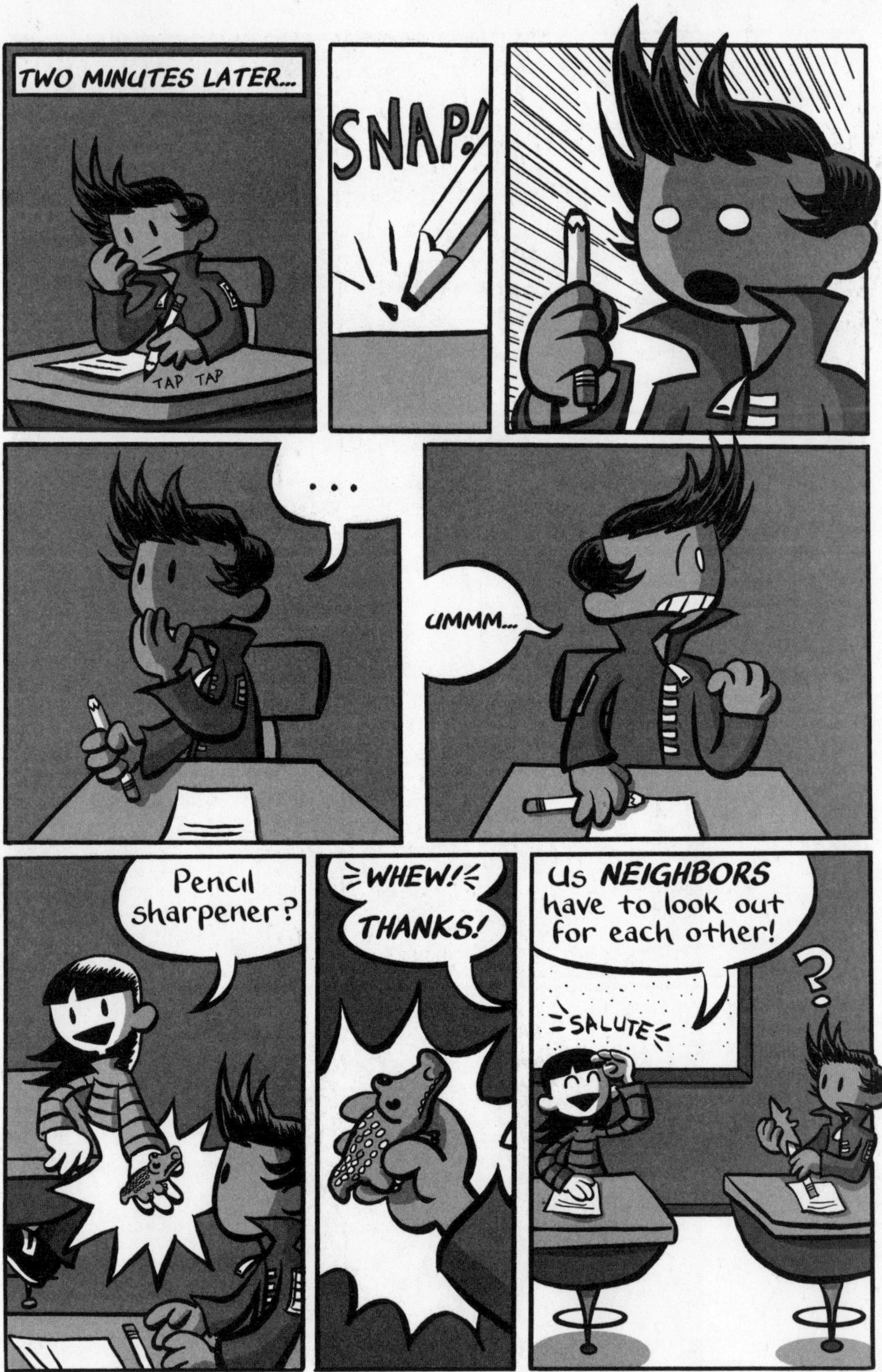
TWO MINUTES LATER...
TAP TAP
SNAP!
...
UMMM...
Pencil sharpener?
WHEW!
THANKS!
Us NEIGHBORS have to look out for each other!
SALUTE
?
END!

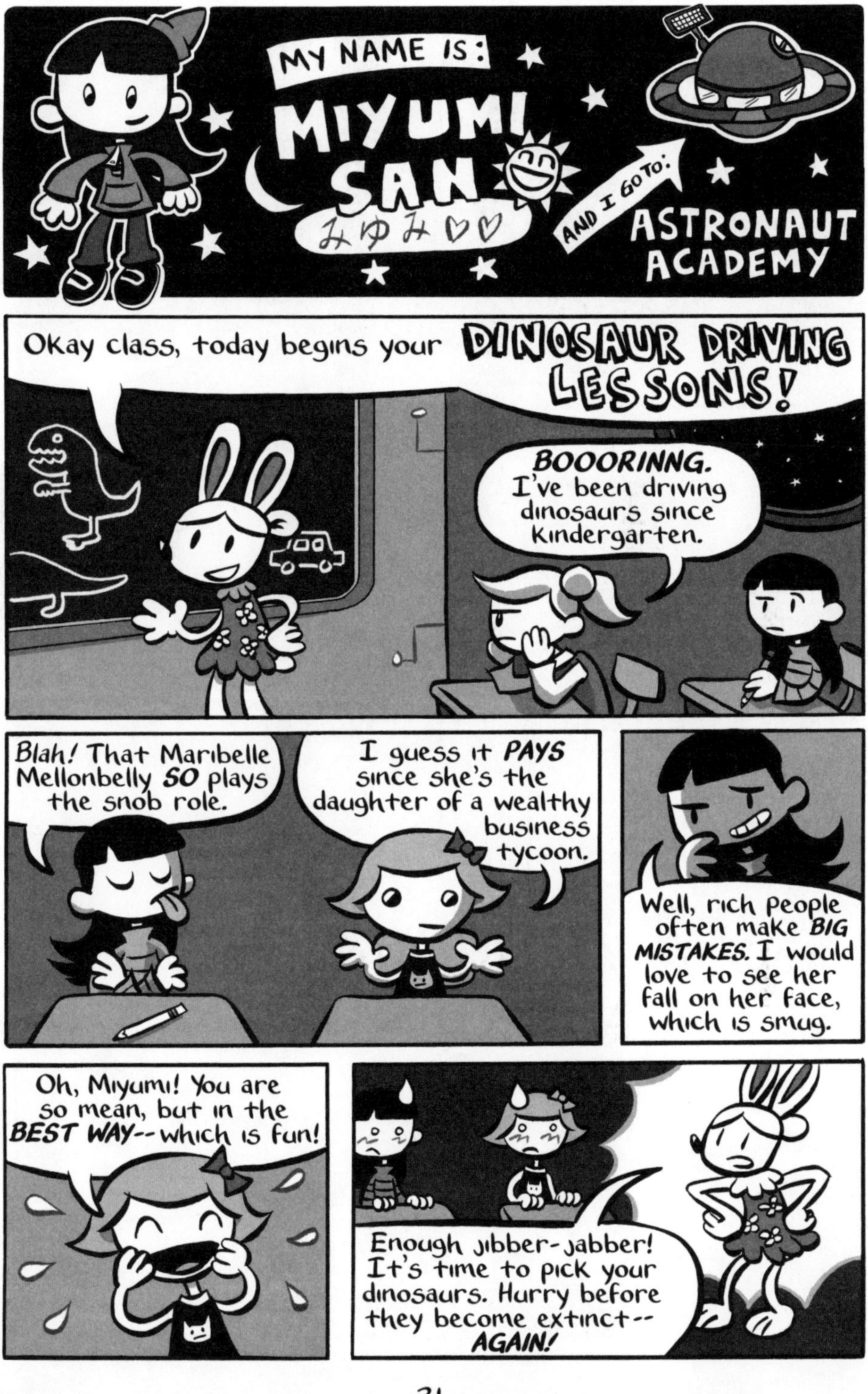
MY NAME IS:
MIYUMI SAN
みゆみ♡♡
AND I GO TO:
ASTRONAUT ACADEMY
Okay class, today begins your DINOSAUR DRIVING LESSONS!
BOOORINNG. I've been driving dinosaurs since Kindergarten.
Blah! That Maribelle Mellonbelly SO plays the snob role.
I guess it PAYS since she's the daughter of a wealthy business tycoon.
Well, rich people often make BIG MISTAKES. I would love to see her fall on her face, which is smug.
Oh, Miyumi! You are so mean, but in the BEST WAY-- which is fun!
Enough jibber-jabber! It's time to pick your dinosaurs. Hurry before they become extinct-- AGAIN!

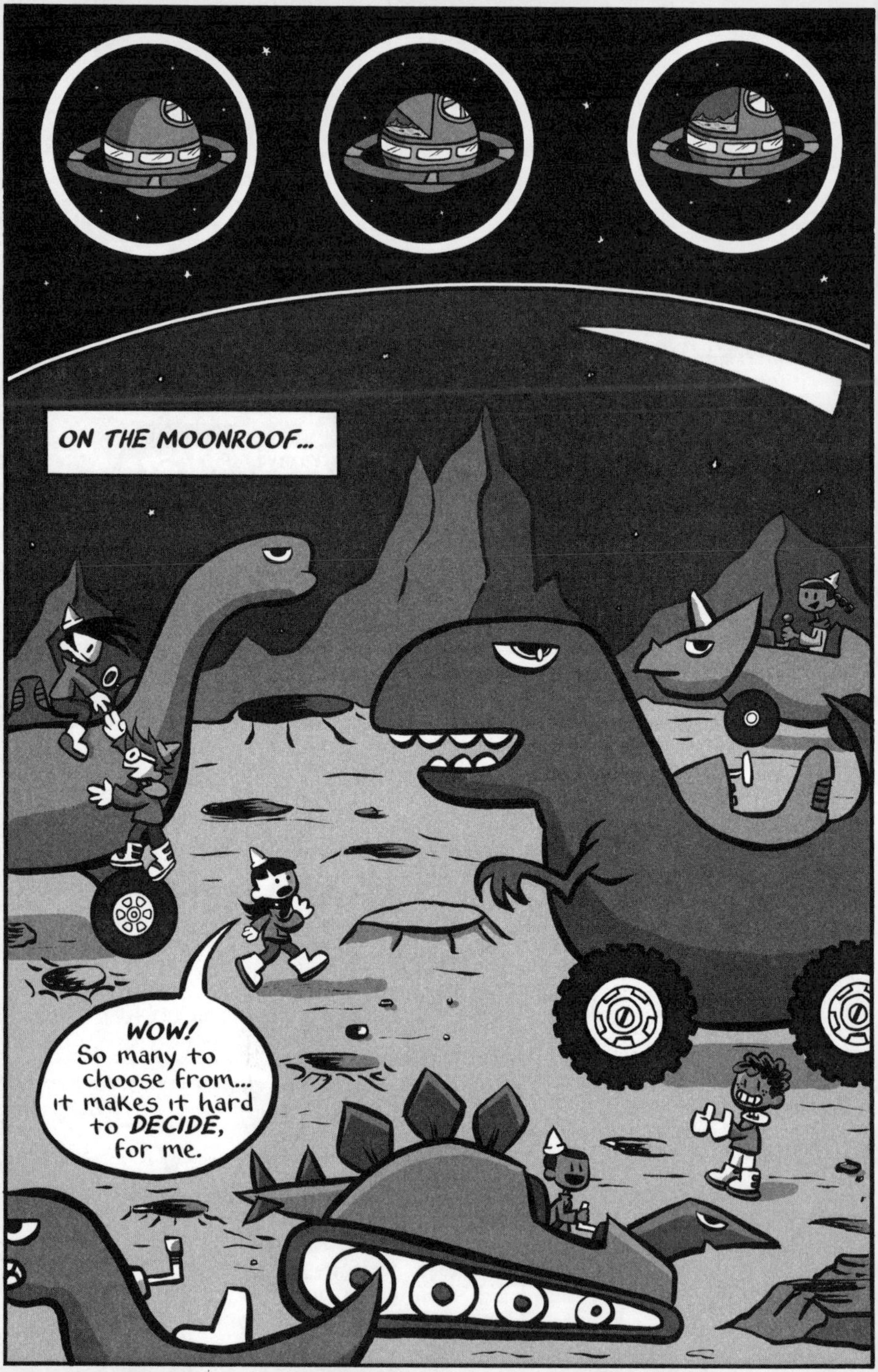
ON THE MOONROOF...
WOW! So many to choose from... it makes it hard to DECIDE, for me.

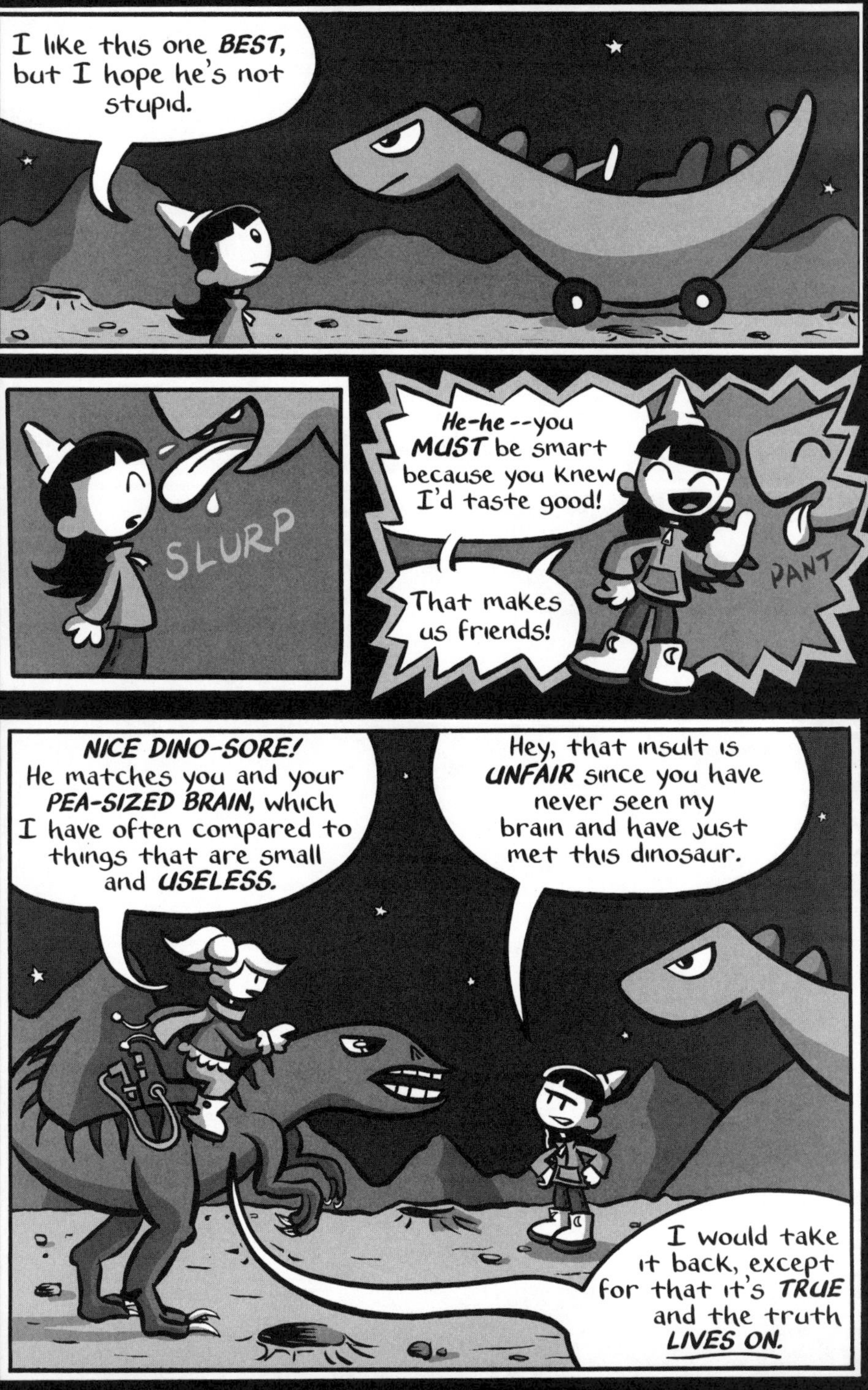
I like this one **BEST**, but I hope he's not stupid.
SLURP
He-he--you **MUST** be smart because you knew I'd taste good!
That makes us friends!
PANT
NICE DINO-SORE! He matches you and your **PEA-SIZED BRAIN,** which I have often compared to things that are small and **USELESS.**
Hey, that insult is **UNFAIR** since you have never seen my brain and have just met this dinosaur.
I would take it back, except for that it's **TRUE** and the truth **LIVES ON.**

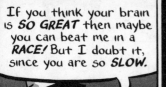
If you think your brain is **SO GREAT** then maybe you can beat me in a **RACE!** But I doubt it, since you are so **SLOW.**

You can't say things like that to **ME!** **I'M RICH!** And I'll race you to **PROVE** how smart I am!

DEAL!

Let the race begin!

Giddy up, dino!

WAIT! You cannot race...it is only your first lesson!

And besides... it's **MY** job to say "let the race begin" since I am the one with the teacher's degree!

Then say it-- because this contest has to be **OFFICIAL** so the world can know that legally I am the best.

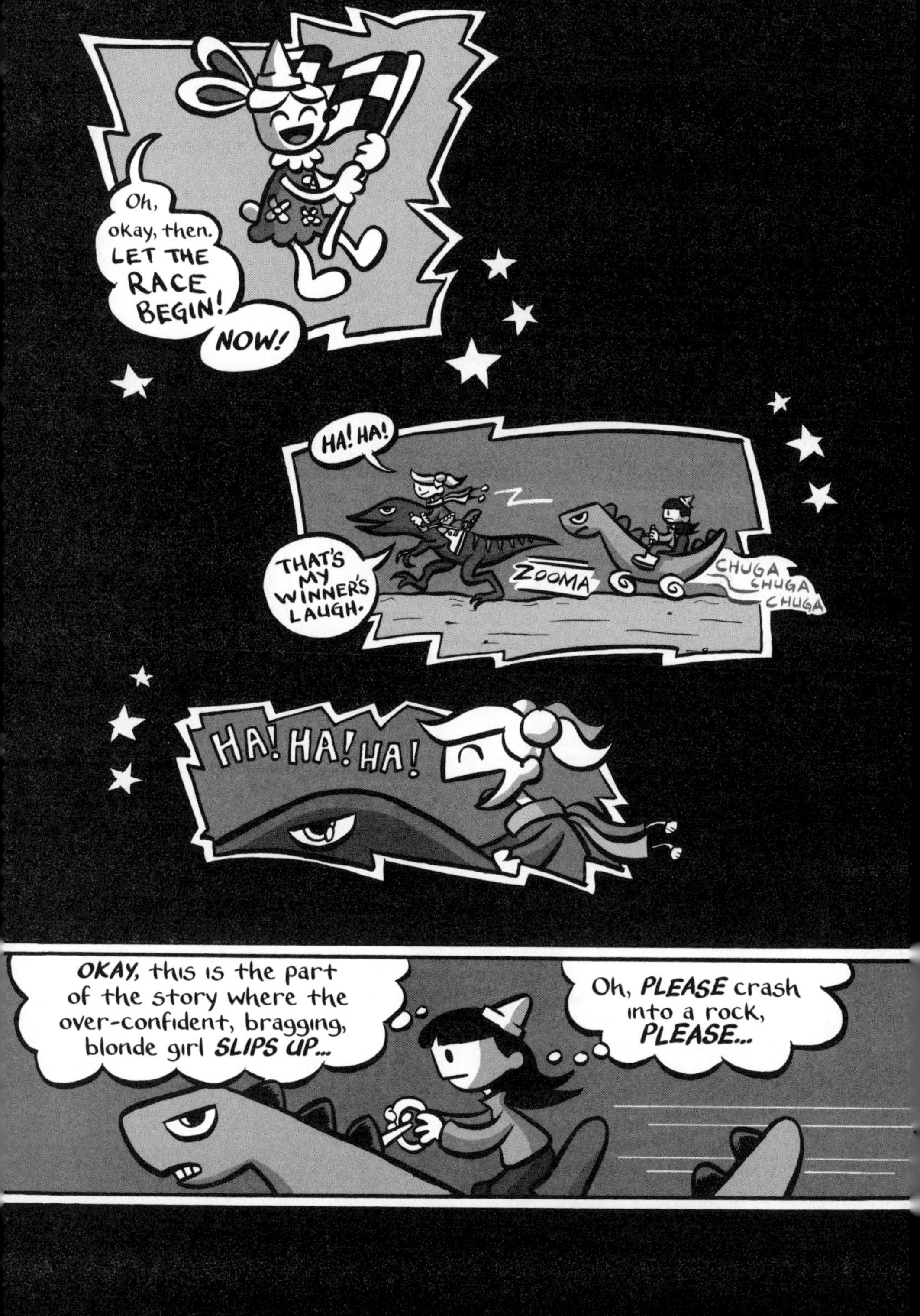
Oh, okay, then. LET THE RACE BEGIN!
NOW!
HA! HA!
THAT'S MY WINNER'S LAUGH.
ZOOMA
CHUGA CHUGA CHUGA
HA! HA! HA!
OKAY, this is the part of the story where the over-confident, bragging, blonde girl SLIPS UP...
Oh, PLEASE crash into a rock, PLEASE...

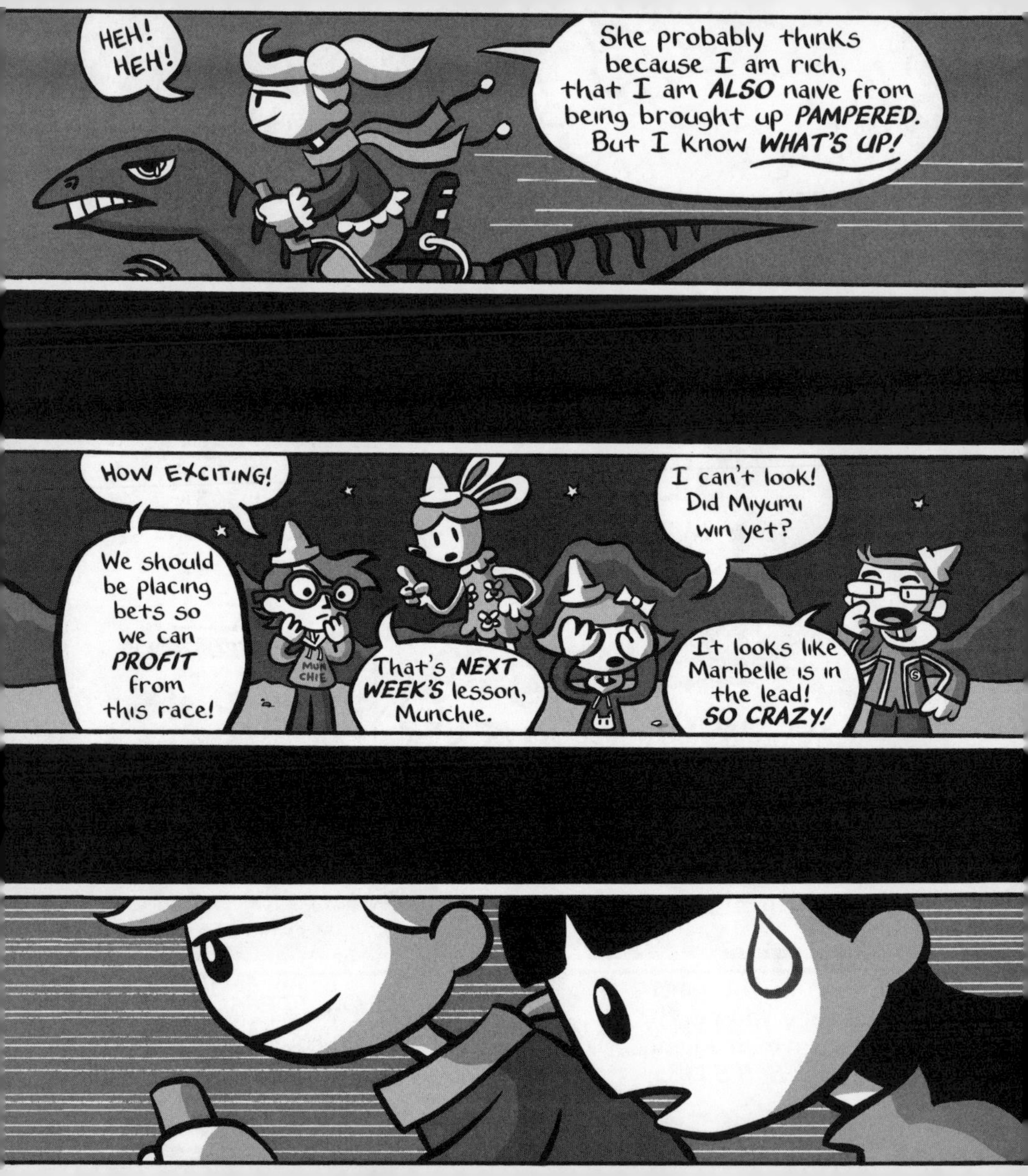
HEH! HEH!
She probably thinks because I am rich, that I am ALSO naive from being brought up PAMPERED. But I know WHAT'S UP!
[redacted]
HOW EXCITING!
We should be placing bets so we can PROFIT from this race!
That's NEXT WEEK'S lesson, Munchie.
I can't look! Did Miyumi win yet?
It looks like Maribelle is in the lead! SO CRAZY!
MUN CHIE
[redacted]

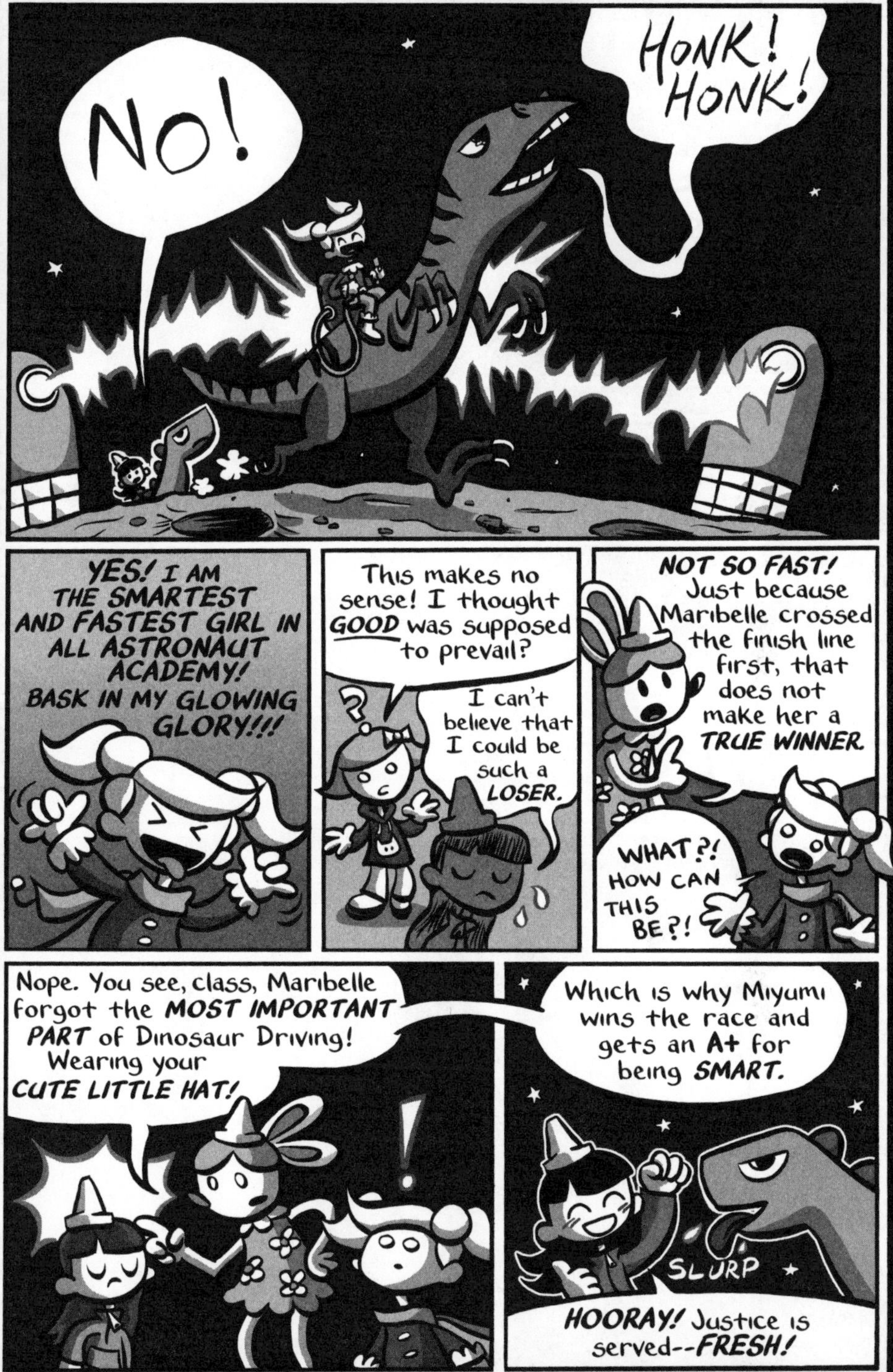

No!
HONK! HONK!
YES! I AM THE SMARTEST AND FASTEST GIRL IN ALL ASTRONAUT ACADEMY! BASK IN MY GLOWING GLORY!!!
This makes no sense! I thought GOOD was supposed to prevail?
?
I can't believe that I could be such a LOSER.
NOT SO FAST! Just because Maribelle crossed the finish line first, that does not make her a TRUE WINNER.
WHAT?! HOW CAN THIS BE?!
Nope. You see, class, Maribelle forgot the MOST IMPORTANT PART of Dinosaur Driving! Wearing your CUTE LITTLE HAT!
!
Which is why Miyumi wins the race and gets an A+ for being SMART.
SLURP
HOORAY! Justice is served--FRESH!

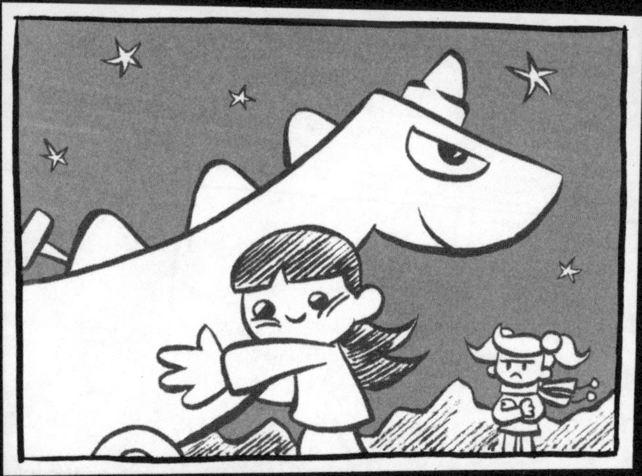

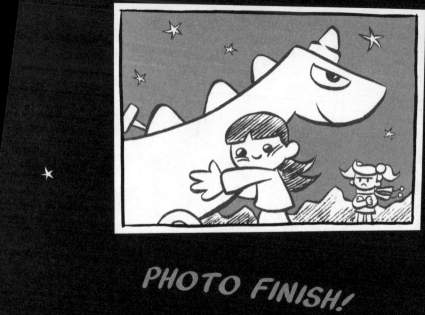

PHOTO FINISH!

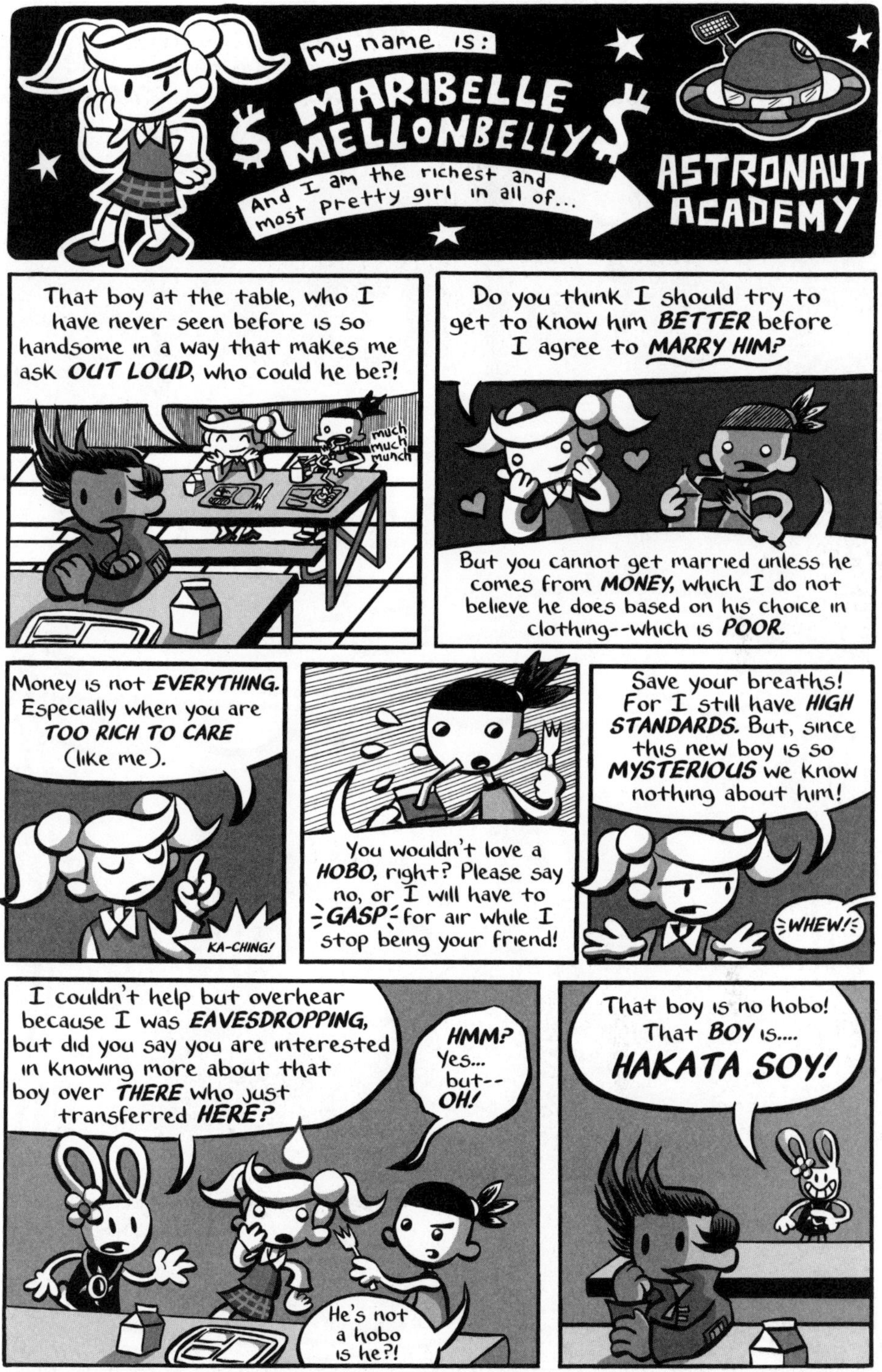
my name is:
$ MARIBELLE MELLONBELLY $
And I am the richest and most pretty girl in all of...
ASTRONAUT ACADEMY
That boy at the table, who I have never seen before is so handsome in a way that makes me ask OUT LOUD, who could he be?!
much much munch
Do you think I should try to get to know him BETTER before I agree to MARRY HIM?
But you cannot get married unless he comes from MONEY, which I do not believe he does based on his choice in clothing--which is POOR.
Money is not EVERYTHING. Especially when you are TOO RICH TO CARE (like me).
KA-CHING!
You wouldn't love a HOBO, right? Please say no, or I will have to GASP for air while I stop being your friend!
Save your breaths! For I still have HIGH STANDARDS. But, since this new boy is so MYSTERIOUS we know nothing about him!
WHEW!
I couldn't help but overhear because I was EAVESDROPPING, but did you say you are interested in knowing more about that boy over THERE who just transferred HERE?
HMM? Yes... but-- OH!
He's not a hobo is he?!
That boy is no hobo! That BOY is.... HAKATA SOY!

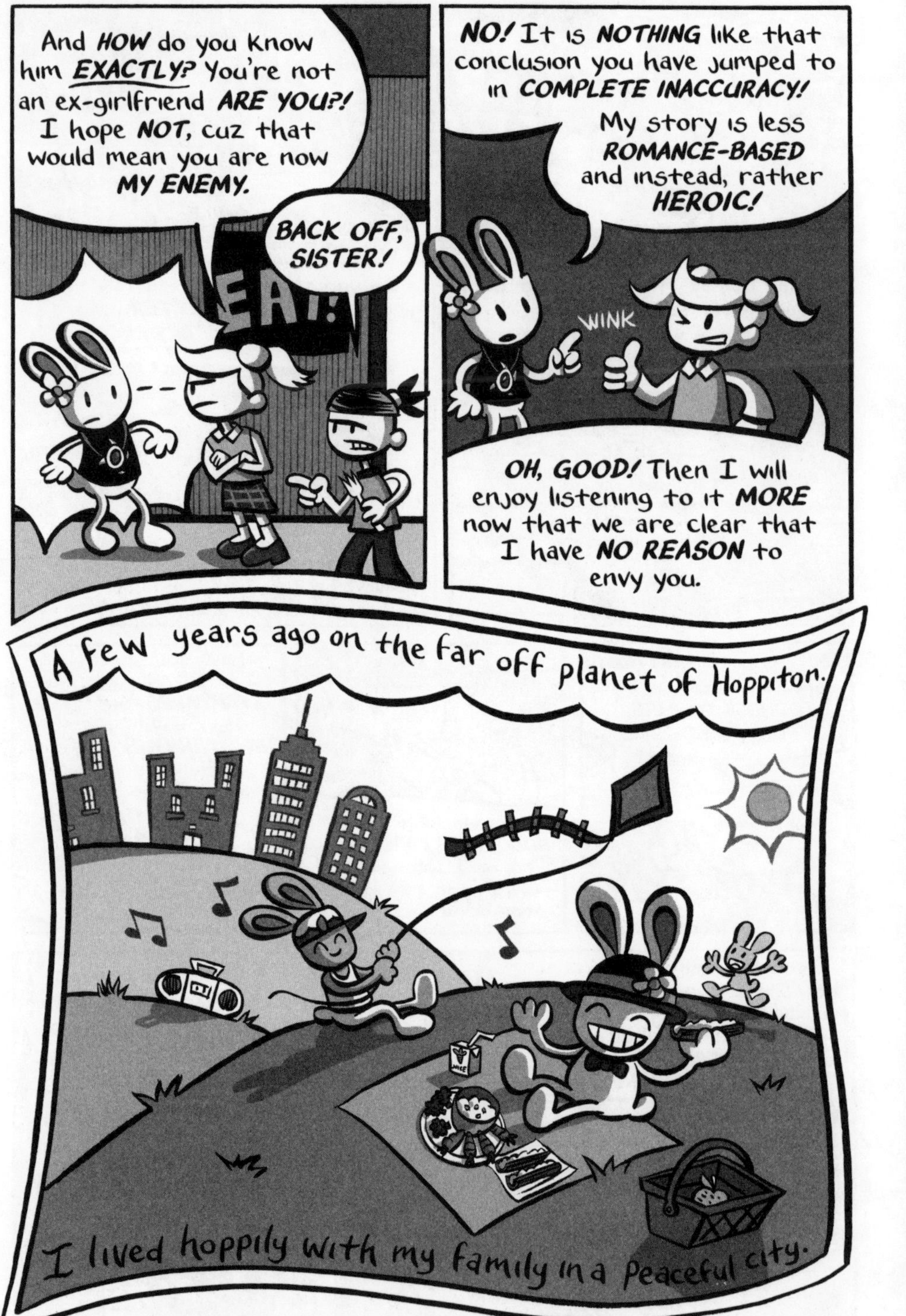
And HOW do you know him EXACTLY? You're not an ex-girlfriend ARE YOU?! I hope NOT, cuz that would mean you are now MY ENEMY.
BACK OFF, SISTER!
EAT
NO! It is NOTHING like that conclusion you have jumped to in COMPLETE INACCURACY!
My story is less ROMANCE-BASED and instead, rather HEROIC!
WINK
OH, GOOD! Then I will enjoy listening to it MORE now that we are clear that I have NO REASON to envy you.
A few years ago on the far off planet of Hoppiton.
I lived hoppily with my family in a peaceful city.

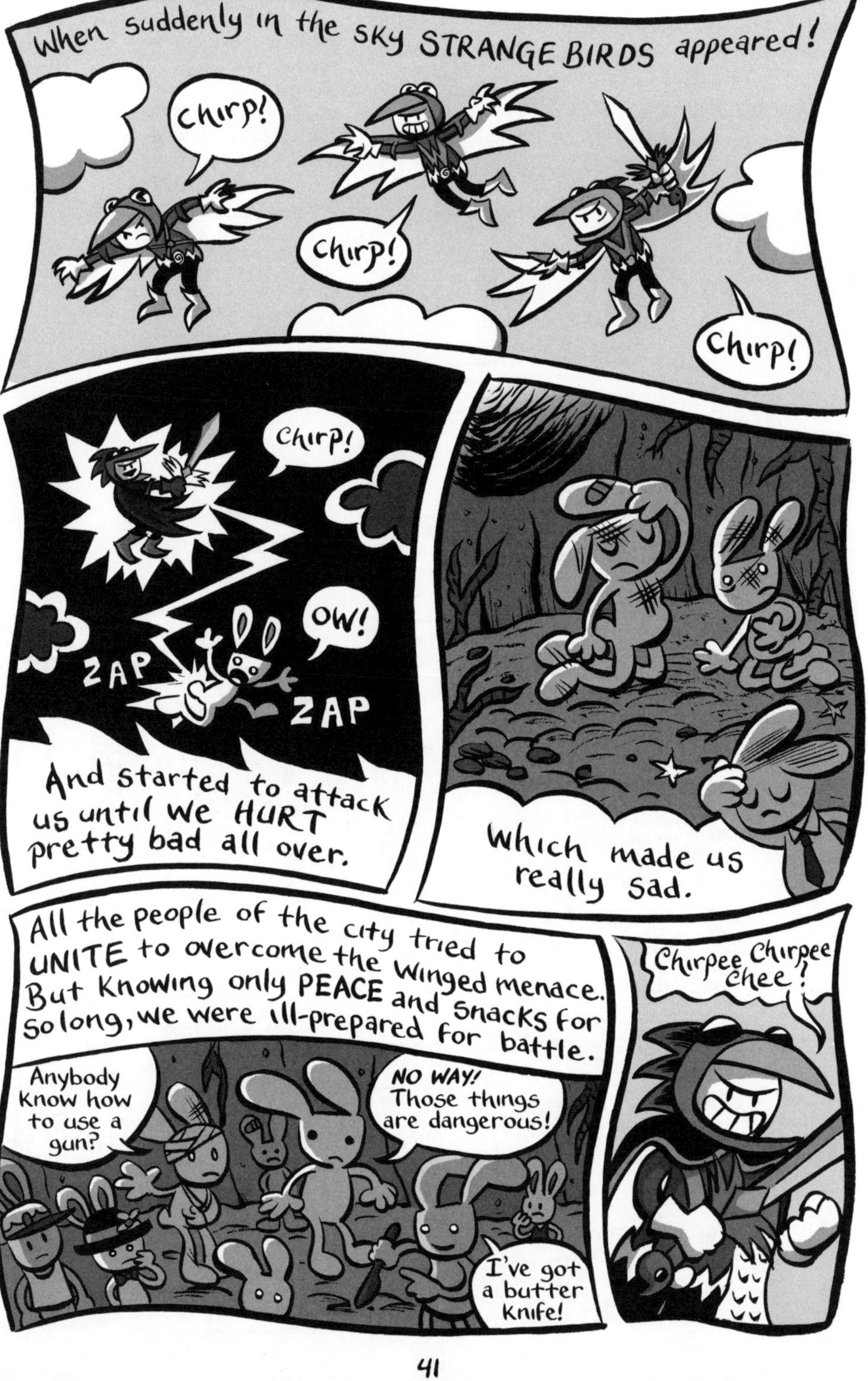
When suddenly in the sky STRANGE BIRDS appeared!
Chirp!
Chirp!
Chirp!
Chirp!
ZAP
OW!
ZAP
And started to attack us until we HURT pretty bad all over.
Which made us really sad.
All the people of the city tried to UNITE to overcome the winged menace. But knowing only PEACE and snacks for so long, we were ill-prepared for battle.
Anybody know how to use a gun?
NO WAY! Those things are dangerous!
I've got a butter knife!
Chirpee Chirpee Chee?

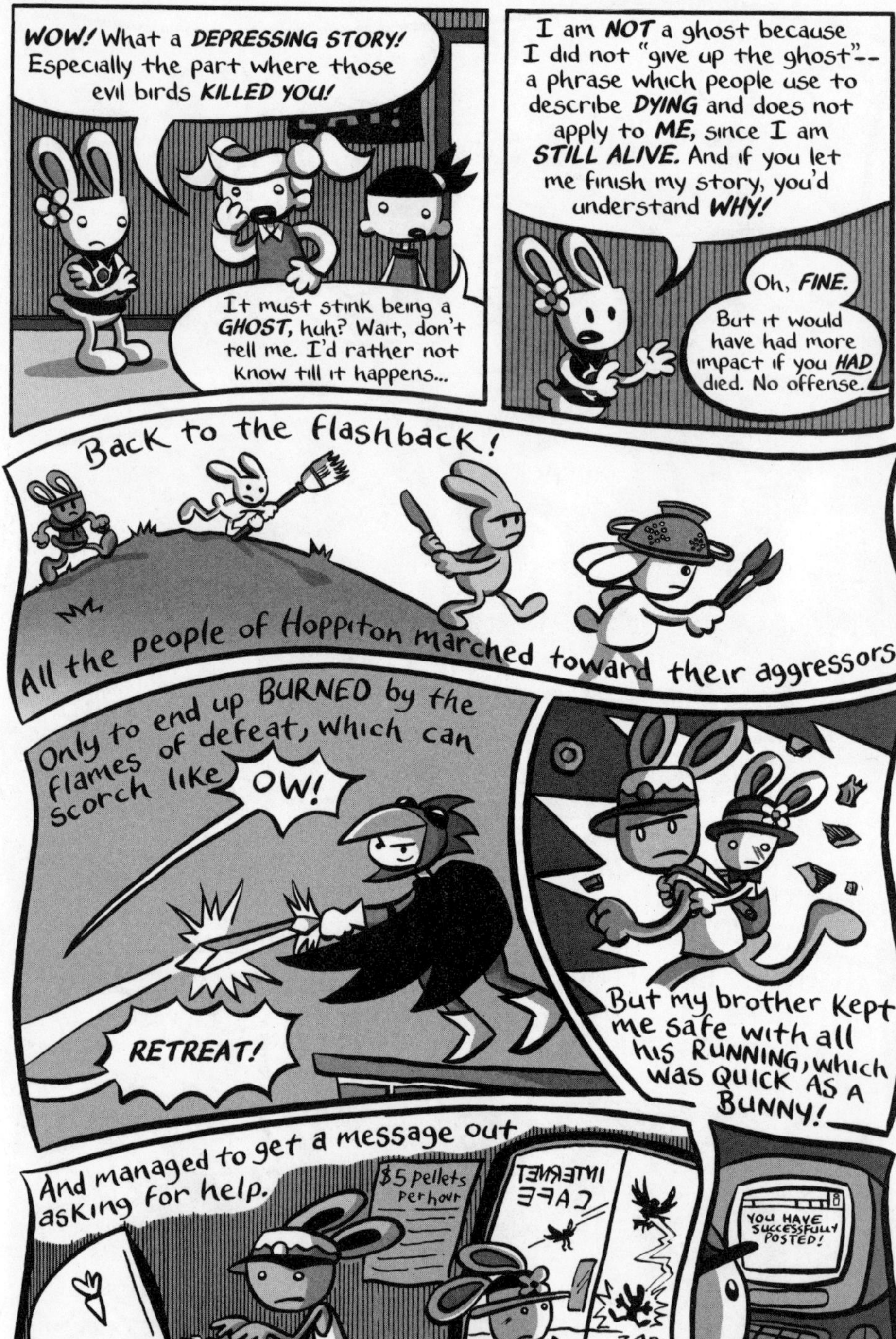
WOW! What a DEPRESSING STORY! Especially the part where those evil birds KILLED YOU!
It must stink being a GHOST, huh? Wait, don't tell me. I'd rather not know till it happens...
I am NOT a ghost because I did not "give up the ghost"-- a phrase which people use to describe DYING and does not apply to ME, since I am STILL ALIVE. And if you let me finish my story, you'd understand WHY!
Oh, FINE.
But it would have had more impact if you HAD died. No offense.
Back to the flashback!
All the people of Hoppiton marched toward their aggressors.
Only to end up BURNED by the flames of defeat, which can scorch like
OW!
RETREAT!
But my brother kept me safe with all his RUNNING, which was QUICK AS A BUNNY!
And managed to get a message out asking for help.
$5 pellets per hour
INTERNET CAFE
ZAP
gulp
YOU HAVE SUCCESSFULLY POSTED!

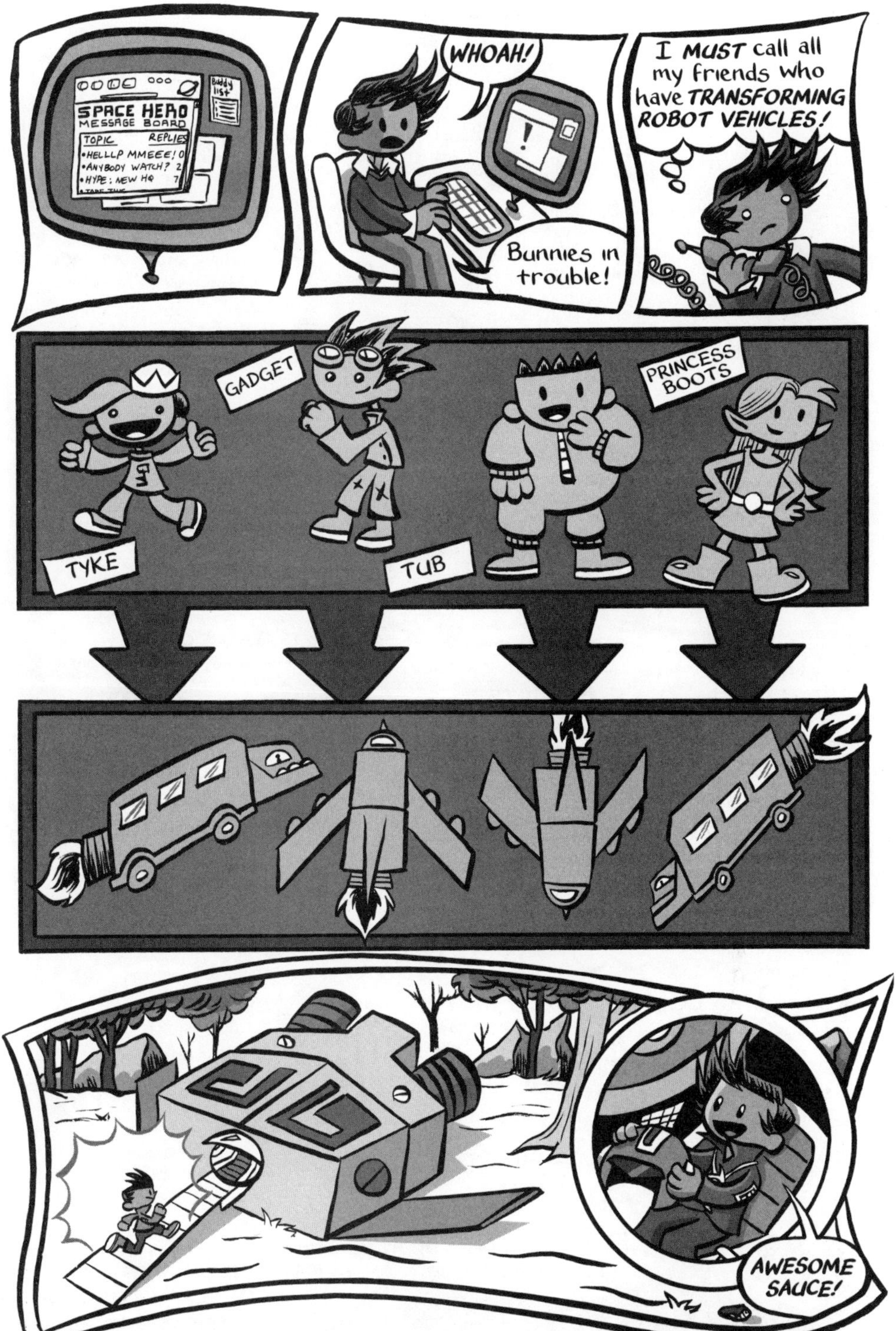
SPACE HERO
MESSAGE BOARD
TOPIC
REPLIES
•HELLLP MMEEE! 0
•ANYBODY WATCH? 2
•HYPE: NEW HQ 7
WHOAH!
Bunnies in trouble!
I MUST call all my friends who have TRANSFORMING ROBOT VEHICLES!
GADGET
PRINCESS BOOTS
TYKE
TUB
AWESOME SAUCE!

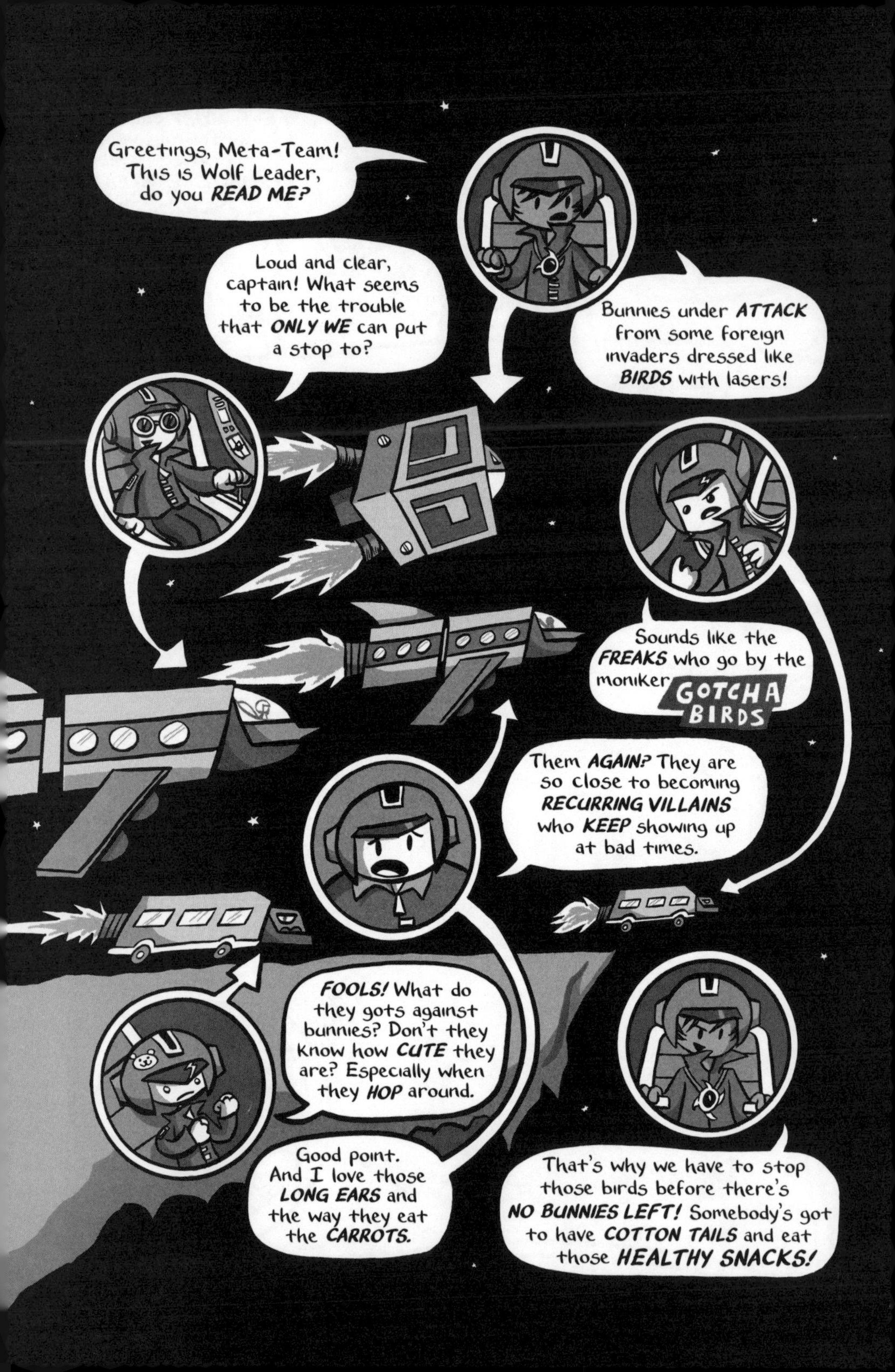
Greetings, Meta-Team! This is Wolf Leader, do you READ ME?
Loud and clear, captain! What seems to be the trouble that ONLY WE can put a stop to?
Bunnies under ATTACK from some foreign invaders dressed like BIRDS with lasers!
Sounds like the FREAKS who go by the moniker GOTCHA BIRDS
Them AGAIN? They are so close to becoming RECURRING VILLAINS who KEEP showing up at bad times.
FOOLS! What do they gots against bunnies? Don't they know how CUTE they are? Especially when they HOP around.
Good point. And I love those LONG EARS and the way they eat the CARROTS.
That's why we have to stop those birds before there's NO BUNNIES LEFT! Somebody's got to have COTTON TAILS and eat those HEALTHY SNACKS!

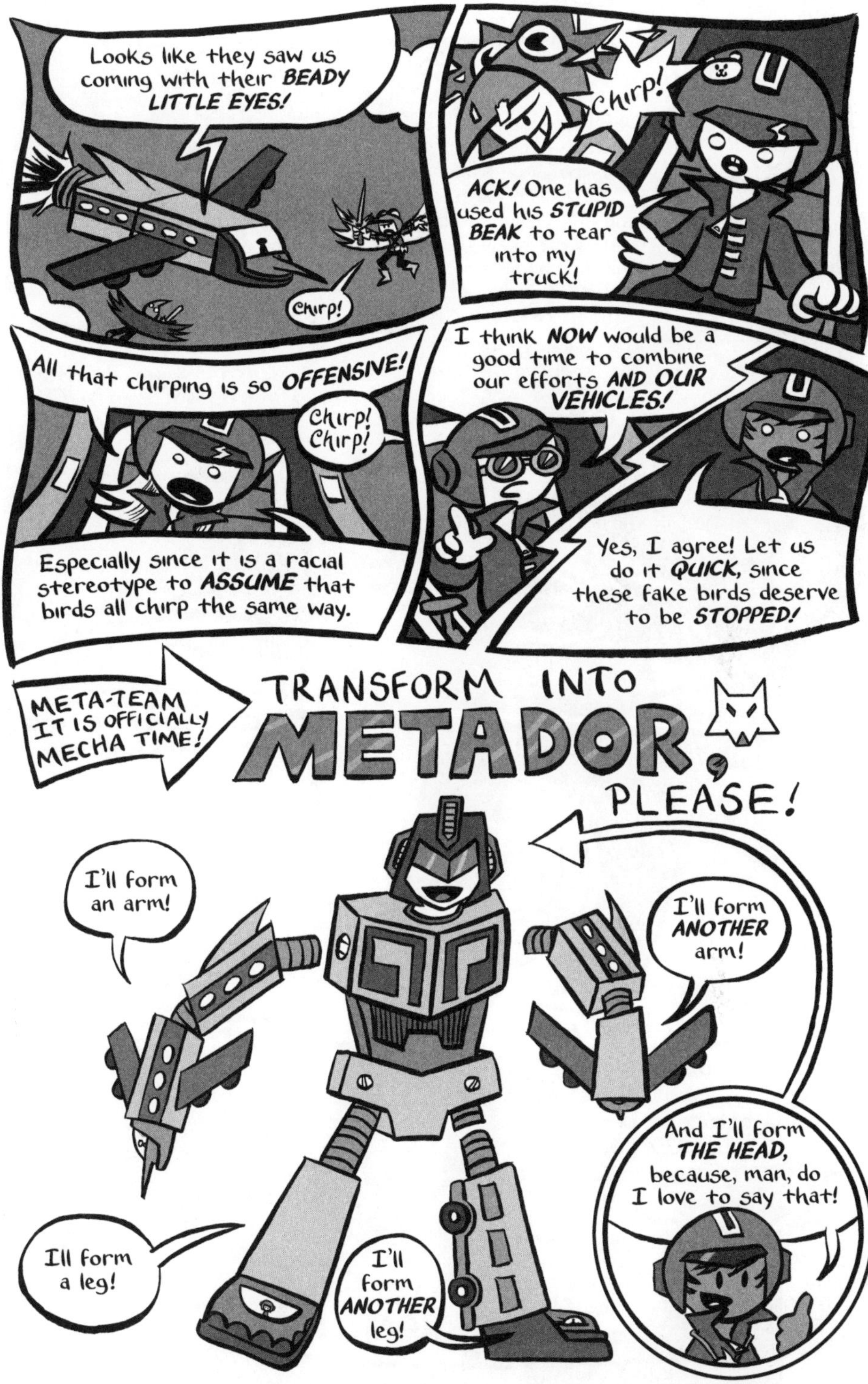
Looks like they saw us coming with their BEADY LITTLE EYES!
Chirp!
Chirp!
ACK! One has used his STUPID BEAK to tear into my truck!
All that chirping is so OFFENSIVE!
Chirp! Chirp!
Especially since it is a racial stereotype to ASSUME that birds all chirp the same way.
I think NOW would be a good time to combine our efforts AND OUR VEHICLES!
Yes, I agree! Let us do it QUICK, since these fake birds deserve to be STOPPED!
META-TEAM IT IS OFFICIALLY MECHA TIME!
TRANSFORM INTO METADOR, PLEASE!
I'll form an arm!
I'll form ANOTHER arm!
And I'll form THE HEAD, because, man, do I love to say that!
Ill form a leg!
I'll form ANOTHER leg!

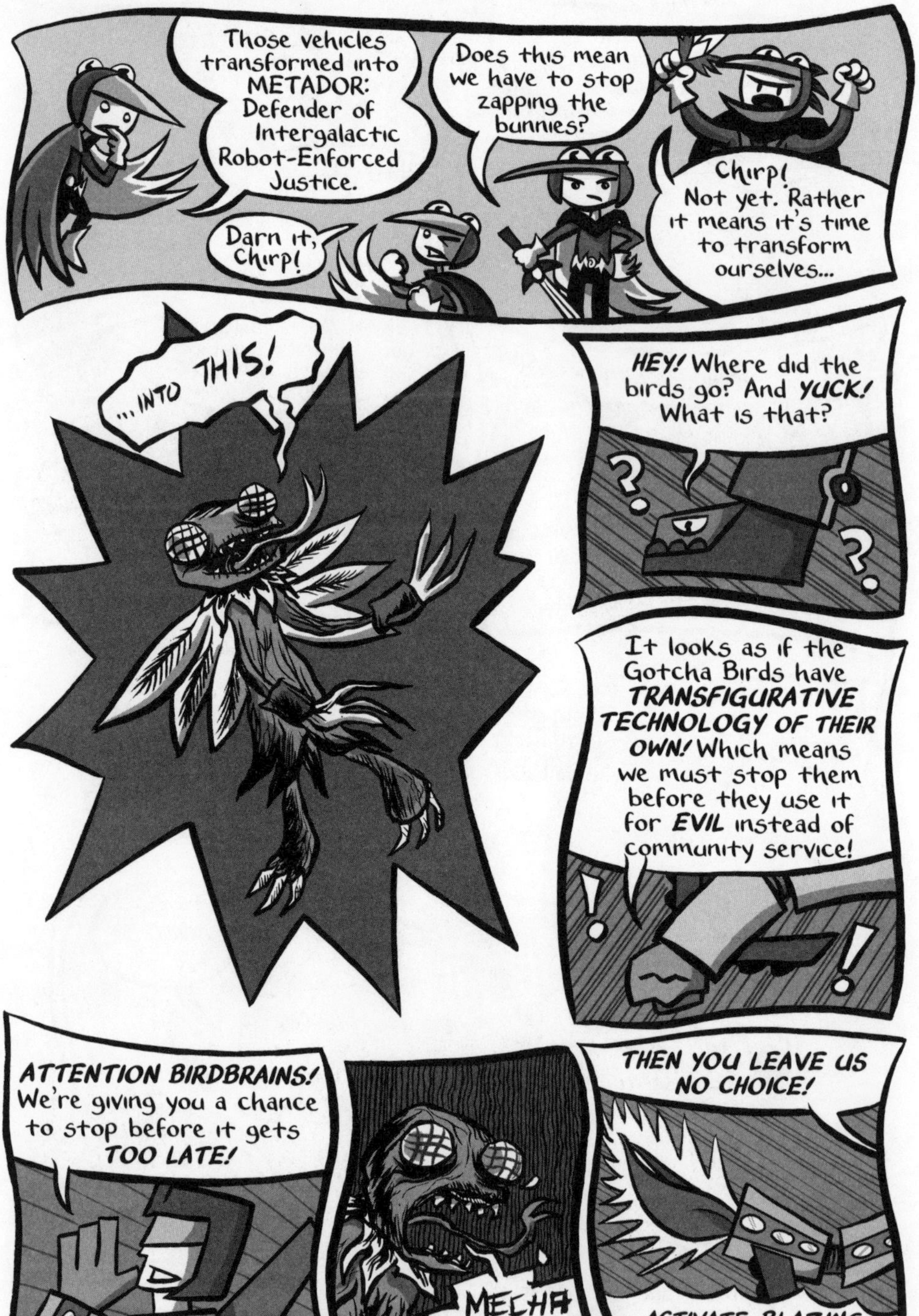
Those vehicles transformed into METADOR: Defender of Intergalactic Robot-Enforced Justice.
Does this mean we have to stop zapping the bunnies?
Darn it, Chirp!
Chirp! Not yet. Rather it means it's time to transform ourselves...
...INTO THIS!
HEY! Where did the birds go? And YUCK! What is that?
It looks as if the Gotcha Birds have TRANSFIGURATIVE TECHNOLOGY OF THEIR OWN! Which means we must stop them before they use it for EVIL instead of community service!
ATTENTION BIRDBRAINS! We're giving you a chance to stop before it gets TOO LATE!
MECHA ROAR!!
THEN YOU LEAVE US NO CHOICE!
ACTIVATE BLAZING MULETA!

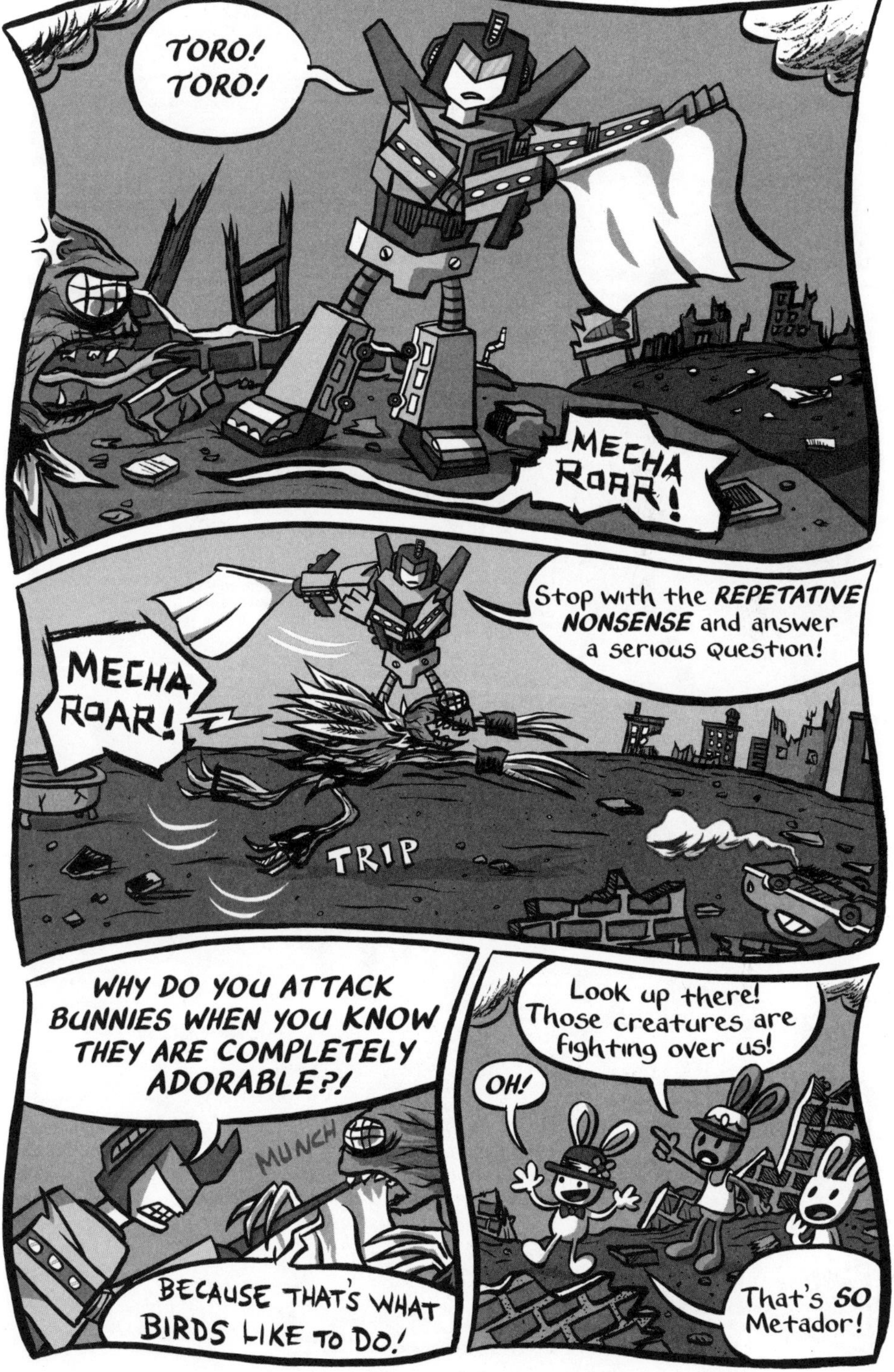
TORO! TORO!
MECHA ROAR!
Stop with the **REPETATIVE NONSENSE** and answer a serious Question!
MECHA ROAR!
TRIP
WHY DO YOU ATTACK BUNNIES WHEN YOU KNOW THEY ARE COMPLETELY ADORABLE?!
MUNCH
BECAUSE THAT'S WHAT BIRDS LIKE TO DO!
Look up there! Those creatures are fighting over us!
OH!
That's **SO** Metador!

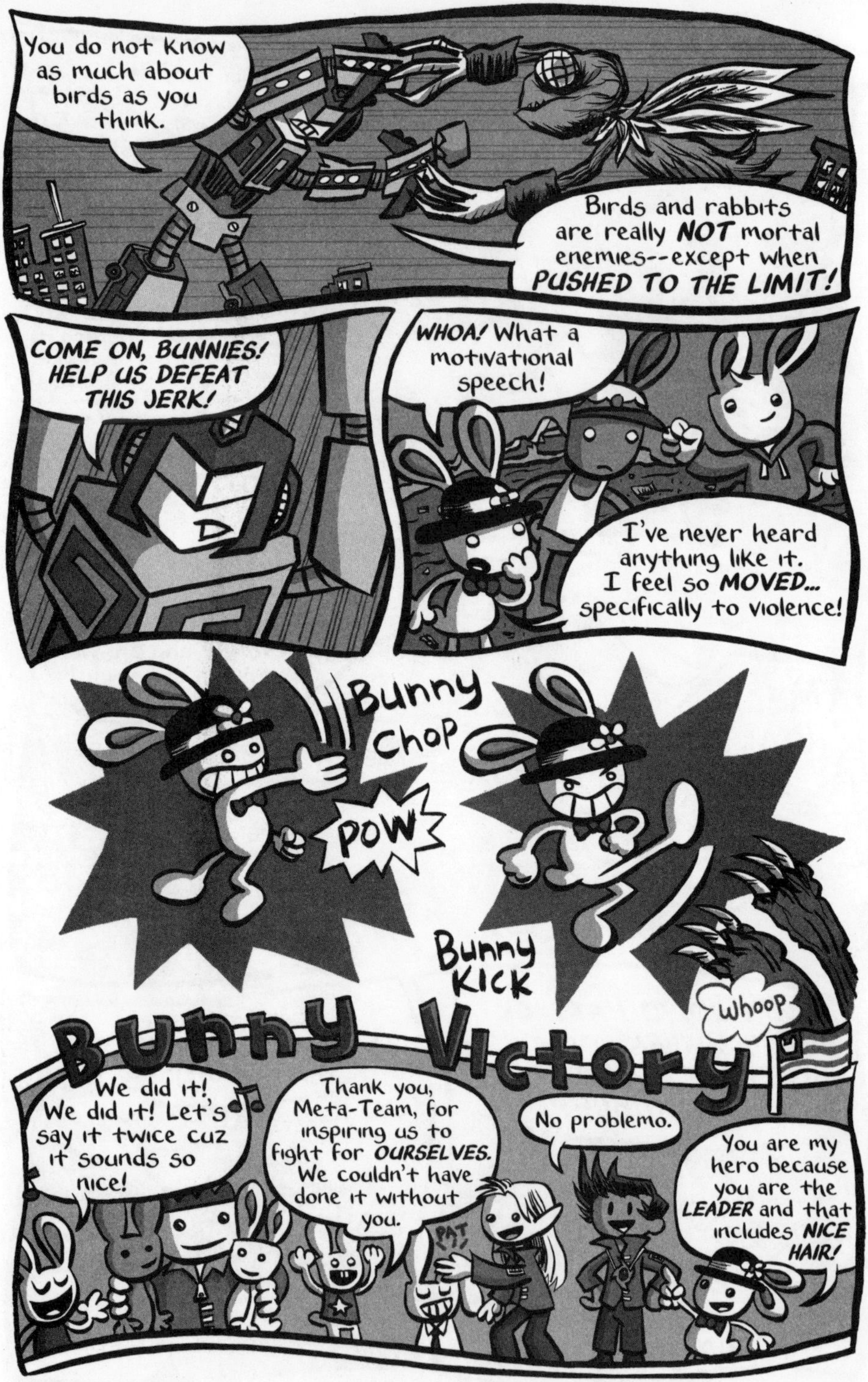
You do not know as much about birds as you think.
Birds and rabbits are really NOT mortal enemies--except when PUSHED TO THE LIMIT!
COME ON, BUNNIES! HELP US DEFEAT THIS JERK!
WHOA! What a motivational speech!
I've never heard anything like it. I feel so MOVED... specifically to violence!
Bunny Chop
POW
Bunny Kick
Whoop
Bunny Victory
We did it! We did it! Let's say it twice cuz it sounds so nice!
Thank you, Meta-Team, for inspiring us to fight for OURSELVES. We couldn't have done it without you.
PAT
No problemo.
You are my hero because you are the LEADER and that includes NICE HAIR!

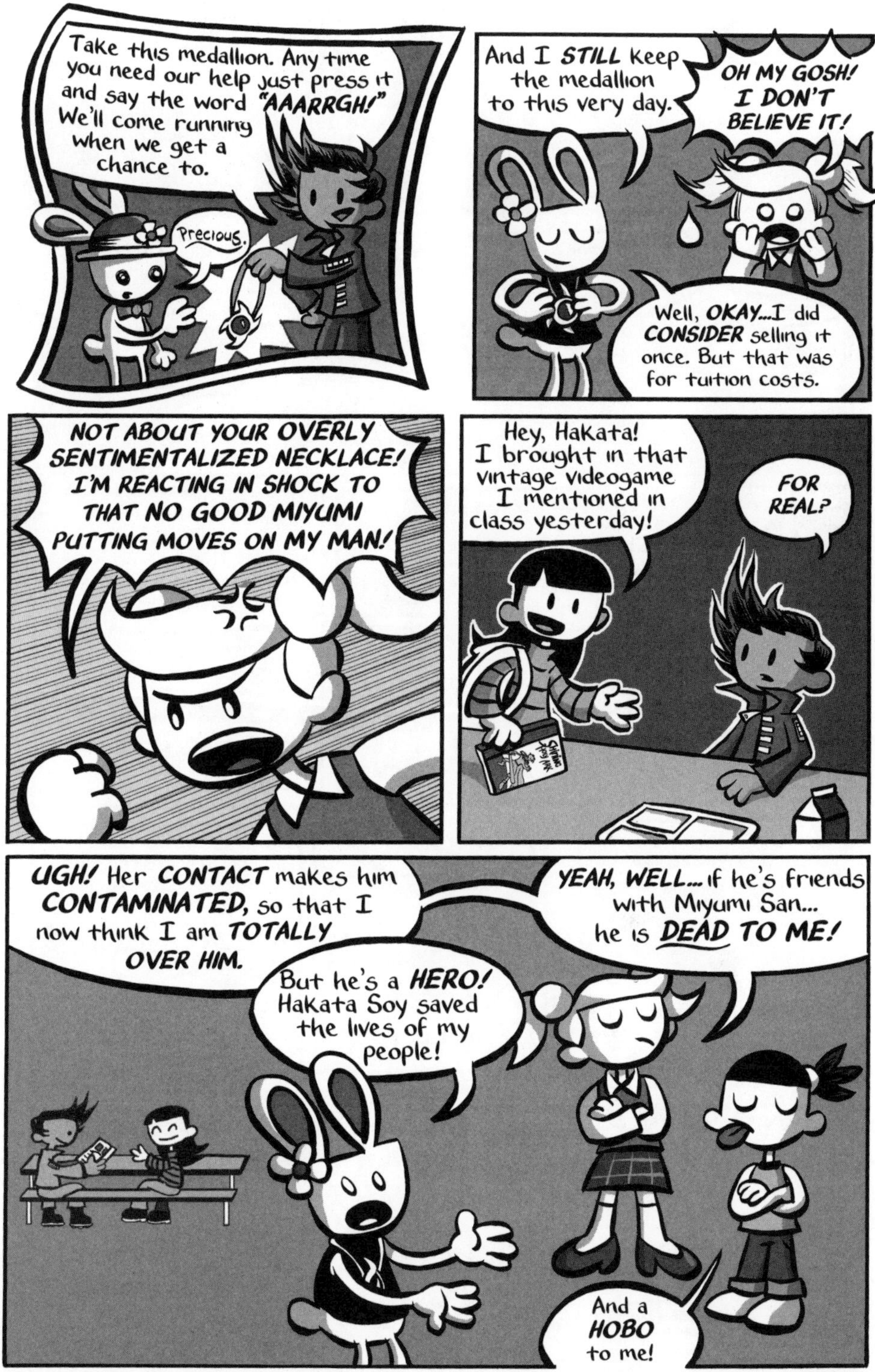
Take this medallion. Any time you need our help just press it and say the word "AAARRGH!" We'll come running when we get a chance to.
Precious.
And I STILL keep the medallion to this very day.
OH MY GOSH! I DON'T BELIEVE IT!
Well, OKAY...I did CONSIDER selling it once. But that was for tuition costs.
NOT ABOUT YOUR OVERLY SENTIMENTALIZED NECKLACE! I'M REACTING IN SHOCK TO THAT NO GOOD MIYUMI PUTTING MOVES ON MY MAN!
Hey, Hakata! I brought in that vintage videogame I mentioned in class yesterday!
FOR REAL?
UGH! Her CONTACT makes him CONTAMINATED, so that I now think I am TOTALLY OVER HIM.
YEAH, WELL... if he's friends with Miyumi San... he is DEAD TO ME!
But he's a HERO! Hakata Soy saved the lives of my people!
And a HOBO to me!
END!

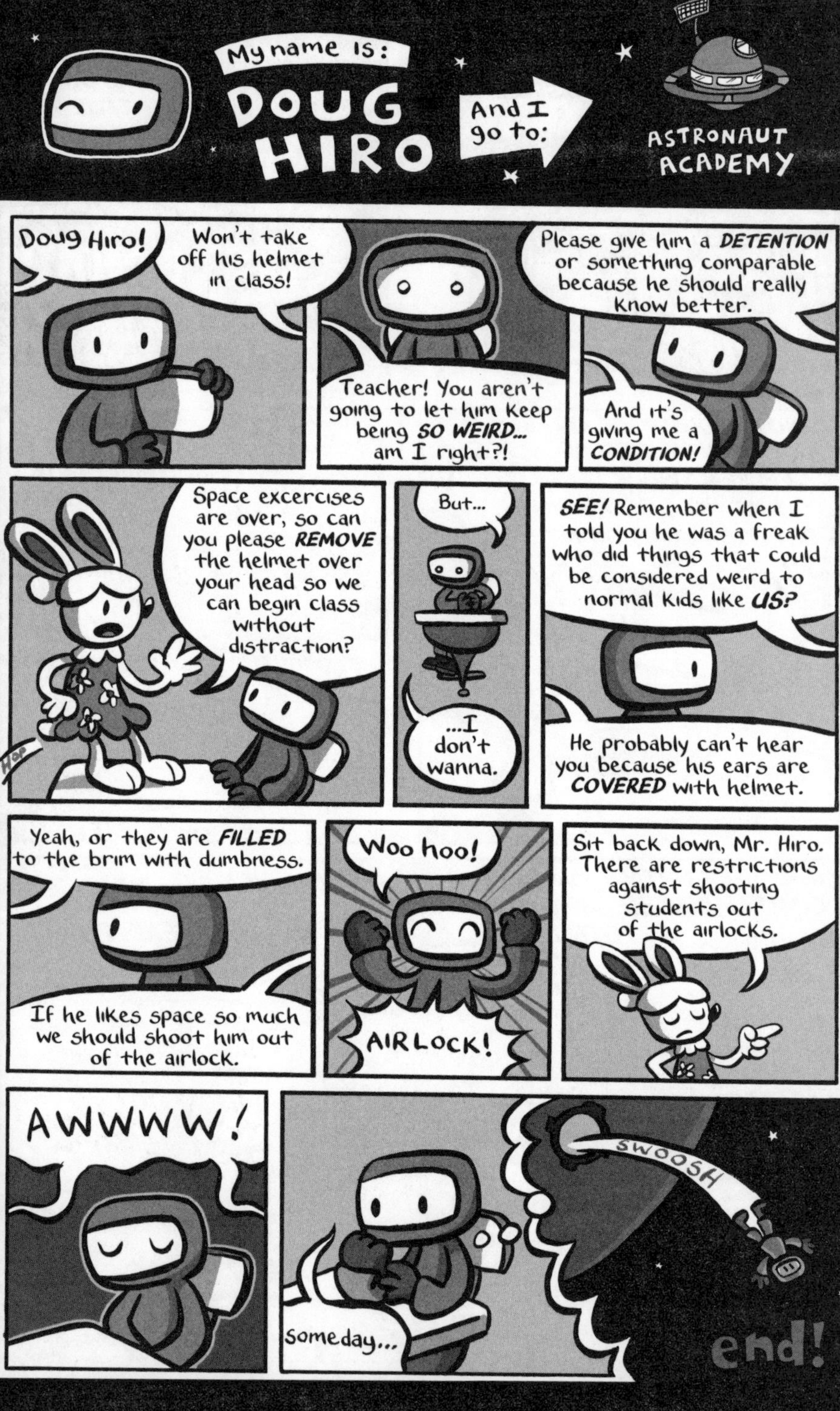
My name is:
DOUG HIRO
And I go to:
ASTRONAUT ACADEMY
Doug Hiro!
Won't take off his helmet in class!
Teacher! You aren't going to let him keep being SO WEIRD... am I right?!
Please give him a DETENTION or something comparable because he should really know better.
And it's giving me a CONDITION!
Space excercises are over, so can you please REMOVE the helmet over your head so we can begin class without distraction?
But...
...I don't wanna.
SEE! Remember when I told you he was a freak who did things that could be considered weird to normal kids like US?
He probably can't hear you because his ears are COVERED with helmet.
Yeah, or they are FILLED to the brim with dumbness.
If he likes space so much we should shoot him out of the airlock.
Woo hoo!
AIRLOCK!
Sit back down, Mr. Hiro. There are restrictions against shooting students out of the airlocks.
AWWWW!
Someday...
SWOOSH
end!

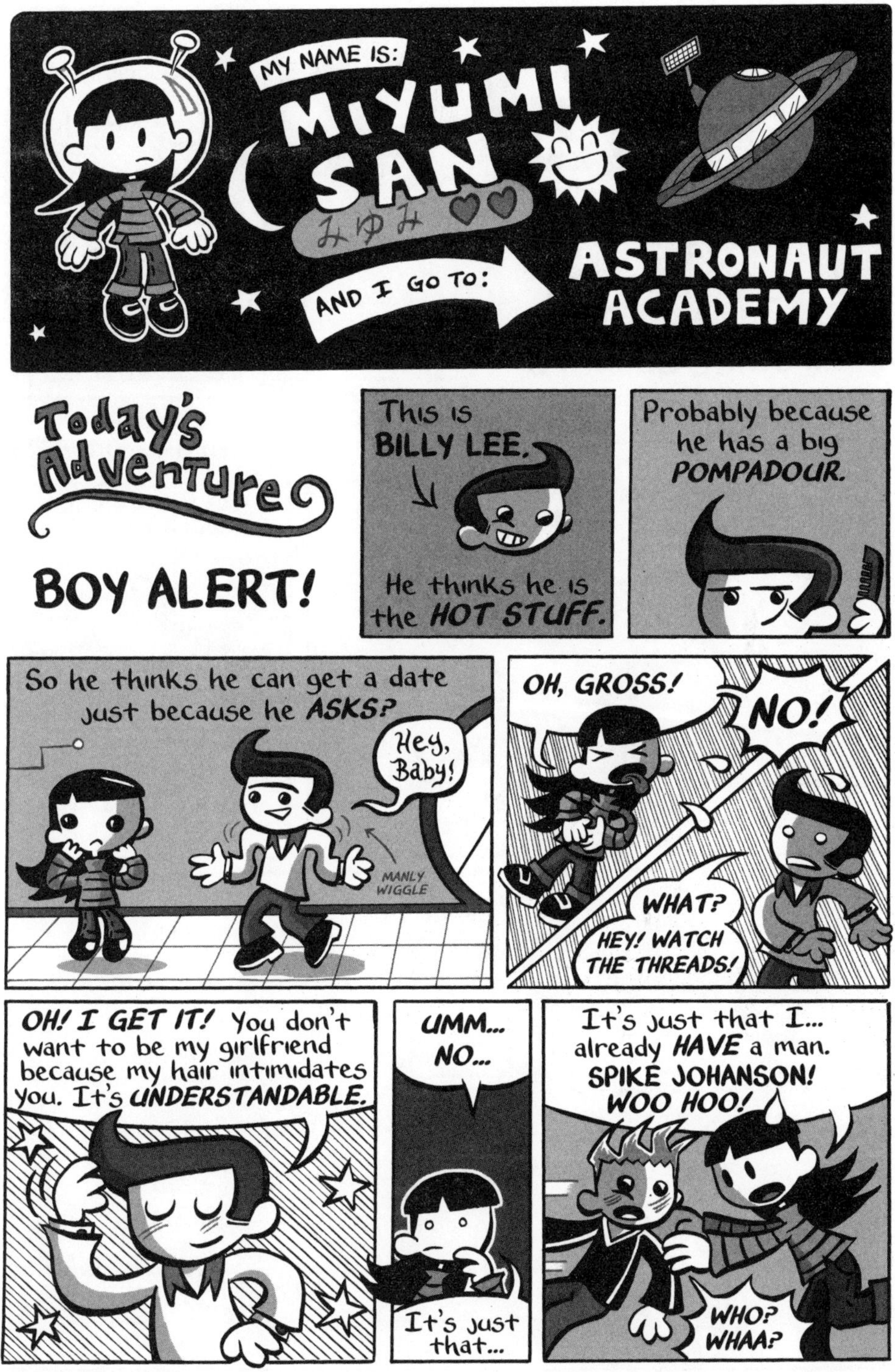
MY NAME IS:
MIYUMI SAN
みゆみ
AND I GO TO:
ASTRONAUT ACADEMY
Today's Adventure
BOY ALERT!
This is BILLY LEE.
He thinks he is the HOT STUFF.
Probably because he has a big POMPADOUR.
So he thinks he can get a date just because he ASKS?
Hey, Baby!
MANLY WIGGLE
OH, GROSS!
NO!
WHAT?
HEY! WATCH THE THREADS!
OH! I GET IT! You don't want to be my girlfriend because my hair intimidates you. It's UNDERSTANDABLE.
UMM... NO...
It's just that...
It's just that I... already HAVE a man. SPIKE JOHANSON! WOO HOO!
WHO? WHAA?

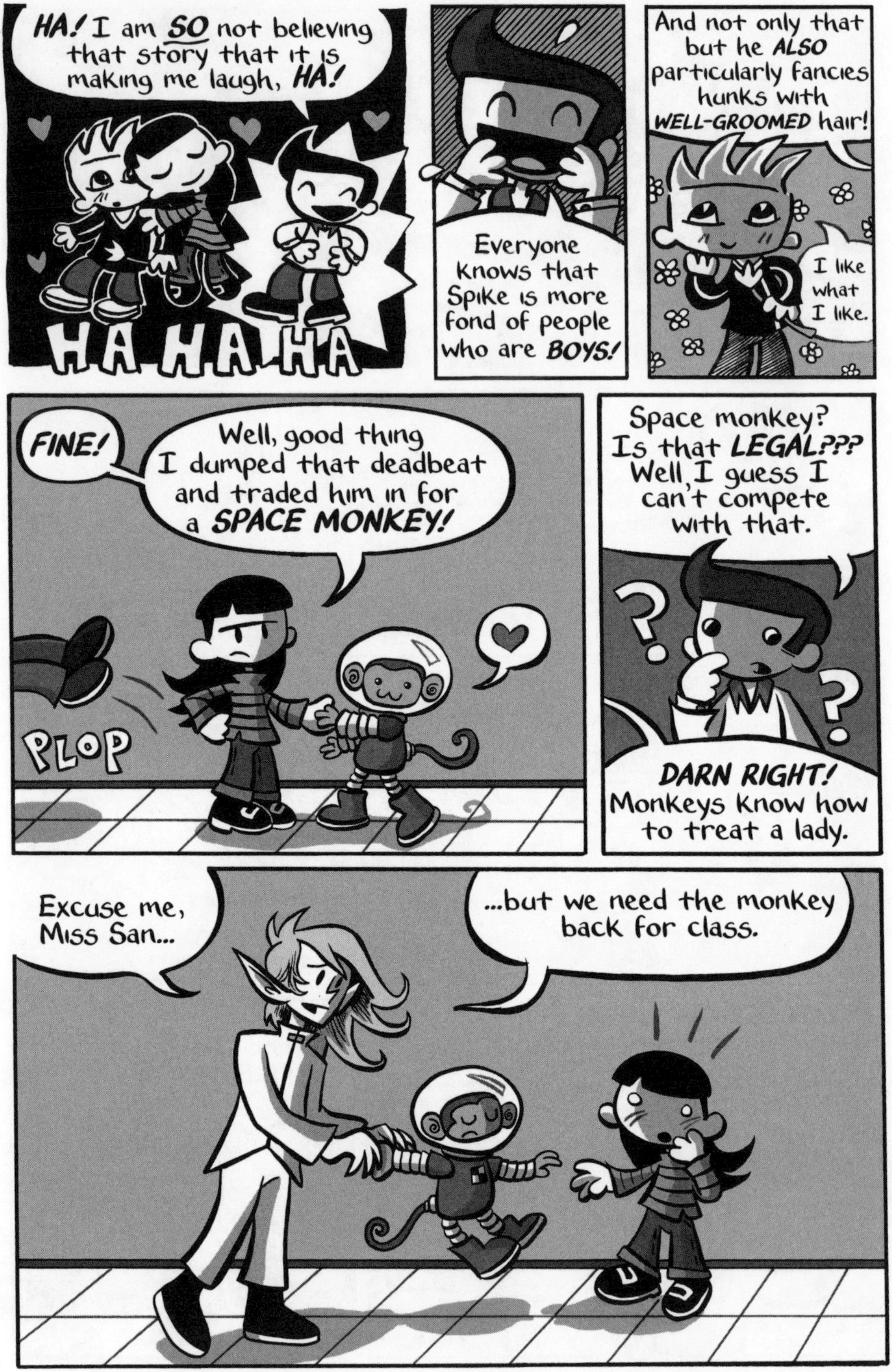
HA! I am SO not believing that story that it is making me laugh, HA!
HA HA HA HA
Everyone knows that Spike is more fond of people who are BOYS!
And not only that but he ALSO particularly fancies hunks with WELL-GROOMED hair!
I like what I like.
FINE!
Well, good thing I dumped that deadbeat and traded him in for a SPACE MONKEY!
PLOP
Space monkey? Is that LEGAL??? Well, I guess I can't compete with that.
DARN RIGHT! Monkeys know how to treat a lady.
Excuse me, Miss San...
...but we need the monkey back for class.

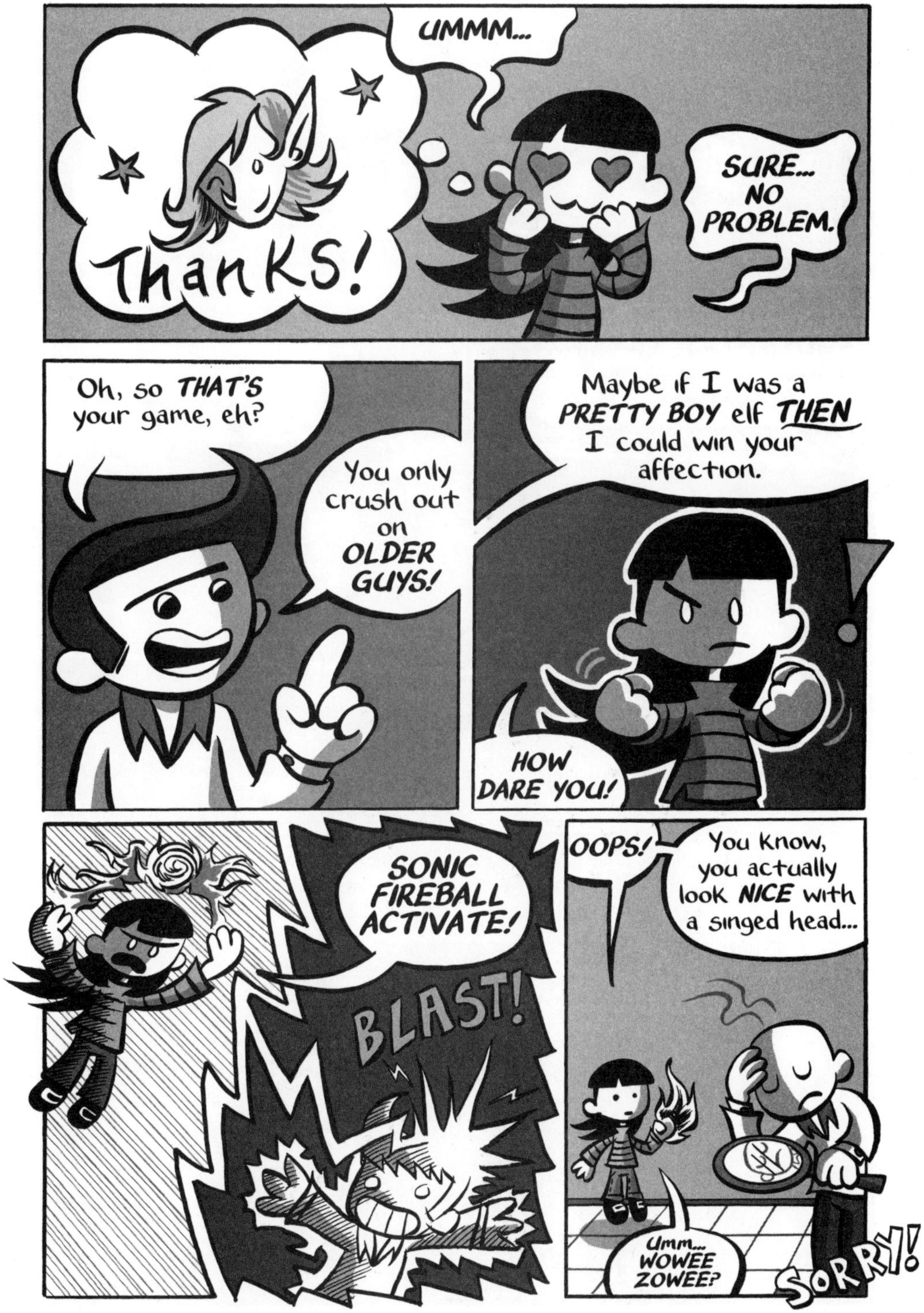
Thanks!
UMMM...
SURE... NO PROBLEM.
Oh, so THAT'S your game, eh?
You only crush out on OLDER GUYS!
Maybe if I was a PRETTY BOY elf THEN I could win your affection.
!
HOW DARE YOU!
SONIC FIREBALL ACTIVATE!
BLAST!
OOPS!
You know, you actually look NICE with a singed head...
Umm... WOWEE ZOWEE?
SORRY!

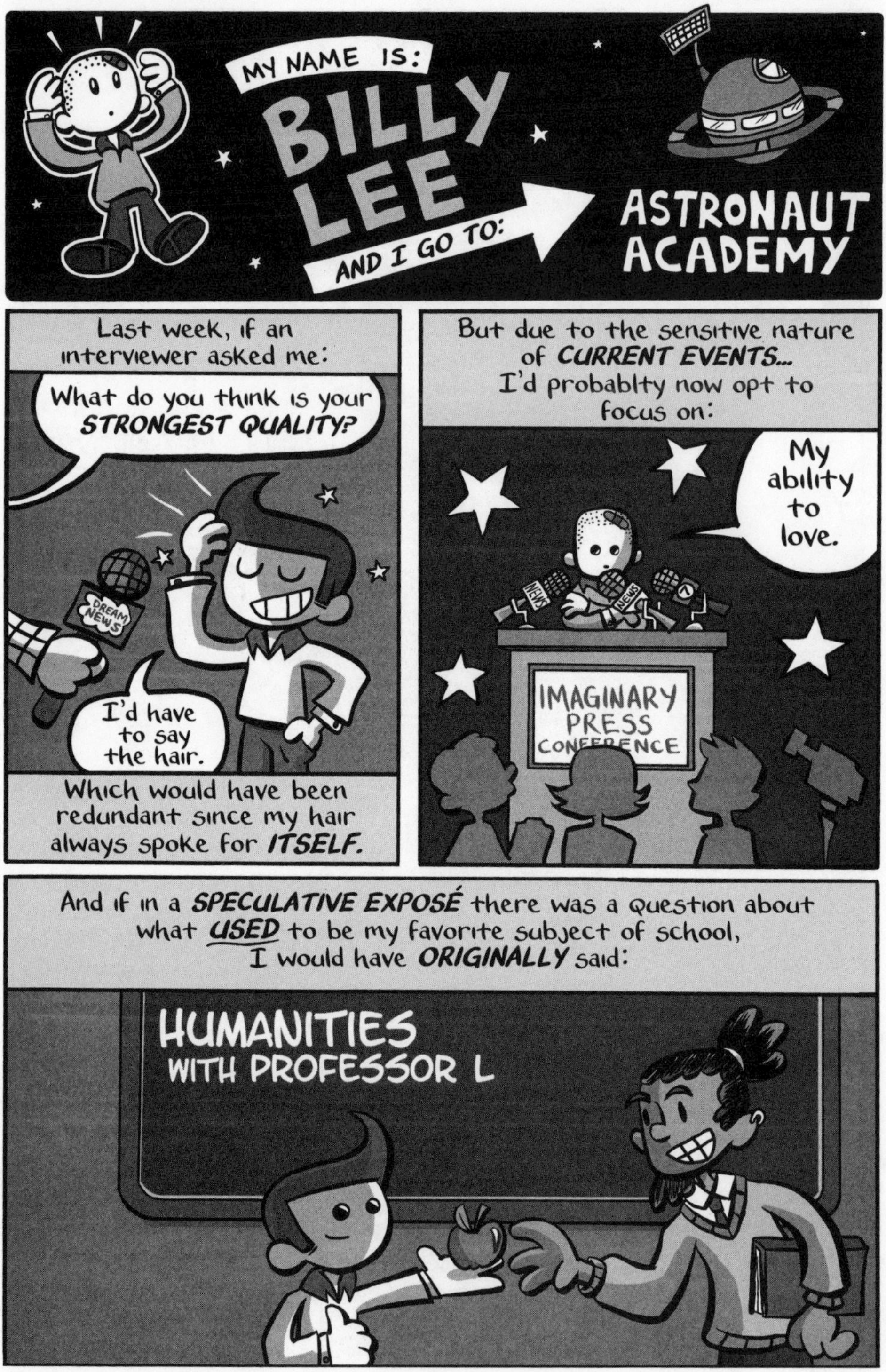
MY NAME IS:
BILLY LEE
AND I GO TO:
ASTRONAUT ACADEMY
Last week, if an interviewer asked me:
What do you think is your STRONGEST QUALITY?
DREAM NEWS
I'd have to say the hair.
Which would have been redundant since my hair always spoke for ITSELF.
But due to the sensitive nature of CURRENT EVENTS... I'd probablty now opt to focus on:
My ability to love.
IMAGINARY PRESS CONFERENCE
And if in a SPECULATIVE EXPOSÉ there was a question about what USED to be my favorite subject of school, I would have ORIGINALLY said:
HUMANITIES WITH PROFESSOR L

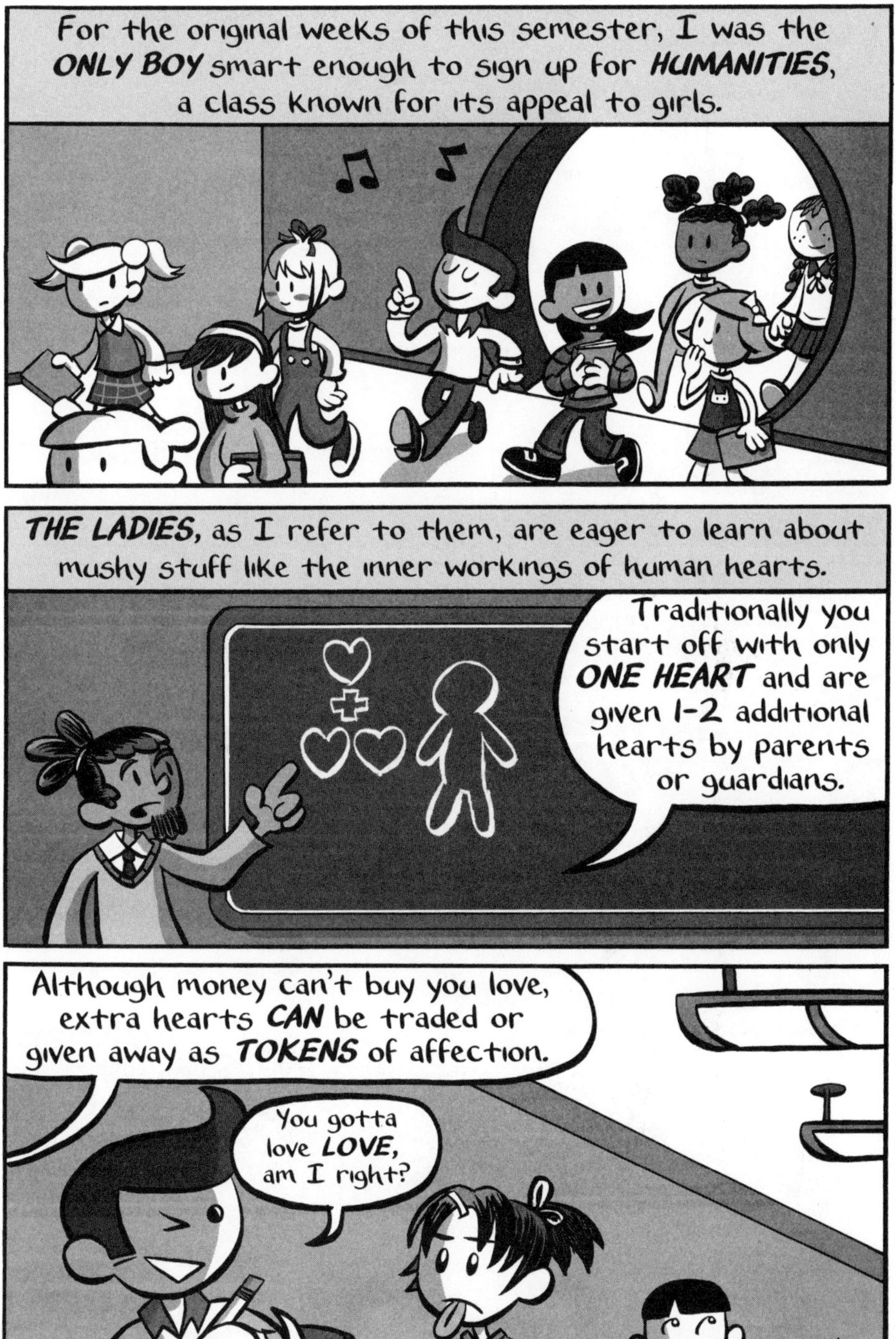
For the original weeks of this semester, I was the ONLY BOY smart enough to sign up for HUMANITIES, a class known for its appeal to girls.
THE LADIES, as I refer to them, are eager to learn about mushy stuff like the inner workings of human hearts.
Traditionally you start off with only ONE HEART and are given 1-2 additional hearts by parents or guardians.
Although money can't buy you love, extra hearts CAN be traded or given away as TOKENS of affection.
You gotta love LOVE, am I right?
I'm a FAN.

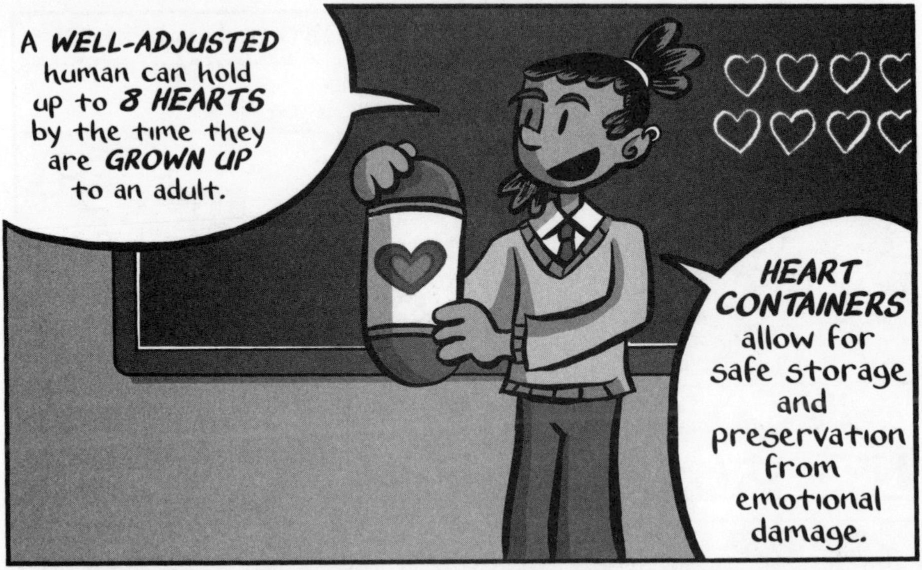
A WELL-ADJUSTED human can hold up to 8 HEARTS by the time they are GROWN UP to an adult.
HEART CONTAINERS allow for safe storage and preservation from emotional damage.

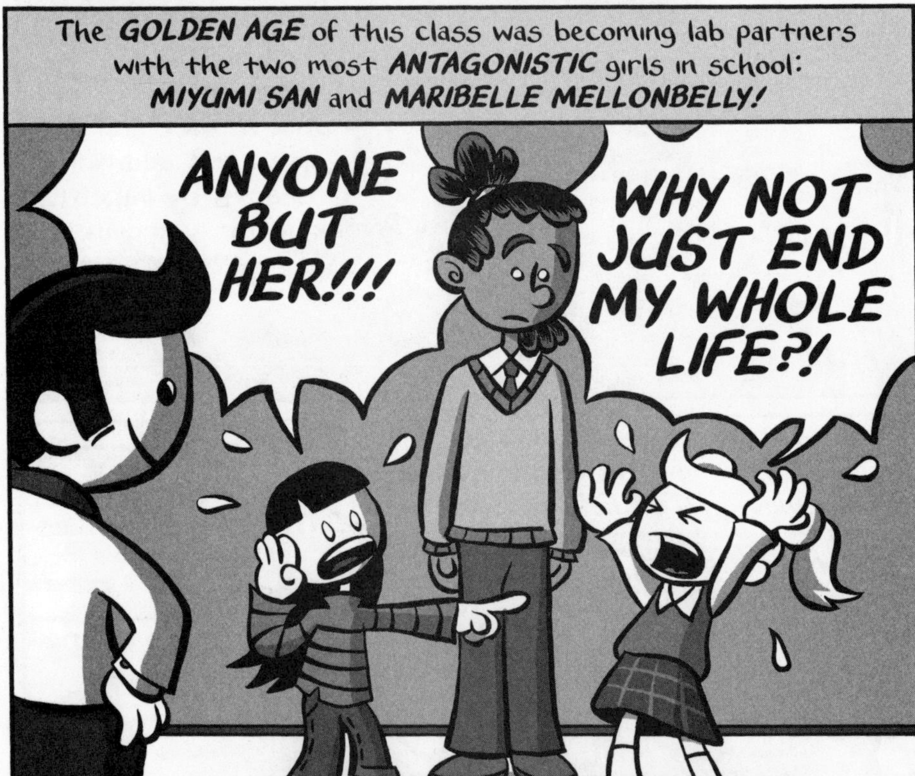
The GOLDEN AGE of this class was becoming lab partners with the two most ANTAGONISTIC girls in school: MIYUMI SAN and MARIBELLE MELLONBELLY!
ANYONE BUT HER!!!
WHY NOT JUST END MY WHOLE LIFE?!

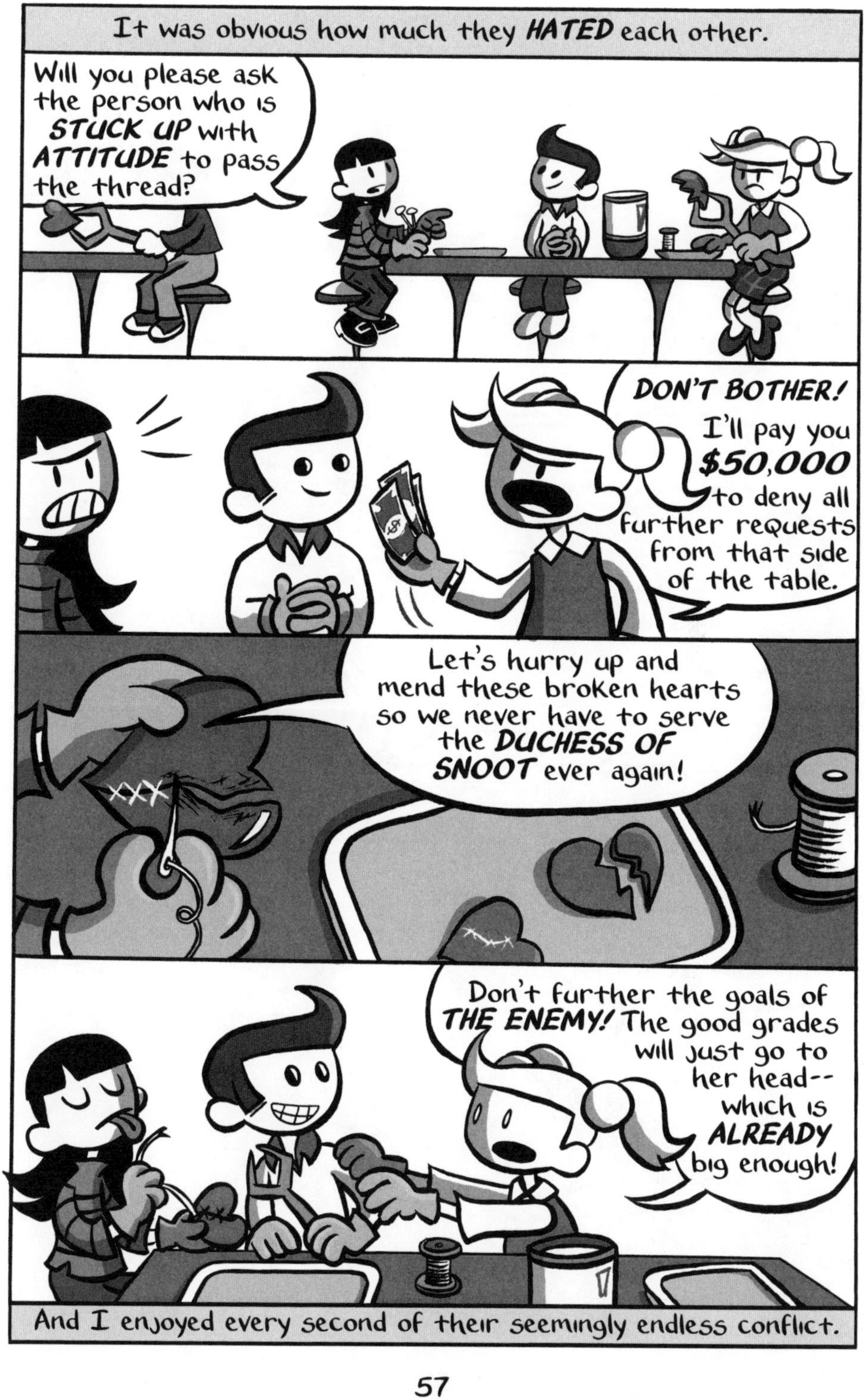
It was obvious how much they HATED each other.
Will you please ask the person who is STUCK UP with ATTITUDE to pass the thread?
DON'T BOTHER! I'll pay you $50,000 to deny all further requests from that side of the table.
Let's hurry up and mend these broken hearts so we never have to serve the DUCHESS OF SNOOT ever again!
Don't further the goals of THE ENEMY! The good grades will just go to her head--which is ALREADY big enough!
And I enjoyed every second of their seemingly endless conflict.

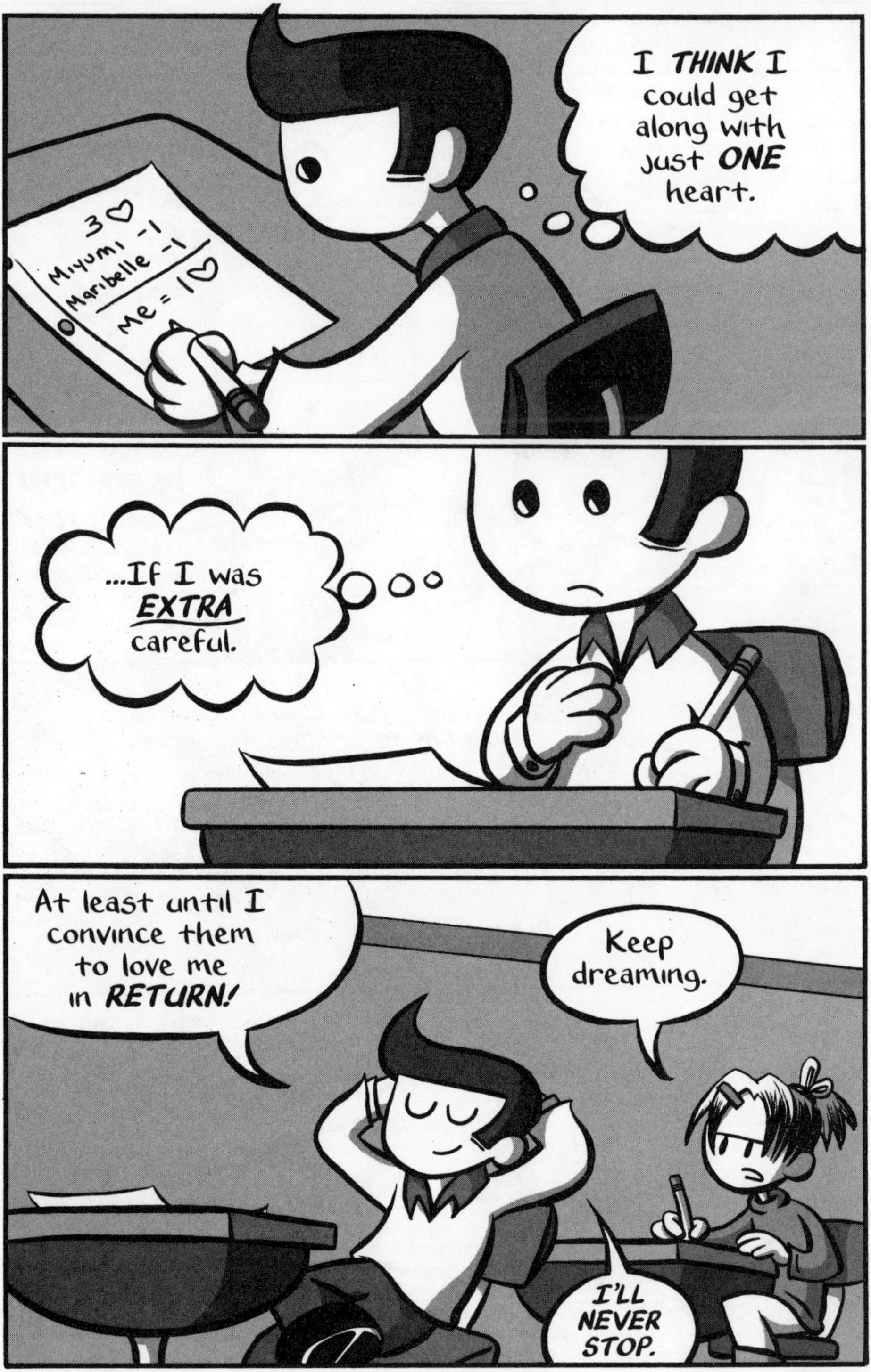
3 ♡
Miyumi -1
Maribelle -1
Me = 1♡
I THINK I could get along with just ONE heart.
...If I was EXTRA careful.
At least until I convince them to love me in RETURN!
Keep dreaming.
I'LL NEVER STOP.

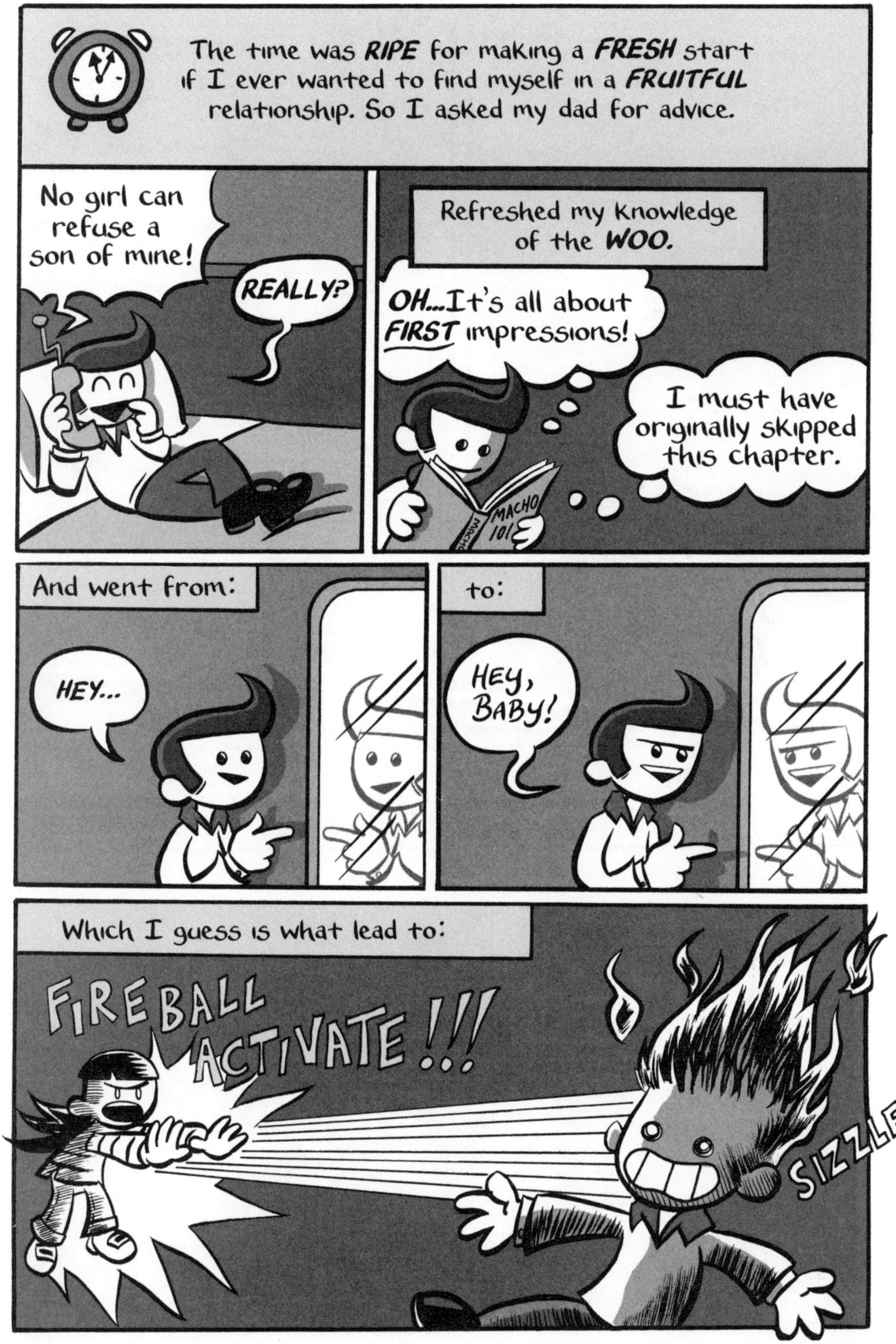
The time was RIPE for making a FRESH start if I ever wanted to find myself in a FRUITFUL relationship. So I asked my dad for advice.
No girl can refuse a son of mine!
REALLY?
Refreshed my knowledge of the WOO.
OH...It's all about FIRST impressions!
I must have originally skipped this chapter.
MACHO 101
And went from:
HEY...
to:
HEY, BABY!
Which I guess is what lead to:
FIREBALL ACTIVATE!!!
SIZZLE

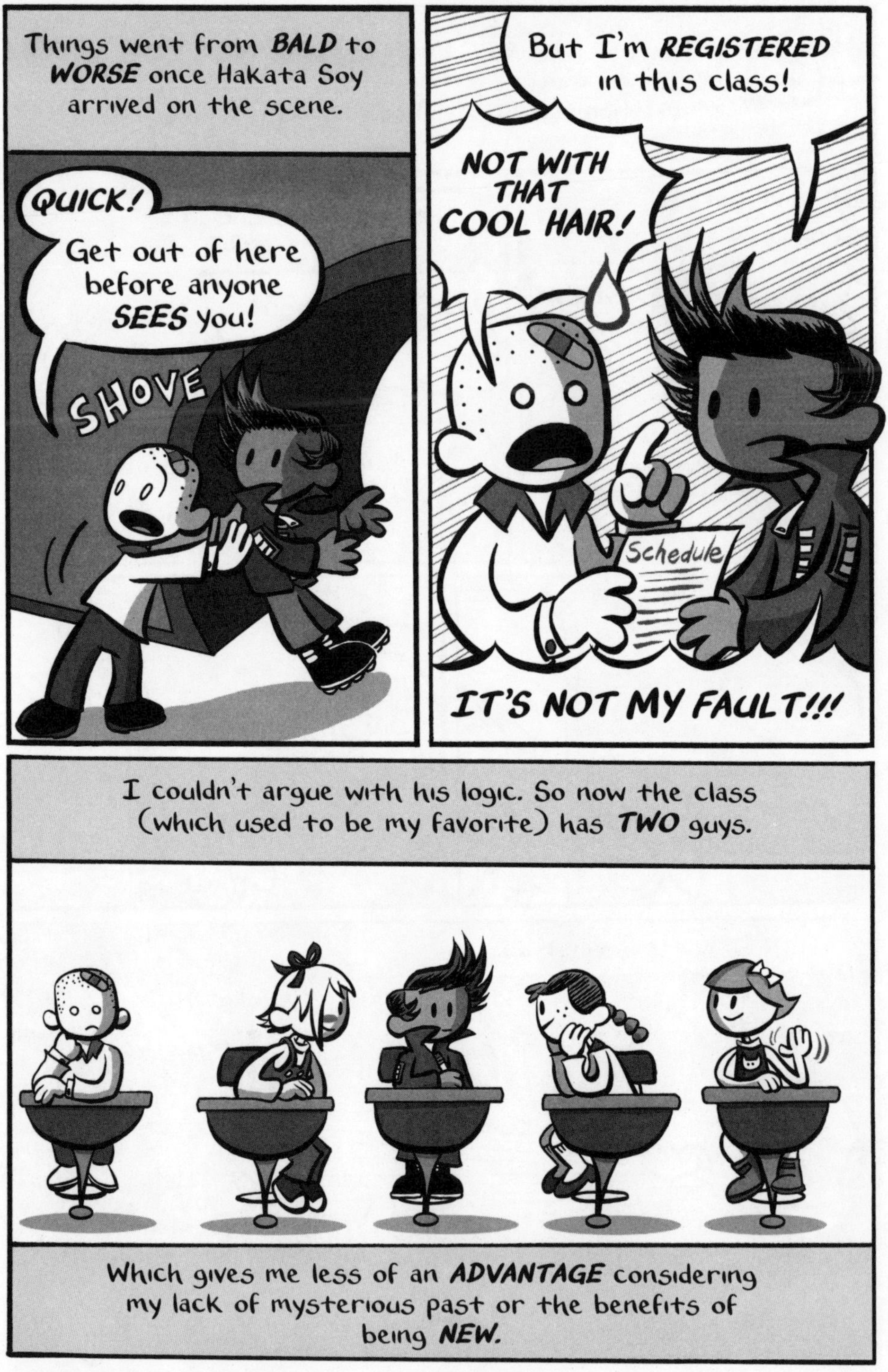
Things went from BALD to WORSE once Hakata Soy arrived on the scene.
QUICK!
Get out of here before anyone SEES you!
SHOVE
But I'm REGISTERED in this class!
NOT WITH THAT COOL HAIR!
Schedule
IT'S NOT MY FAULT!!!
I couldn't argue with his logic. So now the class (which used to be my favorite) has TWO guys.
Which gives me less of an ADVANTAGE considering my lack of mysterious past or the benefits of being NEW.

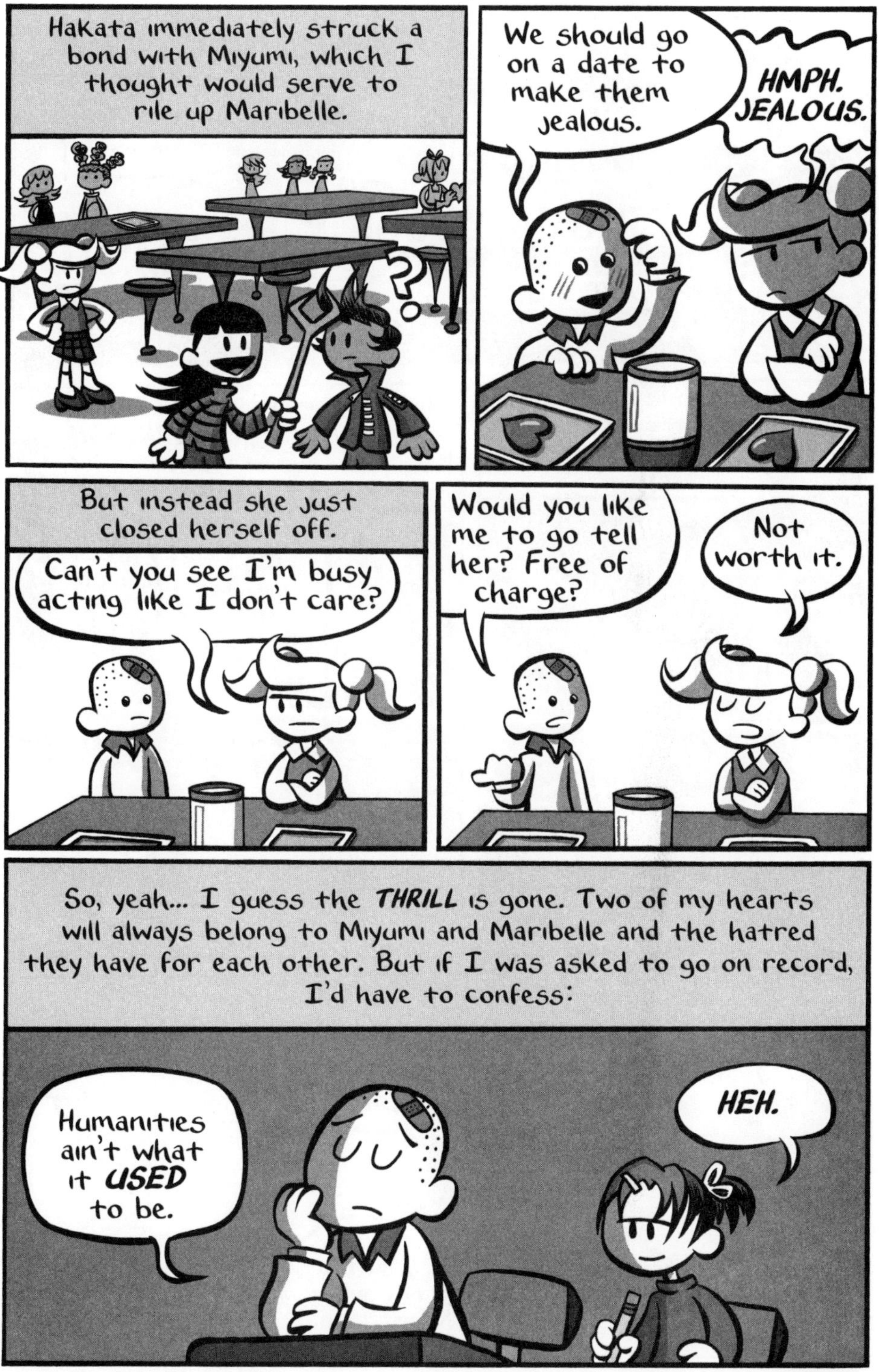
Hakata immediately struck a bond with Miyumi, which I thought would serve to rile up Maribelle.
We should go on a date to make them jealous.
HMPH. JEALOUS.
But instead she just closed herself off.
Can't you see I'm busy acting like I don't care?
Would you like me to go tell her? Free of charge?
Not worth it.
So, yeah... I guess the THRILL is gone. Two of my hearts will always belong to Miyumi and Maribelle and the hatred they have for each other. But if I was asked to go on record, I'd have to confess:
Humanities ain't what it USED to be.
HEH.

END!

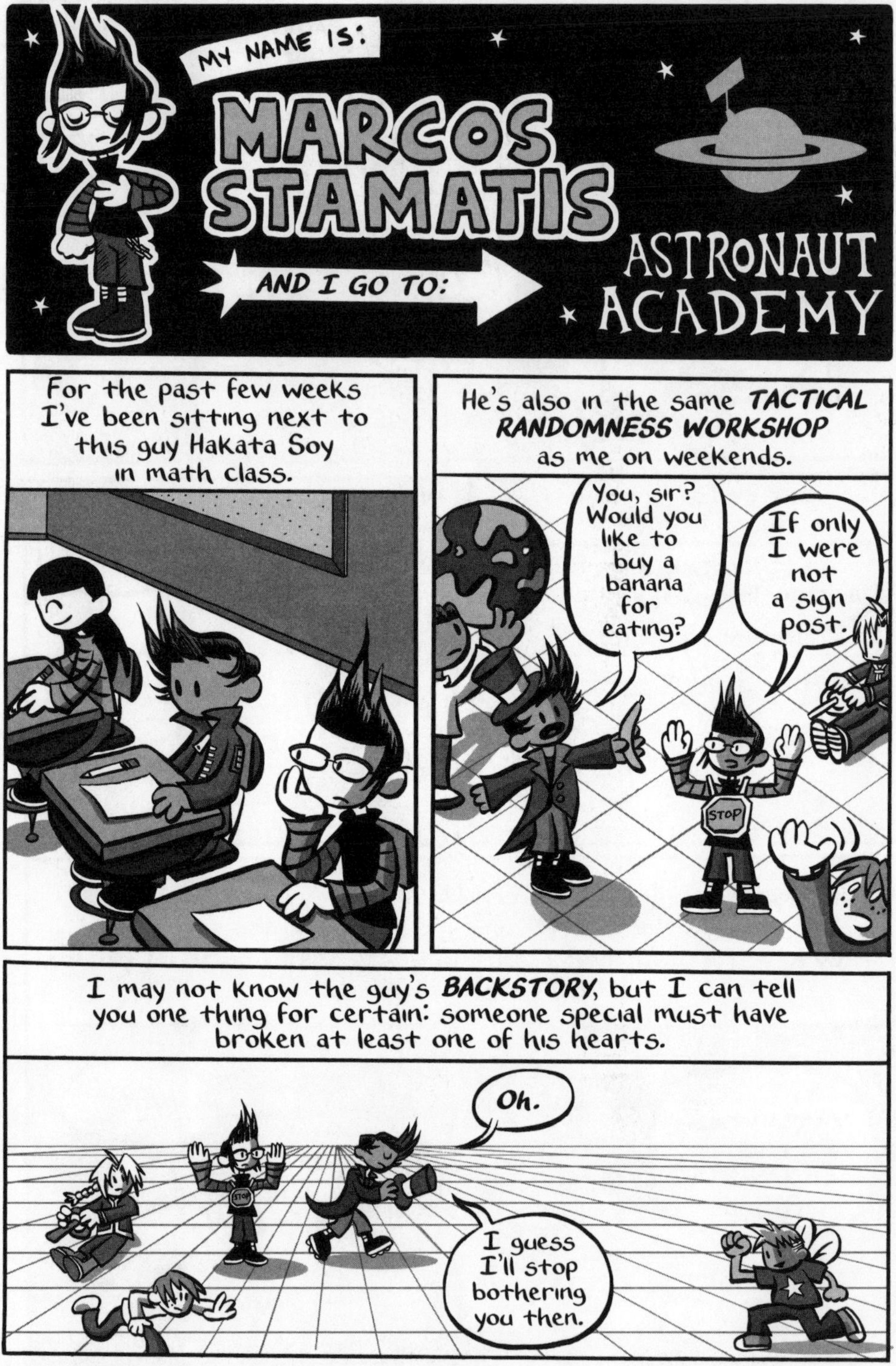
MY NAME IS:
MARCOS STAMATIS
AND I GO TO:
ASTRONAUT ACADEMY
For the past few weeks I've been sitting next to this guy Hakata Soy in math class.
He's also in the same TACTICAL RANDOMNESS WORKSHOP as me on weekends.
You, sir? Would you like to buy a banana for eating?
If only I were not a sign post.
STOP
I may not know the guy's BACKSTORY, but I can tell you one thing for certain: someone special must have broken at least one of his hearts.
Oh.
I guess I'll stop bothering you then.
STOP

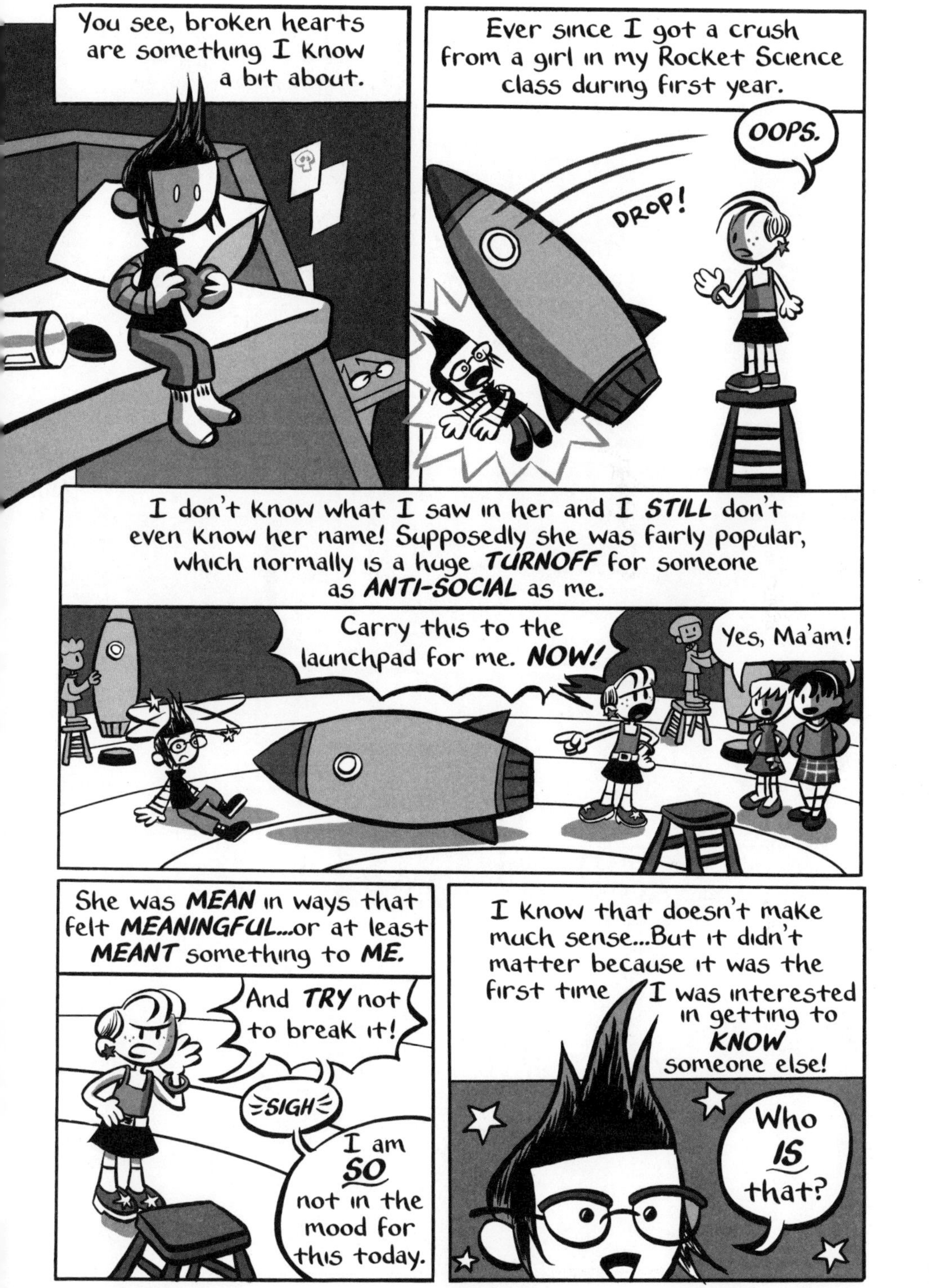

You see, broken hearts are something I know a bit about.
Ever since I got a crush from a girl in my Rocket Science class during first year.
OOPS.
DROP!
I don't know what I saw in her and I STILL don't even know her name! Supposedly she was fairly popular, which normally is a huge TURNOFF for someone as ANTI-SOCIAL as me.
Carry this to the launchpad for me. NOW!
Yes, Ma'am!
She was MEAN in ways that felt MEANINGFUL...or at least MEANT something to ME.
And TRY not to break it!
SIGH
I am SO not in the mood for this today.
I know that doesn't make much sense...But it didn't matter because it was the first time I was interested in getting to KNOW someone else!
Who IS that?

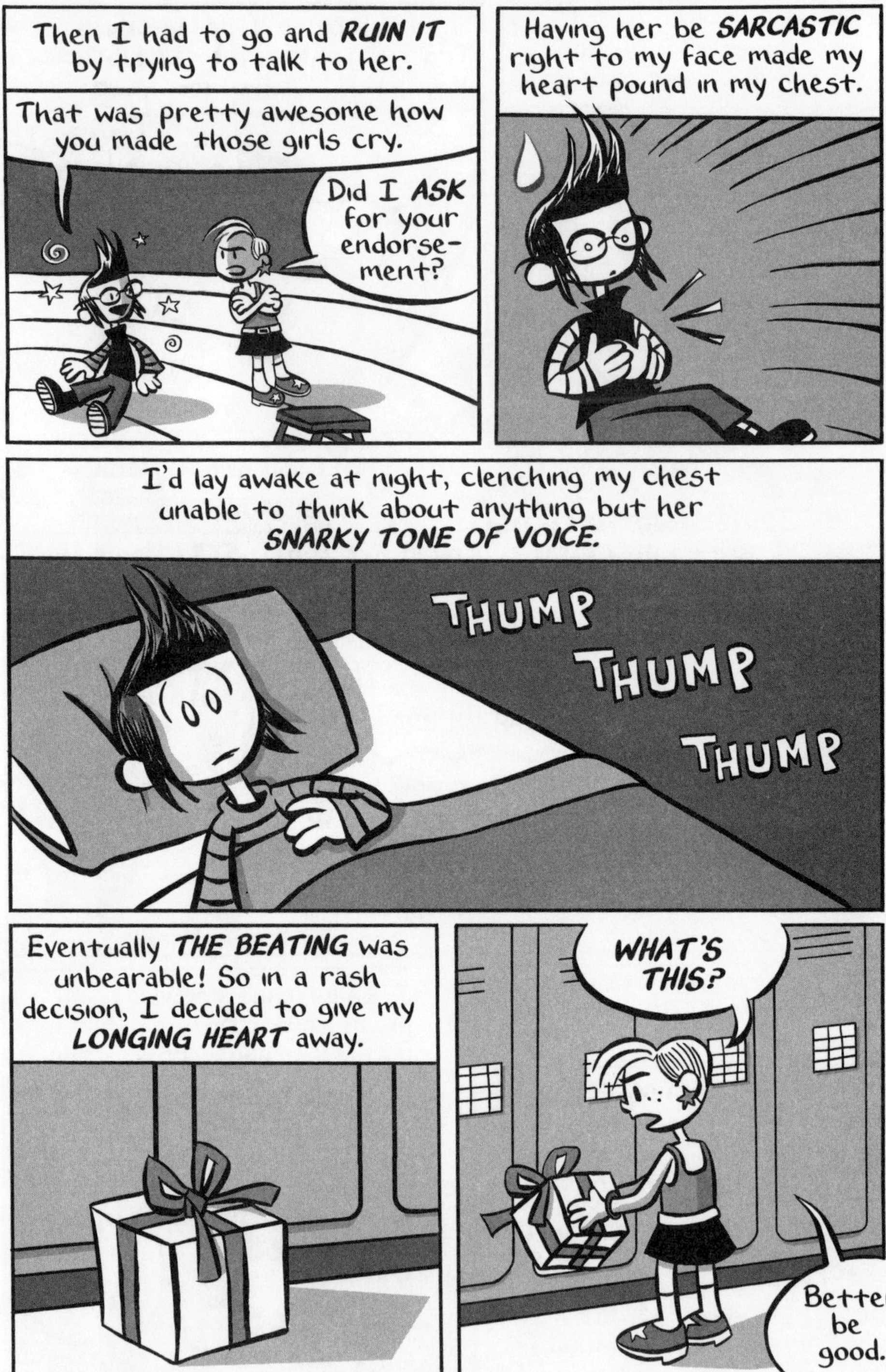
Then I had to go and **RUIN IT** by trying to talk to her.
That was pretty awesome how you made those girls cry.
Did I **ASK** for your endorsement?
Having her be **SARCASTIC** right to my face made my heart pound in my chest.
I'd lay awake at night, clenching my chest unable to think about anything but her **SNARKY TONE OF VOICE.**
THUMP
THUMP
THUMP
Eventually **THE BEATING** was unbearable! So in a rash decision, I decided to give my **LONGING HEART** away.
WHAT'S THIS?
Better be good.

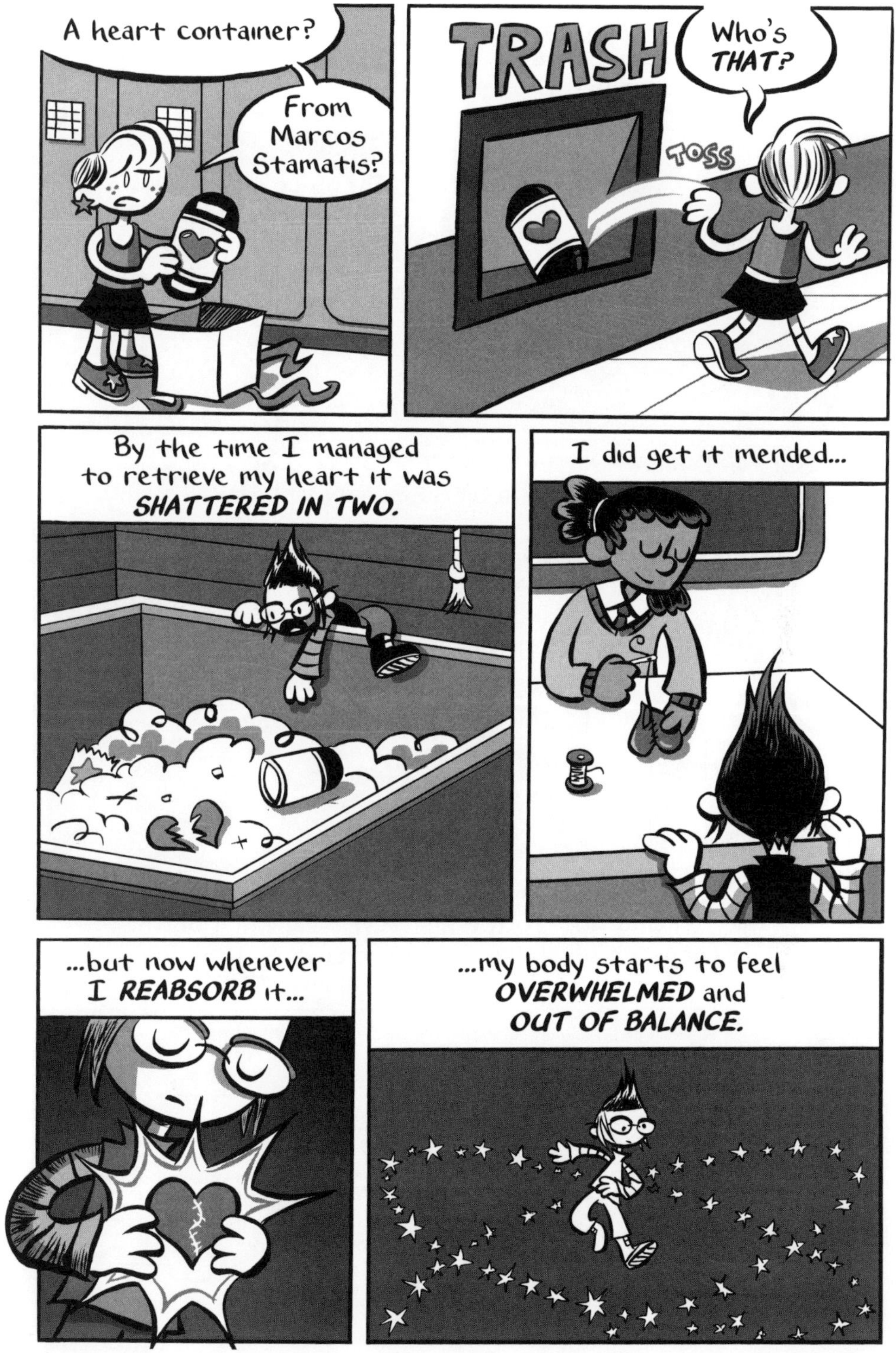
A heart container?
From Marcos Stamatis?
TRASH
Who's THAT?
TOSS
By the time I managed to retrieve my heart it was SHATTERED IN TWO.
I did get it mended...
...but now whenever I REABSORB it...
...my body starts to feel OVERWHELMED and OUT OF BALANCE.

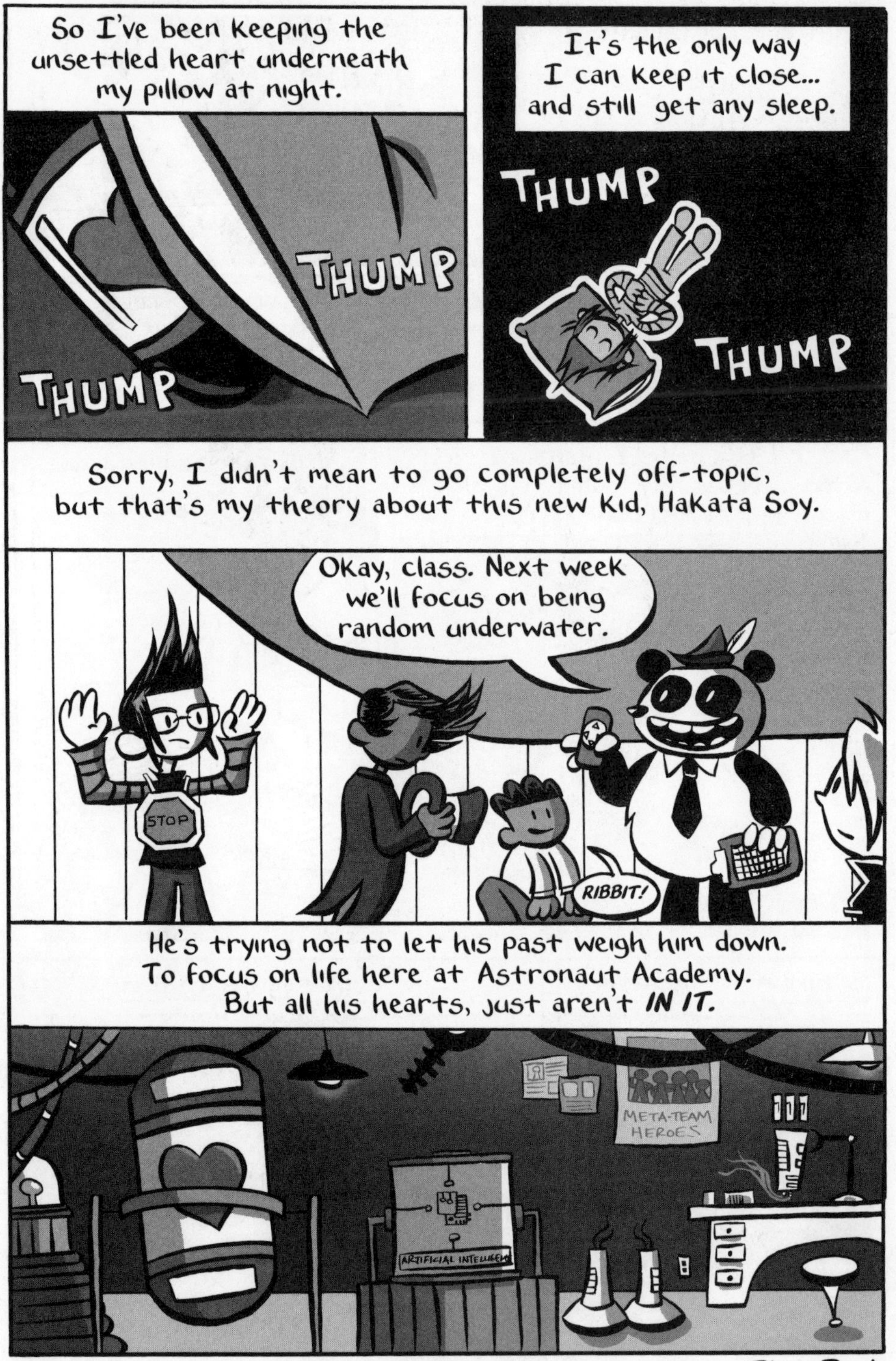
So I've been keeping the unsettled heart underneath my pillow at night.
THUMP
THUMP
It's the only way I can keep it close... and still get any sleep.
THUMP
THUMP
Sorry, I didn't mean to go completely off-topic, but that's my theory about this new kid, Hakata Soy.
Okay, class. Next week we'll focus on being random underwater.
STOP
RIBBIT!
He's trying not to let his past weigh him down. To focus on life here at Astronaut Academy. But all his hearts, just aren't *IN IT.*
META-TEAM HEROES

The End.

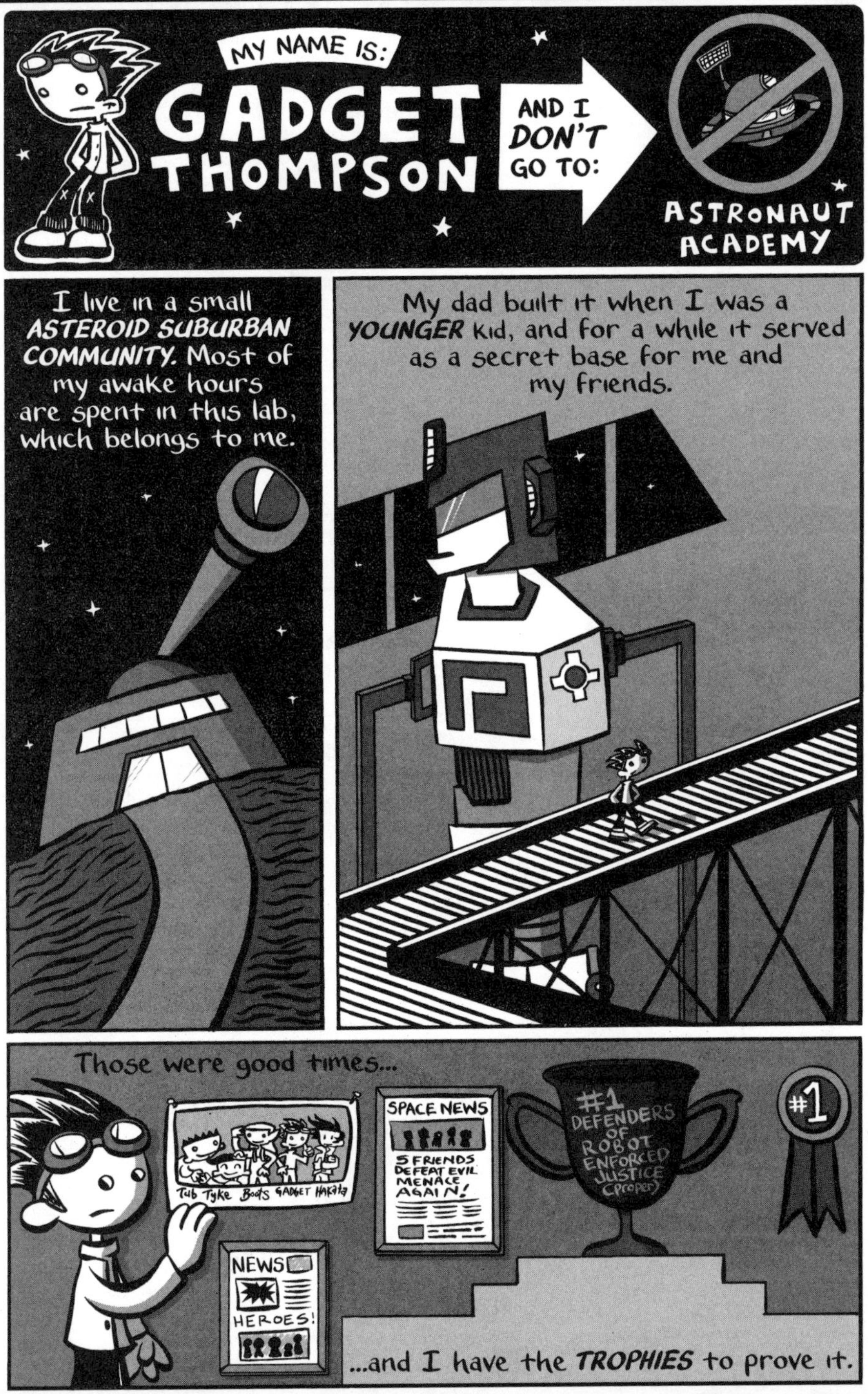

MY NAME IS:
GADGET THOMPSON
AND I DON'T GO TO:
ASTRONAUT ACADEMY
I live in a small ASTEROID SUBURBAN COMMUNITY. Most of my awake hours are spent in this lab, which belongs to me.
My dad built it when I was a YOUNGER kid, and for a while it served as a secret base for me and my friends.
Those were good times...
Tub Tyke Boots GADGET Hakata
SPACE NEWS
5 FRIENDS DEFEAT EVIL MENACE AGAIN!
#1 DEFENDERS OF ROBOT ENFORCED JUSTICE (proper)
#1
NEWS
HEROES!
...and I have the TROPHIES to prove it.

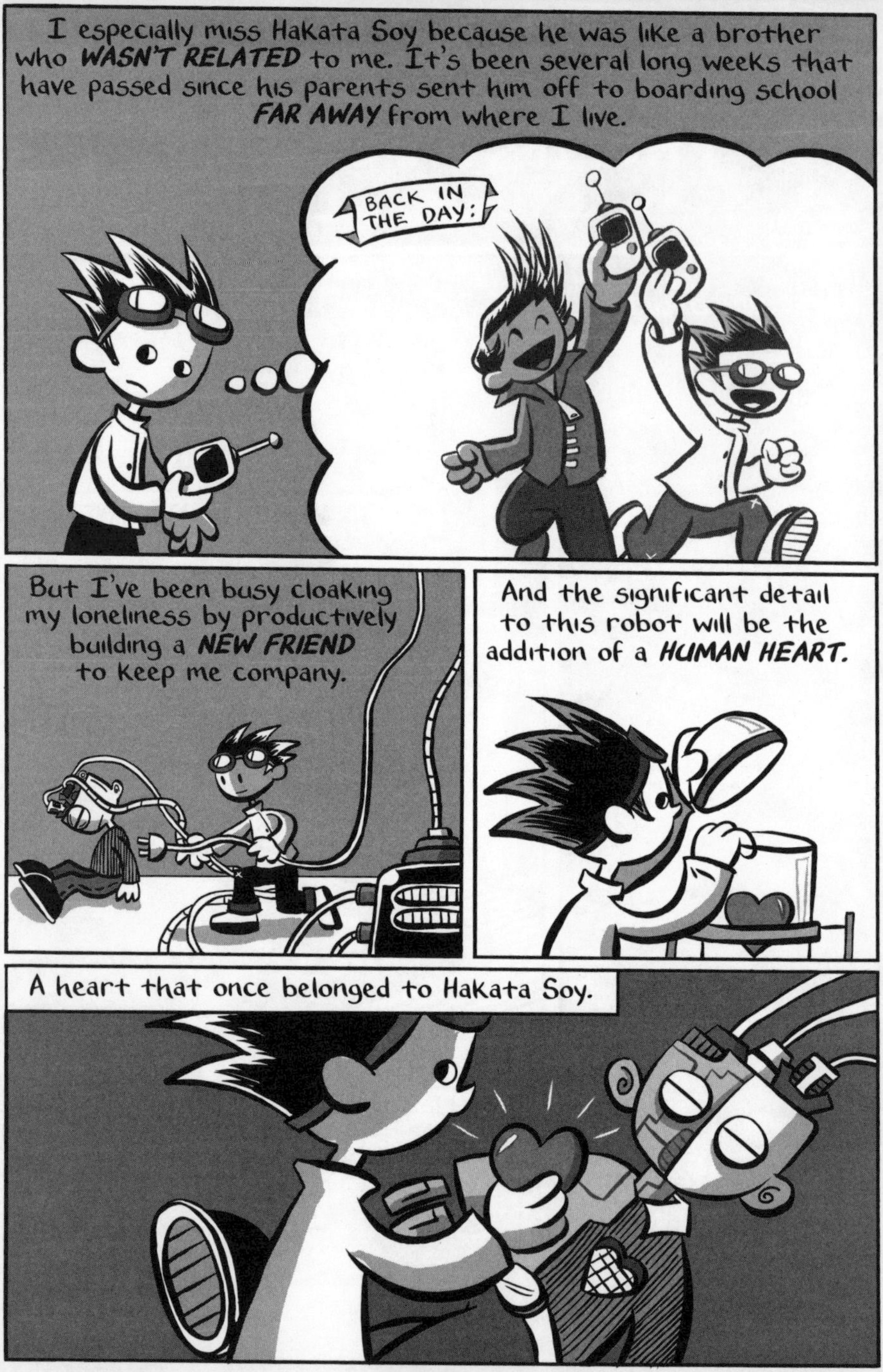
I especially miss Hakata Soy because he was like a brother who **WASN'T RELATED** to me. It's been several long weeks that have passed since his parents sent him off to boarding school **FAR AWAY** from where I live.
BACK IN THE DAY:
But I've been busy cloaking my loneliness by productively building a **NEW FRIEND** to keep me company.
And the significant detail to this robot will be the addition of a **HUMAN HEART.**
A heart that once belonged to Hakata Soy.

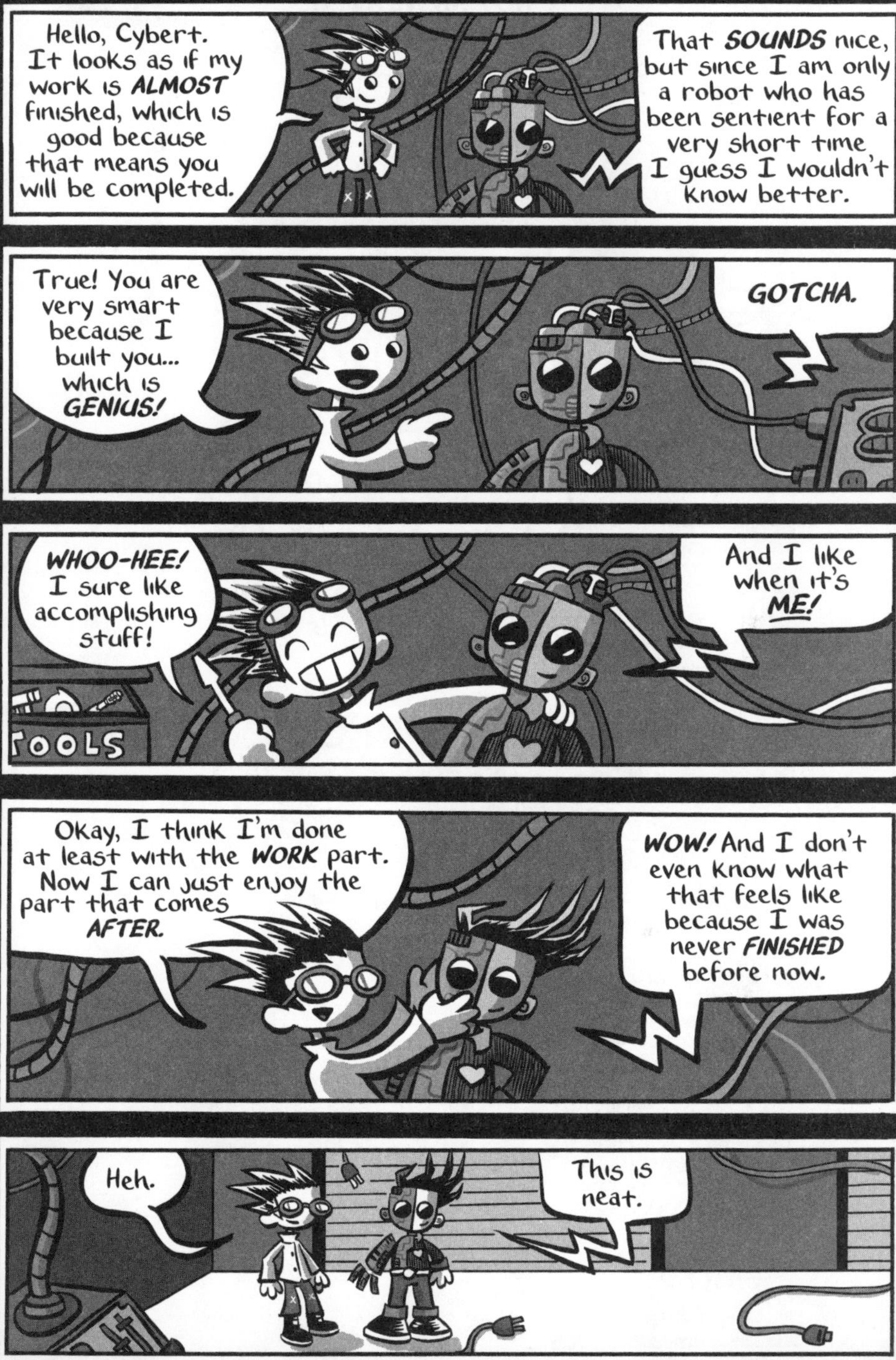
Hello, Cybert. It looks as if my work is ALMOST finished, which is good because that means you will be completed.
That SOUNDS nice, but since I am only a robot who has been sentient for a very short time I guess I wouldn't know better.
True! You are very smart because I built you... which is GENIUS!
GOTCHA.
WHOO-HEE! I sure like accomplishing stuff!
TOOLS
And I like when it's ME!
Okay, I think I'm done at least with the WORK part. Now I can just enjoy the part that comes AFTER.
WOW! And I don't even know what that feels like because I was never FINISHED before now.
Heh.
This is neat.

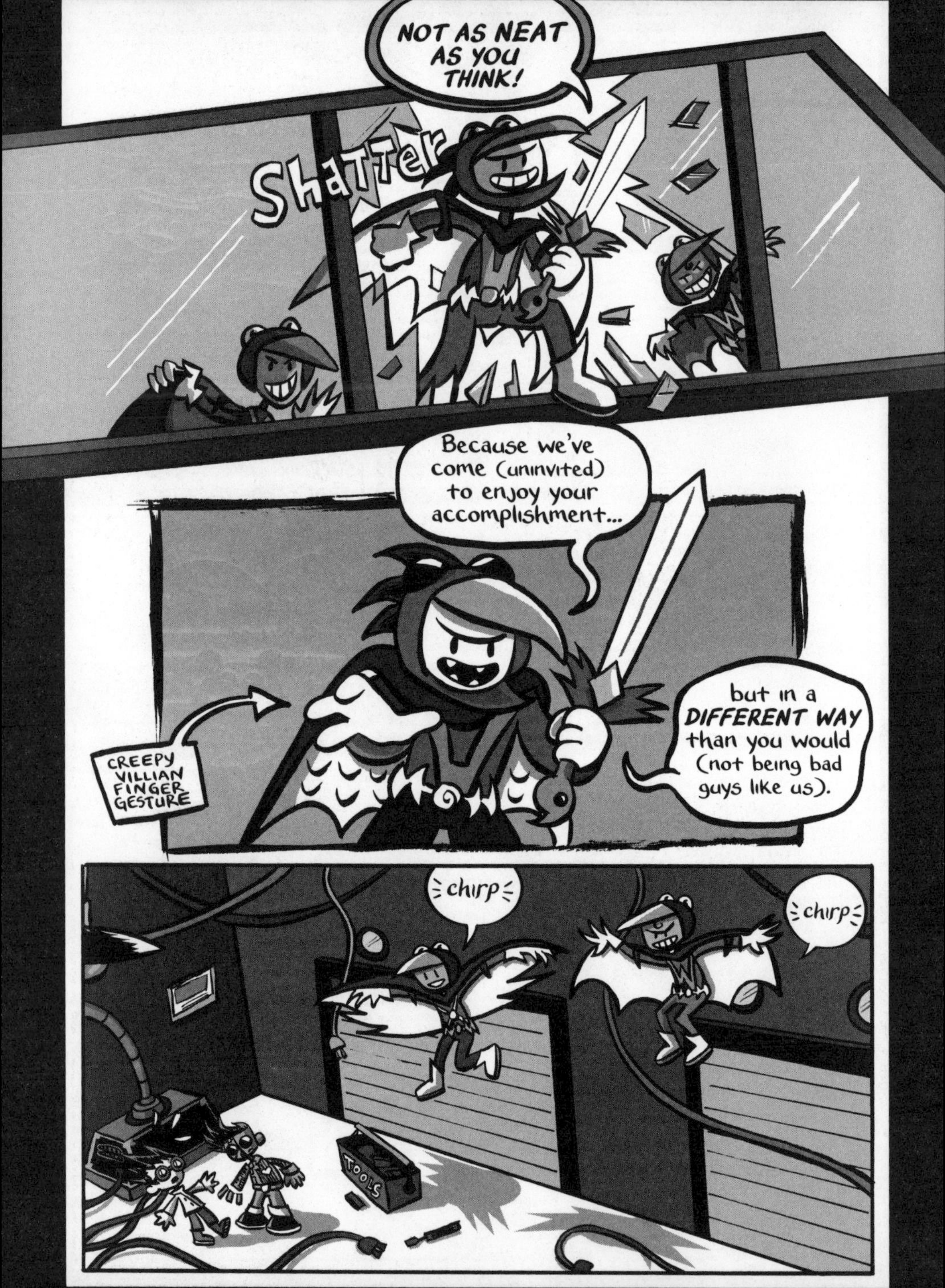
NOT AS NEAT AS YOU THINK!
SHATTER
Because we've come (uninvited) to enjoy your accomplishment...
CREEPY VILLIAN FINGER GESTURE
but in a DIFFERENT WAY than you would (not being bad guys like us).
chirp
chirp
TOOLS

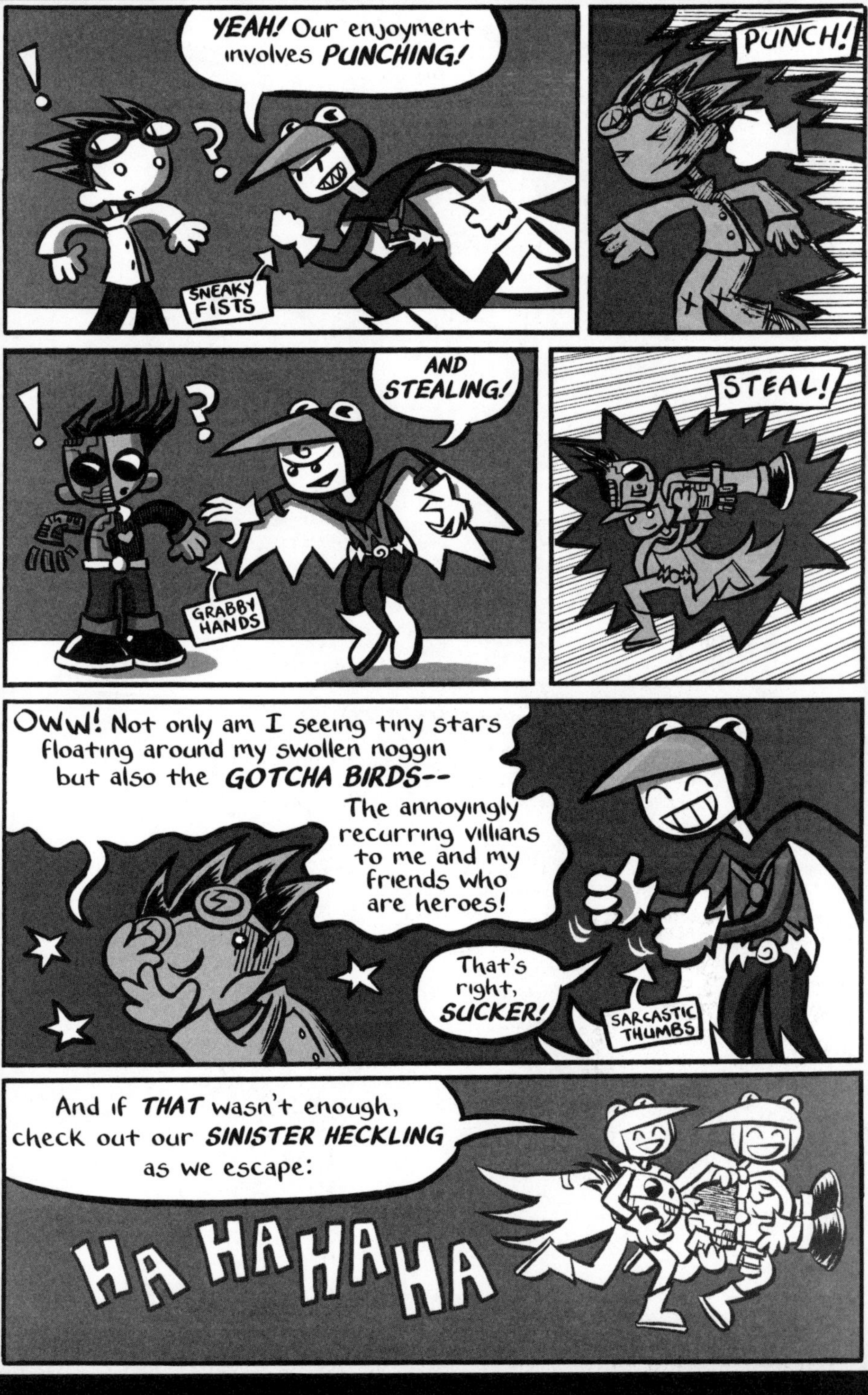
!
?
YEAH! Our enjoyment involves PUNCHING!
SNEAKY FISTS
PUNCH!
!
?
AND STEALING!
GRABBY HANDS
STEAL!
OWW! Not only am I seeing tiny stars floating around my swollen noggin but also the GOTCHA BIRDS--
The annoyingly recurring villians to me and my friends who are heroes!
That's right, SUCKER!
SARCASTIC THUMBS
And if THAT wasn't enough, check out our SINISTER HECKLING as we escape:
HA HA HA HA HA HA

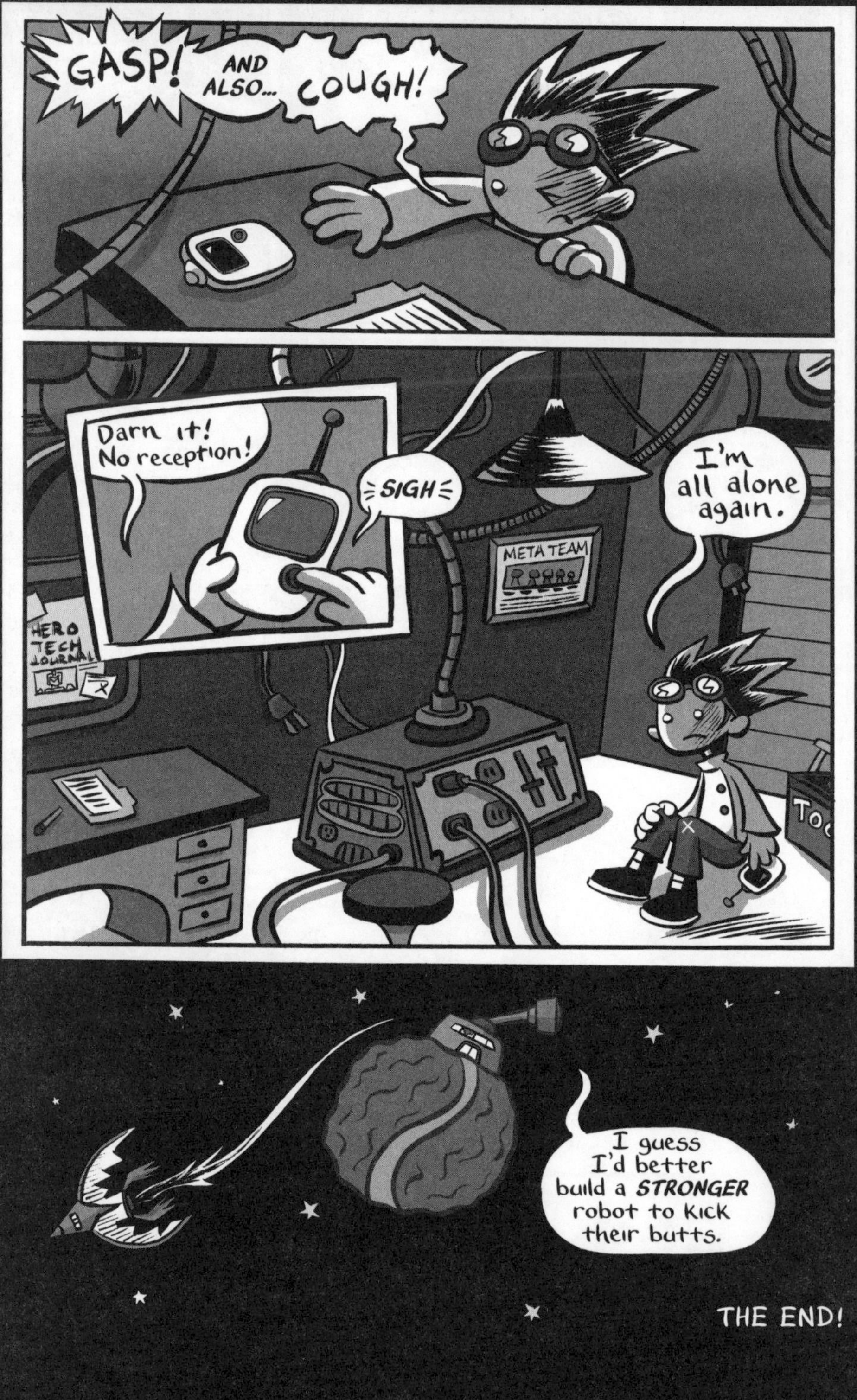
GASP!
AND ALSO... COUGH!
Darn it! No reception!
SIGH
I'm all alone again.
META TEAM
HERO TECH JOURNAL
I guess I'd better build a **STRONGER** robot to kick their butts.
THE END!

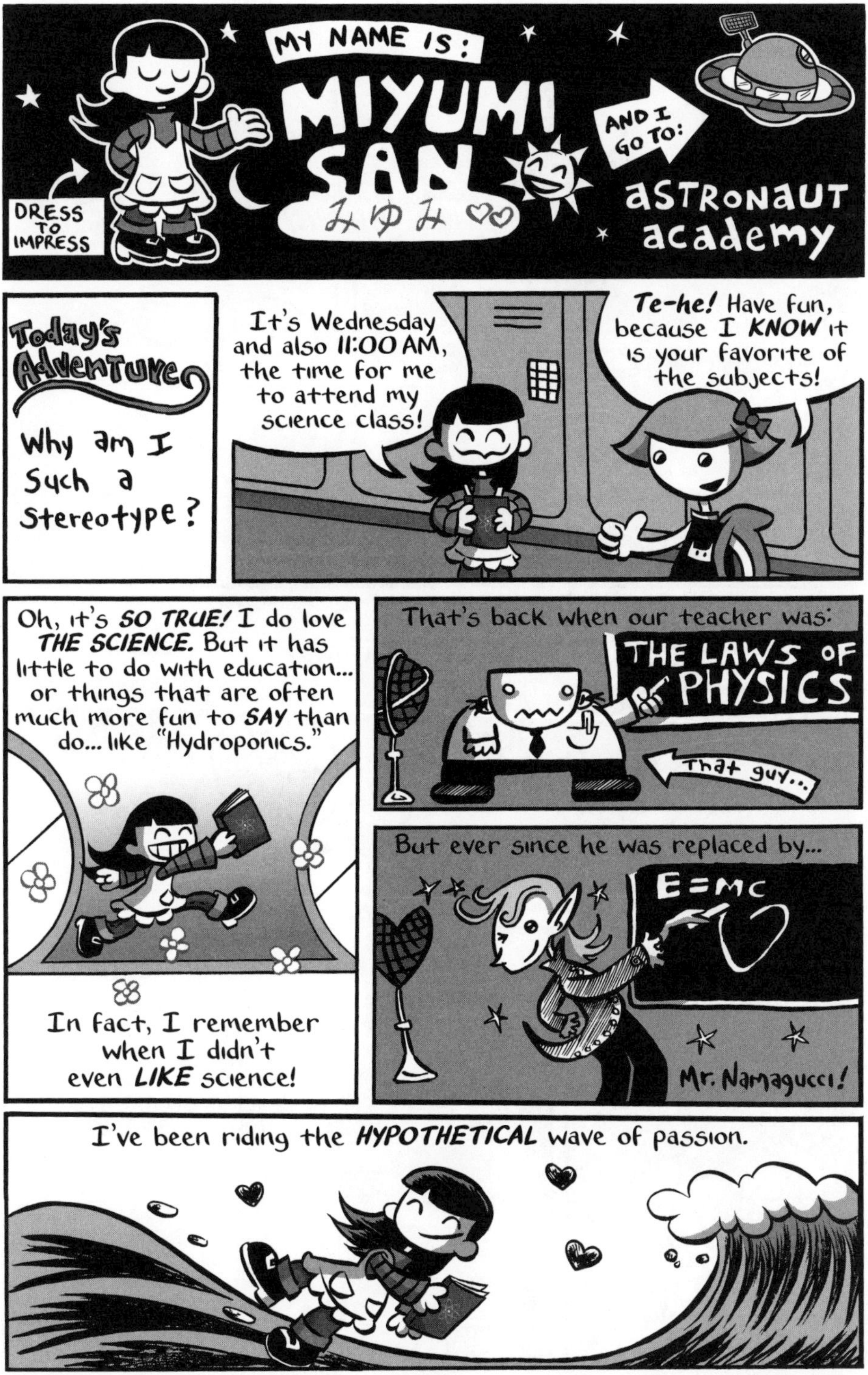

MY NAME IS:
MIYUMI SAN
みゆみ ♡♡
AND I GO TO:
astronaut academy
DRESS TO IMPRESS
Today's Adventure
Why am I such a stereotype?
It's Wednesday and also 11:00 AM, the time for me to attend my science class!
Te-he! Have fun, because I KNOW it is your favorite of the subjects!
Oh, it's SO TRUE! I do love THE SCIENCE. But it has little to do with education... or things that are often much more fun to SAY than do... like "Hydroponics."
In fact, I remember when I didn't even LIKE science!
That's back when our teacher was:
THE LAWS OF PHYSICS
That guy...
But ever since he was replaced by...
E=MC
Mr. Namagucci!
I've been riding the HYPOTHETICAL wave of passion.

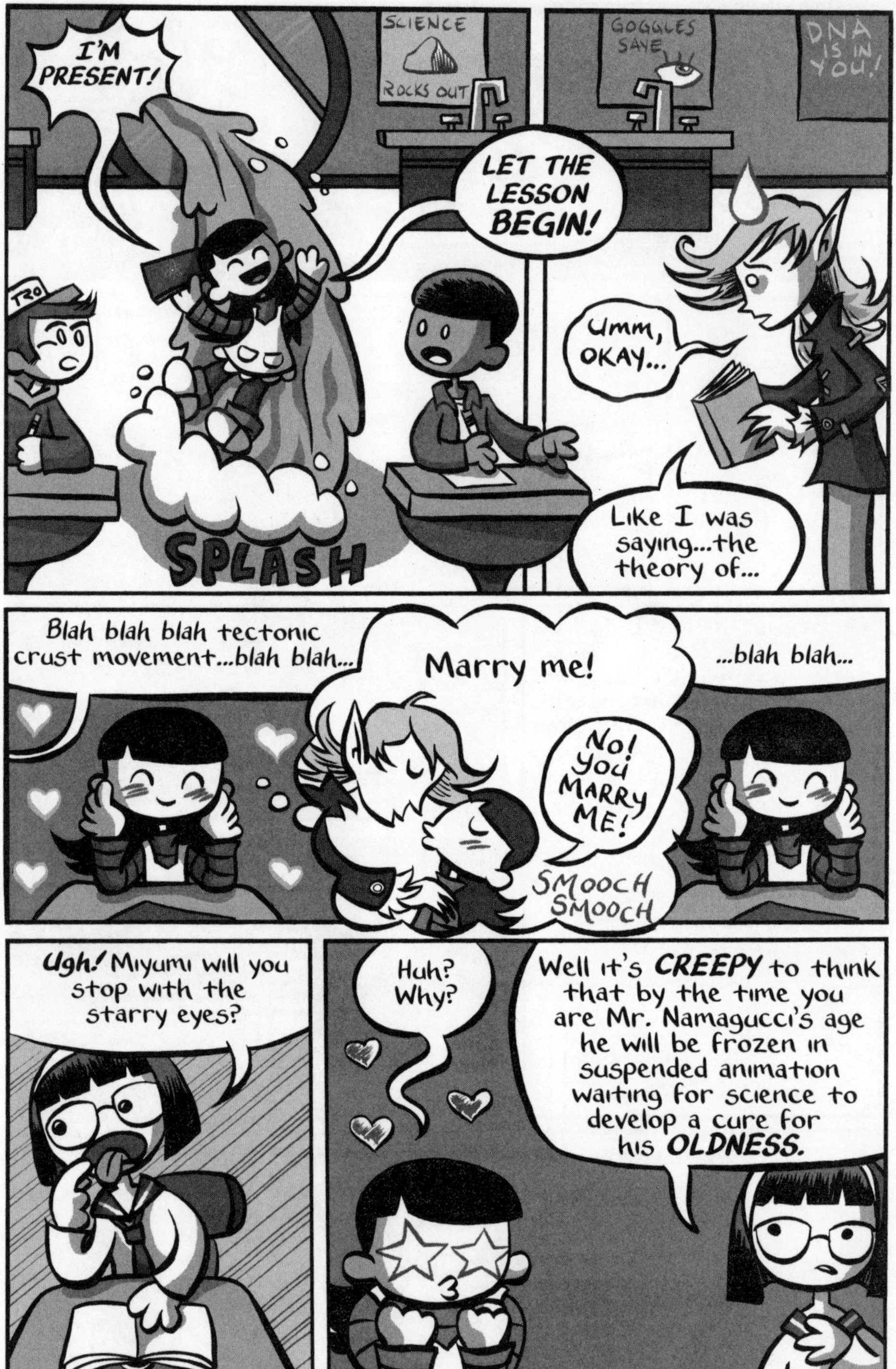
SCIENCE ROCKS OUT
GOGGLES SAVE
DNA IS IN YOU!
I'M PRESENT!
LET THE LESSON BEGIN!
TRO
SPLASH
Umm, OKAY...
Like I was saying...the theory of...
Blah blah blah tectonic crust movement...blah blah...
Marry me!
No! You MARRY ME!
SMOOCH SMOOCH
...blah blah...
Ugh! Miyumi will you stop with the starry eyes?
Huh? Why?
Well it's CREEPY to think that by the time you are Mr. Namagucci's age he will be frozen in suspended animation waiting for science to develop a cure for his OLDNESS.

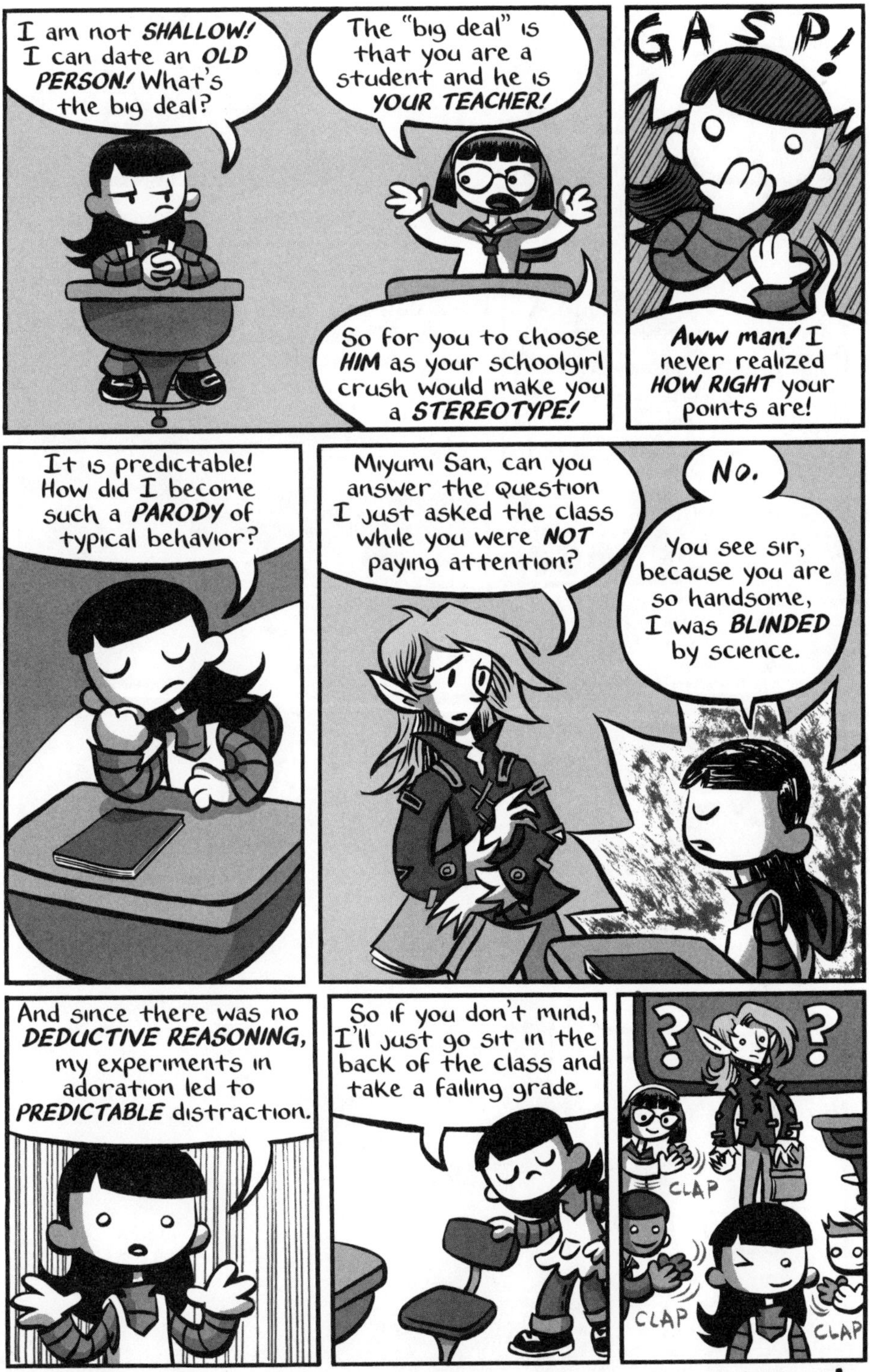
I am not SHALLOW! I can date an OLD PERSON! What's the big deal?
The "big deal" is that you are a student and he is YOUR TEACHER!
So for you to choose HIM as your schoolgirl crush would make you a STEREOTYPE!
GASP!
Aww man! I never realized HOW RIGHT your points are!
It is predictable! How did I become such a PARODY of typical behavior?
Miyumi San, can you answer the question I just asked the class while you were NOT paying attention?
No.
You see sir, because you are so handsome, I was BLINDED by science.
And since there was no DEDUCTIVE REASONING, my experiments in adoration led to PREDICTABLE distraction.
So if you don't mind, I'll just go sit in the back of the class and take a failing grade.
? ?
CLAP
CLAP
CLAP
♥end♥

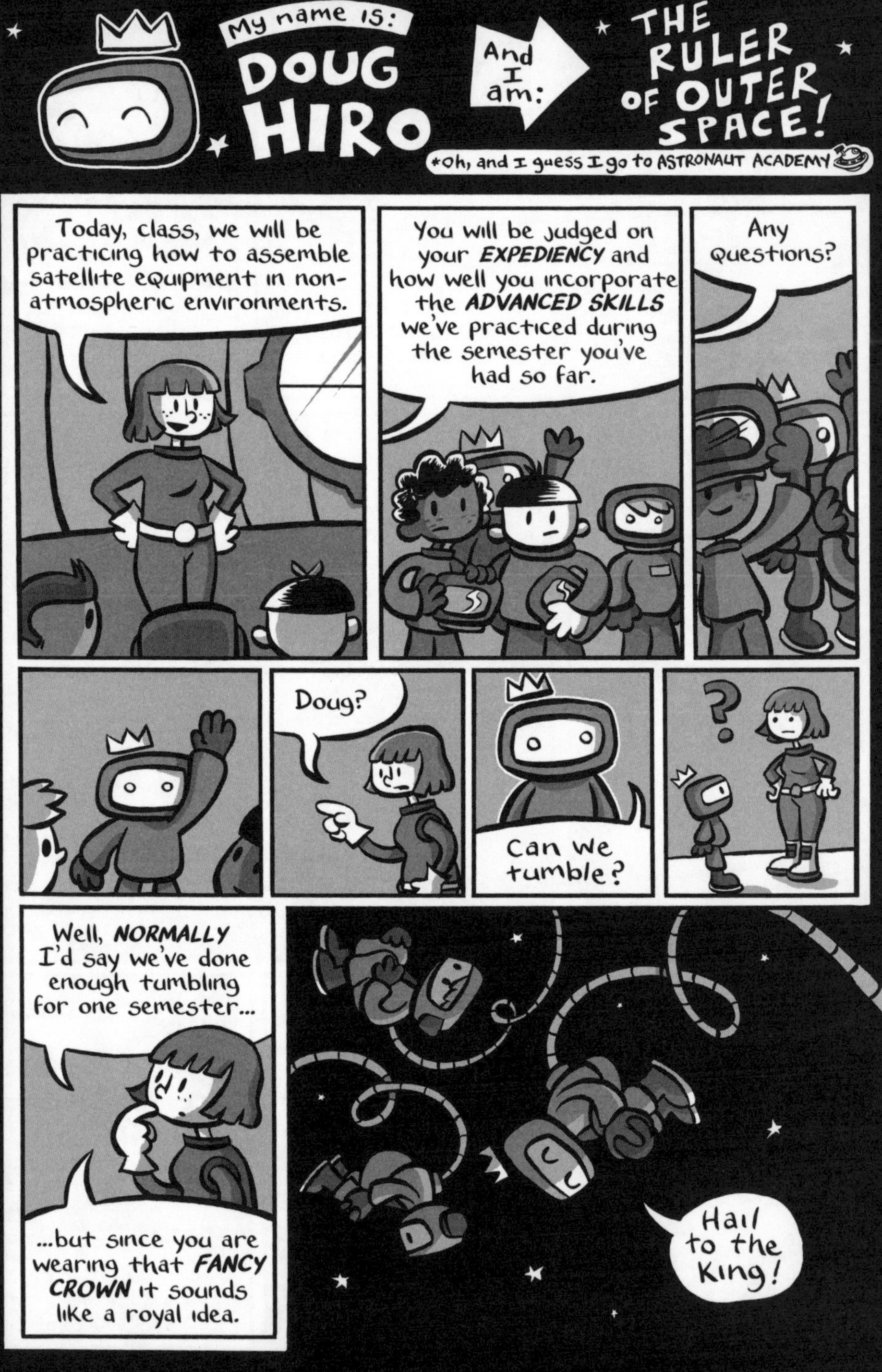

My name is:
DOUG HIRO
And I am:
THE RULER OF OUTER SPACE!
*Oh, and I guess I go to ASTRONAUT ACADEMY
Today, class, we will be practicing how to assemble satellite equipment in non-atmospheric environments.
You will be judged on your EXPEDIENCY and how well you incorporate the ADVANCED SKILLS we've practiced during the semester you've had so far.
Any Questions?
Doug?
Can we tumble?
?
Well, NORMALLY I'd say we've done enough tumbling for one semester...
...but since you are wearing that FANCY CROWN it sounds like a royal idea.
Hail to the King!

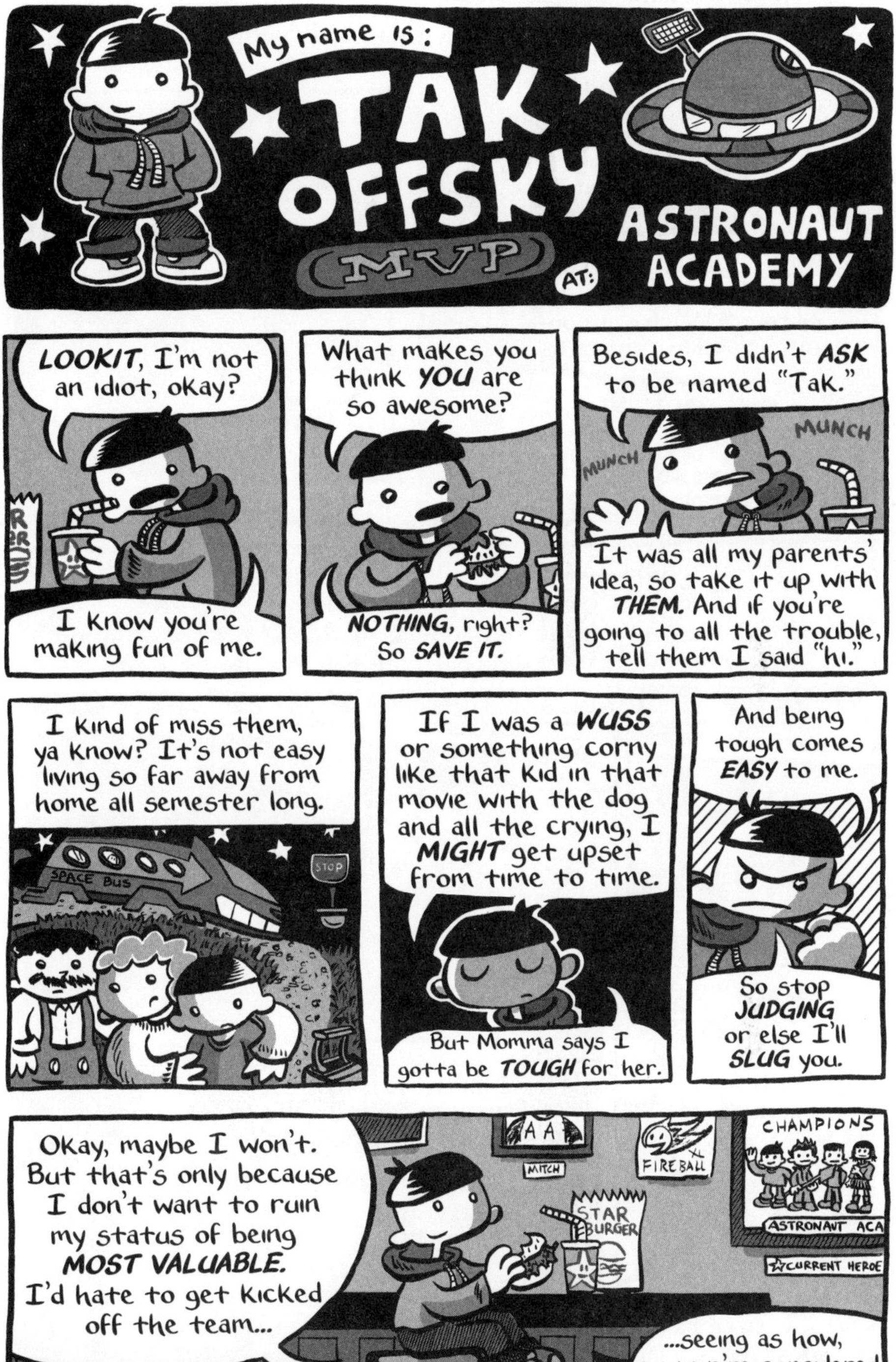
My name is:
TAK OFFSKY
MVP
AT:
ASTRONAUT ACADEMY
LOOKIT, I'm not an idiot, okay?
I know you're making fun of me.
What makes you think YOU are so awesome?
NOTHING, right? So SAVE IT.
Besides, I didn't ASK to be named "Tak."
MUNCH
MUNCH
It was all my parents' idea, so take it up with THEM. And if you're going to all the trouble, tell them I said "hi."
I kind of miss them, ya know? It's not easy living so far away from home all semester long.
SPACE BUS
STOP
If I was a WUSS or something corny like that kid in that movie with the dog and all the crying, I MIGHT get upset from time to time.
But Momma says I gotta be TOUGH for her.
And being tough comes EASY to me.
So stop JUDGING or else I'll SLUG you.
Okay, maybe I won't. But that's only because I don't want to ruin my status of being MOST VALUABLE. I'd hate to get kicked off the team...
AA
MITCH
FIREBALL
CHAMPIONS
ASTRONAUT ACA
CURRENT HEROE
STAR BURGER
...seeing as how, now, we're considered so UNBEATABLE.

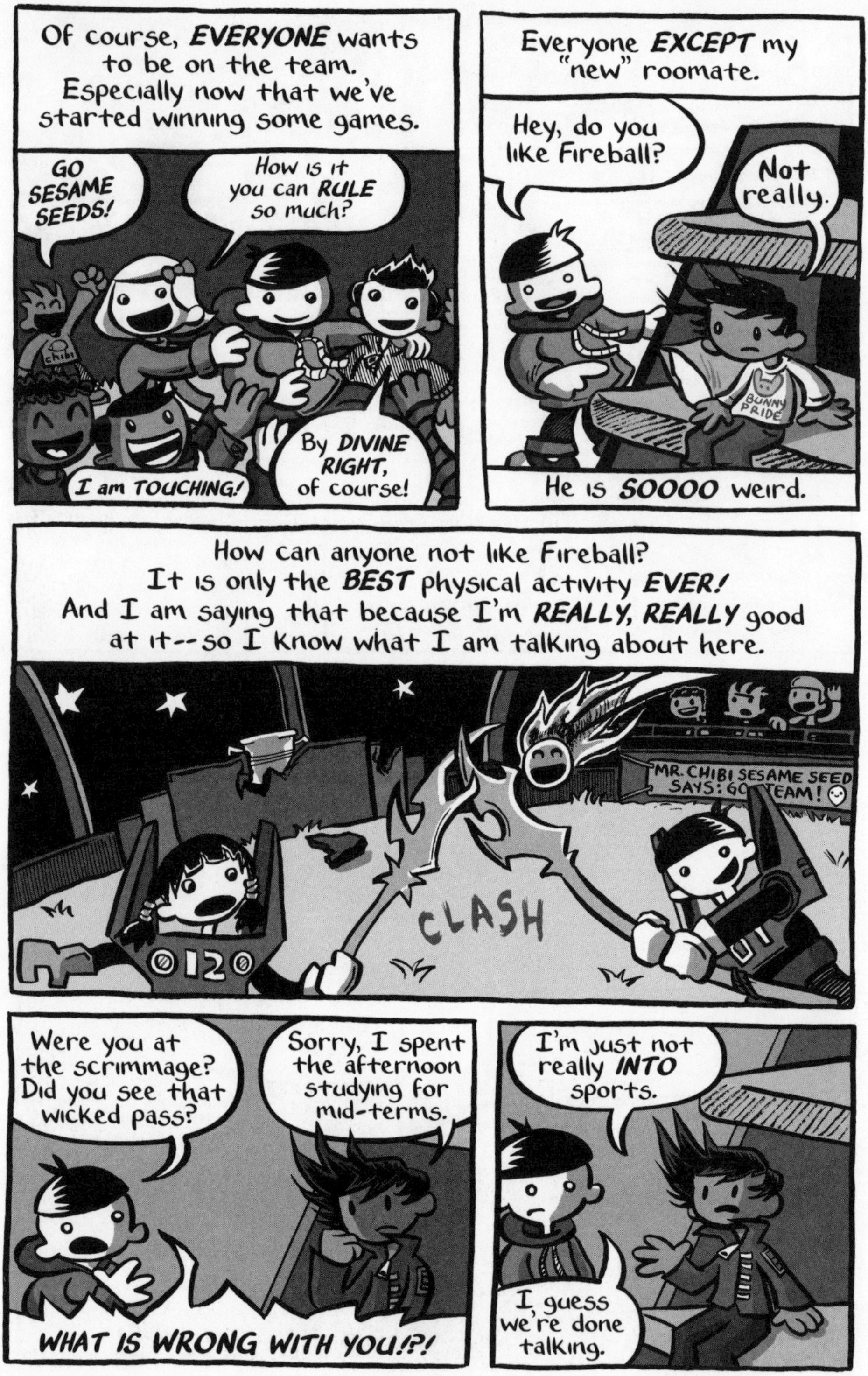

Of course, EVERYONE wants to be on the team. Especially now that we've started winning some games.
GO SESAME SEEDS!
How is it you can RULE so much?
CHIBI
I am TOUCHING!
By DIVINE RIGHT, of course!
Everyone EXCEPT my "new" roomate.
Hey, do you like Fireball?
Not really.
BUNNY PRIDE
He is SOOOO weird.
How can anyone not like Fireball? It is only the BEST physical activity EVER! And I am saying that because I'm REALLY, REALLY good at it--so I know what I am talking about here.
MR. CHIBI SESAME SEED SAYS: GO TEAM!
CLASH
12
Were you at the scrimmage? Did you see that wicked pass?
Sorry, I spent the afternoon studying for mid-terms.
WHAT IS WRONG WITH YOU!?!
I'm just not really INTO sports.
I guess we're done talking.

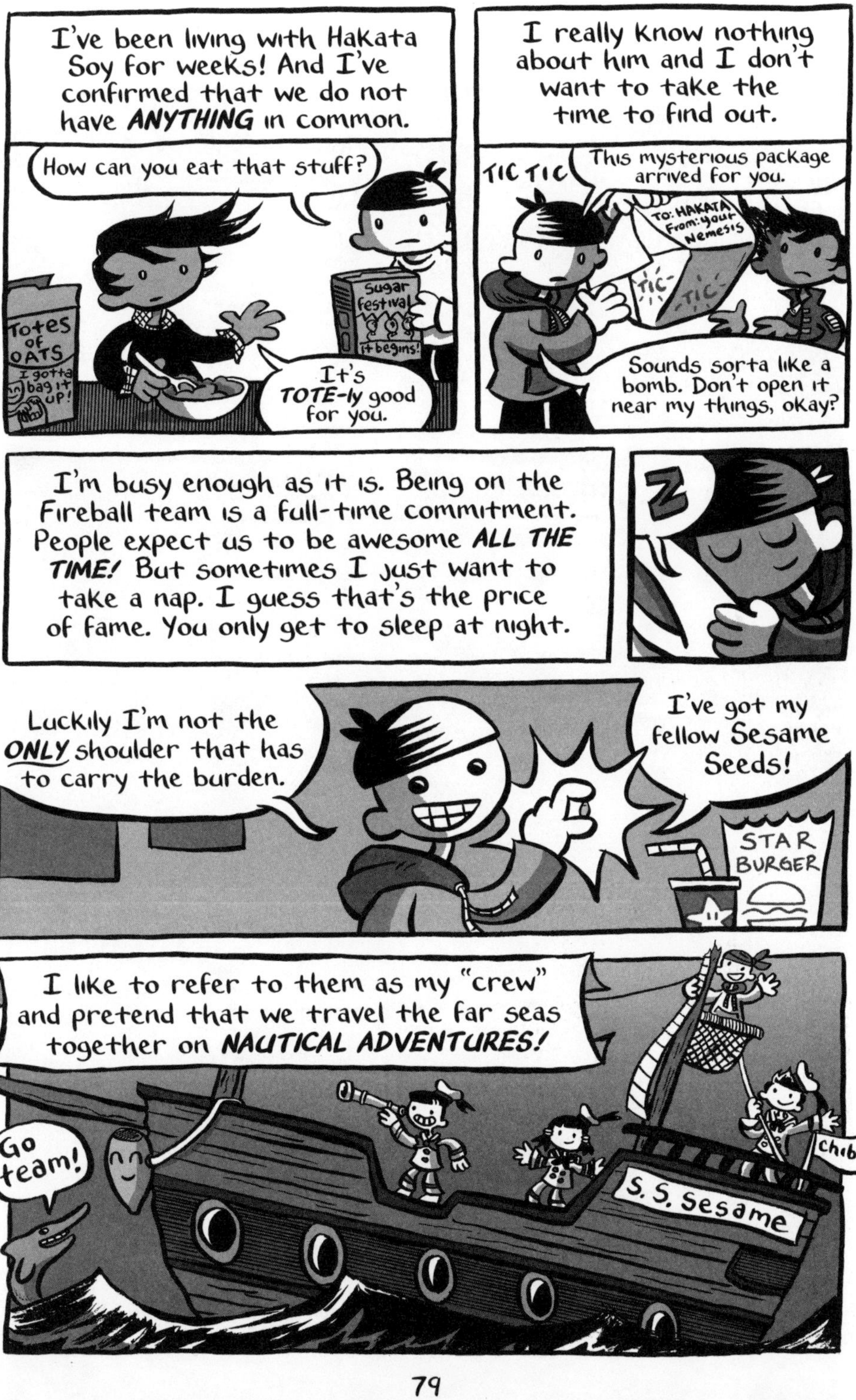
I've been living with Hakata Soy for weeks! And I've confirmed that we do not have ANYTHING in common.
How can you eat that stuff?
Totes of Oats
I gotta bag it up!
Sugar festival
it begins!
It's TOTE-ly good for you.
I really know nothing about him and I don't want to take the time to find out.
TIC TIC
This mysterious package arrived for you.
To: HAKATA From: your Nemesis
TIC
TIC
Sounds sorta like a bomb. Don't open it near my things, okay?
I'm busy enough as it is. Being on the Fireball team is a full-time commitment. People expect us to be awesome ALL THE TIME! But sometimes I just want to take a nap. I guess that's the price of fame. You only get to sleep at night.
Z
Luckily I'm not the ONLY shoulder that has to carry the burden.
I've got my fellow Sesame Seeds!
STAR BURGER
I like to refer to them as my "crew" and pretend that we travel the far seas together on NAUTICAL ADVENTURES!
Go team!
Chibi
S. S. Sesame

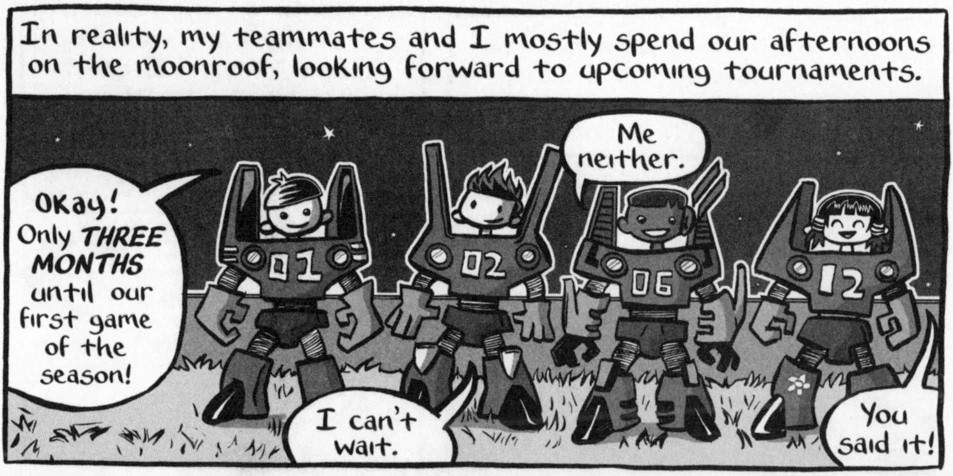
In reality, my teammates and I mostly spend our afternoons on the moonroof, looking forward to upcoming tournaments.
01
02
06
12
Okay! Only **THREE MONTHS** until our first game of the season!
I can't wait.
Me neither.
You said it!

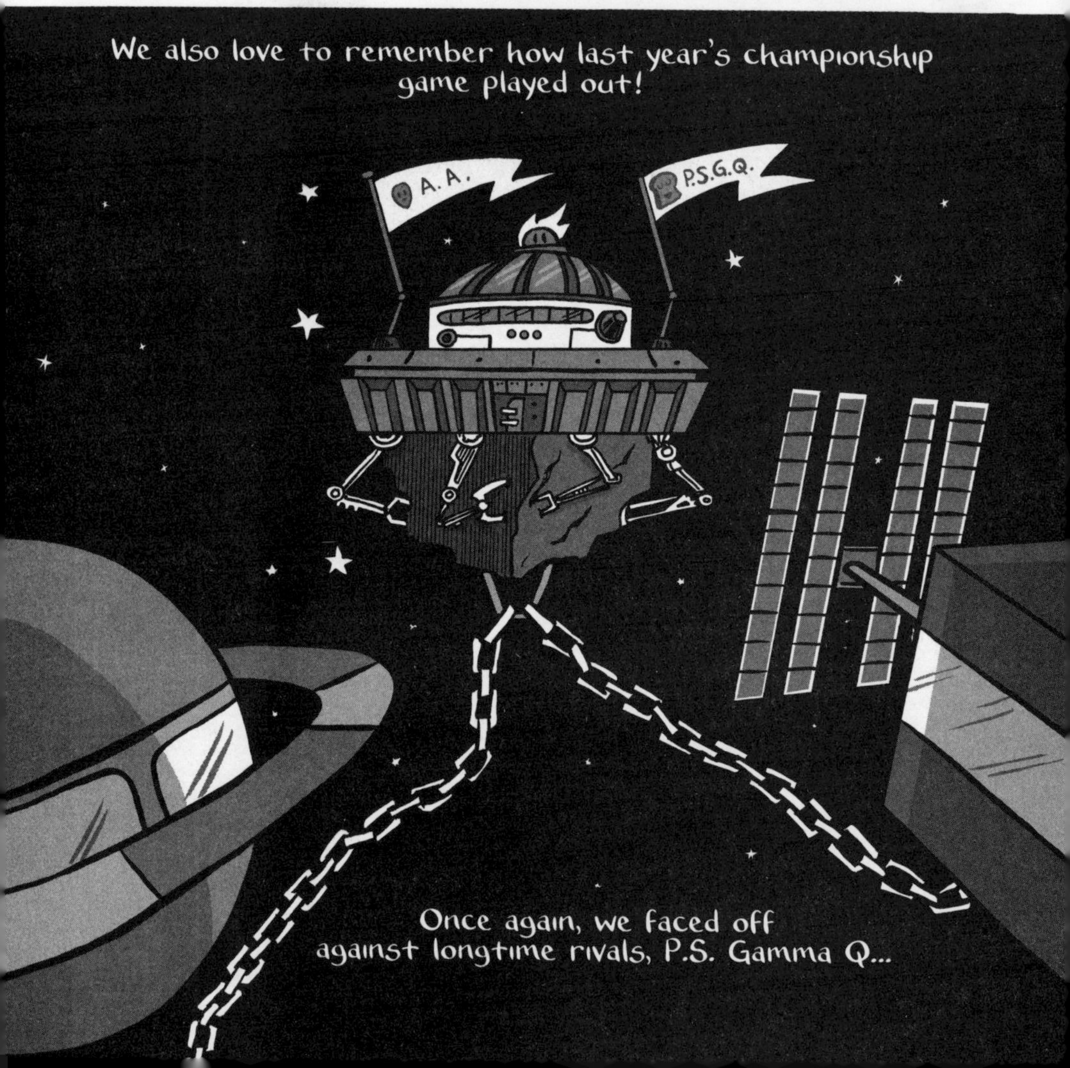
We also love to remember how last year's championship game played out!
A. A.
P.S.G.Q.
Once again, we faced off against longtime rivals, P.S. Gamma Q...

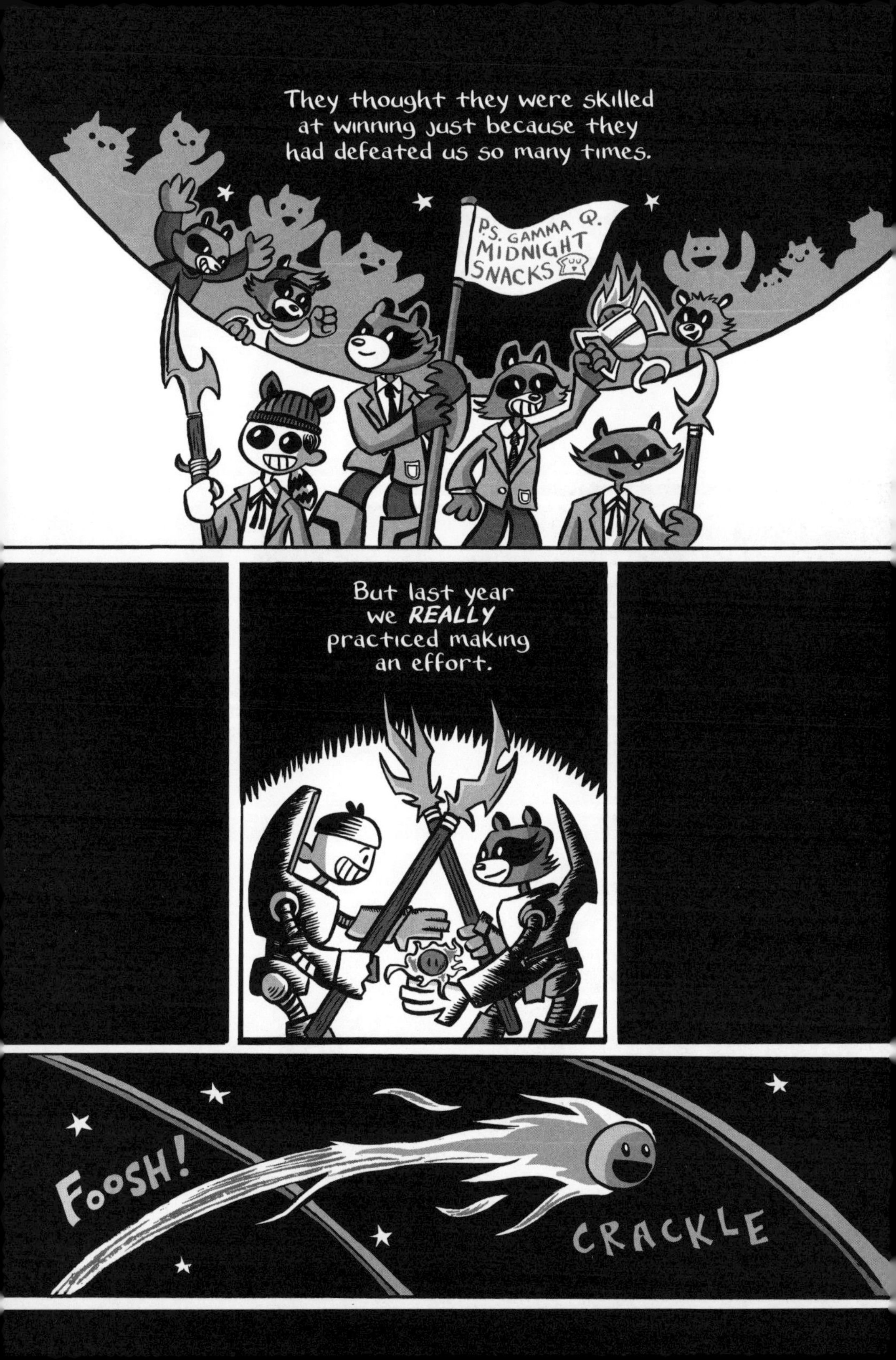
They thought they were skilled at winning just because they had defeated us so many times.
P.S. GAMMA Q. MIDNIGHT SNACKS
But last year we *REALLY* practiced making an effort.
FOOSH!
CRACKLE

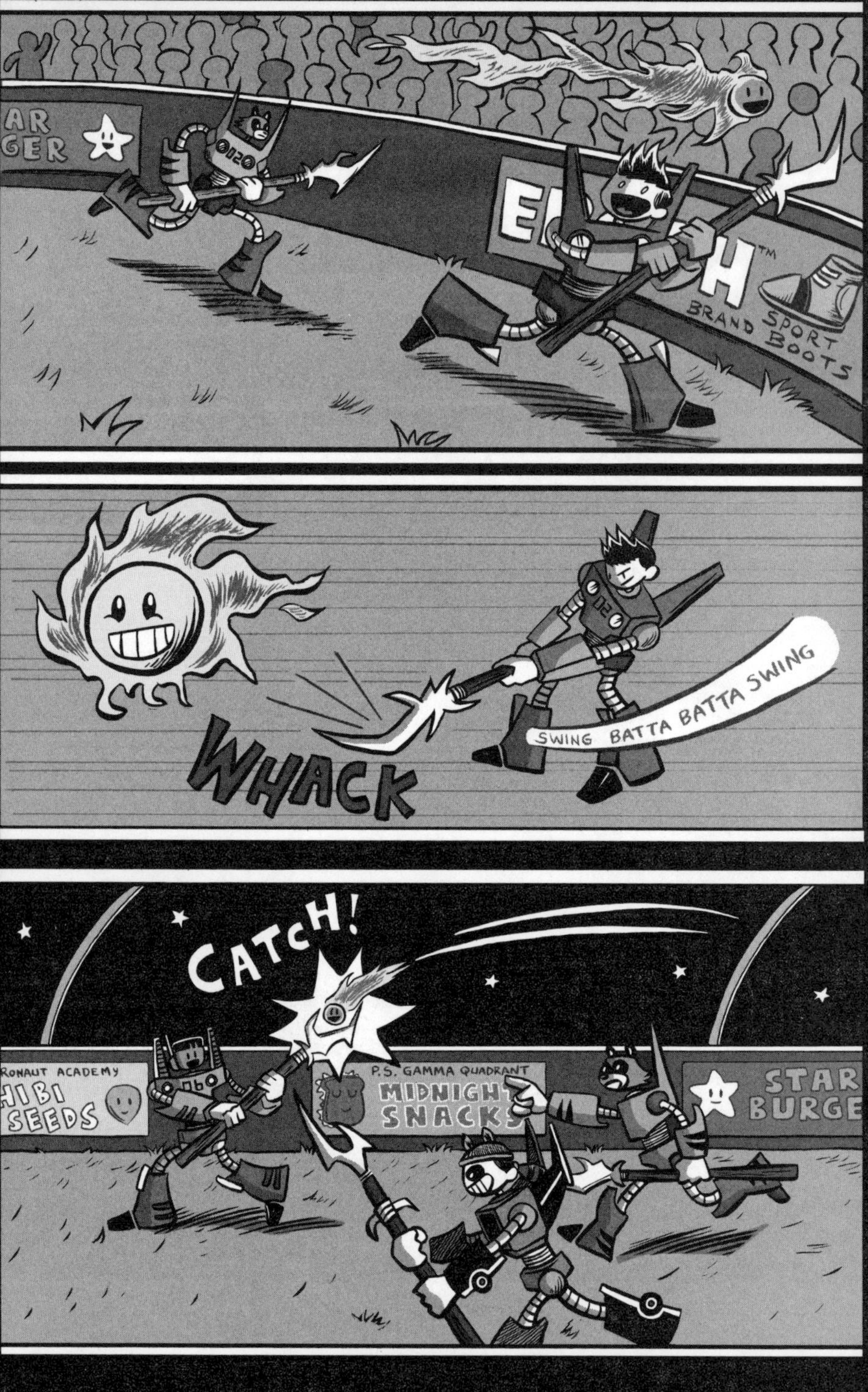
BRAND SPORT BOOTS
WHACK
SWING BATTA BATTA SWING
CATCH!
P.S. GAMMA QUADRANT
MIDNIGHT SNACKS

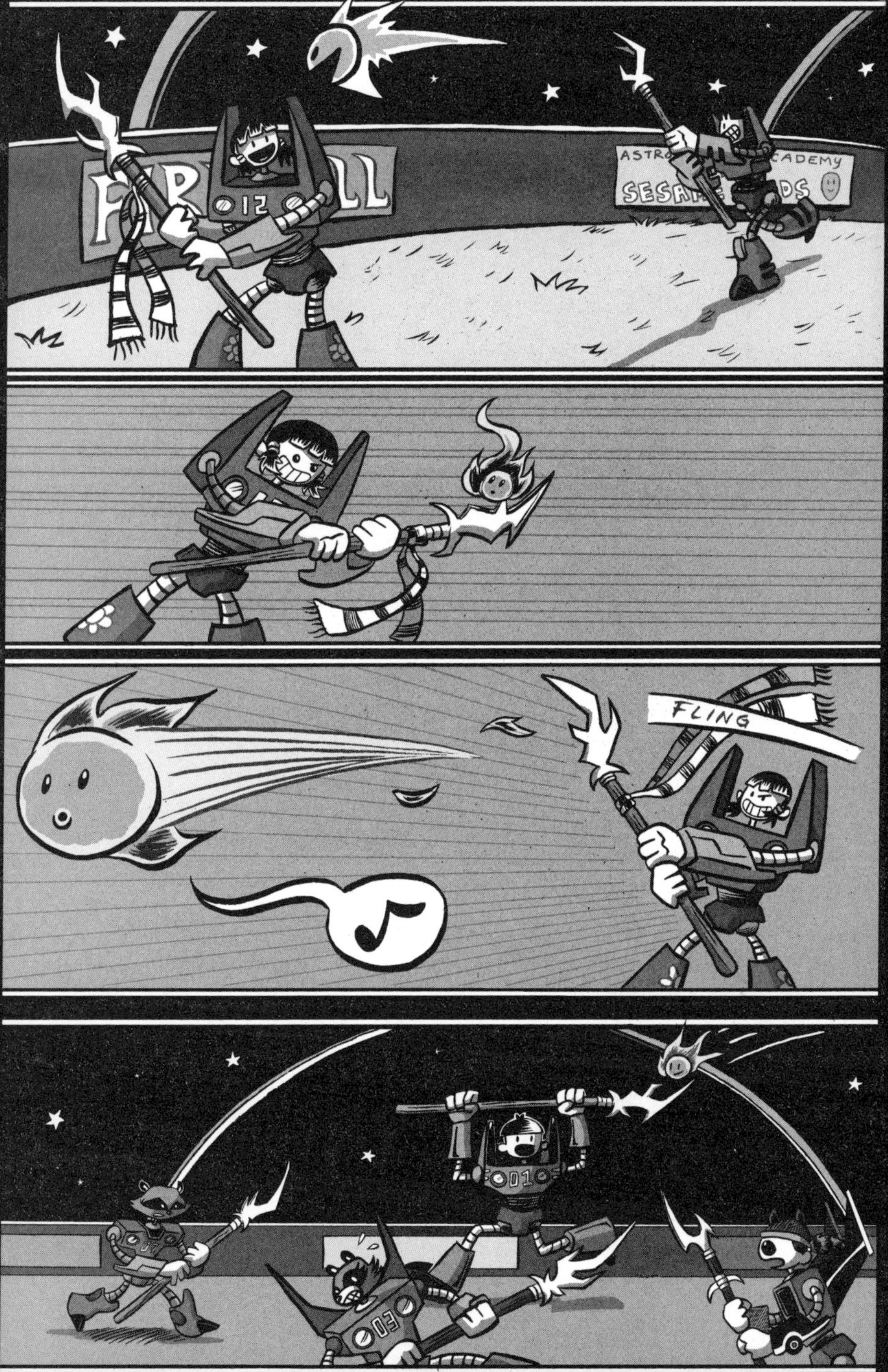
12
FLING

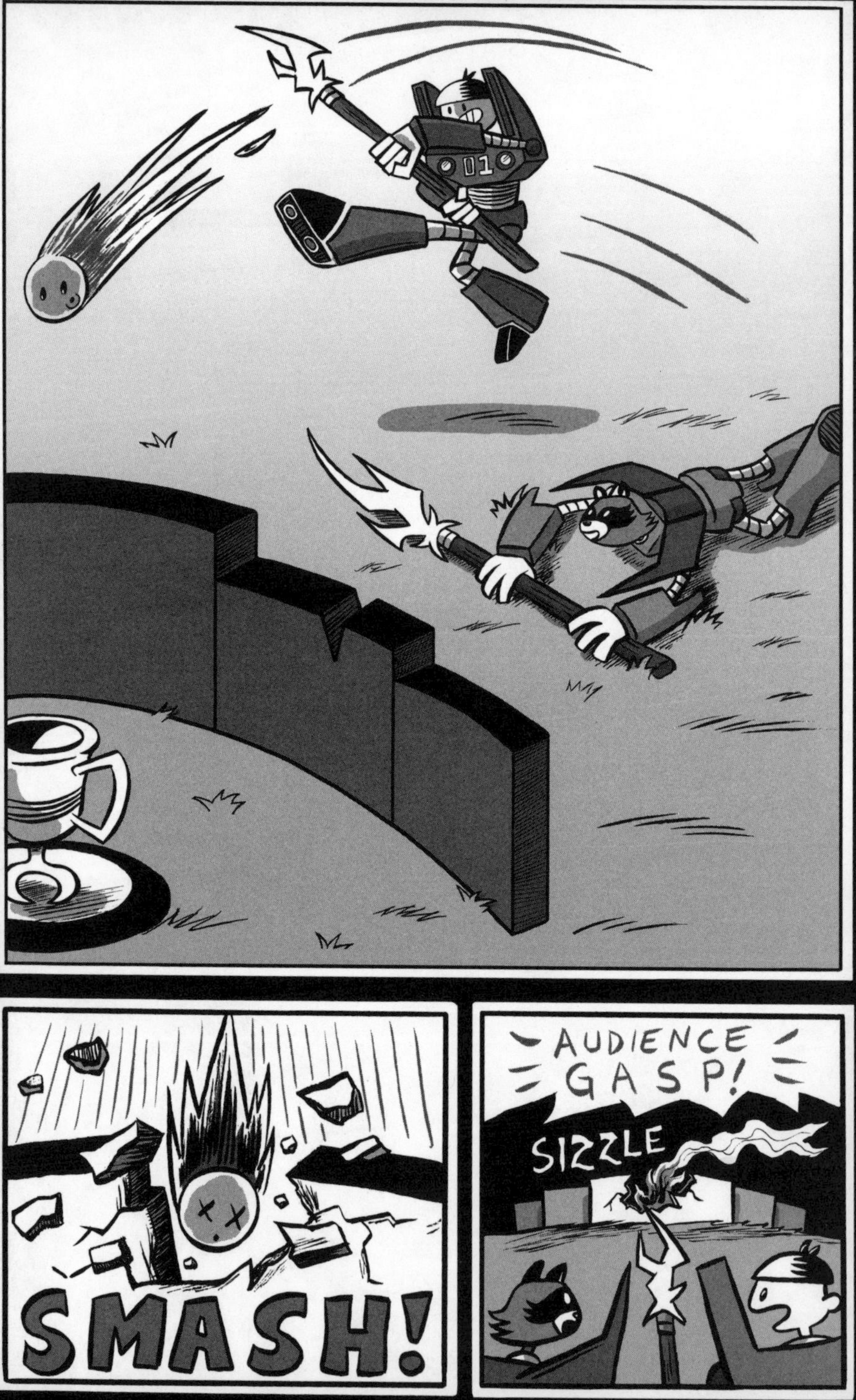
01
SMASH!
AUDIENCE GASP!
SIZZLE

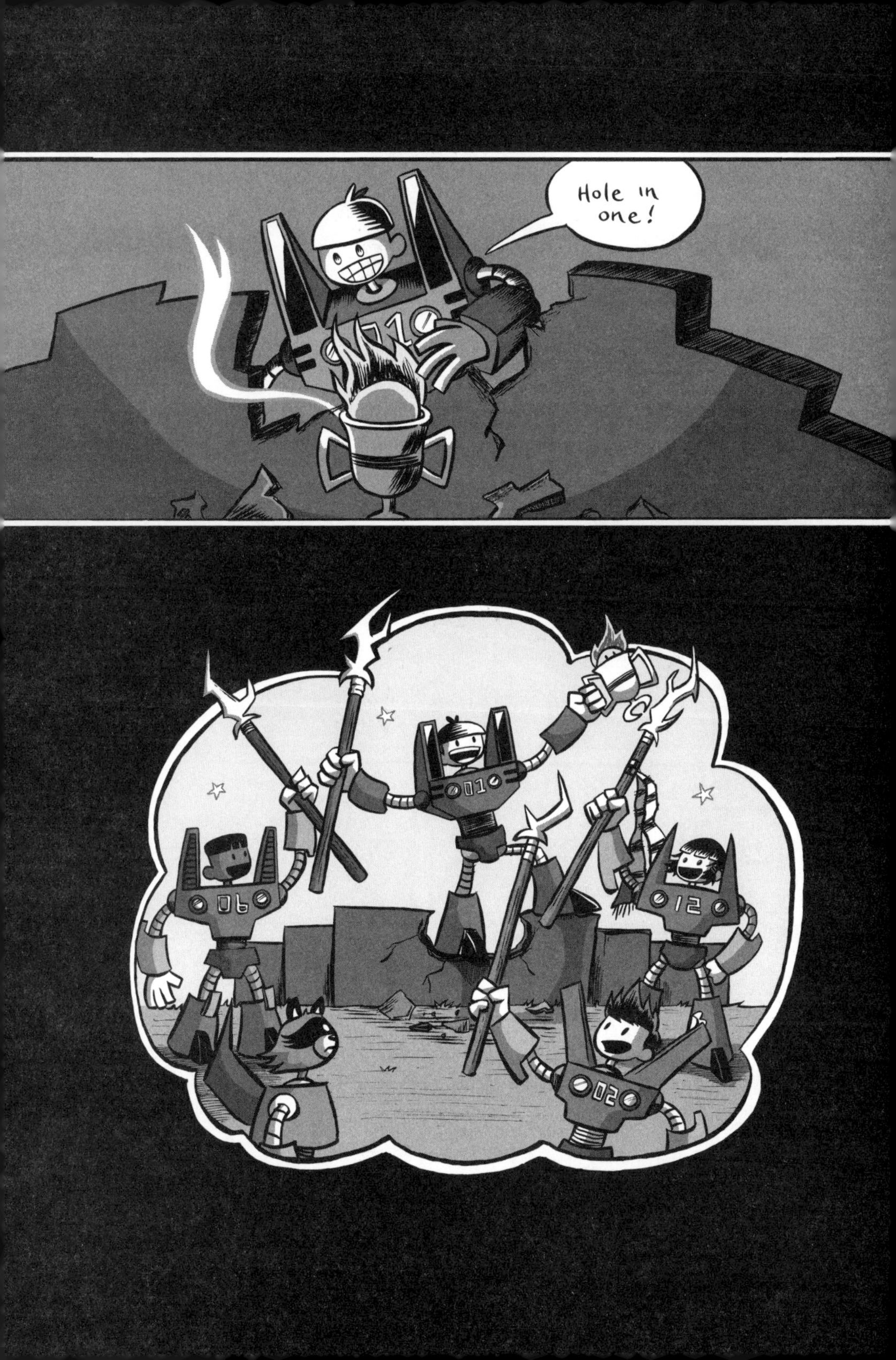
Hole in one!

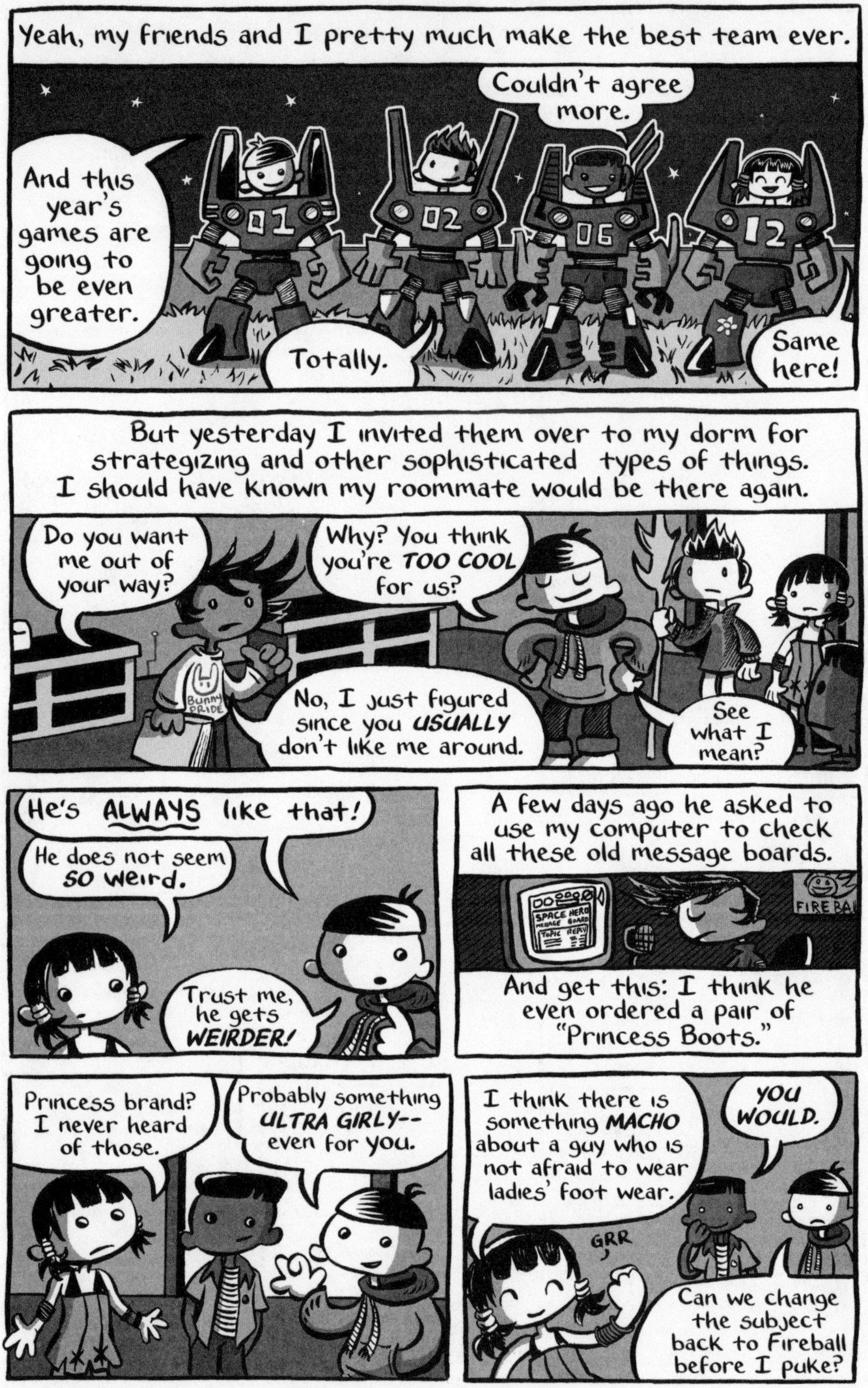
Yeah, my friends and I pretty much make the best team ever.
And this year's games are going to be even greater.
Totally.
Couldn't agree more.
Same here!
01
02
06
12
But yesterday I invited them over to my dorm for strategizing and other sophisticated types of things. I should have known my roommate would be there again.
Do you want me out of my way?
Why? You think you're TOO COOL for us?
BUNNY PRIDE
No, I just figured since you USUALLY don't like me around.
See what I mean?
He's ALWAYS like that!
He does not seem SO weird.
Trust me, he gets WEIRDER!
A few days ago he asked to use my computer to check all these old message boards.
SPACE HERO MESSAGE BOARD
TOPIC REPLY
FIREBAL
And get this: I think he even ordered a pair of "Princess Boots."
Princess brand? I never heard of those.
Probably something ULTRA GIRLY-- even for you.
I think there is something MACHO about a guy who is not afraid to wear ladies' foot wear.
YOU WOULD.
GRR
Can we change the subject back to Fireball before I puke?

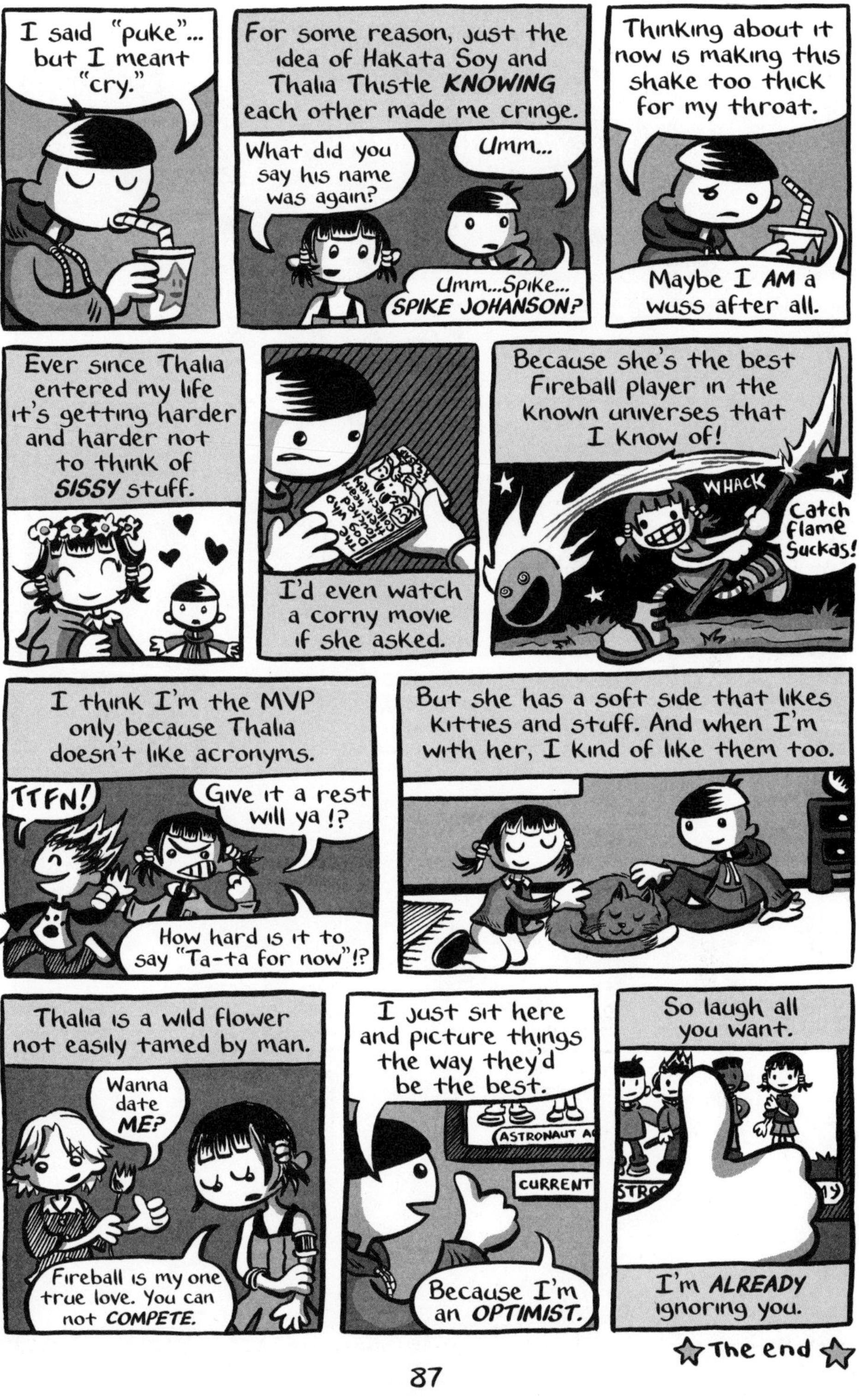
I said "puke"... but I meant "cry."
For some reason, just the idea of Hakata Soy and Thalia Thistle KNOWING each other made me cringe.
What did you say his name was again?
Umm...
Umm...Spike... SPIKE JOHANSON?
Thinking about it now is making this shake too thick for my throat.
Maybe I AM a wuss after all.
Ever since Thalia entered my life it's getting harder and harder not to think of SISSY stuff.
I'd even watch a corny movie if she asked.
Because she's the best Fireball player in the known universes that I know of!
WHACK
Catch flame Suckas!
I think I'm the MVP only because Thalia doesn't like acronyms.
TTFN!
Give it a rest will ya !?
How hard is it to say "Ta-ta for now"!?
But she has a soft side that likes kitties and stuff. And when I'm with her, I kind of like them too.
Thalia is a wild flower not easily tamed by man.
Wanna date ME?
Fireball is my one true love. You can not COMPETE.
I just sit here and picture things the way they'd be the best.
CURRENT
Because I'm an OPTIMIST.
So laugh all you want.
I'm ALREADY ignoring you.
The end

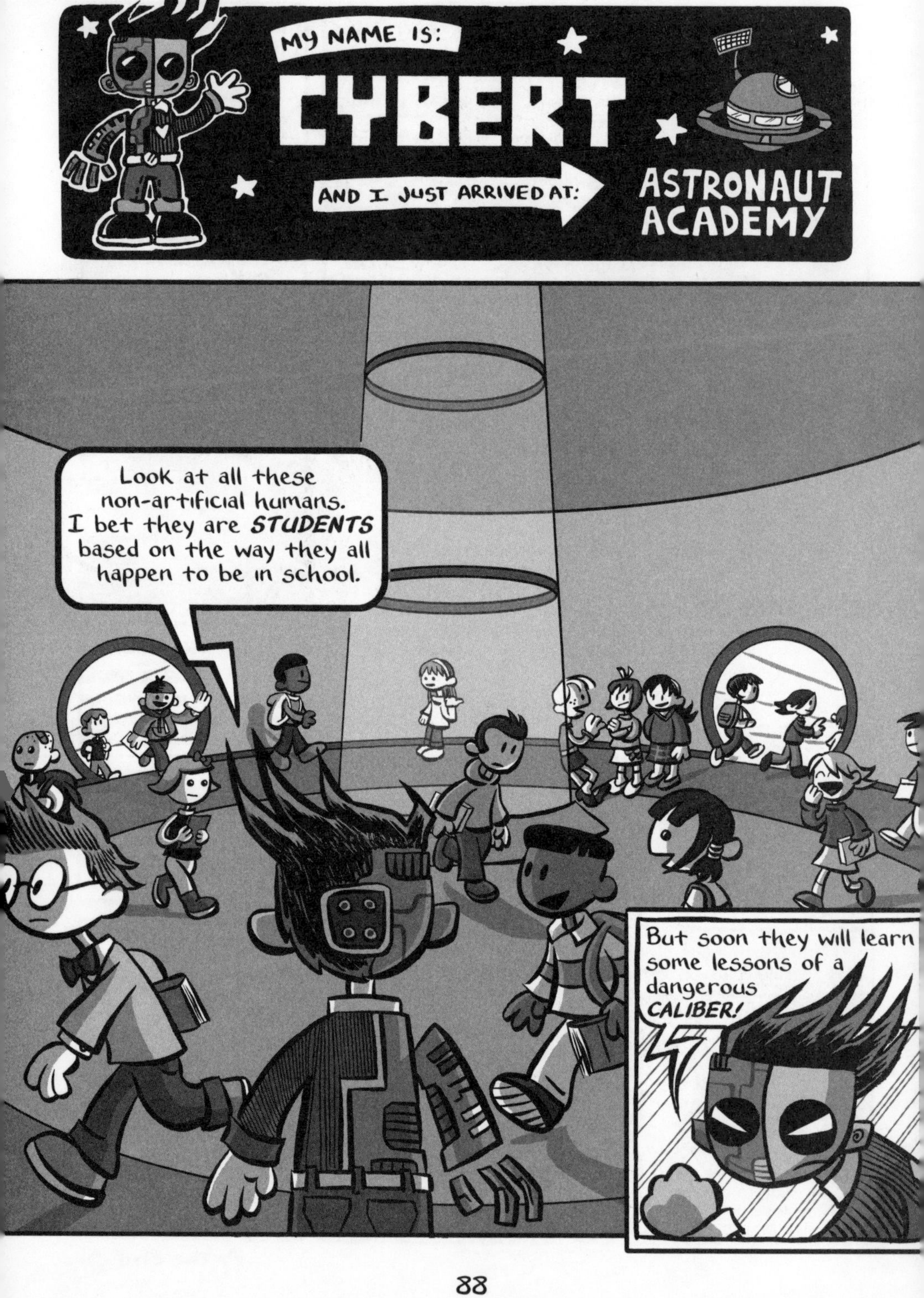
MY NAME IS:
CYBERT
AND I JUST ARRIVED AT:
ASTRONAUT ACADEMY
Look at all these non-artificial humans. I bet they are STUDENTS based on the way they all happen to be in school.
But soon they will learn some lessons of a dangerous CALIBER!

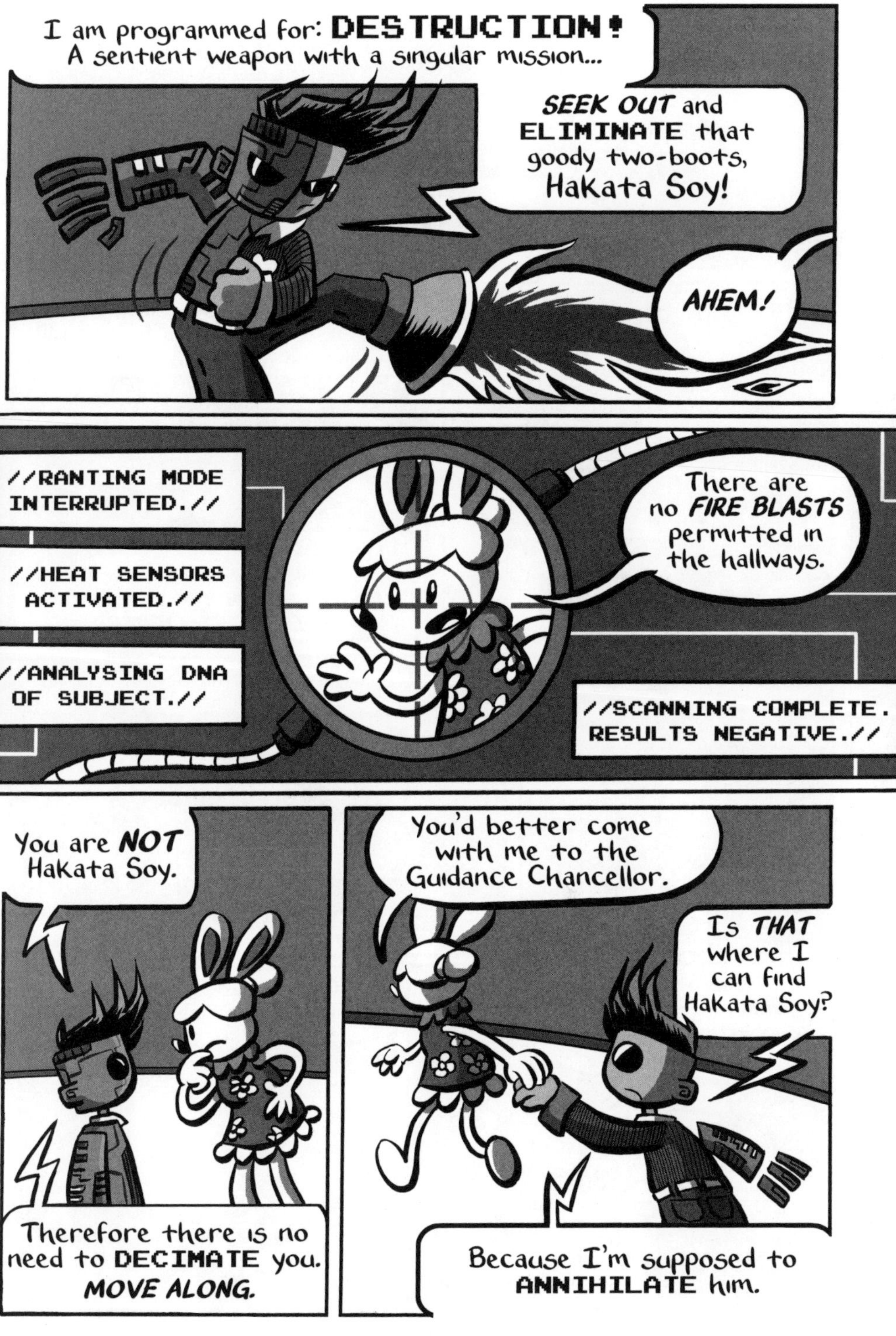

I am programmed for: DESTRUCTION! A sentient weapon with a singular mission...
SEEK OUT and ELIMINATE that goody two-boots, Hakata Soy!
AHEM!
//RANTING MODE INTERRUPTED.//
//HEAT SENSORS ACTIVATED.//
//ANALYSING DNA OF SUBJECT.//
There are no FIRE BLASTS permitted in the hallways.
//SCANNING COMPLETE. RESULTS NEGATIVE.//
You are NOT Hakata Soy.
Therefore there is no need to DECIMATE you. MOVE ALONG.
You'd better come with me to the Guidance Chancellor.
Is THAT where I can find Hakata Soy?
Because I'm supposed to ANNIHILATE him.

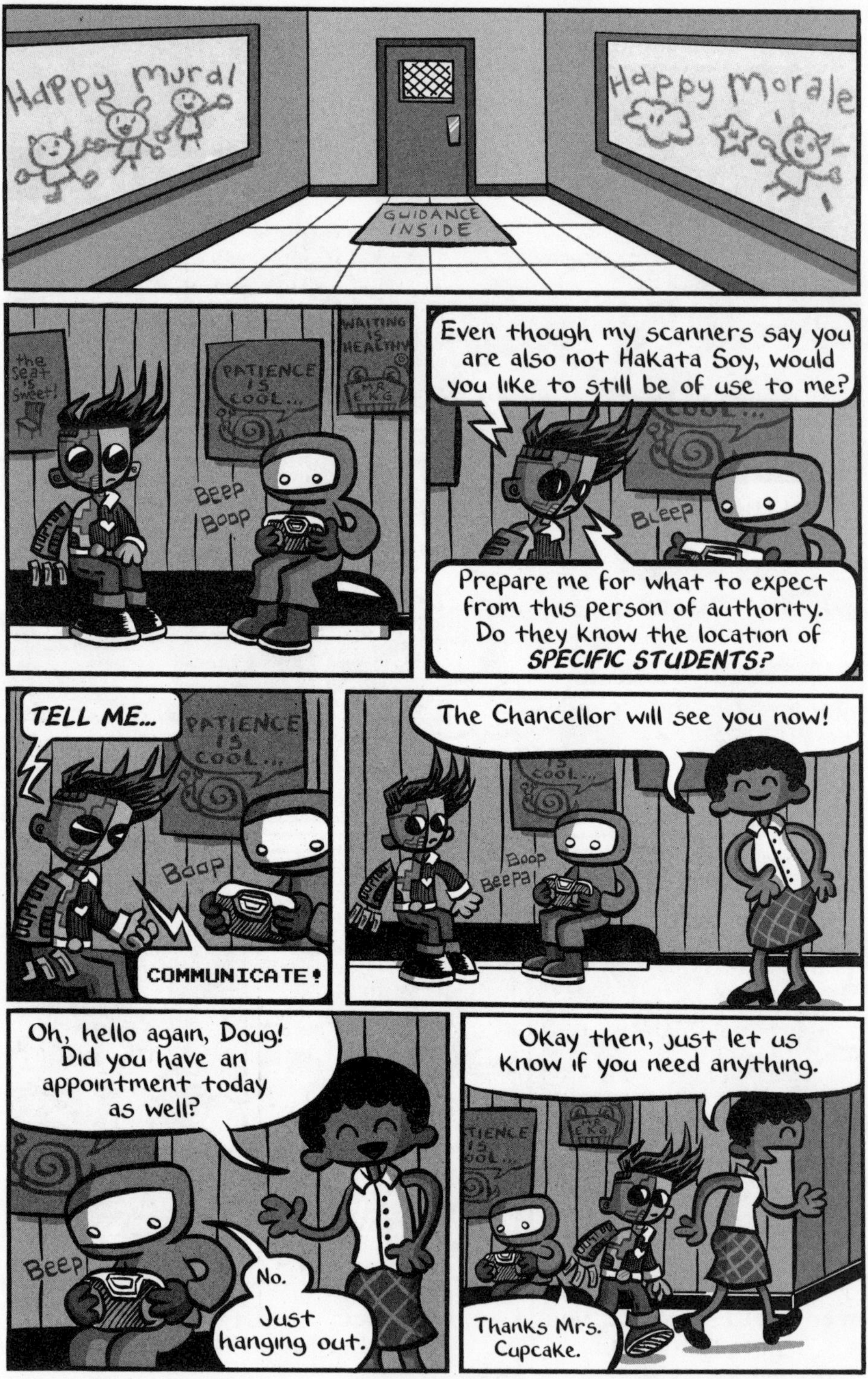
Happy Mural
GUIDANCE INSIDE
Happy Morale
the seat is sweet!
PATIENCE IS COOL...
WAITING IS HEALTHY
Beep
Boop
Even though my scanners say you are also not HaKata Soy, would you like to still be of use to me?
Bleep
Prepare me for what to expect from this person of authority. Do they Know the location of *SPECIFIC STUDENTS?*
TELL ME...
PATIENCE IS COOL...
Boop
COMMUNICATE!
The Chancellor will see you now!
Boop
Oh, hello again, Doug! Did you have an appointment today as well?
Beep
No. Just hanging out.
Okay then, just let us know if you need anything.
Thanks Mrs. Cupcake.

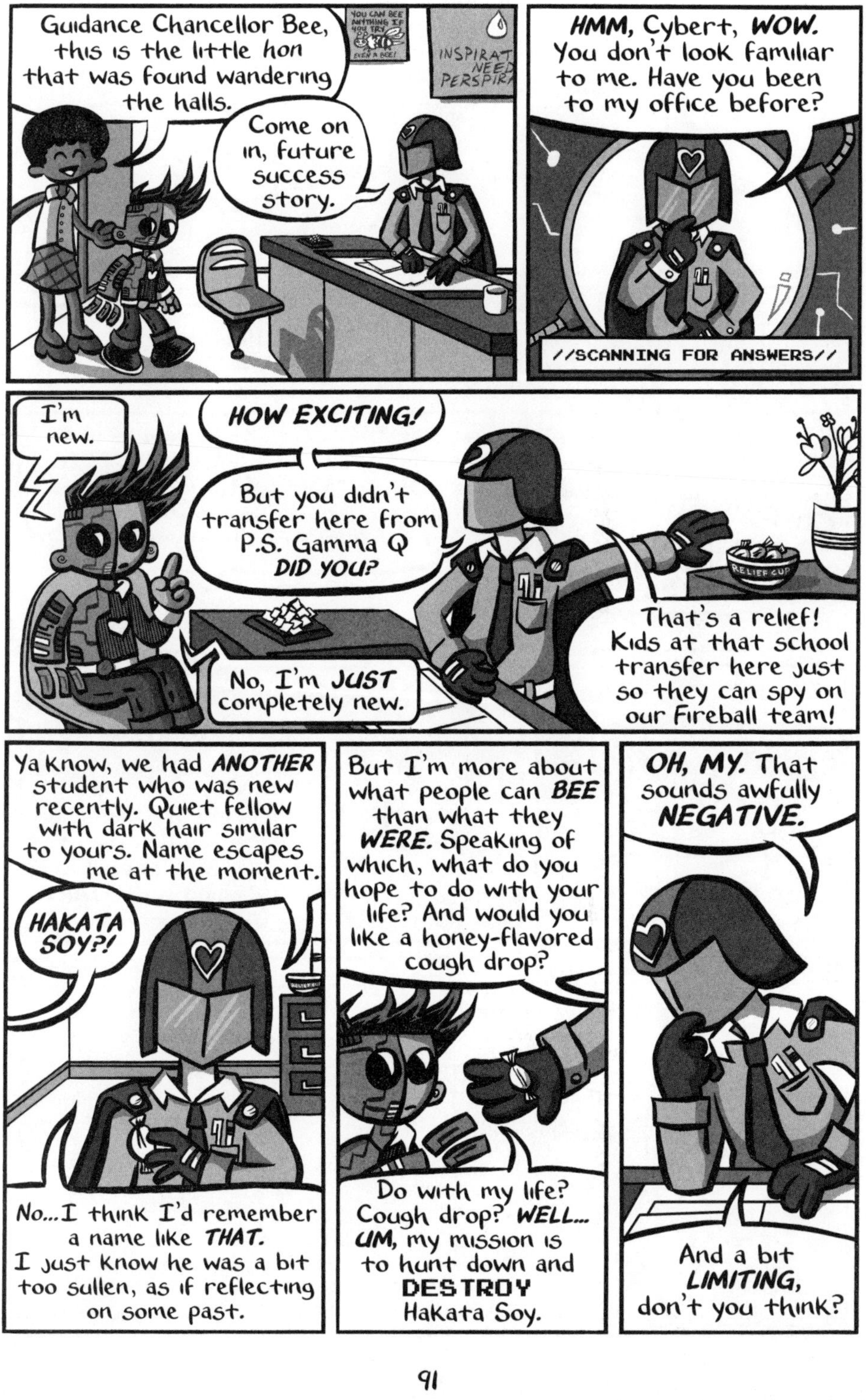
Guidance Chancellor Bee, this is the little hon that was found wandering the halls.
Come on in, future success story.
HMM, Cybert, WOW. You don't look familiar to me. Have you been to my office before?
//SCANNING FOR ANSWERS//
I'm new.
HOW EXCITING!
But you didn't transfer here from P.S. Gamma Q DID YOU?
No, I'm JUST completely new.
RELIEF CUP
That's a relief! Kids at that school transfer here just so they can spy on our Fireball team!
Ya know, we had ANOTHER student who was new recently. Quiet fellow with dark hair similar to yours. Name escapes me at the moment.
HAKATA SOY?!
No...I think I'd remember a name like THAT. I just know he was a bit too sullen, as if reflecting on some past.
But I'm more about what people can BEE than what they WERE. Speaking of which, what do you hope to do with your life? And would you like a honey-flavored cough drop?
Do with my life? Cough drop? WELL... UM, my mission is to hunt down and DESTROY Hakata Soy.
OH, MY. That sounds awfully NEGATIVE.
And a bit LIMITING, don't you think?

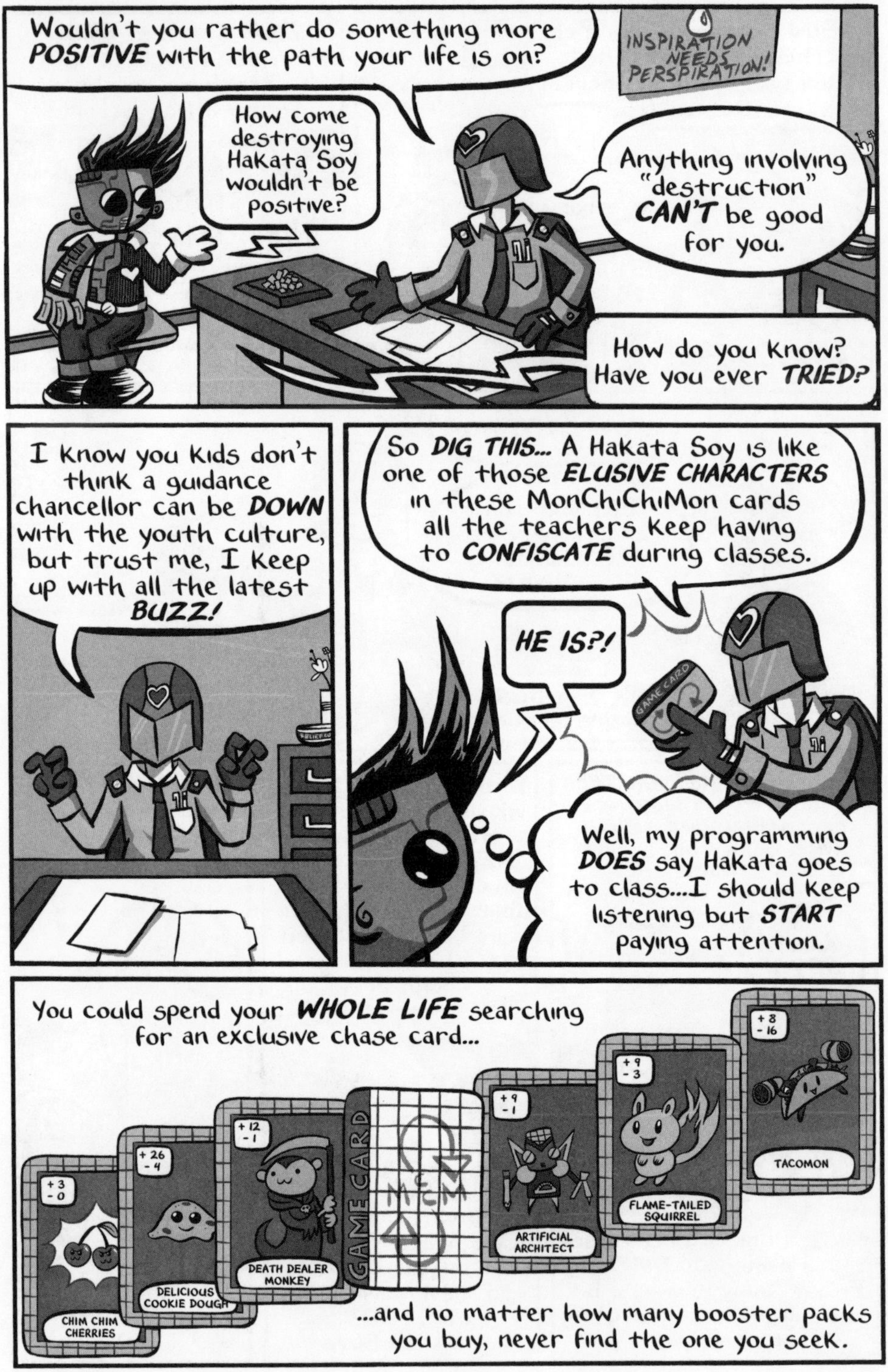
Wouldn't you rather do something more POSITIVE with the path your life is on?
INSPIRATION NEEDS PERSPIRATION!
How come destroying Hakata Soy wouldn't be positive?
Anything involving "destruction" CAN'T be good for you.
How do you know? Have you ever TRIED?
I know you kids don't think a guidance chancellor can be DOWN with the youth culture, but trust me, I keep up with all the latest BUZZ!
So DIG THIS... A Hakata Soy is like one of those ELUSIVE CHARACTERS in these MonChiChiMon cards all the teachers keep having to CONFISCATE during classes.
HE IS?!
GAME CARD
Well, my programming DOES say Hakata goes to class...I should keep listening but START paying attention.
You could spend your WHOLE LIFE searching for an exclusive chase card...
+ 3
- 0
CHIM CHIM CHERRIES
+ 26
- 4
DELICIOUS COOKIE DOUGH
+ 12
- 1
DEATH DEALER MONKEY
GAME CARD
MCM
+ 9
- 1
ARTIFICIAL ARCHITECT
+ 9
- 3
FLAME-TAILED SQUIRREL
+ 8
- 16
TACOMON
...and no matter how many booster packs you buy, never find the one you seek.

95

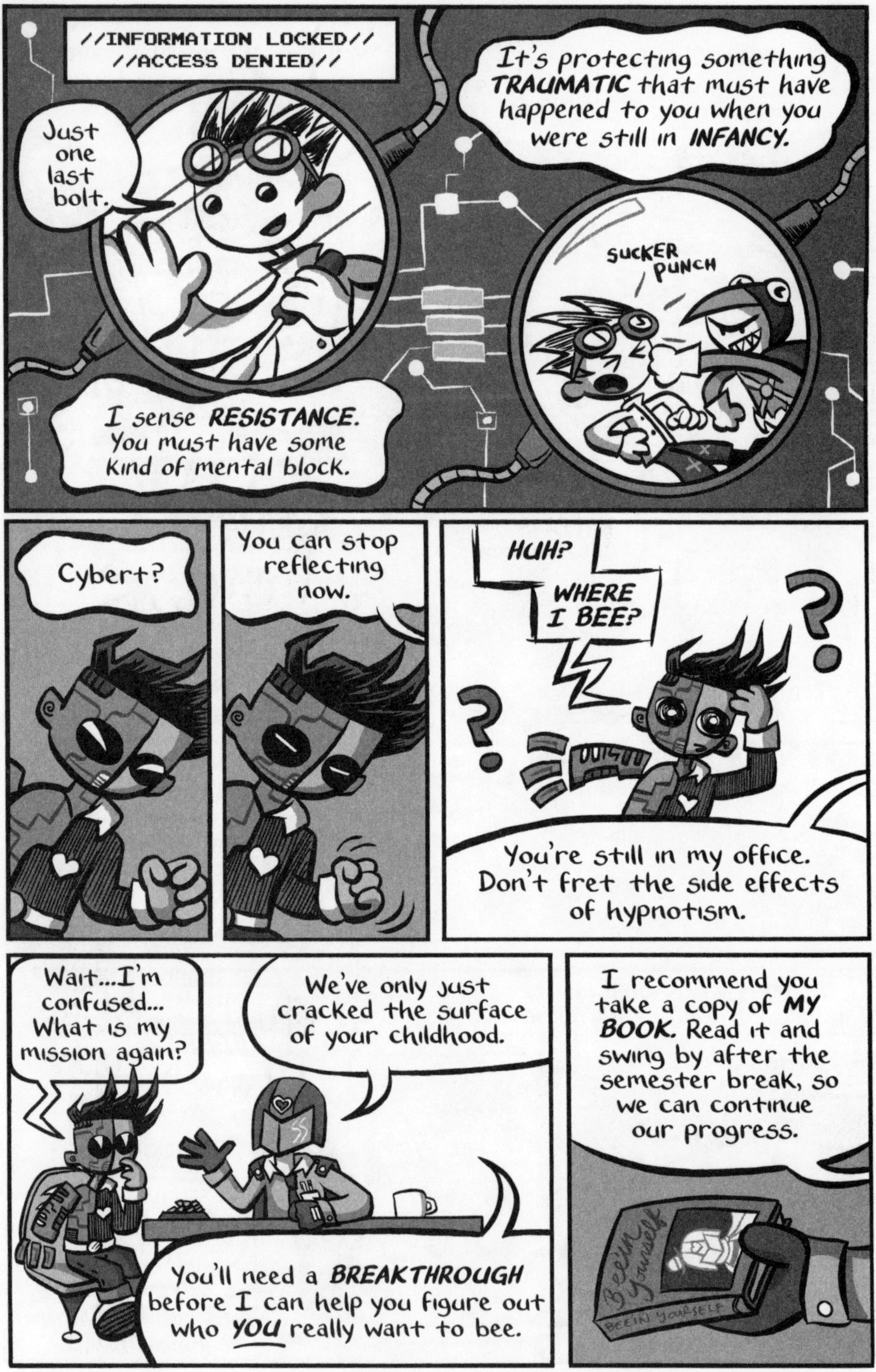
//INFORMATION LOCKED//
//ACCESS DENIED//
Just one last bolt.
It's protecting something TRAUMATIC that must have happened to you when you were still in INFANCY.
SUCKER PUNCH
I sense RESISTANCE. You must have some kind of mental block.
Cybert?
You can stop reflecting now.
HUH?
WHERE I BEE?
You're still in my office. Don't fret the side effects of hypnotism.
Wait...I'm confused... What is my mission again?
We've only just cracked the surface of your childhood.
You'll need a BREAKTHROUGH before I can help you figure out who YOU really want to bee.
I recommend you take a copy of MY BOOK. Read it and swing by after the semester break, so we can continue our progress.
BEEIN' YOURSELF

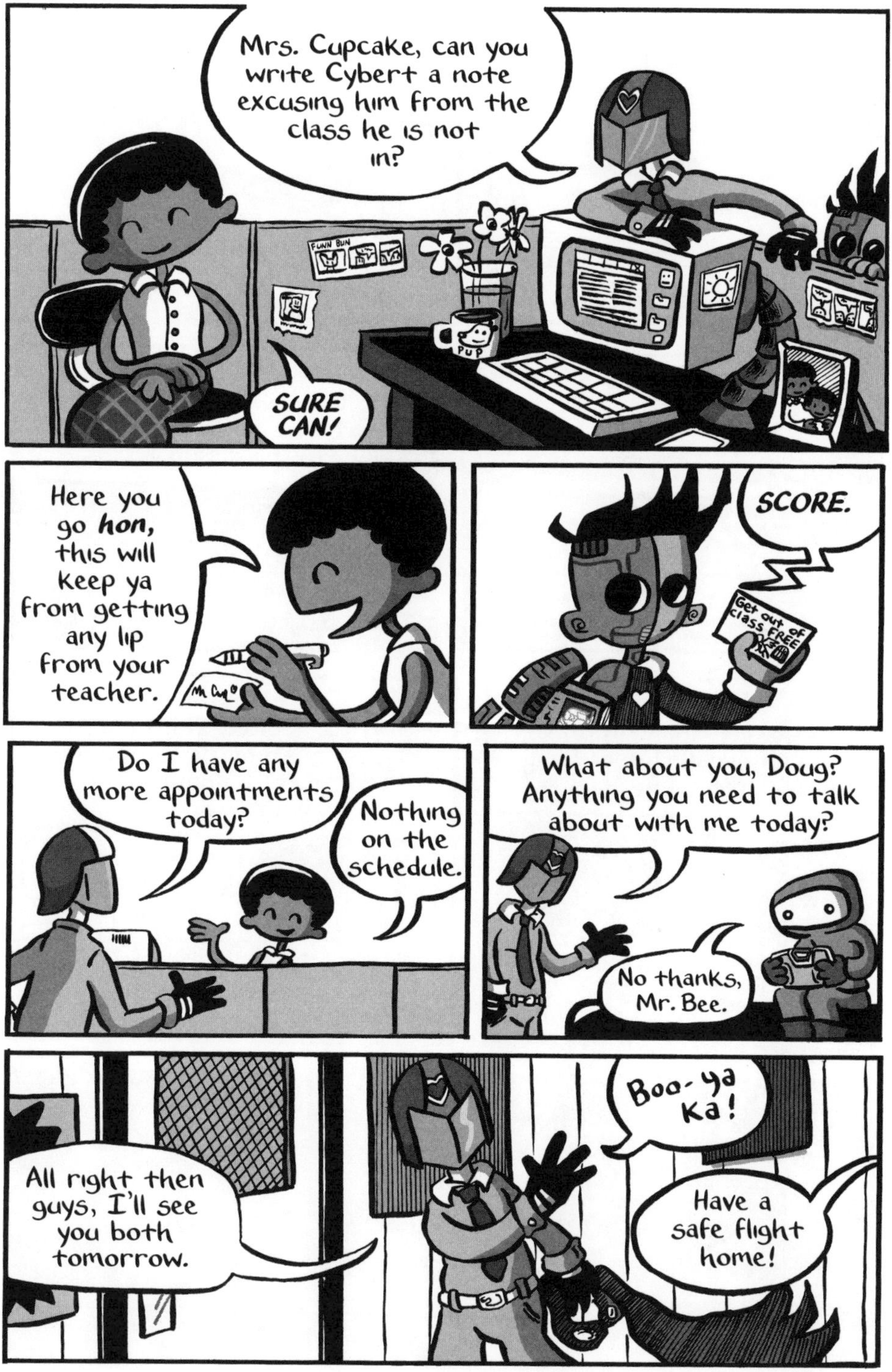
Mrs. Cupcake, can you write Cybert a note excusing him from the class he is not in?
SURE CAN!
FUNN BUN
PUP
Here you go **hon**, this will keep ya from getting any lip from your teacher.
SCORE.
Get out of class FREE
Do I have any more appointments today?
Nothing on the schedule.
What about you, Doug? Anything you need to talk about with me today?
No thanks, Mr. Bee.
Boo-ya Ka!
All right then guys, I'll see you both tomorrow.
Have a safe flight home!

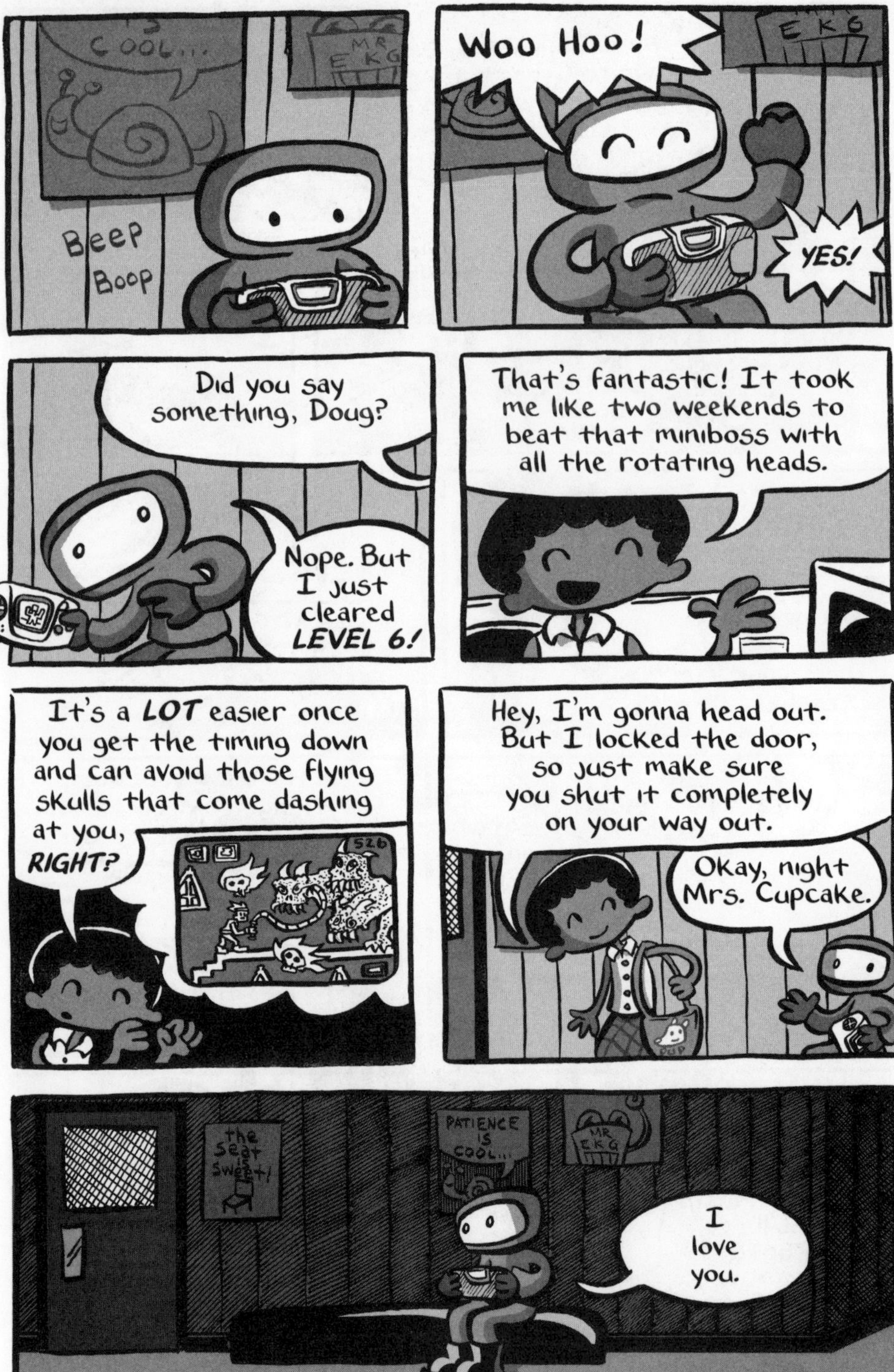
COOL...
MR EKG
Beep
Boop
Woo Hoo!
EKG
YES!
Did you say something, Doug?
Nope. But I just cleared LEVEL 6!
That's fantastic! It took me like two weekends to beat that miniboss with all the rotating heads.
It's a LOT easier once you get the timing down and can avoid those flying skulls that come dashing at you, RIGHT?
526
Hey, I'm gonna head out. But I locked the door, so just make sure you shut it completely on your way out.
Okay, night Mrs. Cupcake.
the seat is sweet!
PATIENCE IS COOL...
MR EKG
I love you.
The end

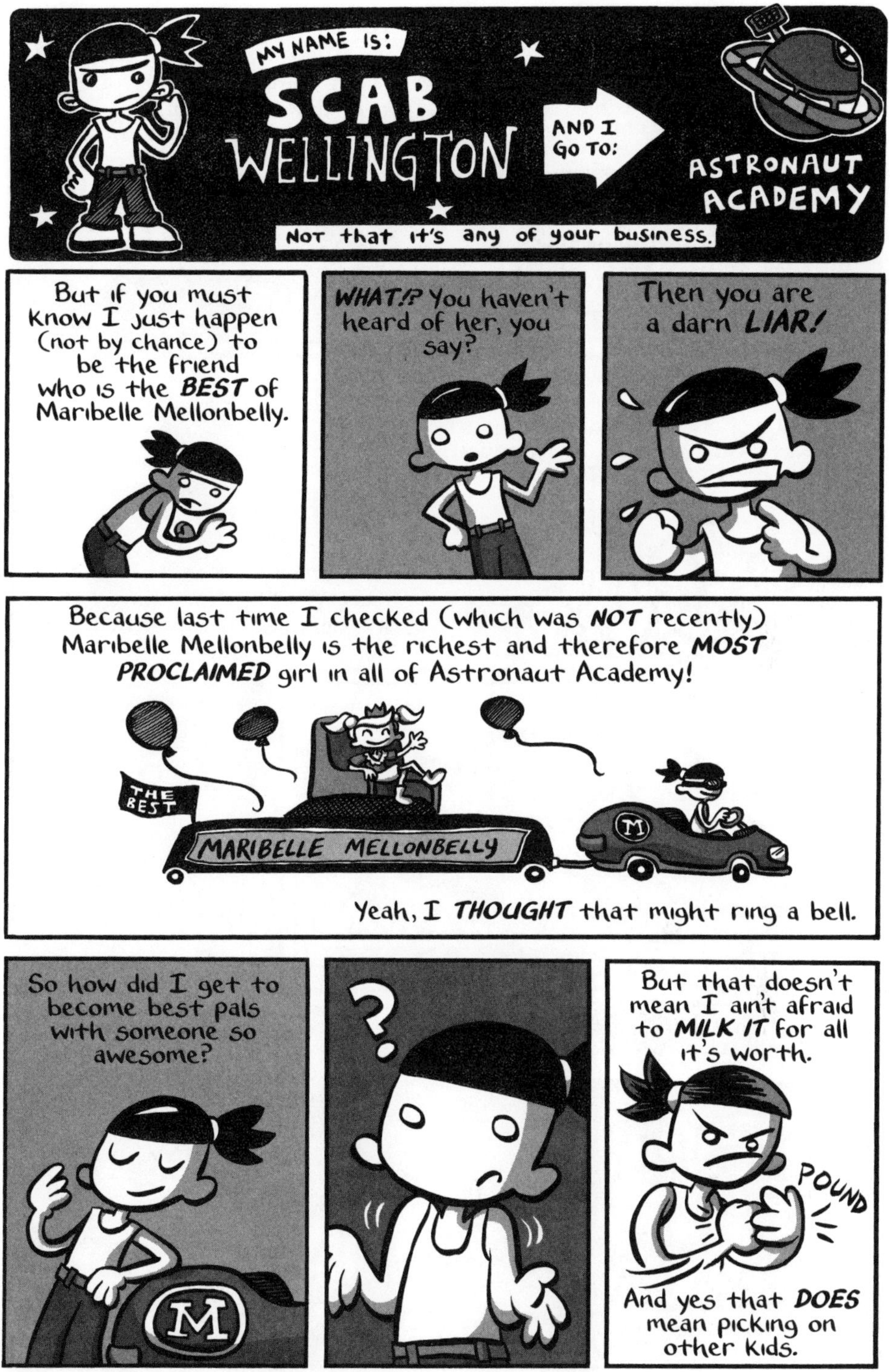

MY NAME IS:
SCAB WELLINGTON
AND I GO TO:
ASTRONAUT ACADEMY
NOT that it's any of your business.
But if you must know I just happen (not by chance) to be the friend who is the BEST of Maribelle Mellonbelly.
WHAT!? You haven't heard of her, you say?
Then you are a darn LIAR!
Because last time I checked (which was NOT recently) Maribelle Mellonbelly is the richest and therefore MOST PROCLAIMED girl in all of Astronaut Academy!
THE BEST
MARIBELLE MELLONBELLY
M
Yeah, I THOUGHT that might ring a bell.
So how did I get to become best pals with someone so awesome?
M
?
But that doesn't mean I ain't afraid to MILK IT for all it's worth.
POUND
And yes that DOES mean picking on other kids.

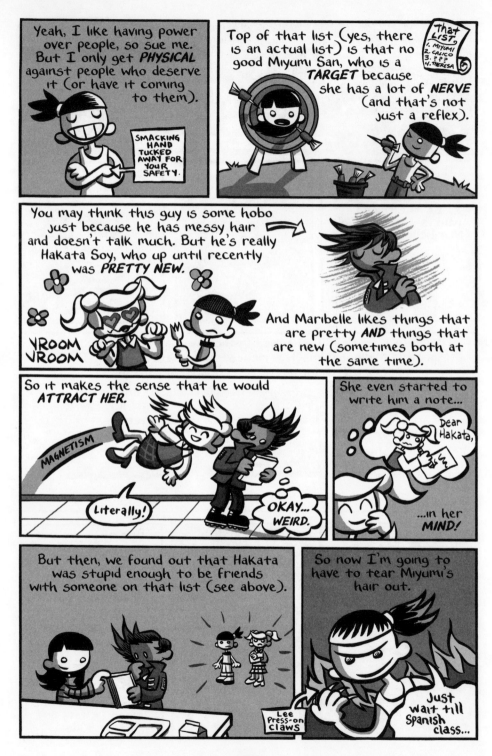

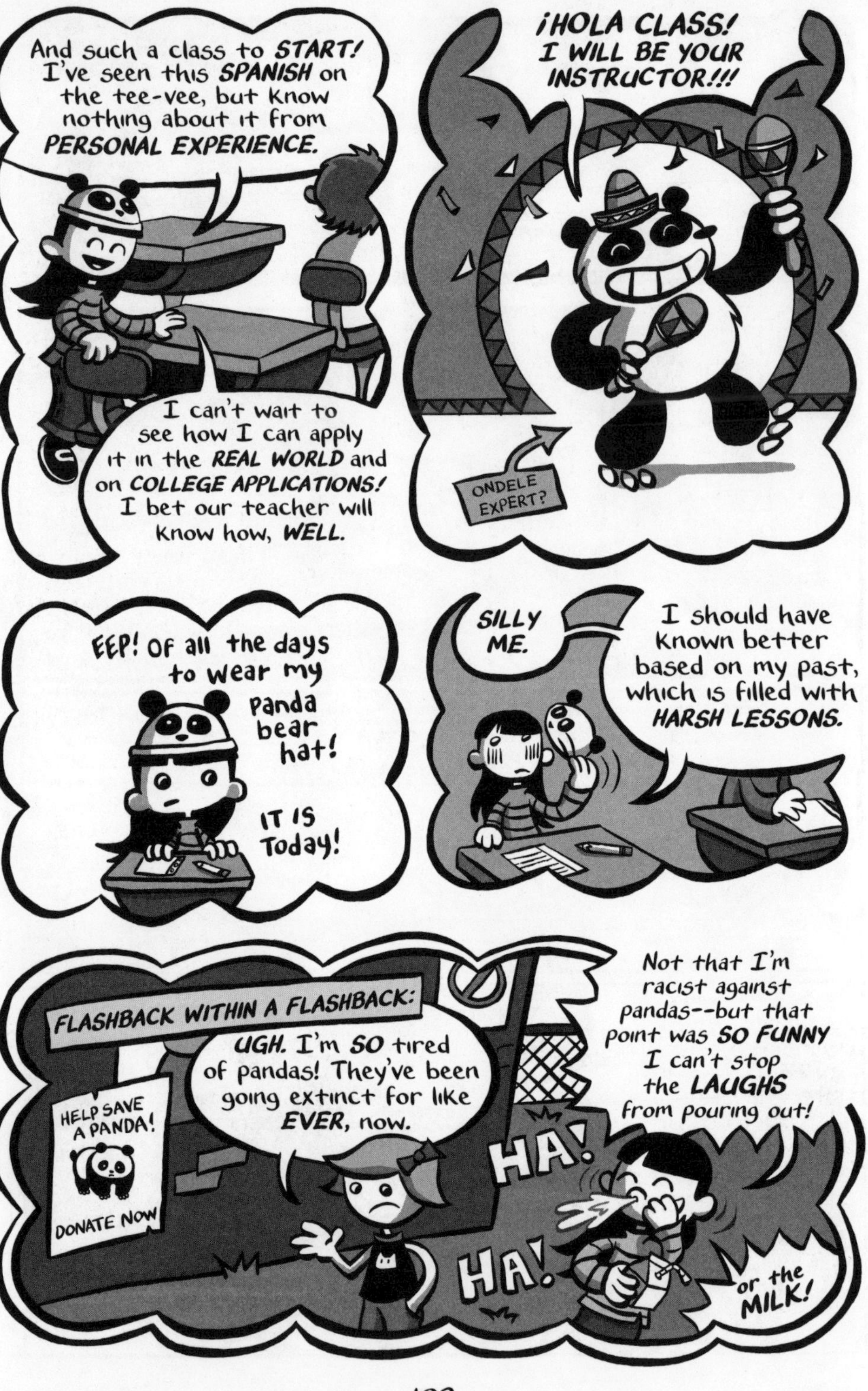

And such a class to START! I've seen this SPANISH on the tee-vee, but know nothing about it from PERSONAL EXPERIENCE.
I can't wait to see how I can apply it in the REAL WORLD and on COLLEGE APPLICATIONS! I bet our teacher will know how, WELL.
¡HOLA CLASS! I WILL BE YOUR INSTRUCTOR!!!
ONDELE EXPERT?
EEP! Of all the days to wear my panda bear hat!
IT IS Today!
SILLY ME.
I should have known better based on my past, which is filled with HARSH LESSONS.
FLASHBACK WITHIN A FLASHBACK:
HELP SAVE A PANDA!
DONATE NOW
UGH. I'm SO tired of pandas! They've been going extinct for like EVER, now.
Not that I'm racist against pandas--but that point was SO FUNNY I can't stop the LAUGHS from pouring out!
HA!
HA!
or the MILK!

*EXTRA FLASHBACK BORDER FOR YOUR PROTECTION

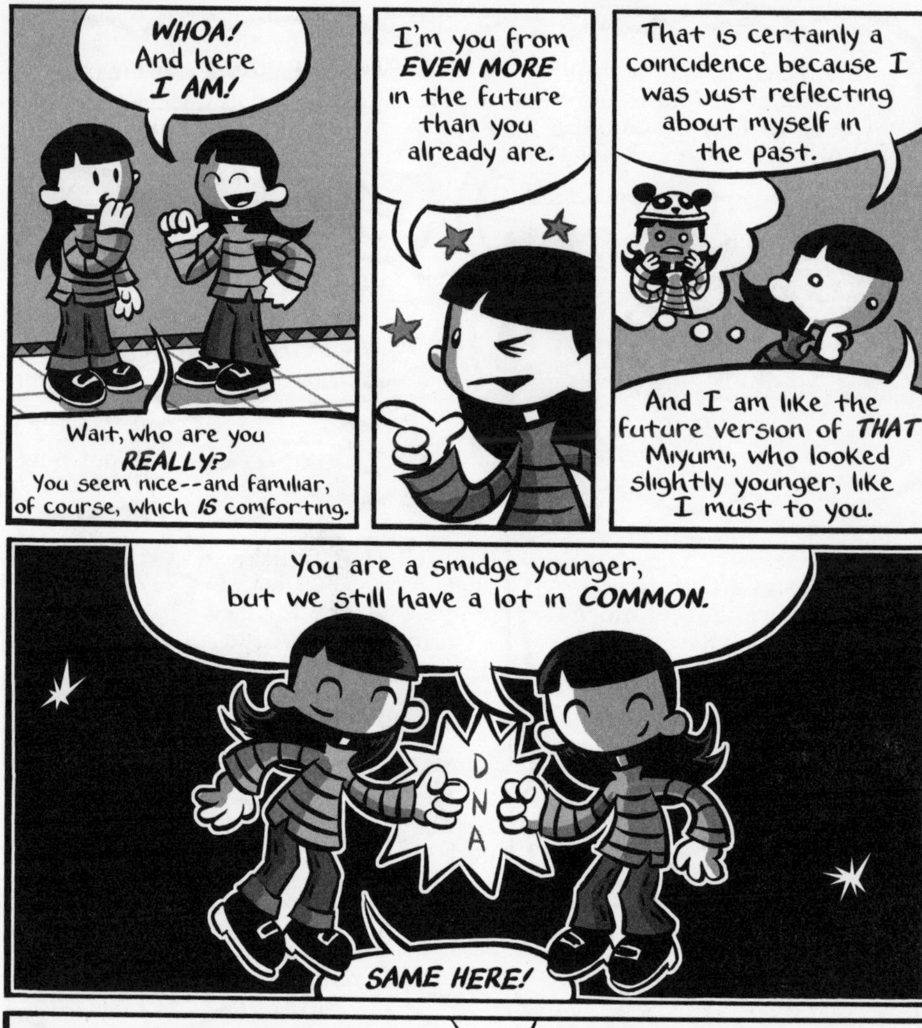
WHOA! And here I AM!
Wait, who are you REALLY? You seem nice--and familiar, of course, which IS comforting.
I'm you from EVEN MORE in the future than you already are.
That is certainly a coincidence because I was just reflecting about myself in the past.
And I am like the future version of THAT Miyumi, who looked slightly younger, like I must to you.
You are a smidge younger, but we still have a lot in COMMON.
DNA
SAME HERE!
But how are we sharing the same TIME AND PLACE in space? Doesn't science make that impossible?
Not for ME because I come from a future where time no longer has the same EFFECT.

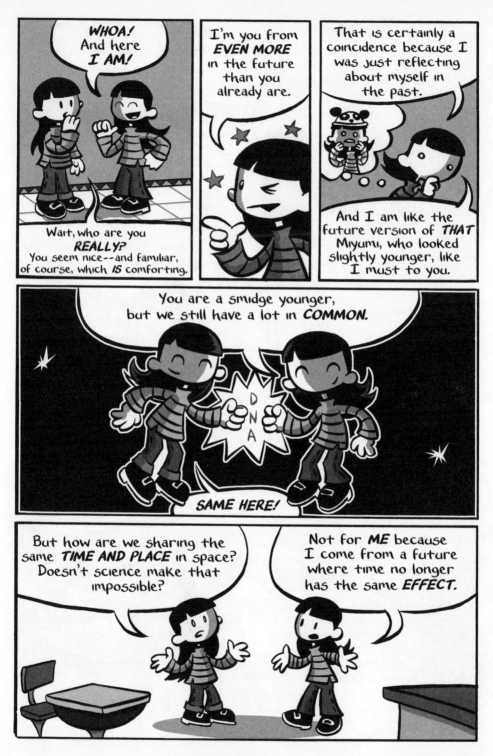

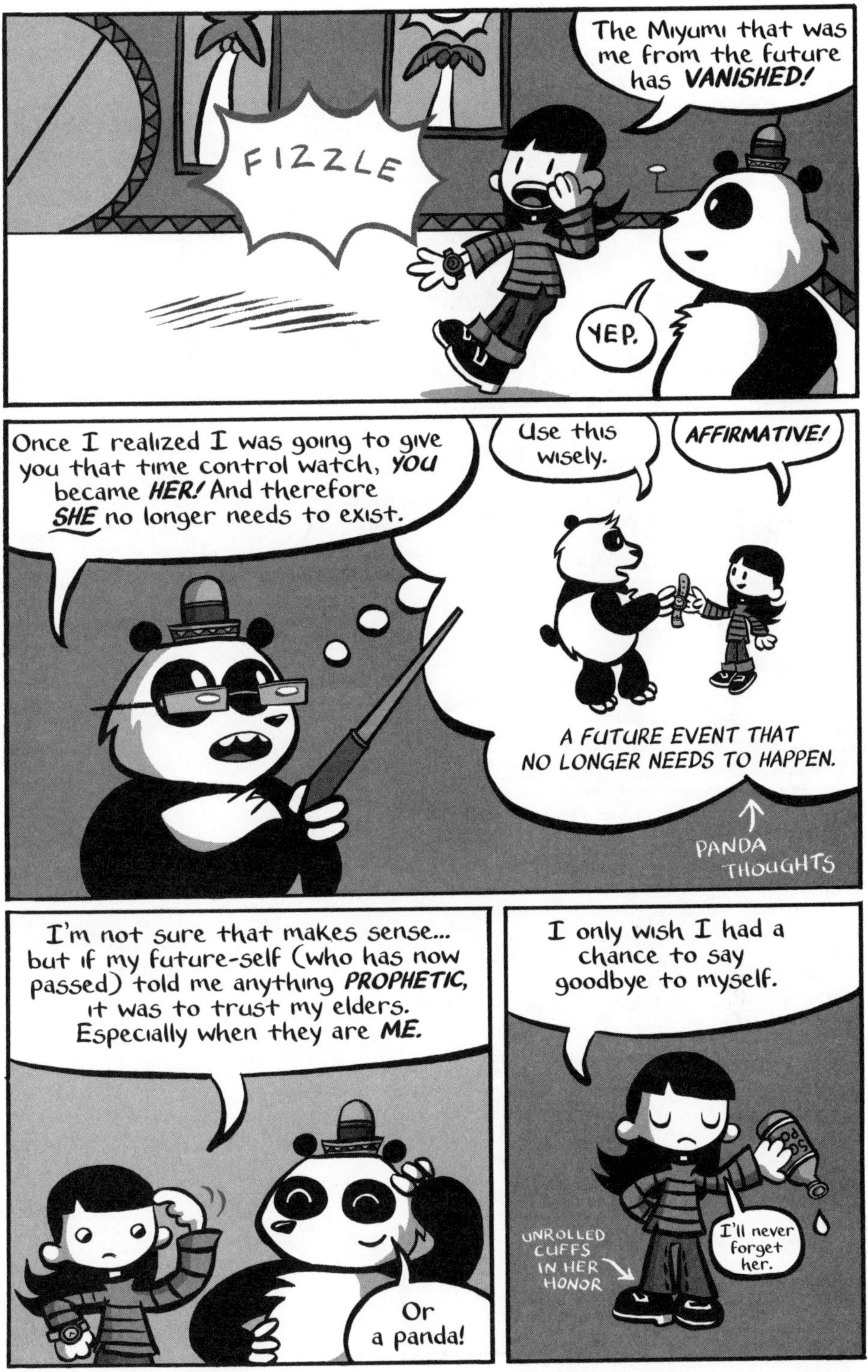
FIZZLE
The Miyumi that was me from the future has VANISHED!
YEP.
Once I realized I was going to give you that time control watch, YOU became HER! And therefore SHE no longer needs to exist.
Use this wisely.
AFFIRMATIVE!
A FUTURE EVENT THAT NO LONGER NEEDS TO HAPPEN.
PANDA THOUGHTS
I'm not sure that makes sense... but if my future-self (who has now passed) told me anything PROPHETIC, it was to trust my elders. Especially when they are ME.
Or a panda!
I only wish I had a chance to say goodbye to myself.
UNROLLED CUFFS IN HER HONOR
I'll never forget her.

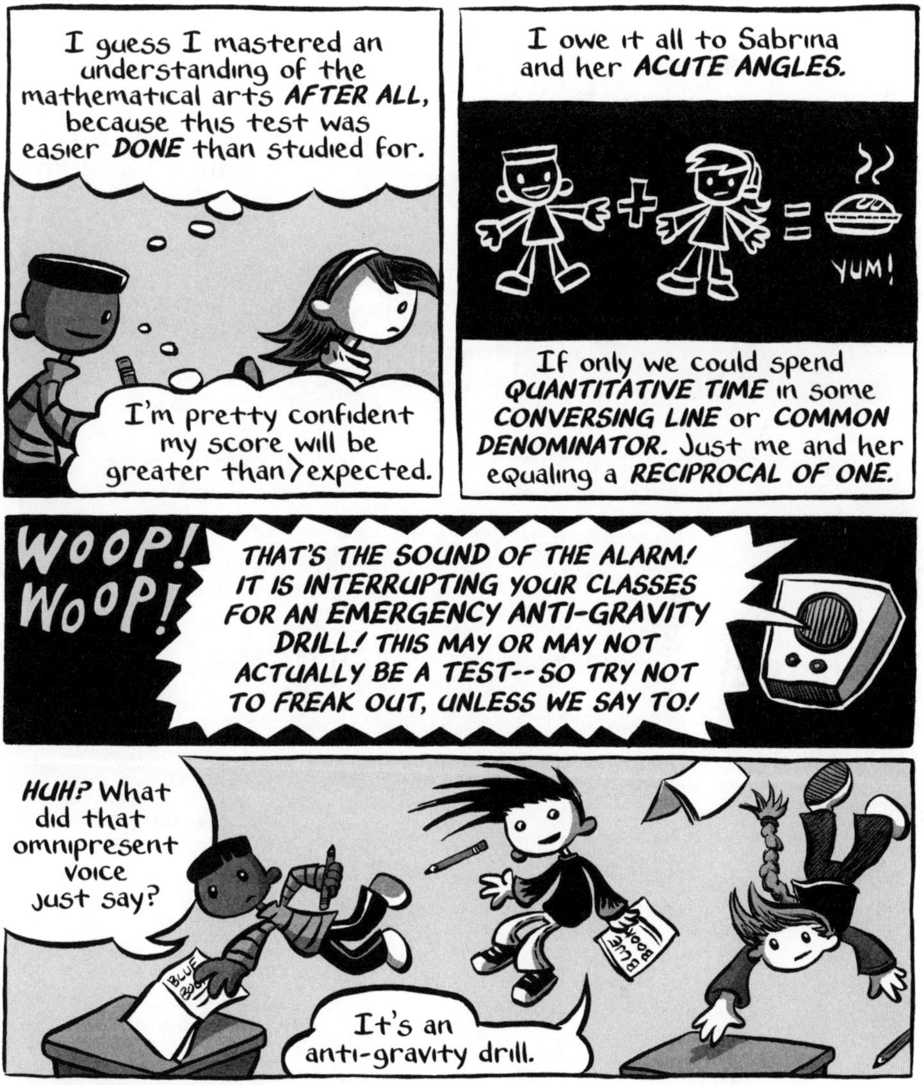
I guess I mastered an understanding of the mathematical arts AFTER ALL, because this test was easier DONE than studied for.
I'm pretty confident my score will be greater than > expected.
I owe it all to Sabrina and her ACUTE ANGLES.
YUM!
If only we could spend QUANTITATIVE TIME in some CONVERSING LINE or COMMON DENOMINATOR. Just me and her equaling a RECIPROCAL OF ONE.
WOOP! WOOP!
THAT'S THE SOUND OF THE ALARM! IT IS INTERRUPTING YOUR CLASSES FOR AN EMERGENCY ANTI-GRAVITY DRILL! THIS MAY OR MAY NOT ACTUALLY BE A TEST--SO TRY NOT TO FREAK OUT, UNLESS WE SAY TO!
HUH? What did that omnipresent voice just say?
BLUE BOOK
BLUE BOOK
It's an anti-gravity drill.
Best day of my life I think.
What about the math exams?
Do they still COUNT?
All right now, hand in your booklets to avoid cheating or losing them in a nearby wormhole.
BLUE BOOK
LET'S GO!

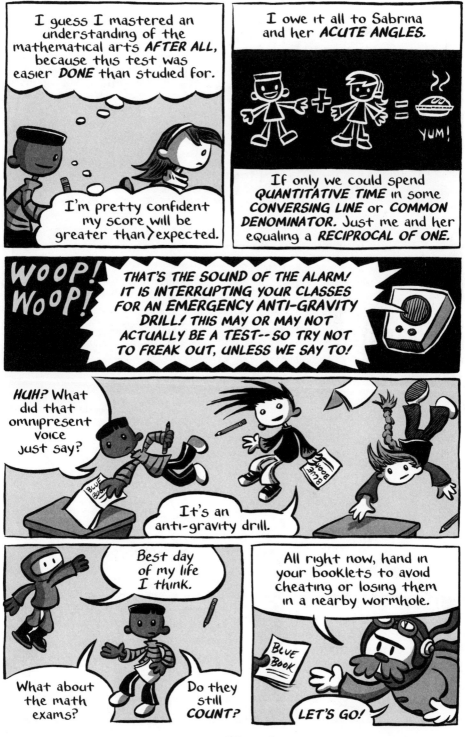

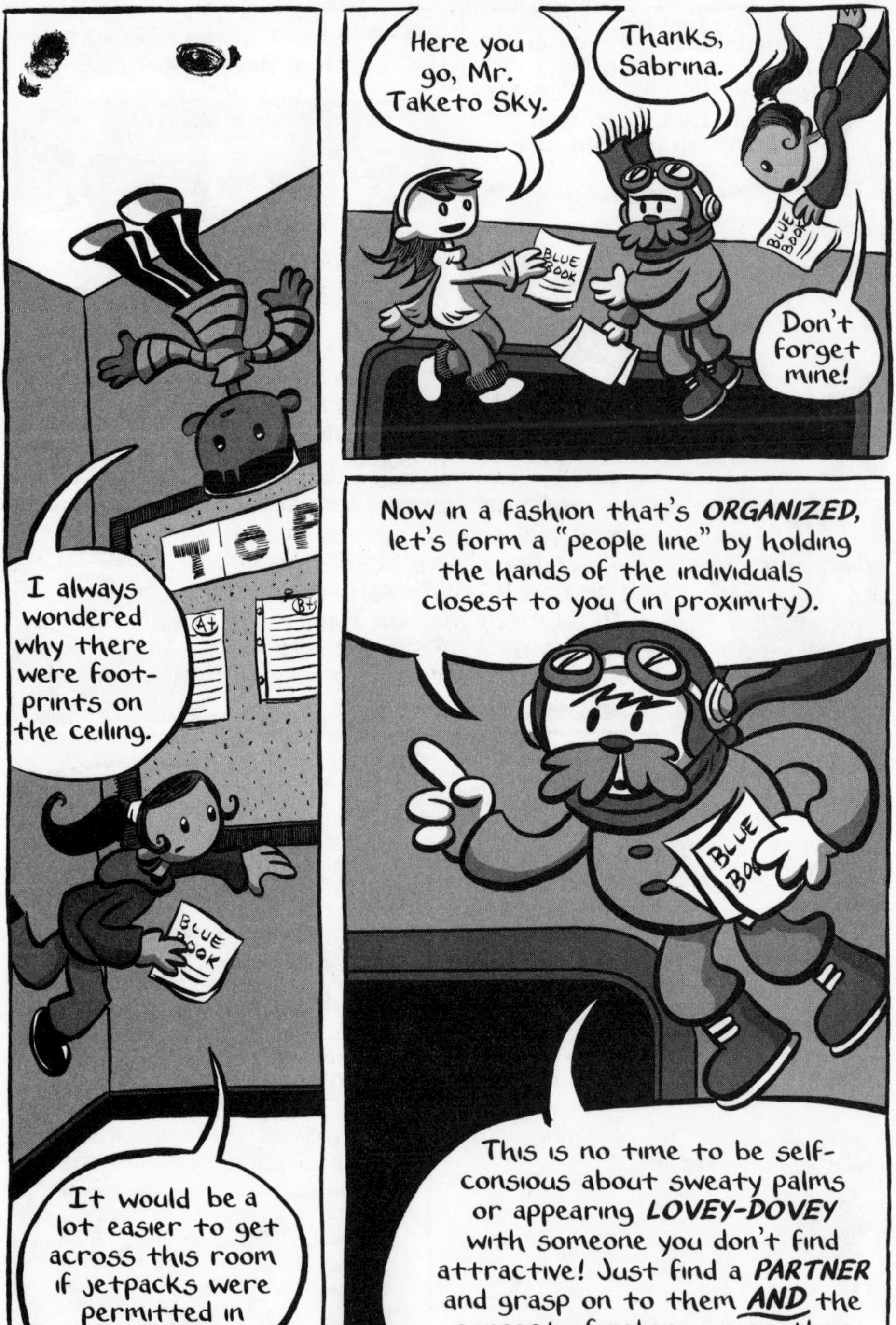
I always wondered why there were foot-prints on the ceiling.
It would be a lot easier to get across this room if jetpacks were permitted in class.
Here you go, Mr. Taketo Sky.
Thanks, Sabrina.
Don't forget mine!
BLUE BOOK
Now in a fashion that's ORGANIZED, let's form a "people line" by holding the hands of the individuals closest to you (in proximity).
This is no time to be self-consious about sweaty palms or appearing LOVEY-DOVEY with someone you don't find attractive! Just find a PARTNER and grasp on to them AND the concept of relying on another person to save your life!

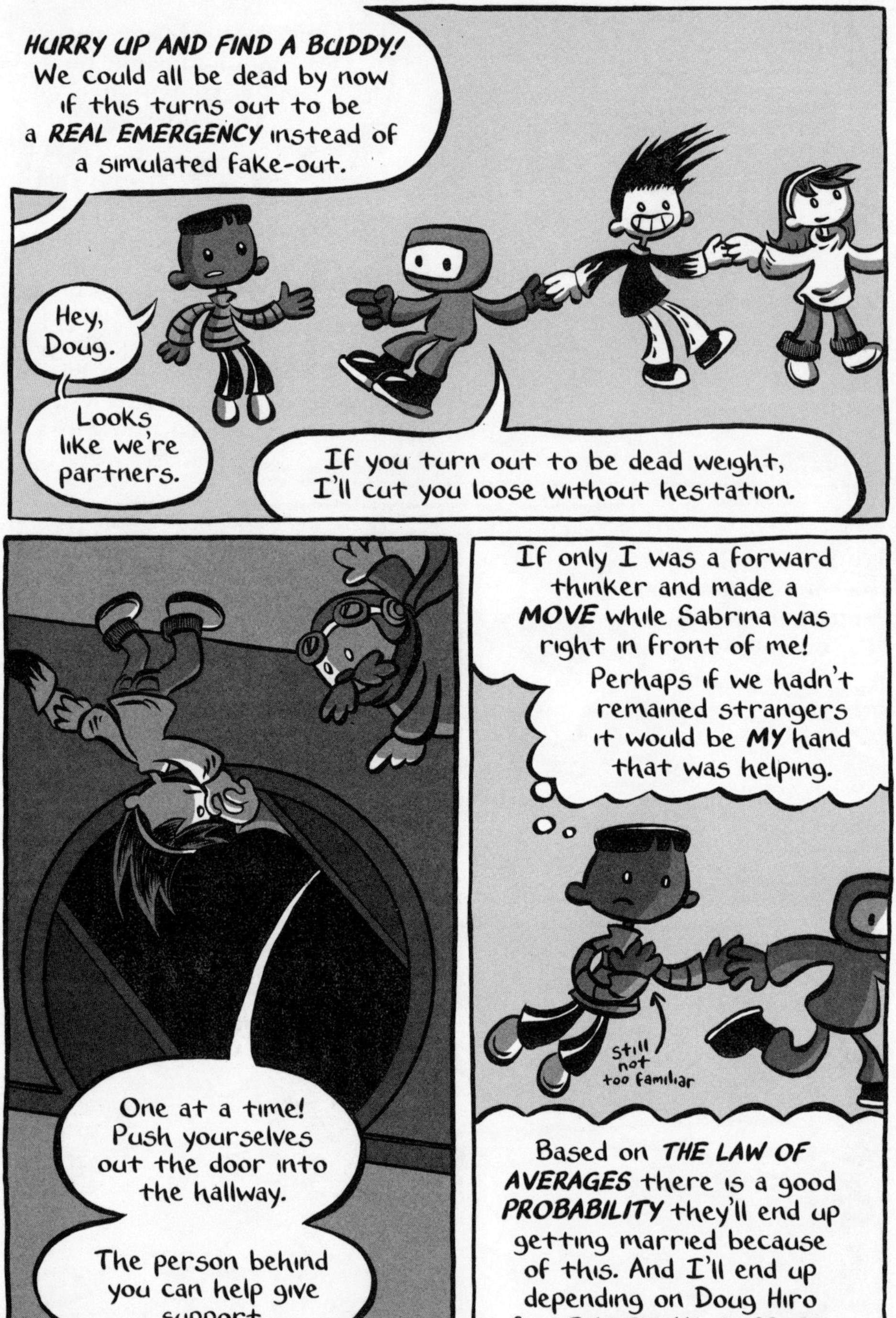
HURRY UP AND FIND A BUDDY! We could all be dead by now if this turns out to be a REAL EMERGENCY instead of a simulated fake-out.
Hey, Doug.
Looks like we're partners.
If you turn out to be dead weight, I'll cut you loose without hesitation.
One at a time! Push yourselves out the door into the hallway.
The person behind you can help give support.
If only I was a forward thinker and made a MOVE while Sabrina was right in front of me!
Perhaps if we hadn't remained strangers it would be MY hand that was helping.
still not too familiar
Based on THE LAW OF AVERAGES there is a good PROBABILITY they'll end up getting married because of this. And I'll end up depending on Doug Hiro for EMOTIONAL SUPPORT.

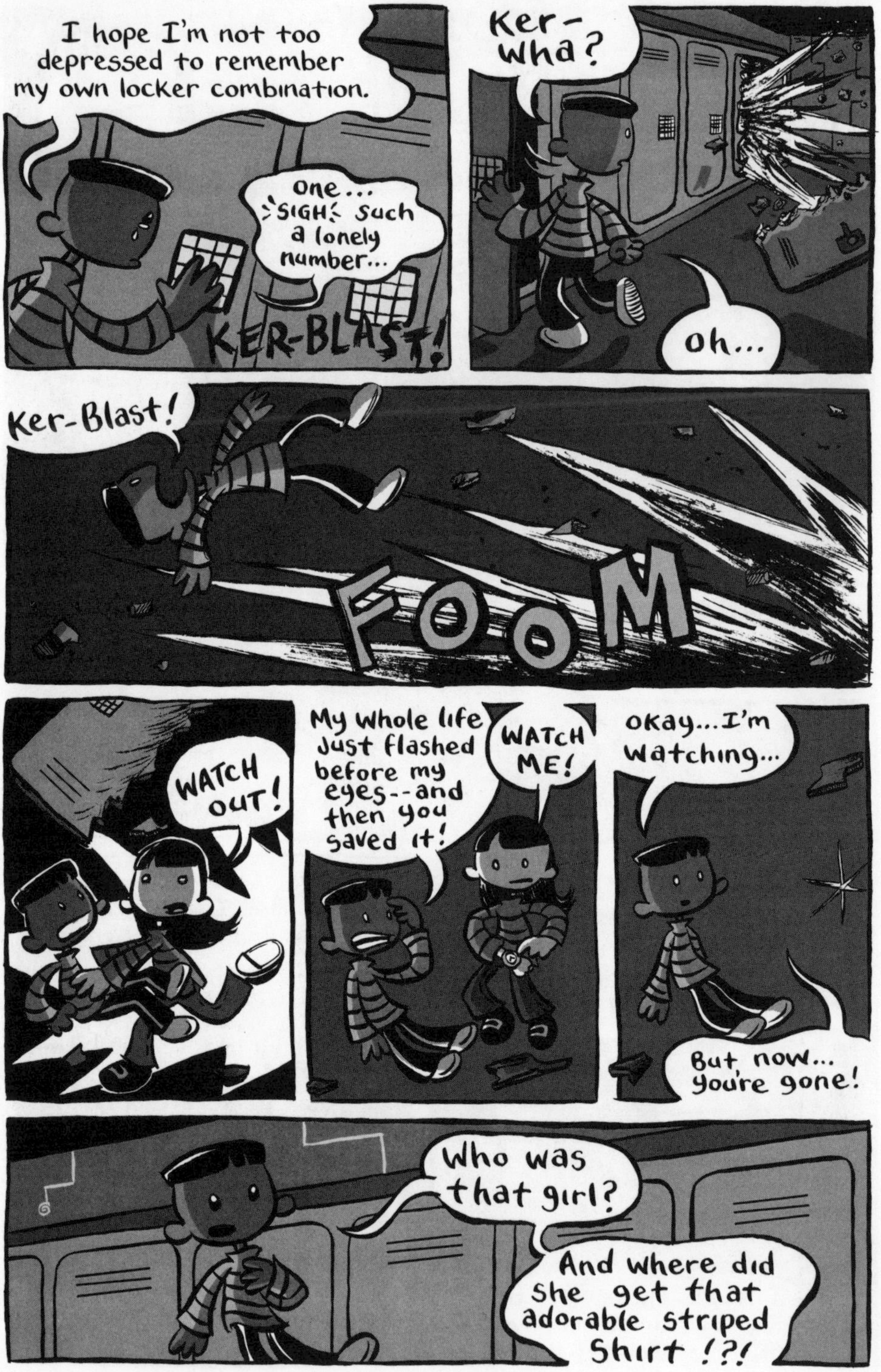
I hope I'm not too depressed to remember my own locker combination.
One... SIGH such a lonely number...
KER-BLAST!
Ker-wha?
Oh...
Ker-Blast!
FOOM
WATCH OUT!
My whole life just flashed before my eyes--and then you saved it!
WATCH ME!
okay...I'm watching...
But now... you're gone!
Who was that girl?
And where did she get that adorable striped shirt !?!

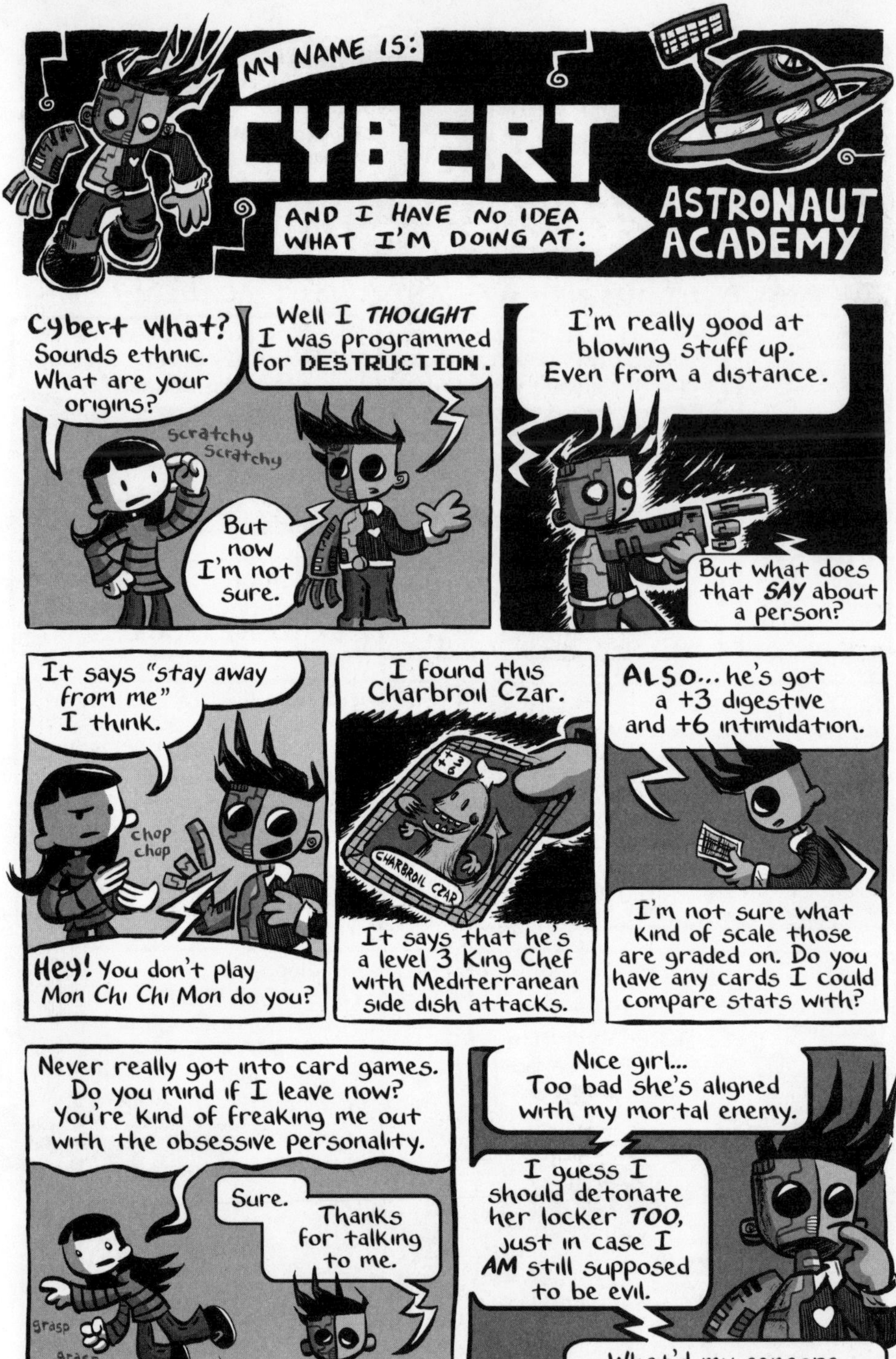
MY NAME IS:
CYBERT
AND I HAVE NO IDEA WHAT I'M DOING AT:
ASTRONAUT ACADEMY
Cybert What? Sounds ethnic. What are your origins?
Well I THOUGHT I was programmed for DESTRUCTION.
Scratchy Scratchy
But now I'm not sure.
I'm really good at blowing stuff up. Even from a distance.
But what does that SAY about a person?
It says "stay away from me" I think.
chop chop
Hey! You don't play Mon Chi Chi Mon do you?
I found this Charbroil Czar.
CHARBROIL CZAR
It says that he's a level 3 King Chef with Mediterranean side dish attacks.
ALSO... he's got a +3 digestive and +6 intimidation.
I'm not sure what kind of scale those are graded on. Do you have any cards I could compare stats with?
Never really got into card games. Do you mind if I leave now? You're kind of freaking me out with the obsessive personality.
Sure.
Thanks for talking to me.
grasp
grasp
Nice girl... Too bad she's aligned with my mortal enemy.
I guess I should detonate her locker TOO, just in case I AM still supposed to be evil.
What'd my sensors say her name was again?

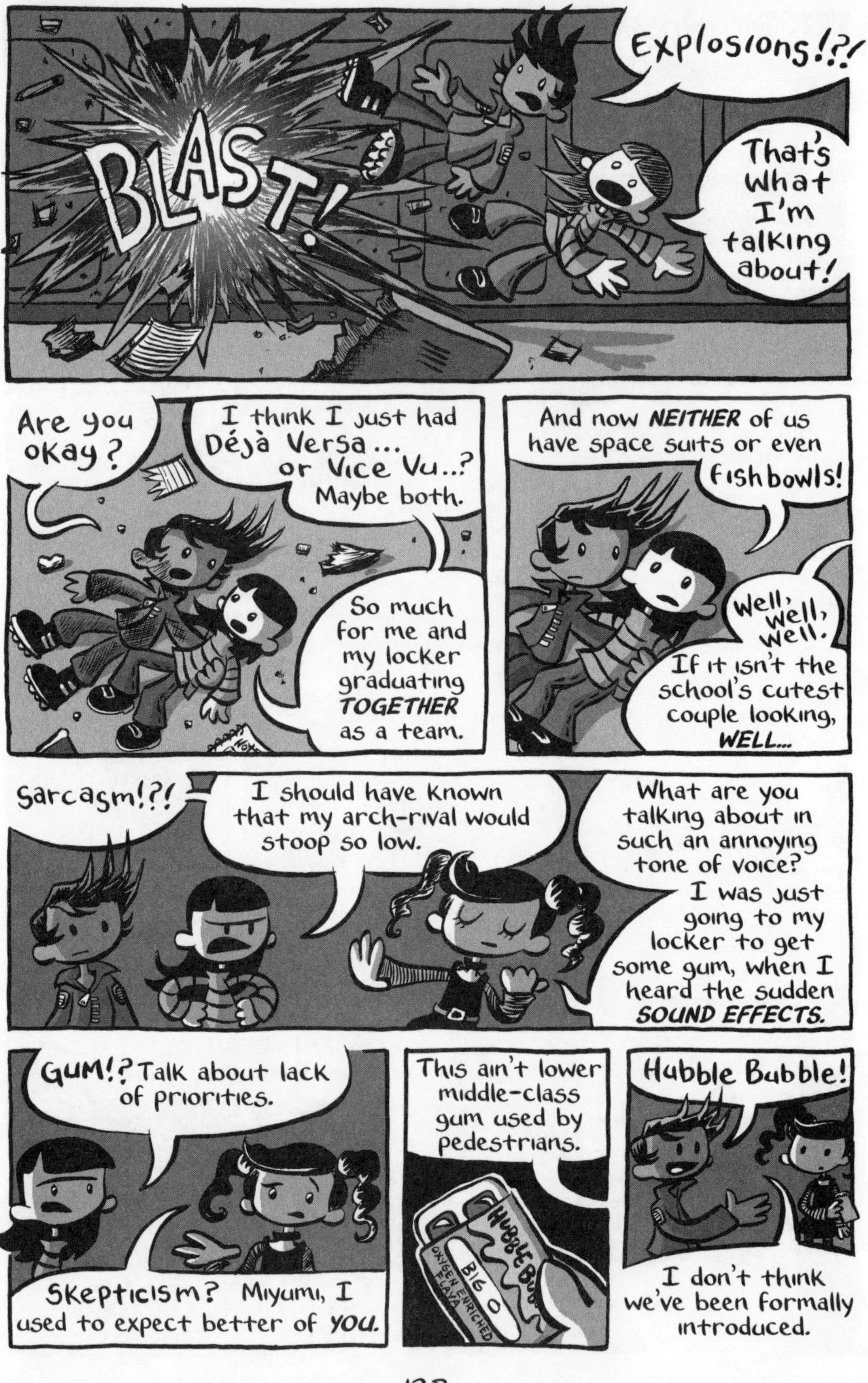
BLAST!
Explosions!?!
That's what I'm talking about!
Are you okay?
I think I just had Déjà Versa... or Vice Vu..? Maybe both.
So much for me and my locker graduating TOGETHER as a team.
And now NEITHER of us have space suits or even fishbowls!
Well, well, well.
If it isn't the school's cutest couple looking, WELL...
Sarcasm!?!
I should have known that my arch-rival would stoop so low.
What are you talking about in such an annoying tone of voice?
I was just going to my locker to get some gum, when I heard the sudden SOUND EFFECTS.
GUM!? Talk about lack of priorities.
Skepticism? Miyumi, I used to expect better of YOU.
This ain't lower middle-class gum used by pedestrians.
HUBBLE BUBB
BIG O
OXYGEN ENRICHED FLAVA
Hubble Bubble!
I don't think we've been formally introduced.

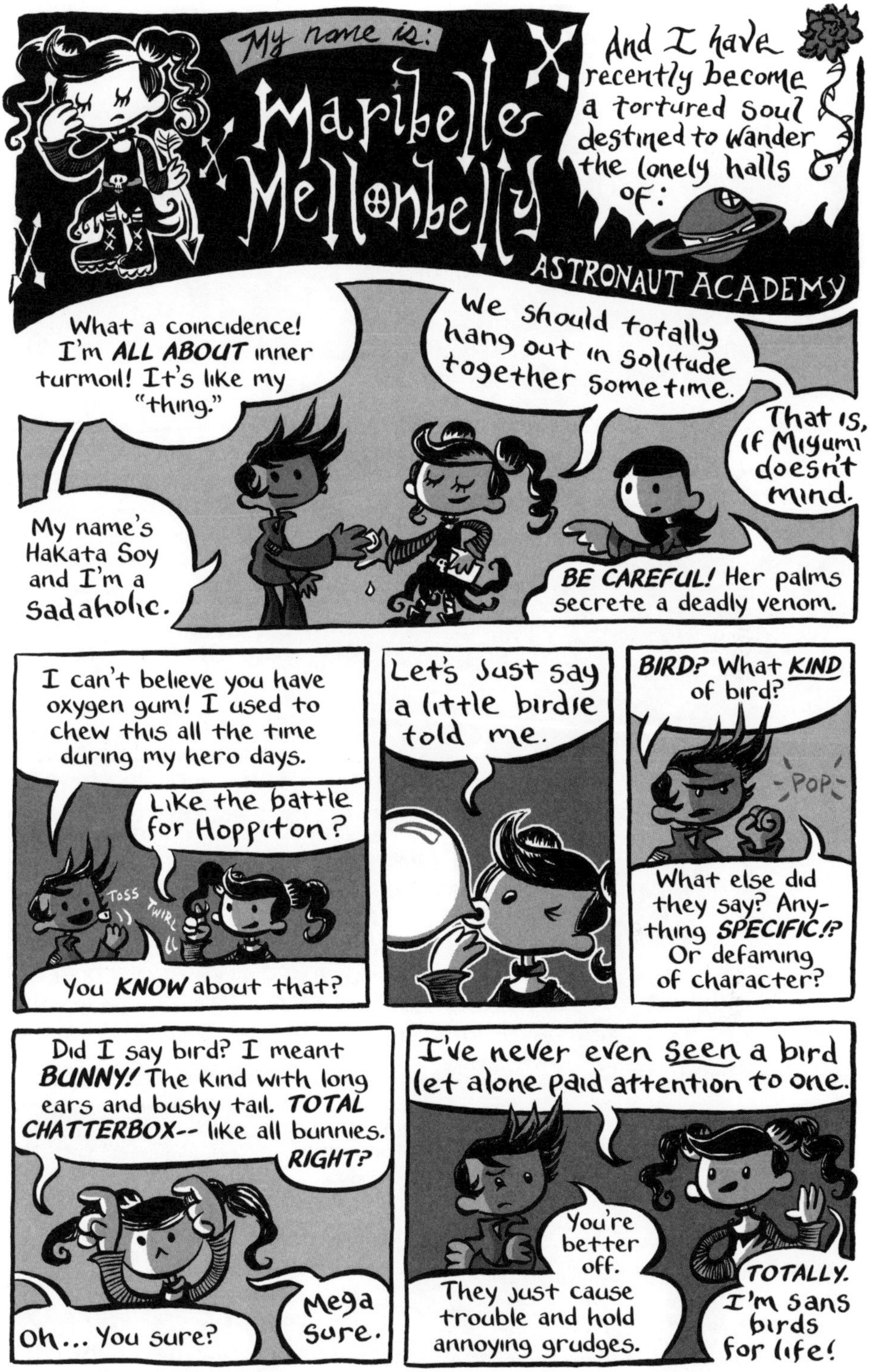
My name is:
Maribelle Mellonbelly
And I have recently become a tortured soul destined to wander the lonely halls of:
ASTRONAUT ACADEMY
What a coincidence! I'm ALL ABOUT inner turmoil! It's like my "thing."
We should totally hang out in solitude together sometime.
That is, if Miyumi doesn't mind.
My name's Hakata Soy and I'm a sadaholic.
BE CAREFUL! Her palms secrete a deadly venom.
I can't believe you have oxygen gum! I used to chew this all the time during my hero days.
Like the battle for Hoppiton?
TOSS
TWIRL
You KNOW about that?
Let's just say a little birdie told me.
BIRD? What KIND of bird?
POP
What else did they say? Anything SPECIFIC!? Or defaming of character?
Did I say bird? I meant BUNNY! The kind with long ears and bushy tail. TOTAL CHATTERBOX-- like all bunnies. RIGHT?
Oh... You sure?
Mega sure.
I've never even seen a bird let alone paid attention to one.
You're better off.
They just cause trouble and hold annoying grudges.
TOTALLY. I'm sans birds for life!

130

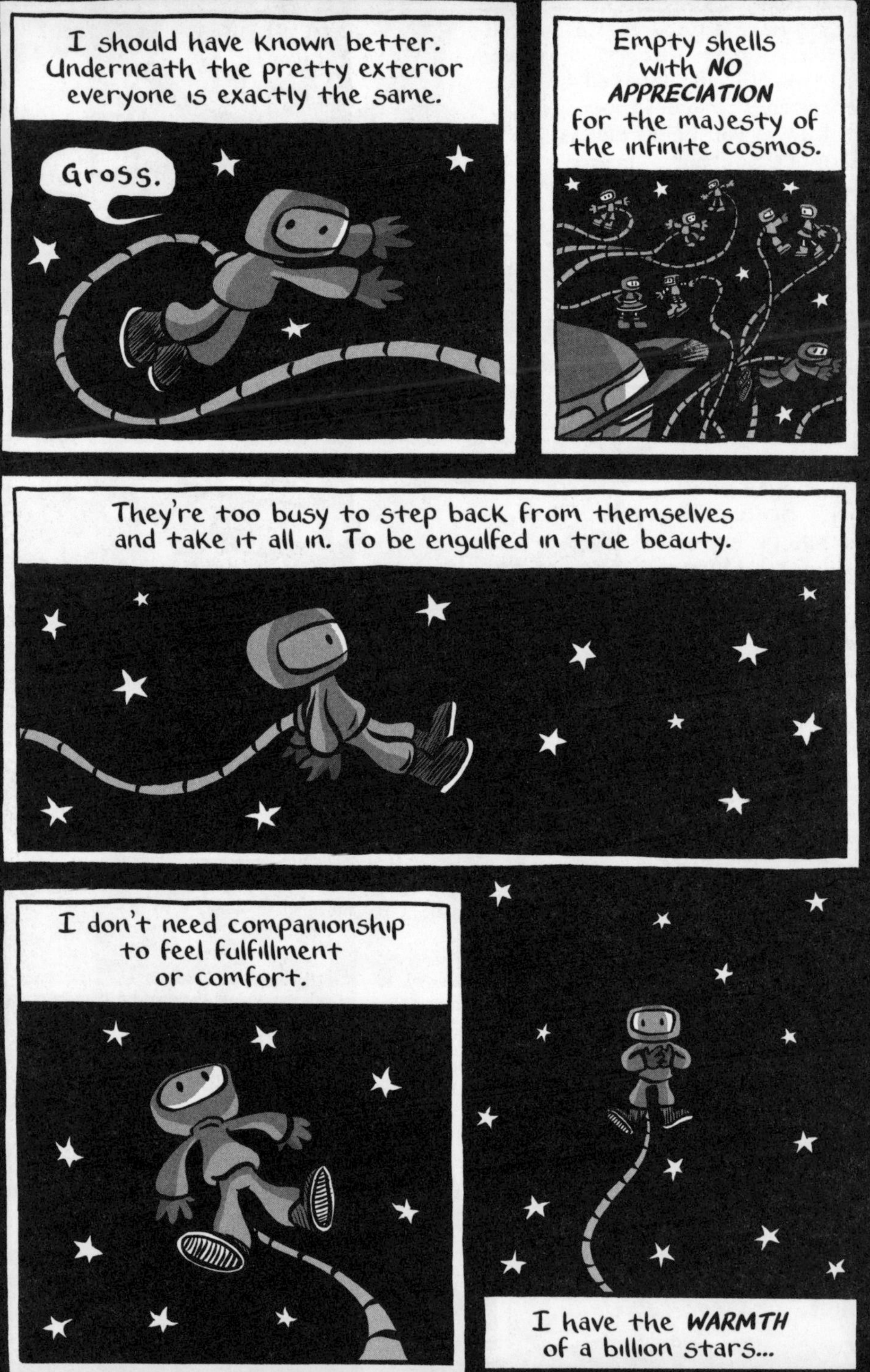
I should have known better. Underneath the pretty exterior everyone is exactly the same.
Gross.
Empty shells with **NO APPRECIATION** for the majesty of the infinite cosmos.
They're too busy to step back from themselves and take it all in. To be engulfed in true beauty.
I don't need companionship to feel fulfillment or comfort.
I have the **WARMTH** of a billion stars...

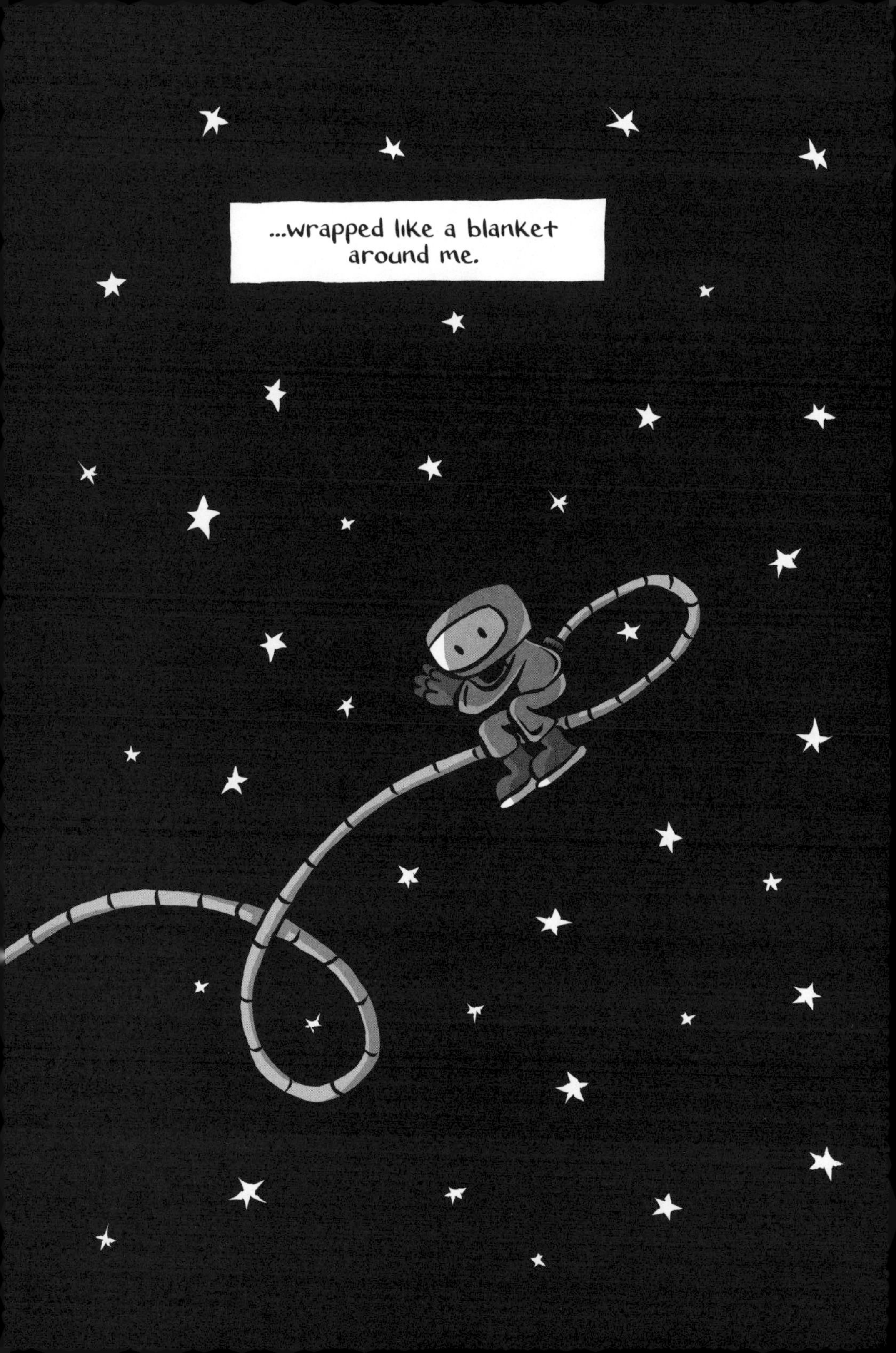
...wrapped like a blanket around me.

140

144

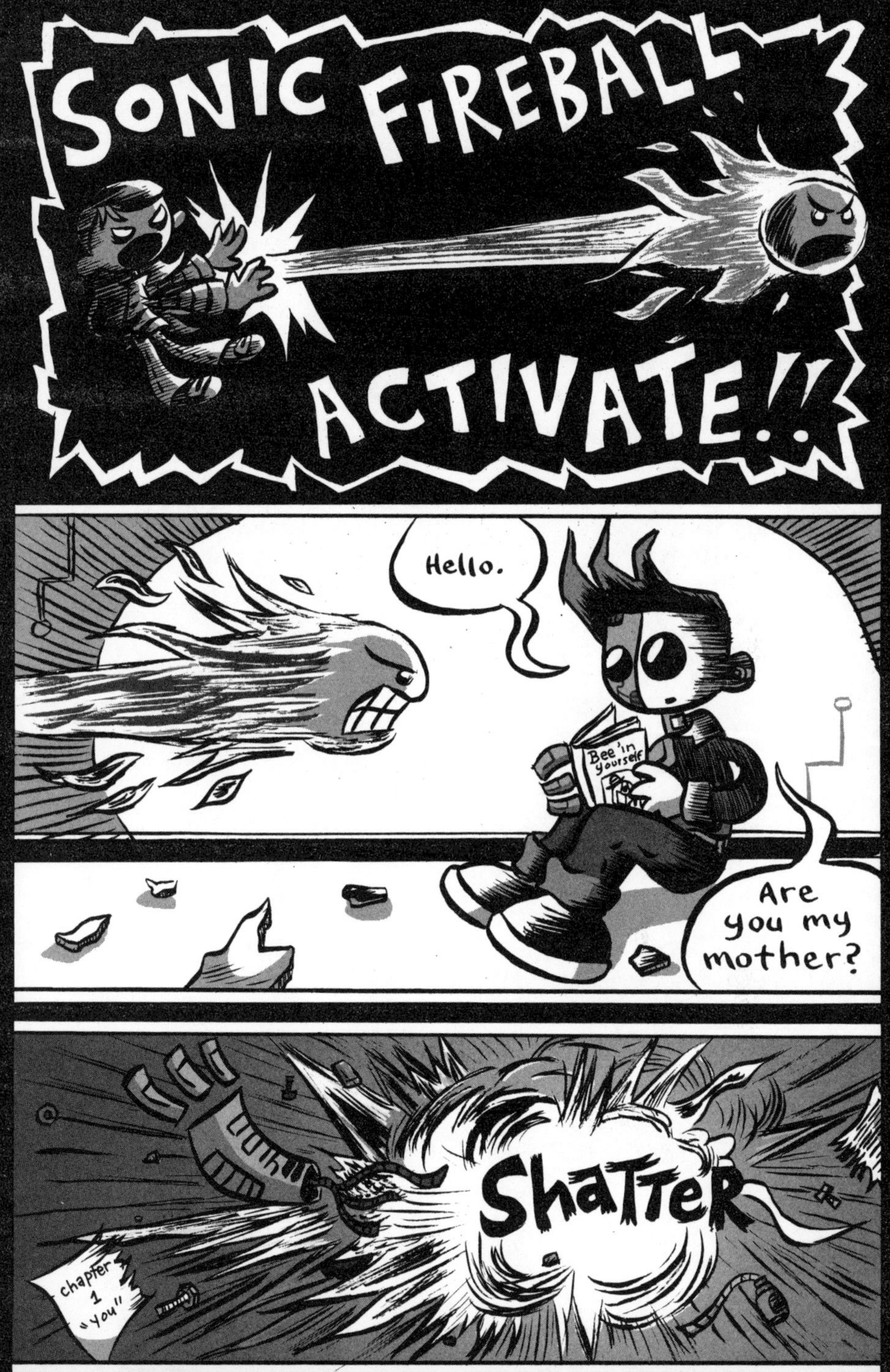
SONIC FIREBALL
ACTIVATE!!
Hello.
Bee 'in yourself
Are you my mother?
SHATTER
chapter 1 "you"

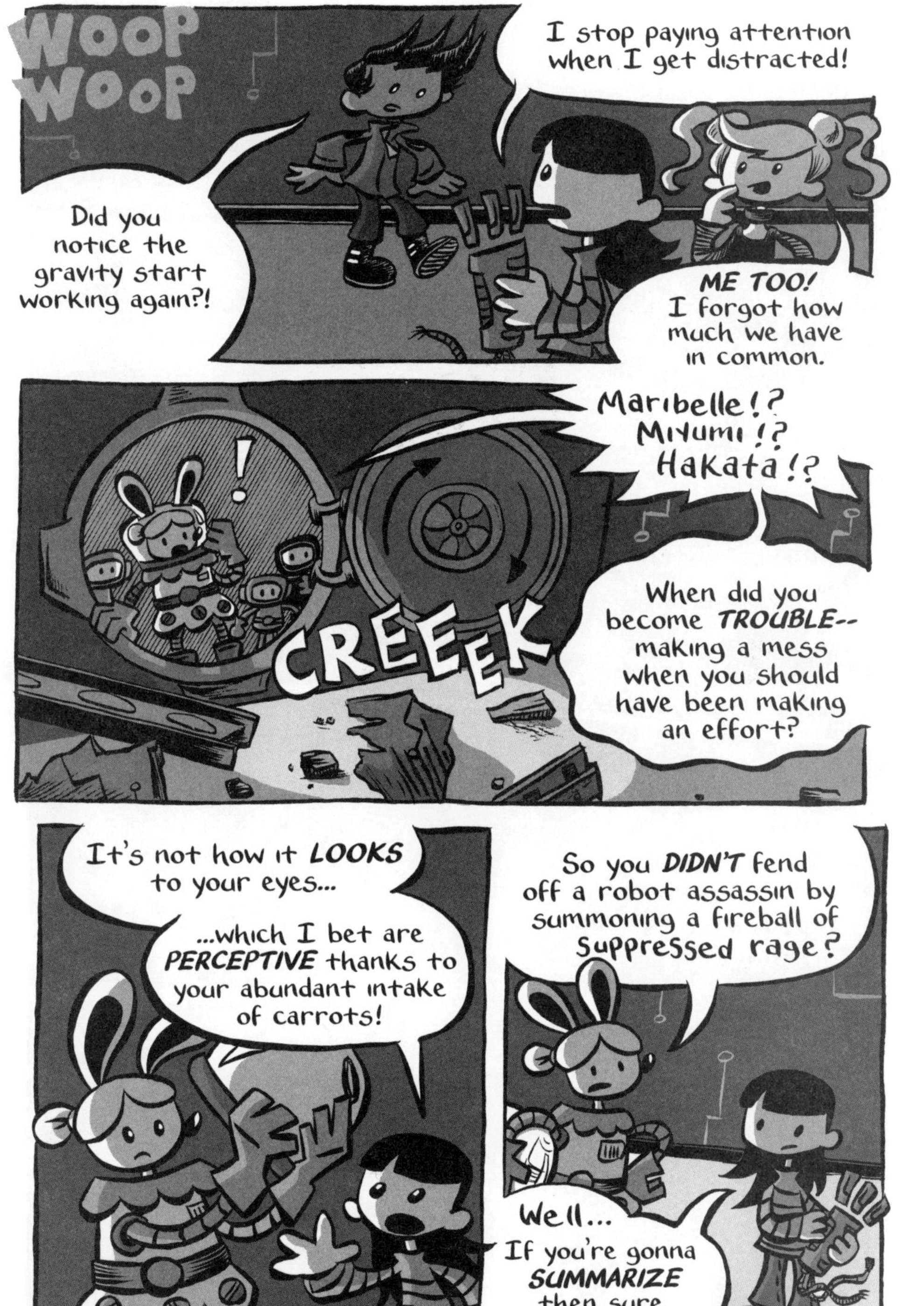
WOOP WOOP
Did you notice the gravity start working again?!
I stop paying attention when I get distracted!
ME TOO! I forgot how much we have in common.
Maribelle!? Miyumi!? Hakata!?
When did you become TROUBLE-- making a mess when you should have been making an effort?
CREEEK
It's not how it LOOKS to your eyes...
...which I bet are PERCEPTIVE thanks to your abundant intake of carrots!
So you DIDN'T fend off a robot assassin by summoning a fireball of suppressed rage?
Well...
If you're gonna SUMMARIZE then sure, I guess...

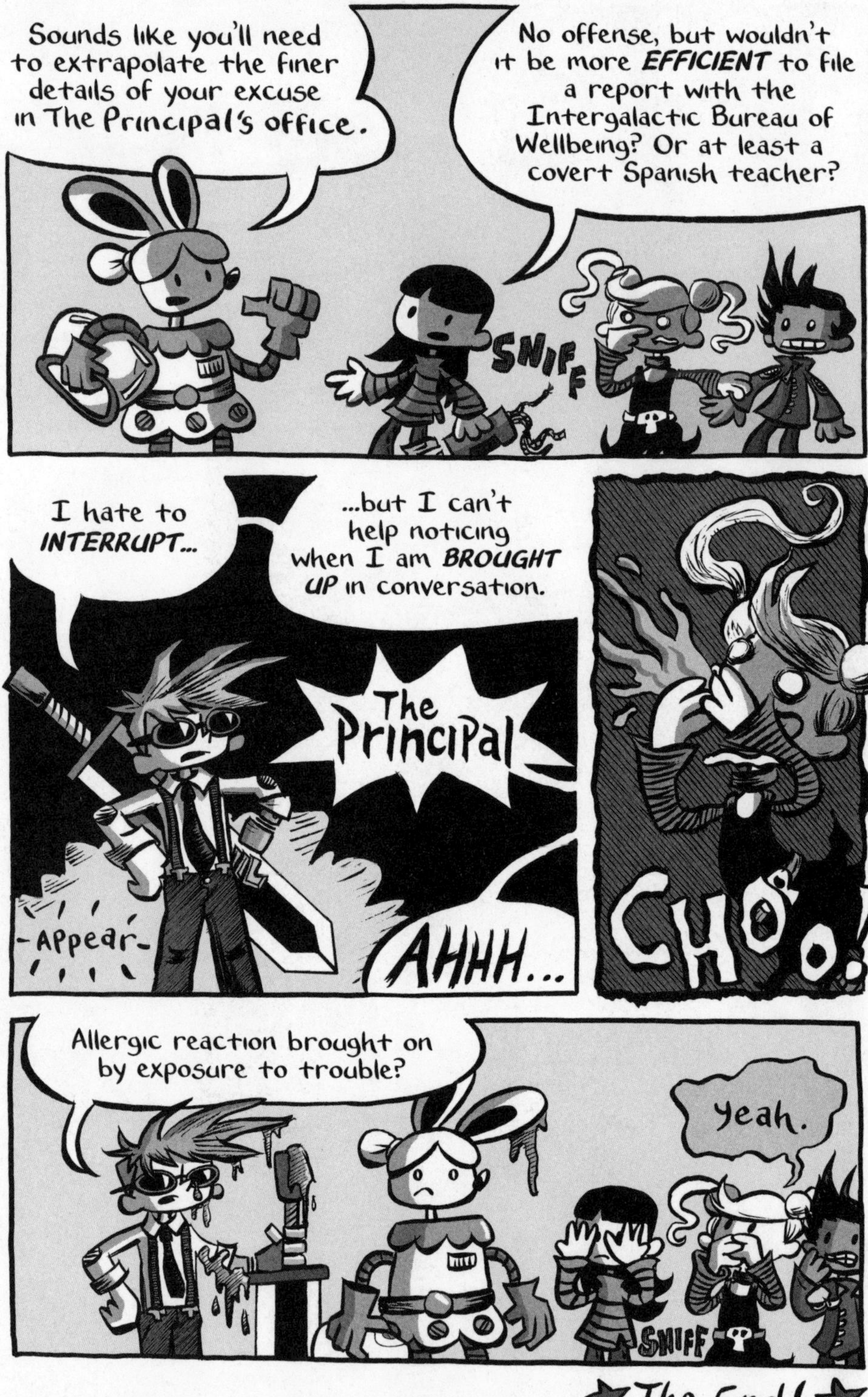
Sounds like you'll need to extrapolate the finer details of your excuse in The Principal's office.
No offense, but wouldn't it be more EFFICIENT to file a report with the Intergalactic Bureau of Wellbeing? Or at least a covert Spanish teacher?
SNIFF
I hate to INTERRUPT...
...but I can't help noticing when I am BROUGHT UP in conversation.
The Principal
-Appear-
AHHH...
CHOO!
Allergic reaction brought on by exposure to trouble?
Yeah.
SNIFF
★The End!★

SCHOOL'S OUT!
But don't head home just yet....

Parent-Teacher Conferences are tonight!
Followed by the Universal Holiday Party!

Don't forget The Principal's farewell
or your epilogues!

PARTY TIME!

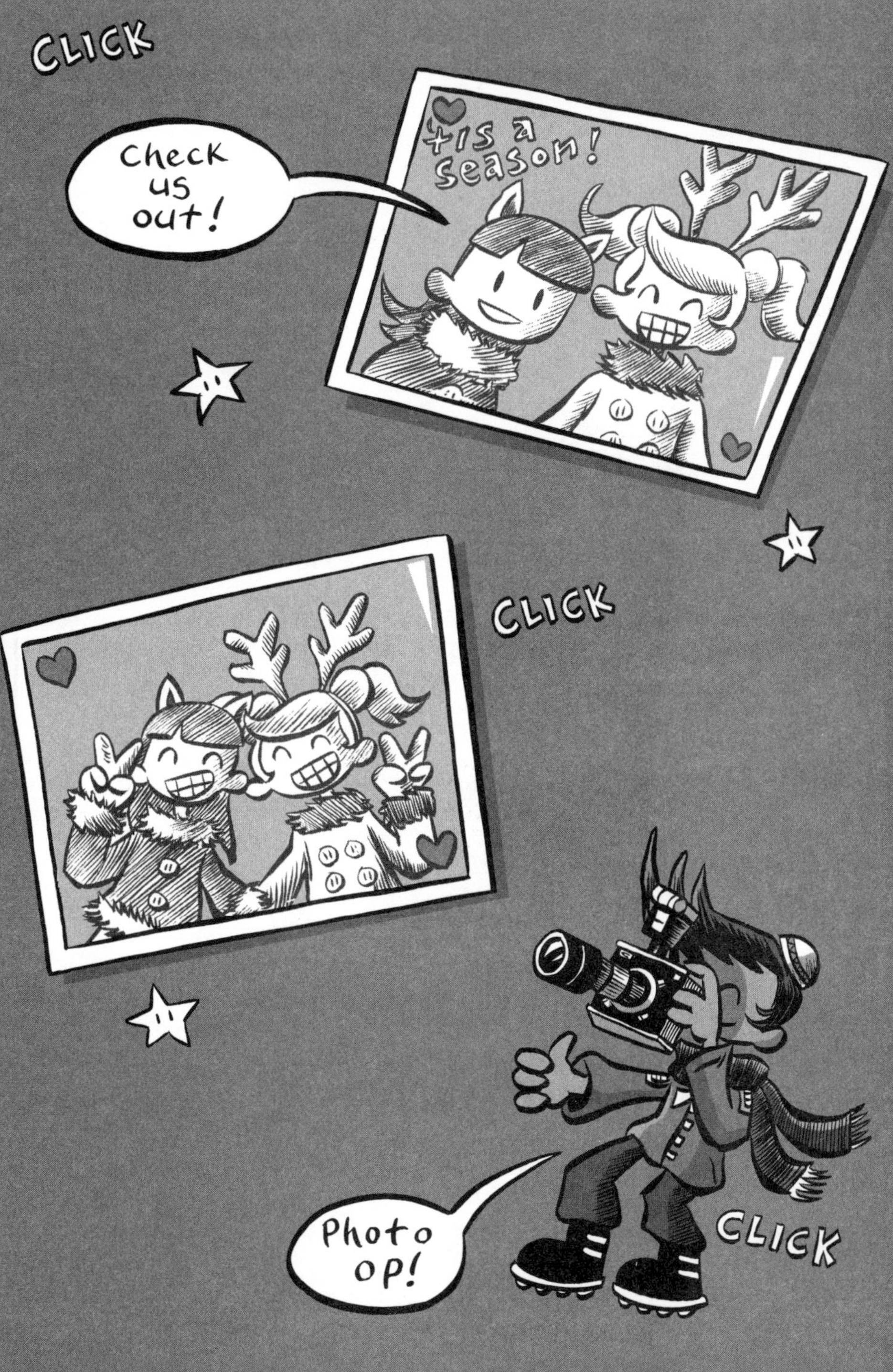
CLICK
Check us out!
'tis a season!
CLICK
Photo op!
CLICK

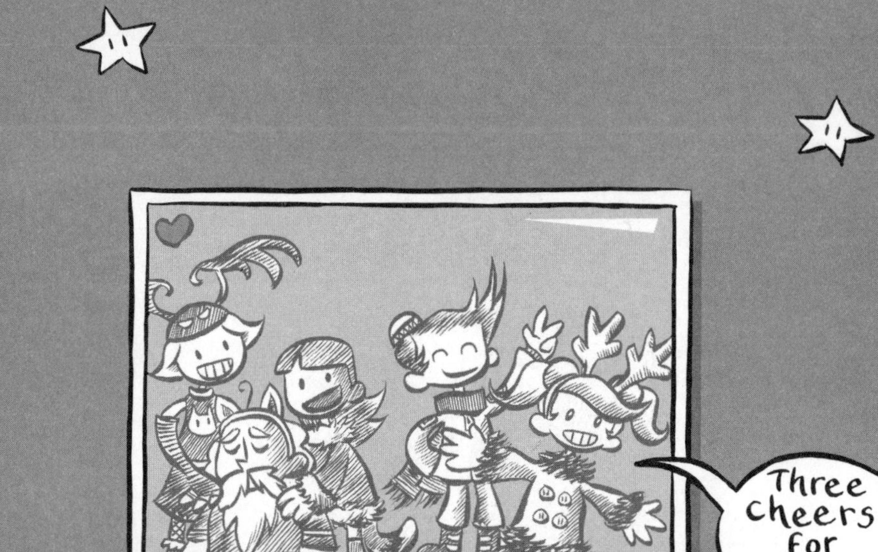
Three cheers for cheese!
SNAP!

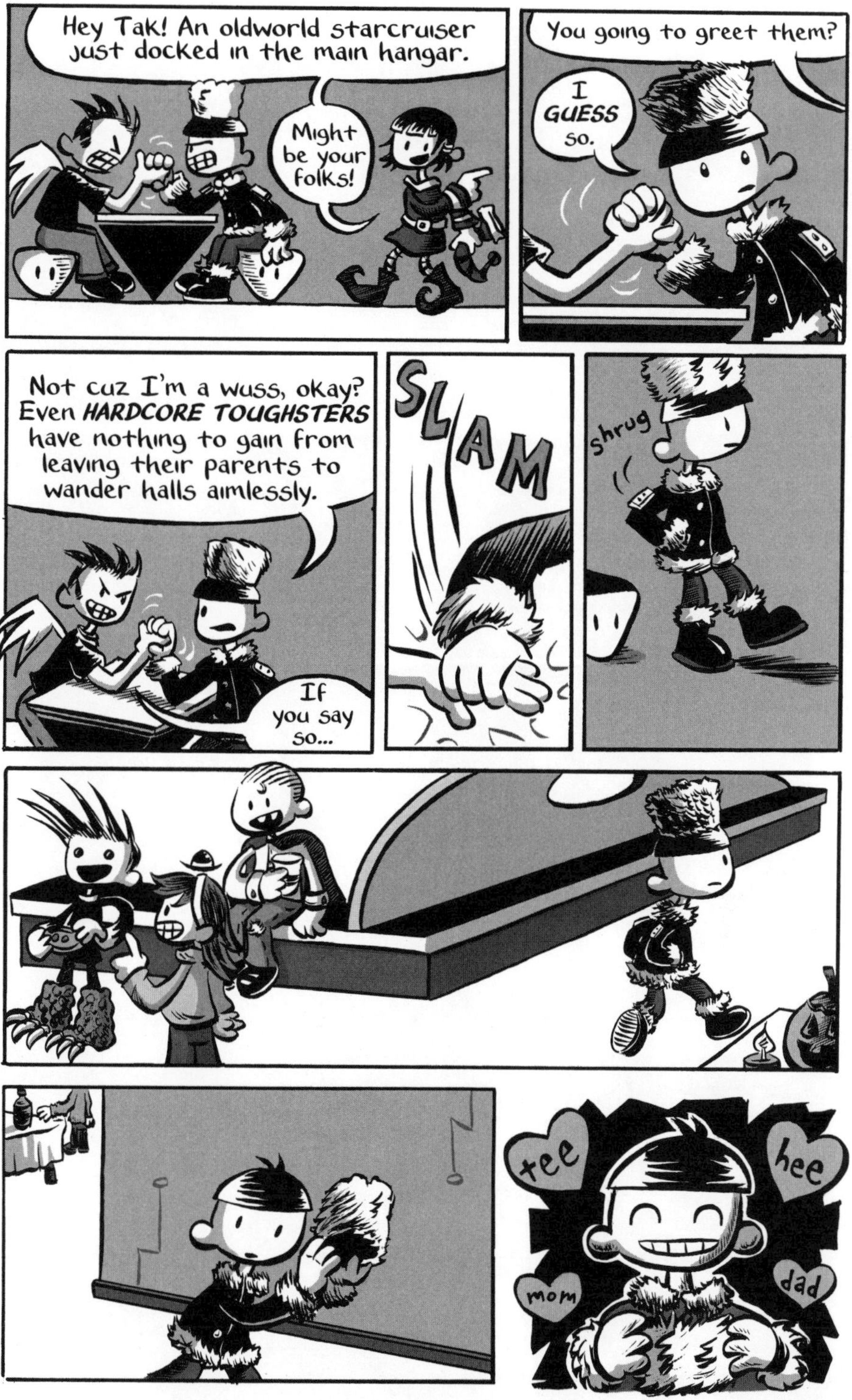
Hey Tak! An oldworld starcruiser just docked in the main hangar.
Might be your folks!
You going to greet them?
I GUESS so.
Not cuz I'm a wuss, okay? Even HARDCORE TOUGHSTERS have nothing to gain from leaving their parents to wander halls aimlessly.
If you say so...
SLAM
shrug
tee
hee
mom
dad

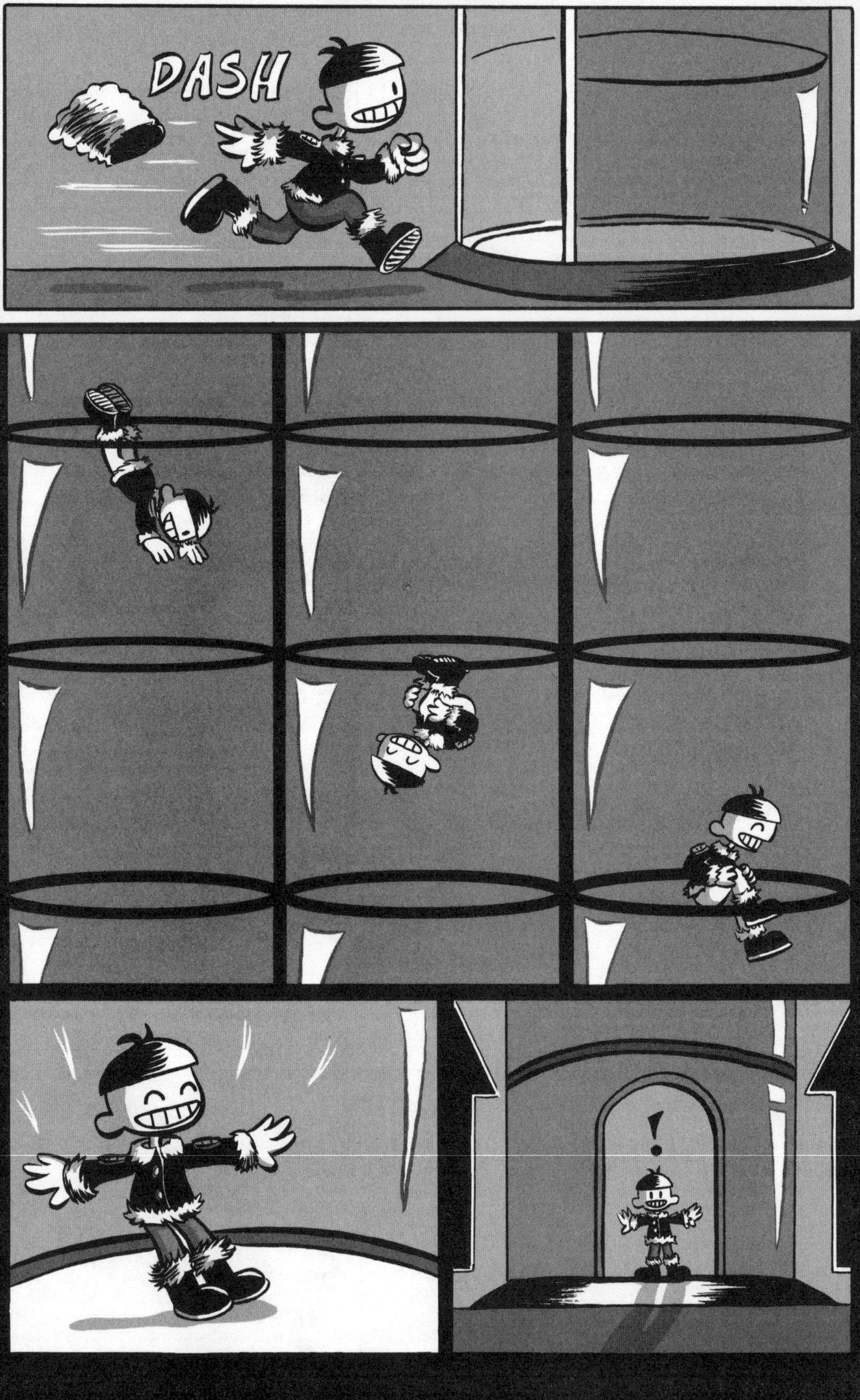
DASH
!

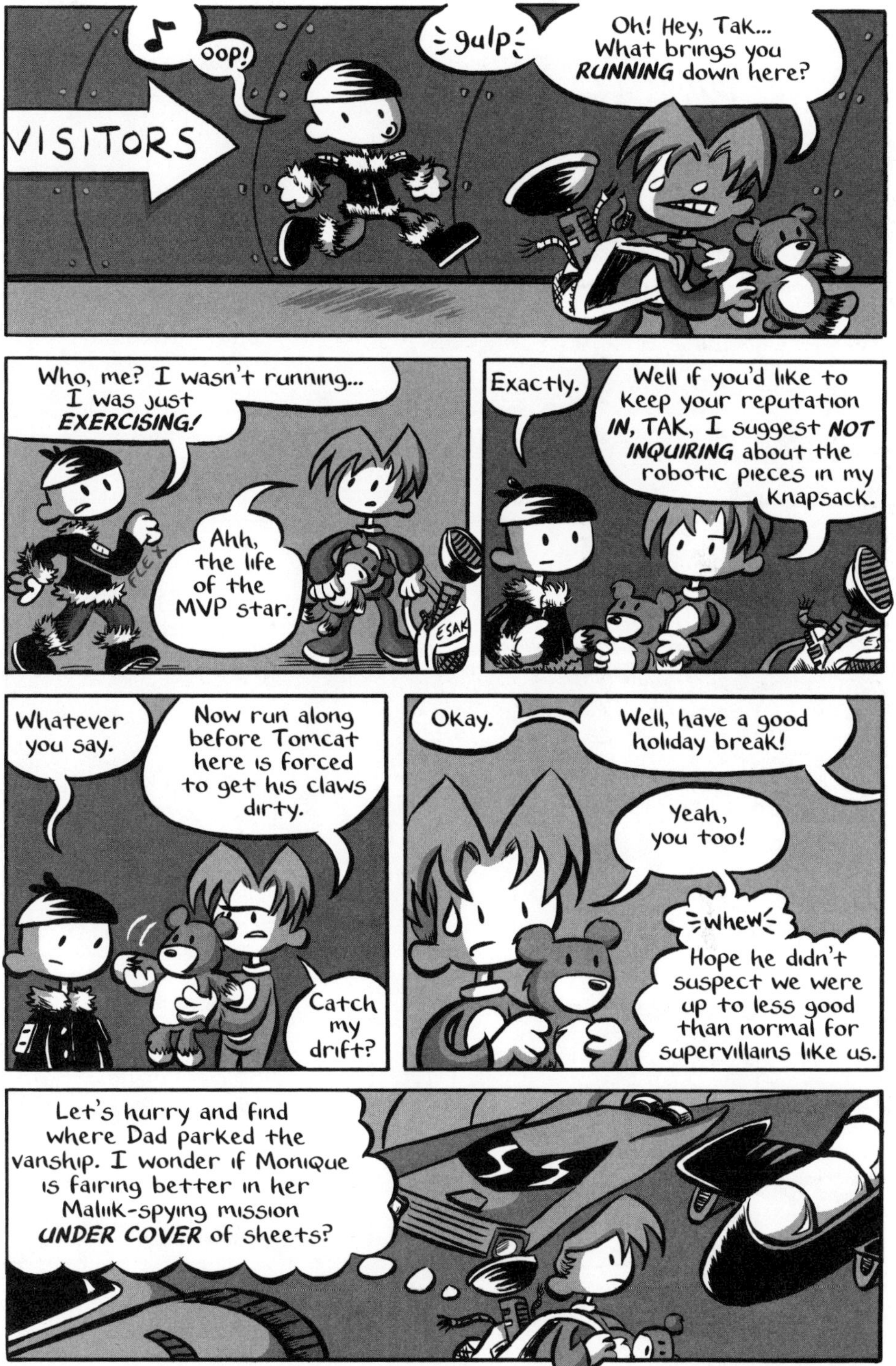
VISITORS
♪ oop!
gulp
Oh! Hey, Tak... What brings you RUNNING down here?
Who, me? I wasn't running... I was just EXERCISING!
FLEX
Ahh, the life of the MVP star.
ESAK
Exactly.
Well if you'd like to keep your reputation IN, TAK, I suggest NOT INQUIRING about the robotic pieces in my knapsack.
Whatever you say.
Now run along before Tomcat here is forced to get his claws dirty.
Catch my drift?
Okay.
Well, have a good holiday break!
Yeah, you too!
whew
Hope he didn't suspect we were up to less good than normal for supervillains like us.
Let's hurry and find where Dad parked the vanship. I wonder if Monique is fairing better in her Maliik-spying mission UNDER COVER of sheets?

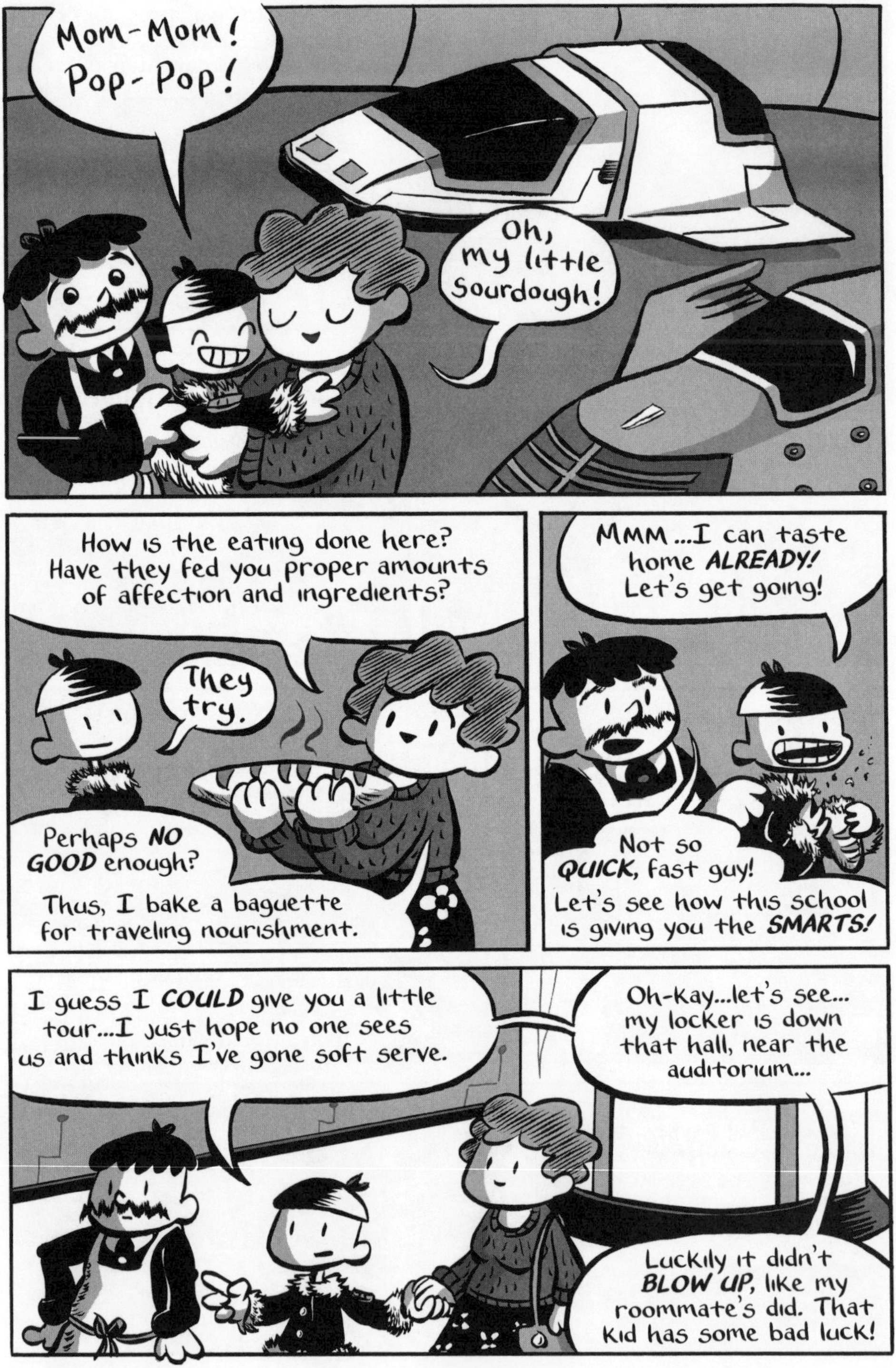

Mom-Mom! Pop-Pop!
Oh, my little Sourdough!
How is the eating done here? Have they fed you proper amounts of affection and ingredients?
They try.
Perhaps NO GOOD enough?
Thus, I bake a baguette for traveling nourishment.
MMM...I can taste home ALREADY! Let's get going!
Not so QUICK, fast guy!
Let's see how this school is giving you the SMARTS!
I guess I COULD give you a little tour...I just hope no one sees us and thinks I've gone soft serve.
Oh-kay...let's see... my locker is down that hall, near the auditorium...
Luckily it didn't BLOW UP, like my roommate's did. That kid has some bad luck!

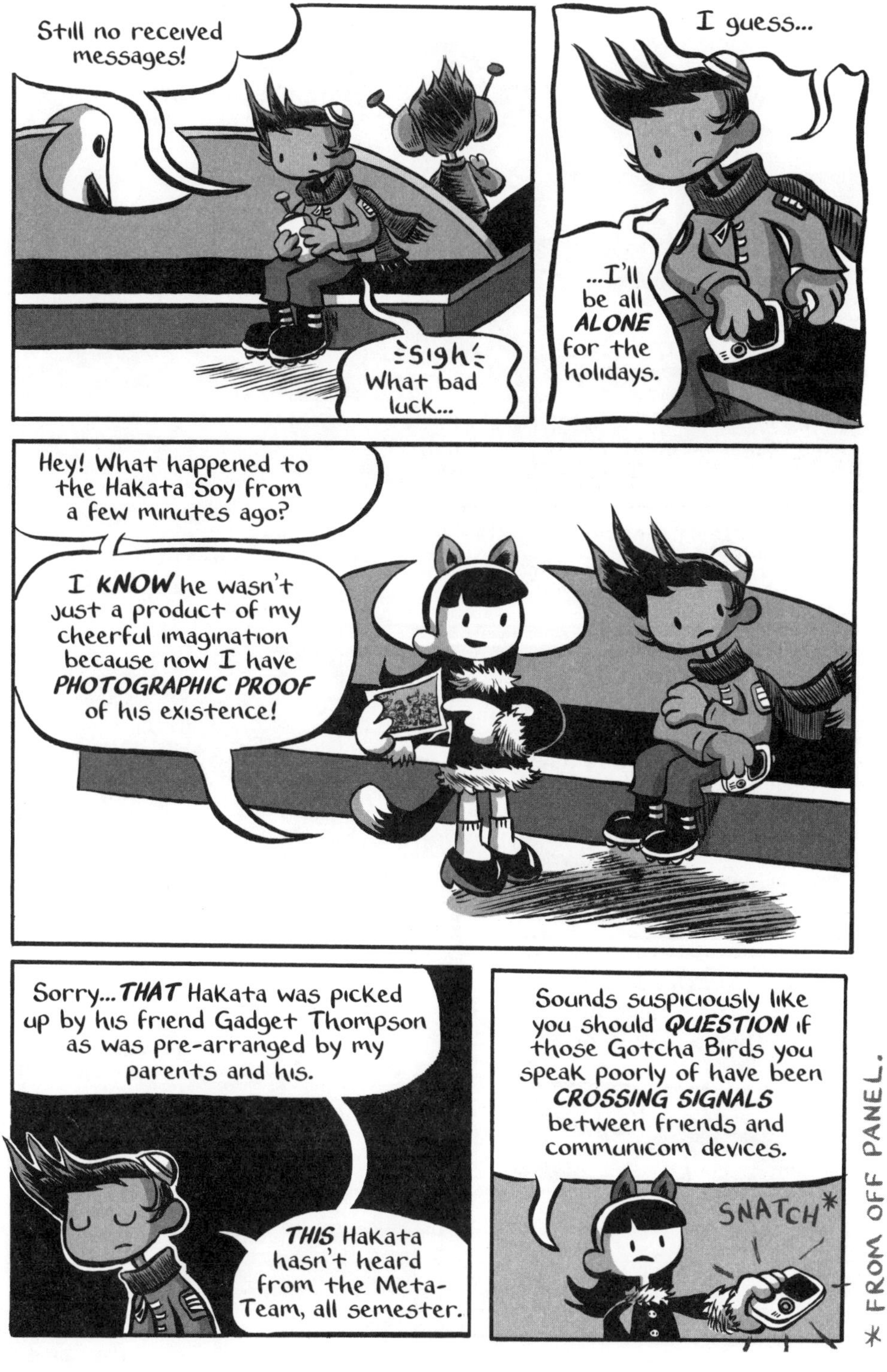
Still no received messages!
I guess...
SIGH What bad luck...
...I'll be all ALONE for the holidays.
Hey! What happened to the Hakata Soy from a few minutes ago?
I KNOW he wasn't just a product of my cheerful imagination because now I have PHOTOGRAPHIC PROOF of his existence!
Sorry... THAT Hakata was picked up by his friend Gadget Thompson as was pre-arranged by my parents and his.
THIS Hakata hasn't heard from the Meta-Team, all semester.
Sounds suspiciously like you should QUESTION if those Gotcha Birds you speak poorly of have been CROSSING SIGNALS between friends and communicom devices.
SNATCH*
* FROM OFF PANEL.

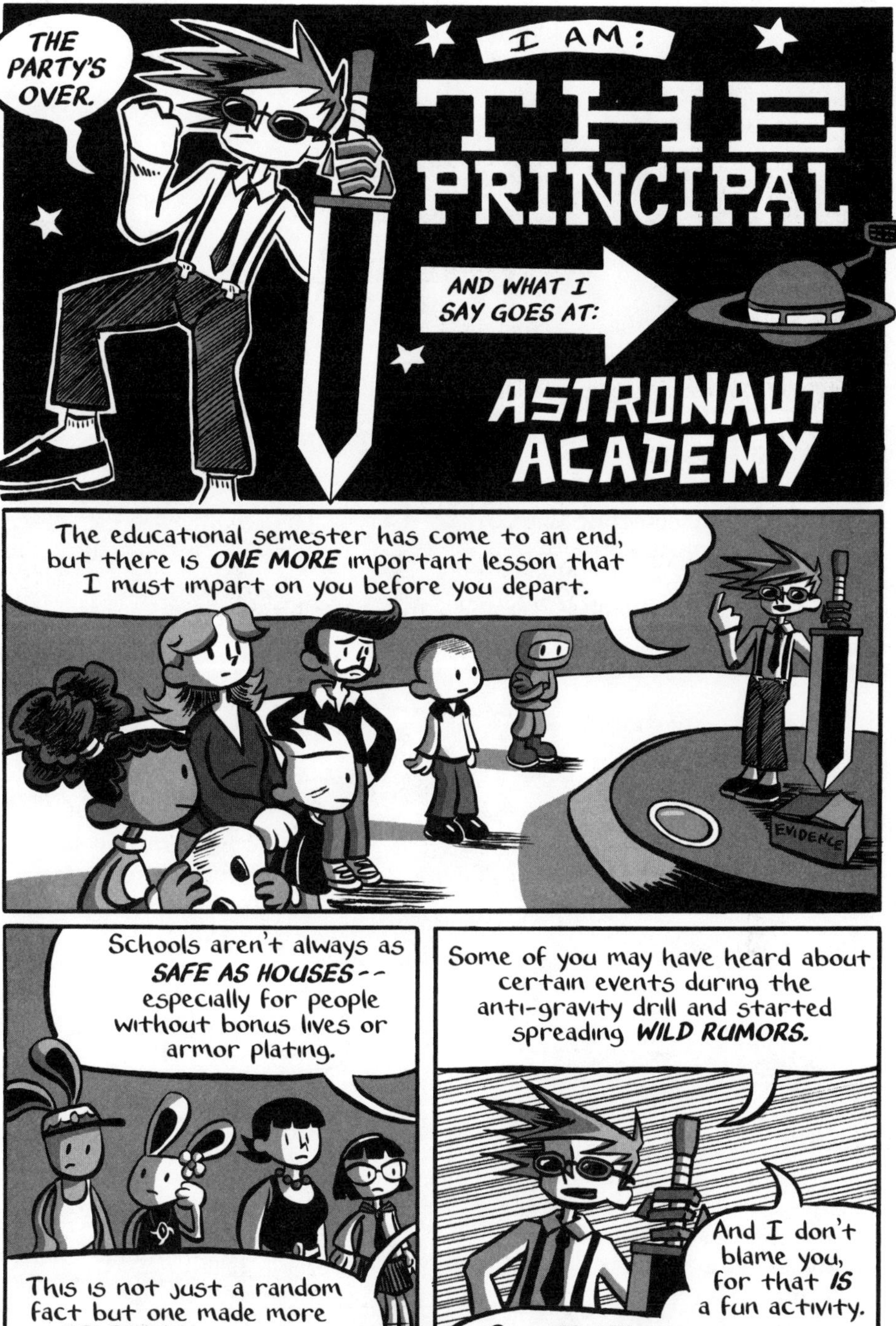
THE PARTY'S OVER.
I AM:
THE PRINCIPAL
AND WHAT I SAY GOES AT:
ASTRONAUT ACADEMY
The educational semester has come to an end, but there is ONE MORE important lesson that I must impart on you before you depart.
EVIDENCE
Schools aren't always as SAFE AS HOUSES-- especially for people without bonus lives or armor plating.
This is not just a random fact but one made more RELEVANT by recent revelations.
Some of you may have heard about certain events during the anti-gravity drill and started spreading WILD RUMORS.
And I don't blame you, for that IS a fun activity.
But TRUTH is more important than having a good time.

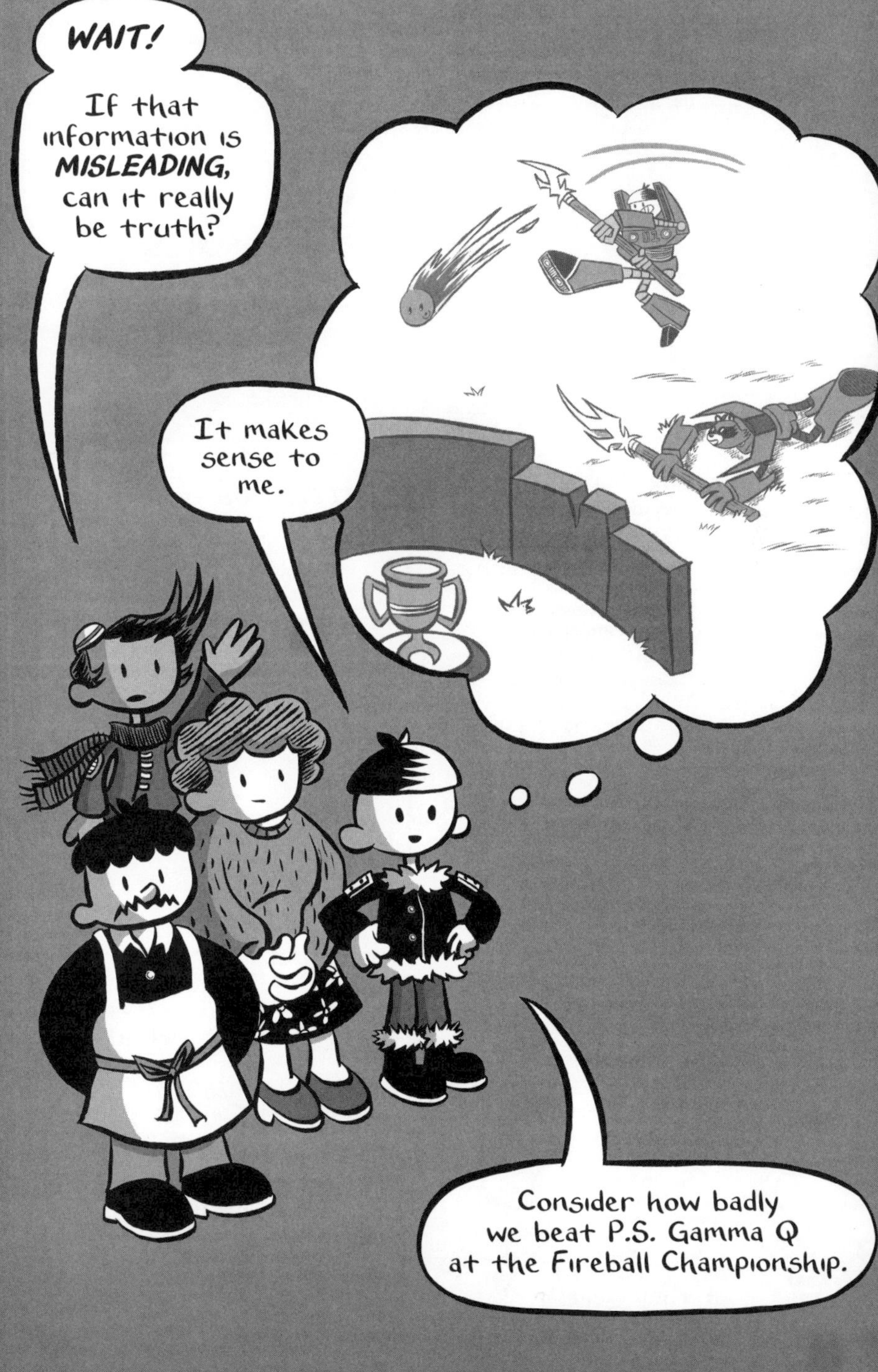
WAIT!
If that information is MISLEADING, can it really be truth?
It makes sense to me.
Consider how badly we beat P.S. Gamma Q at the Fireball Championship.

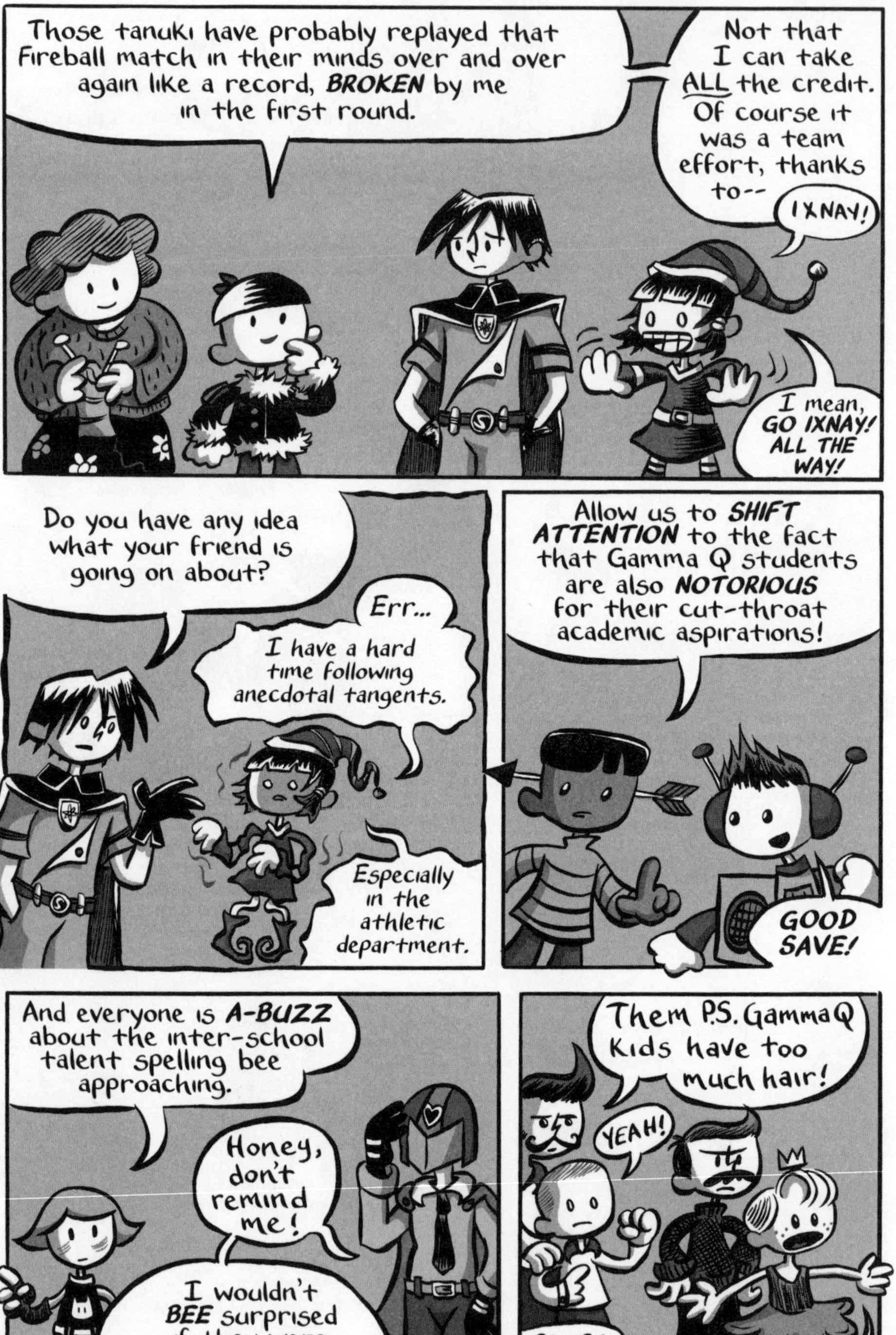

Those tanuki have probably replayed that Fireball match in their minds over and over again like a record, BROKEN by me in the first round.
Not that I can take ALL the credit. Of course it was a team effort, thanks to--
IXNAY!
I mean, GO IXNAY! ALL THE WAY!
Do you have any idea what your friend is going on about?
Err...
I have a hard time following anecdotal tangents.
Especially in the athletic department.
Allow us to SHIFT ATTENTION to the fact that Gamma Q students are also NOTORIOUS for their cut-throat academic aspirations!
GOOD SAVE!
And everyone is A-BUZZ about the inter-school talent spelling bee approaching.
Honey, don't remind me!
I wouldn't BEE surprised if they were trying to sting out the competition!
Them P.S. Gamma Q Kids have too much hair!
YEAH!
PLUS:
They don't like ME! Can you believe the nerve?

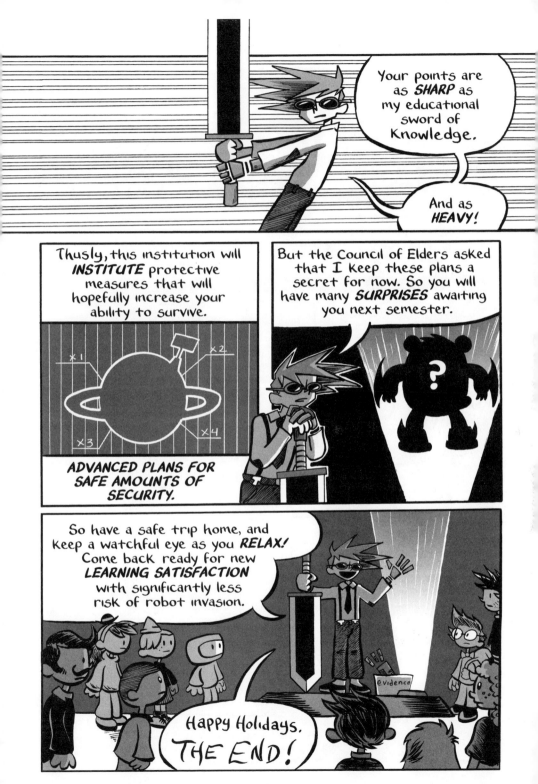

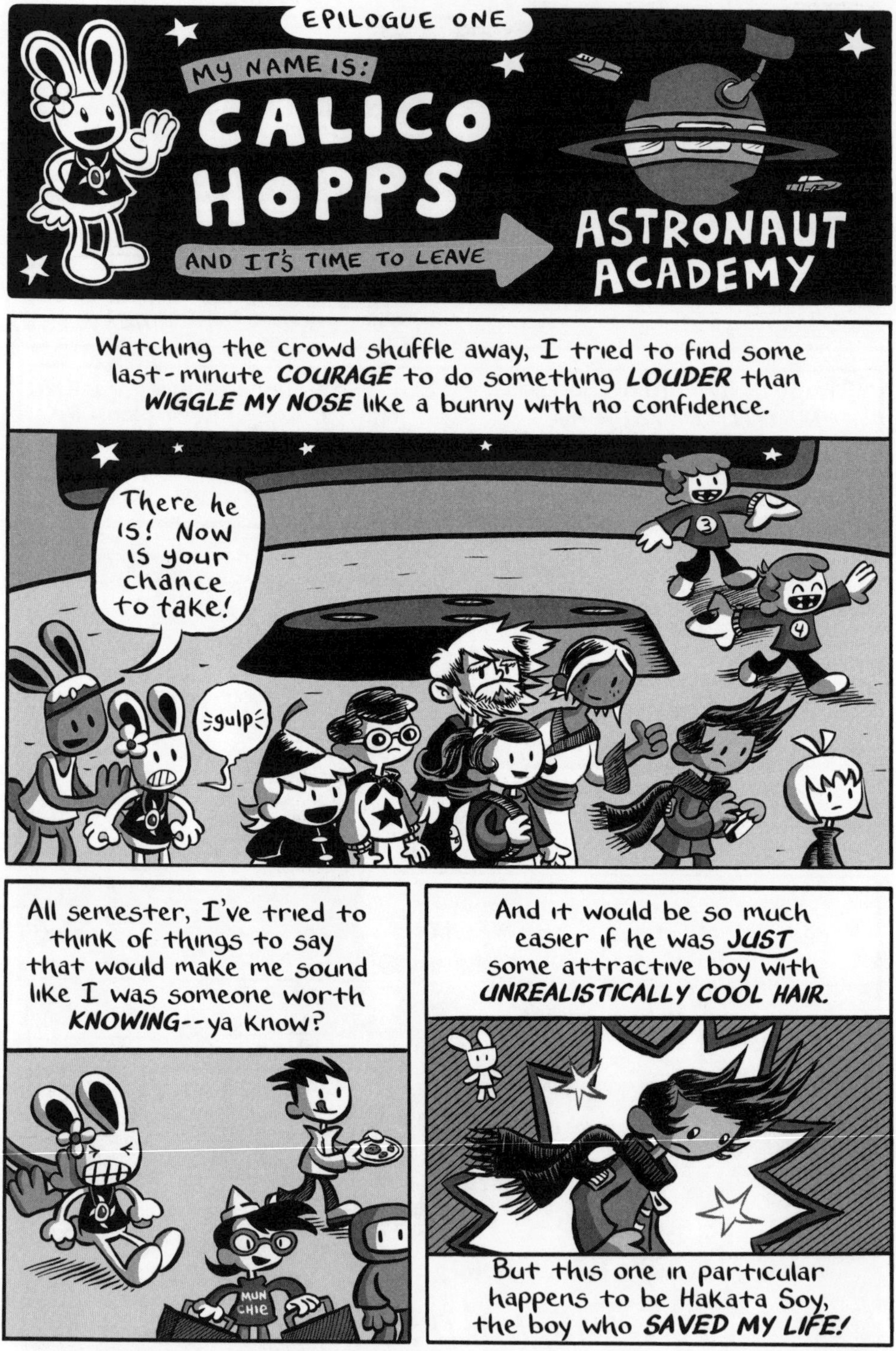
EPILOGUE ONE
MY NAME IS:
CALICO HOPPS
AND IT'S TIME TO LEAVE
ASTRONAUT ACADEMY
Watching the crowd shuffle away, I tried to find some last-minute COURAGE to do something LOUDER than WIGGLE MY NOSE like a bunny with no confidence.
There he is! Now is your chance to take!
gulp
All semester, I've tried to think of things to say that would make me sound like I was someone worth KNOWING--ya know?
MUN CHIE
And it would be so much easier if he was JUST some attractive boy with UNREALISTICALLY COOL HAIR.
But this one in particular happens to be Hakata Soy, the boy who SAVED MY LIFE!

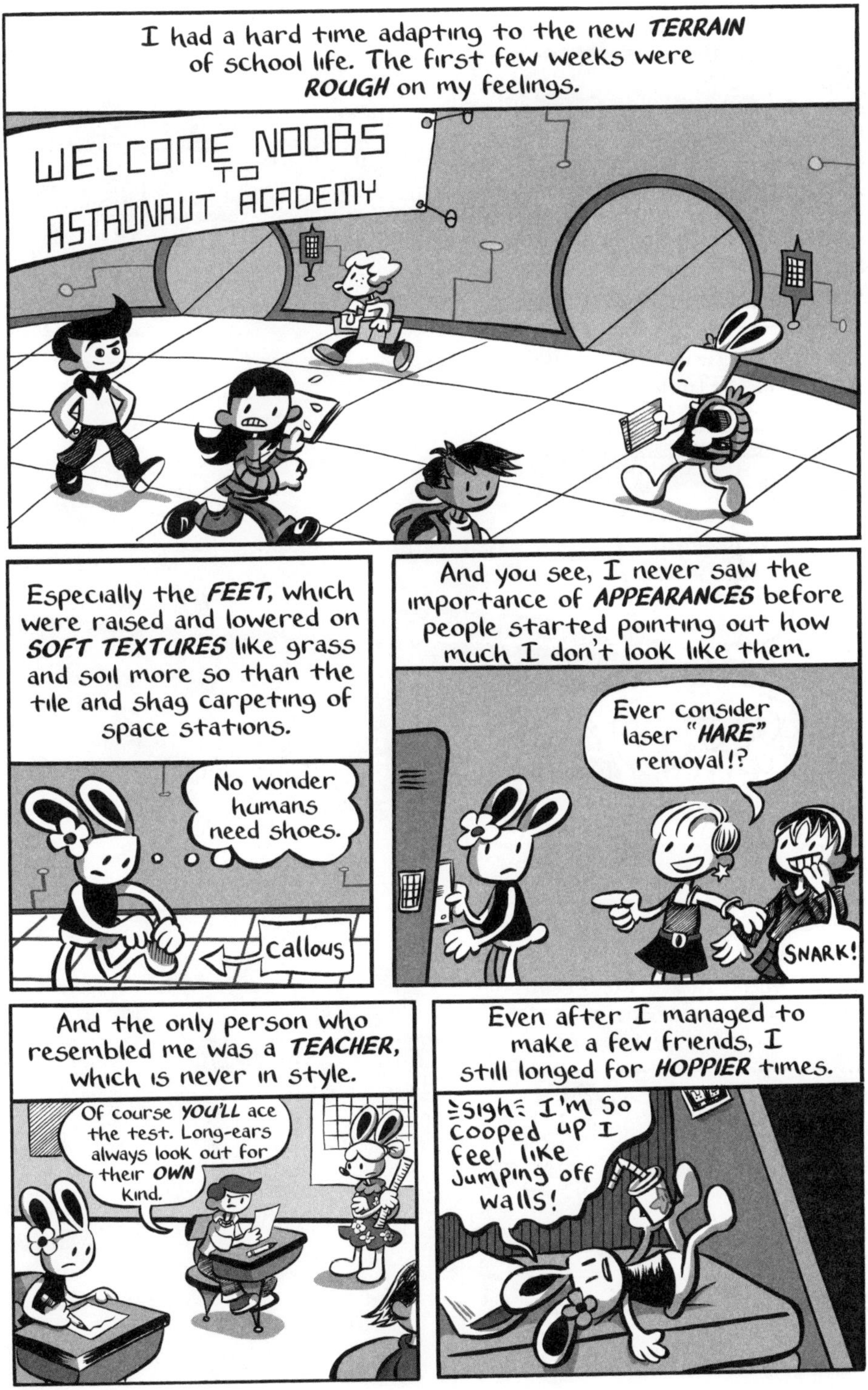
I had a hard time adapting to the new TERRAIN of school life. The first few weeks were ROUGH on my feelings.
WELCOME NOOBS TO ASTRONAUT ACADEMY
Especially the FEET, which were raised and lowered on SOFT TEXTURES like grass and soil more so than the tile and shag carpeting of space stations.
No wonder humans need shoes.
Callous
And you see, I never saw the importance of APPEARANCES before people started pointing out how much I don't look like them.
Ever consider laser "HARE" removal!?
SNARK!
And the only person who resembled me was a TEACHER, which is never in style.
Of course YOU'LL ace the test. Long-ears always look out for their OWN kind.
Even after I managed to make a few friends, I still longed for HOPPIER times.
≡SIGH≡ I'm so cooped up I feel like jumping off walls!

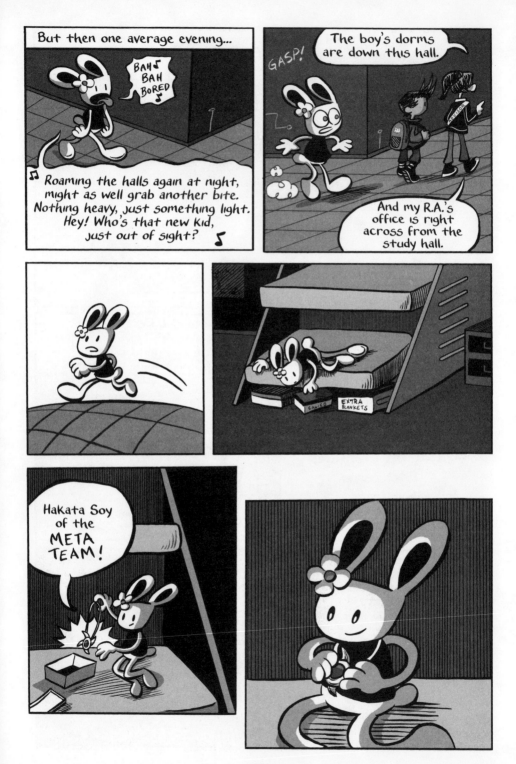

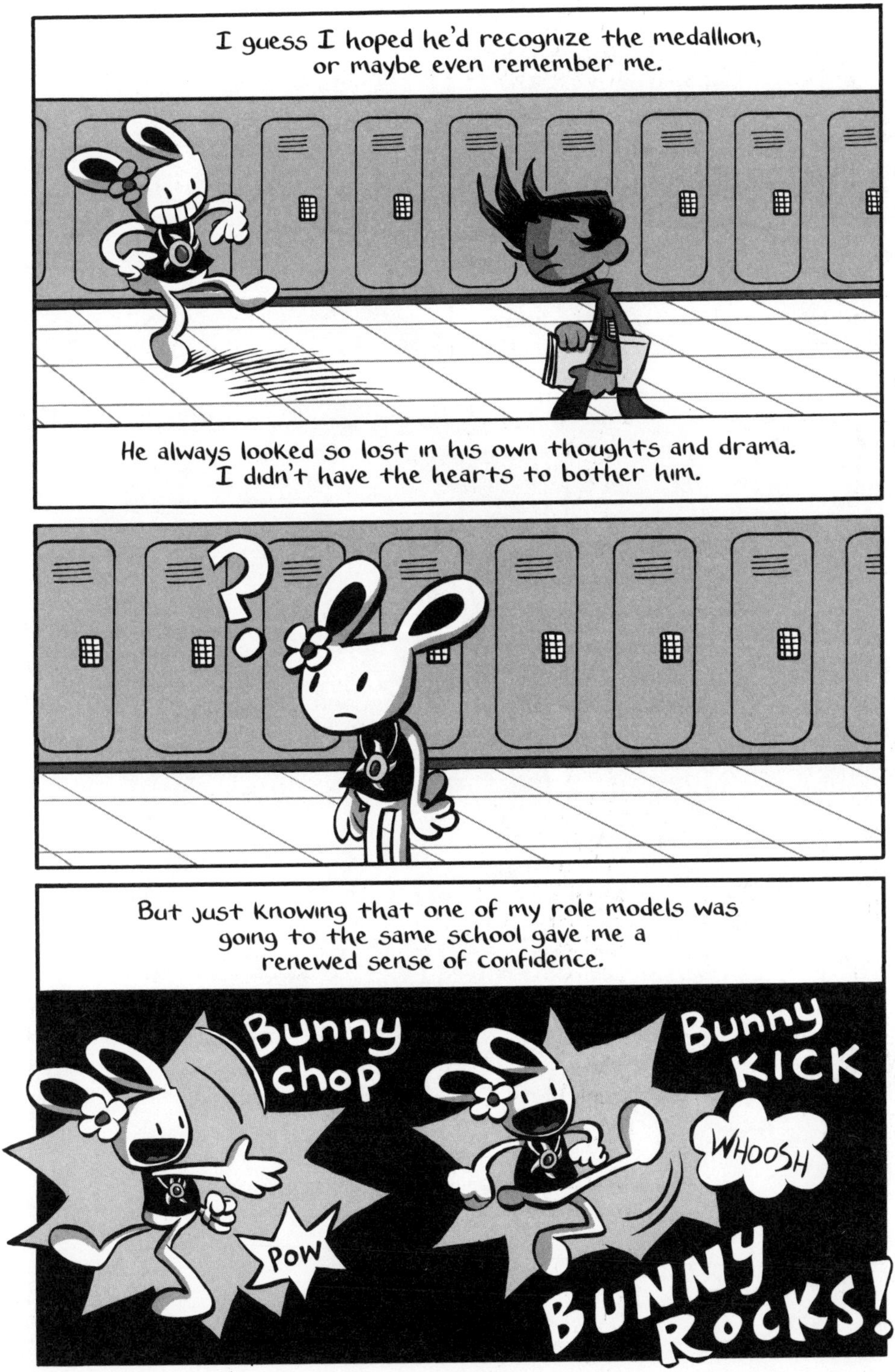
I guess I hoped he'd recognize the medallion, or maybe even remember me.
He always looked so lost in his own thoughts and drama. I didn't have the hearts to bother him.
?
But just knowing that one of my role models was going to the same school gave me a renewed sense of confidence.
Bunny chop
POW
Bunny KICK
WHOOSH
BUNNY ROCKS!

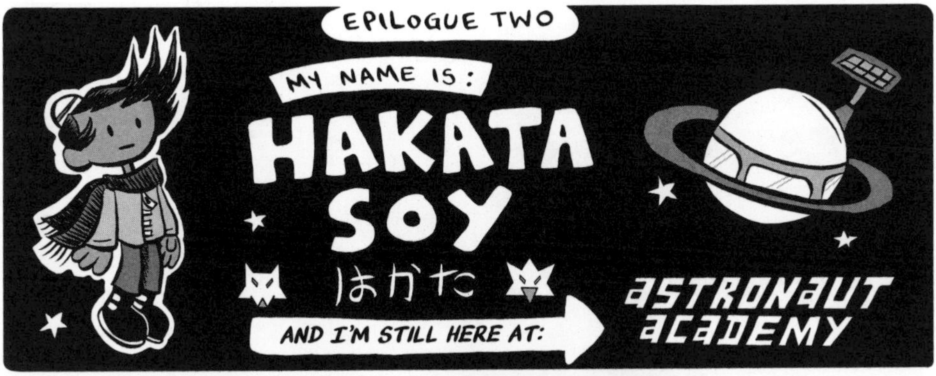
EPILOGUE TWO
MY NAME IS:
HAKATA SOY
はかた
AND I'M STILL HERE AT:
ASTRONAUT ACADEMY

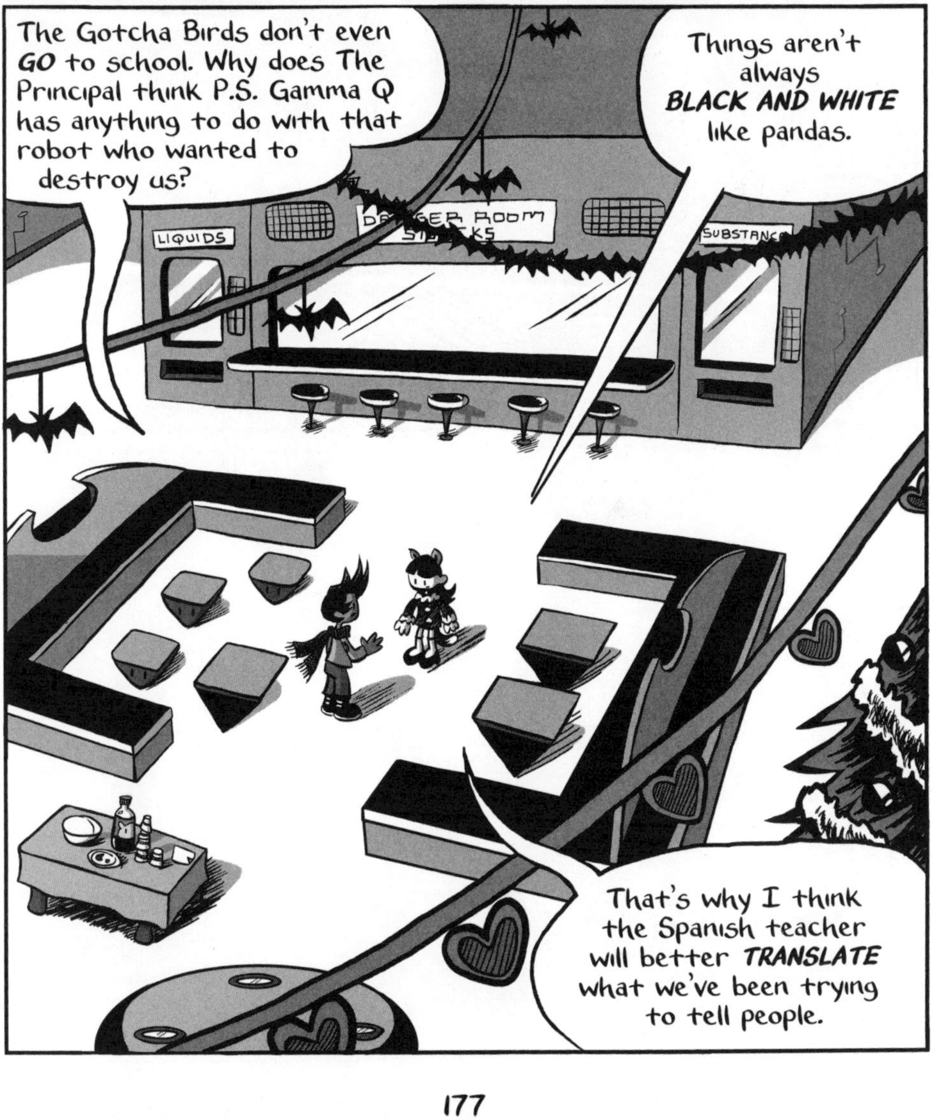
The Gotcha Birds don't even GO to school. Why does The Principal think P.S. Gamma Q has anything to do with that robot who wanted to destroy us?
Things aren't always BLACK AND WHITE like pandas.
LIQUIDS
That's why I think the Spanish teacher will better TRANSLATE what we've been trying to tell people.

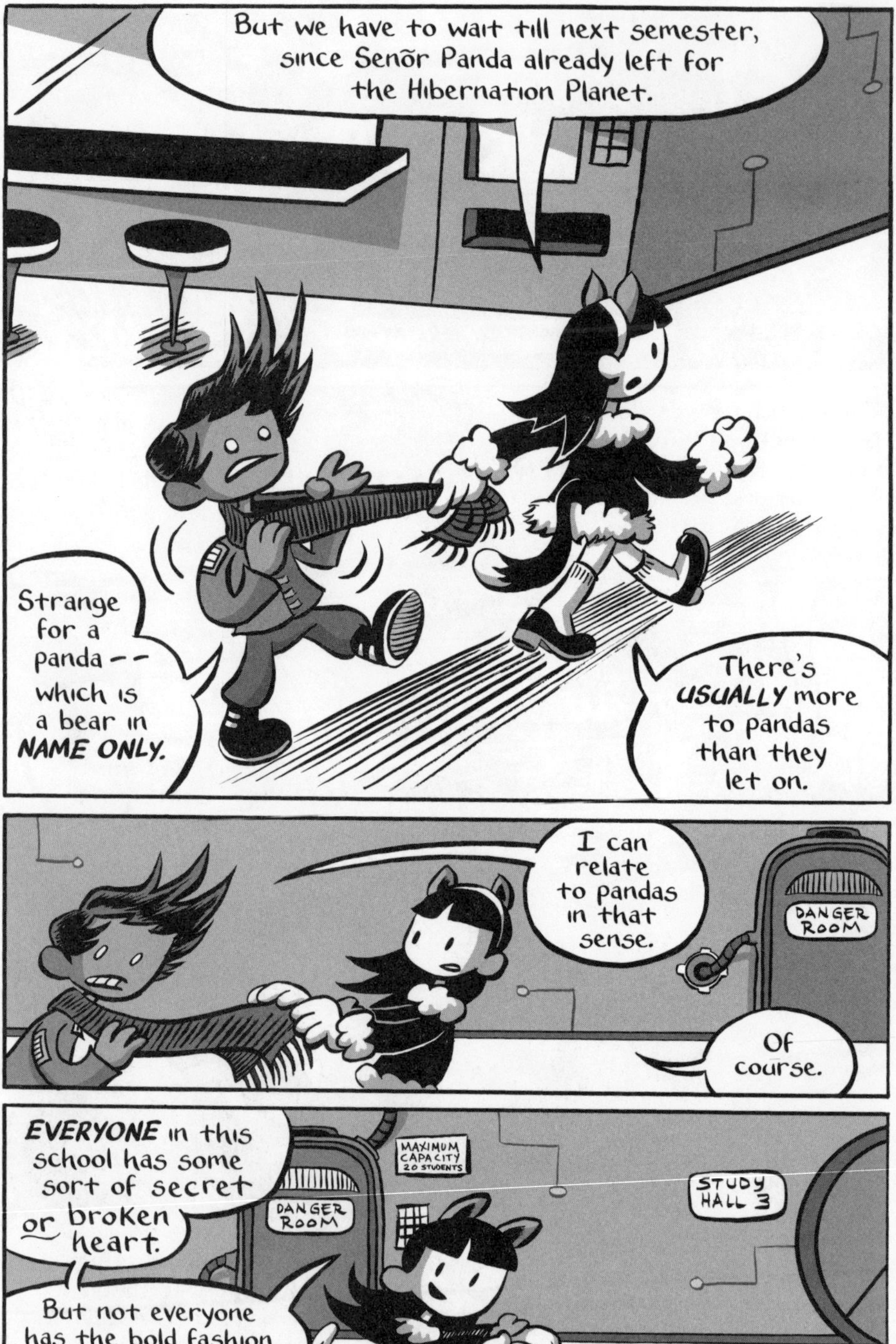

But we have to wait till next semester, since Senõr Panda already left for the Hibernation Planet.
Strange for a panda -- which is a bear in **NAME ONLY.**
There's ***USUALLY*** more to pandas than they let on.
I can relate to pandas in that sense.
DANGER ROOM
Of course.
EVERYONE in this school has some sort of secret or broken heart.
MAXIMUM CAPACITY 20 STUDENTS
DANGER ROOM
STUDY HALL 3
But not everyone has the bold fashion sense to wear their angst on their sleeves.

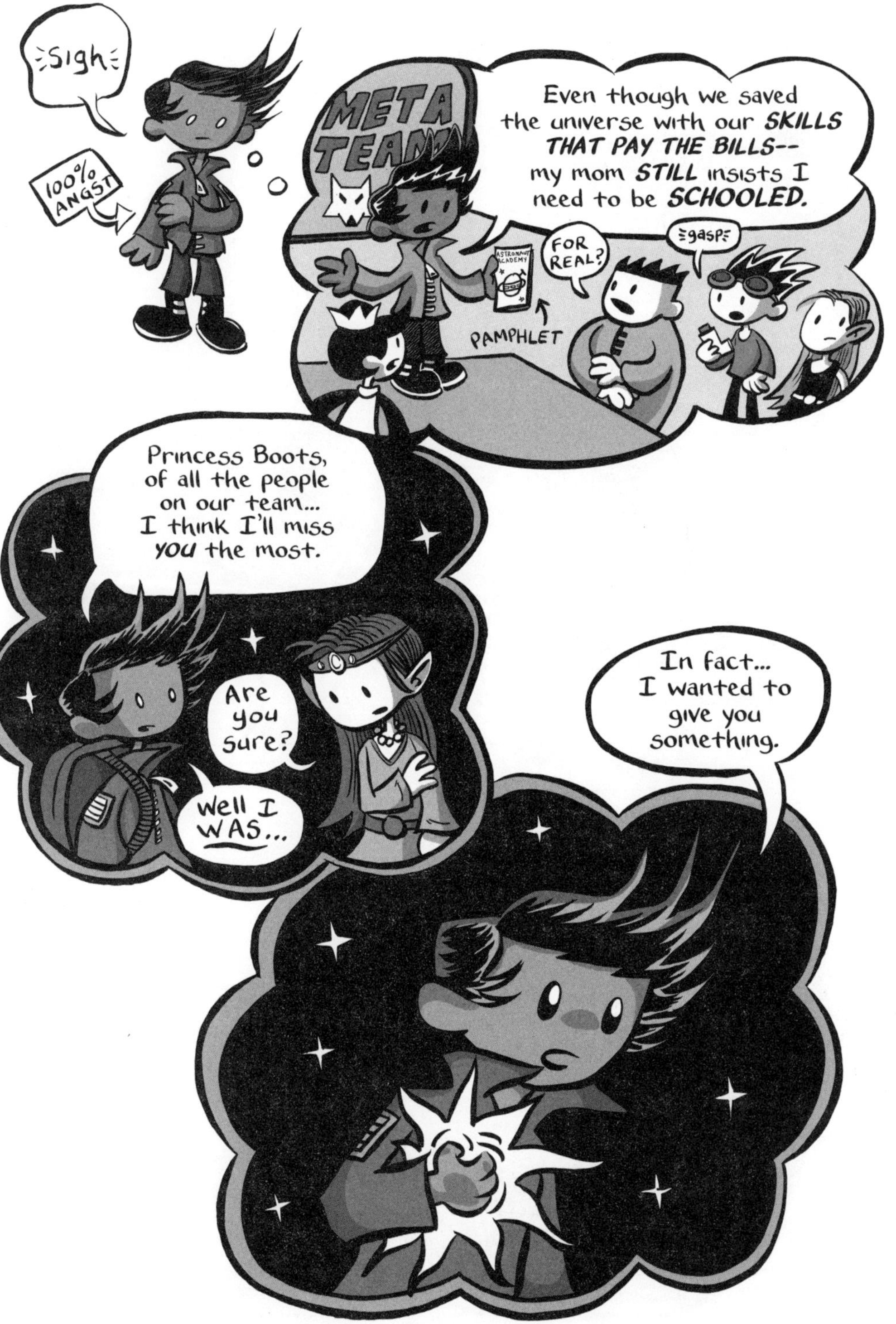
Sigh
100% ANGST
META TEAM
Even though we saved the universe with our SKILLS THAT PAY THE BILLS-- my mom STILL insists I need to be SCHOOLED.
ASTRONAUT ACADEMY
FOR REAL?
gasp
PAMPHLET
Princess Boots, of all the people on our team... I think I'll miss YOU the most.
Are you sure?
Well I WAS...
In fact... I wanted to give you something.

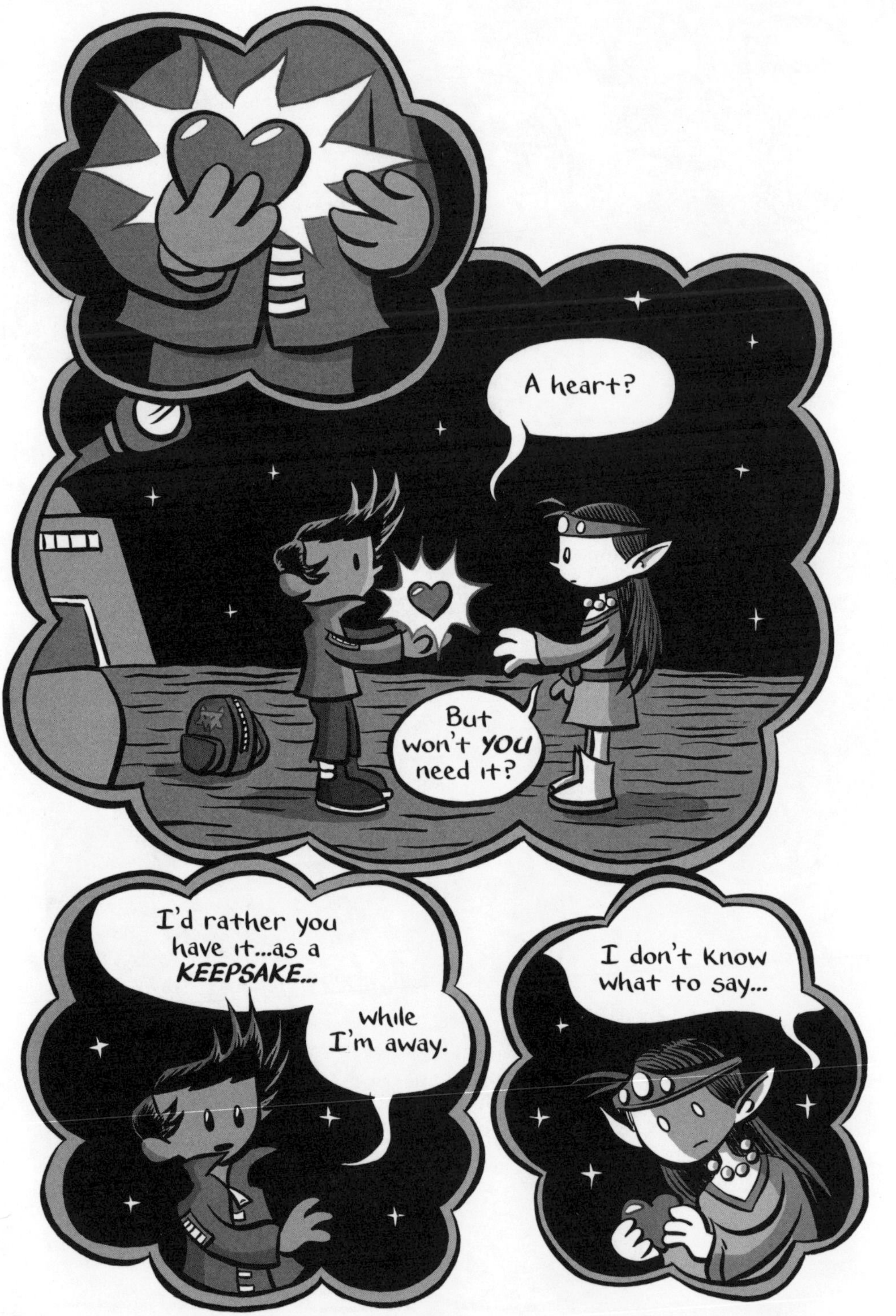

A heart?
But won't YOU need it?
I'd rather you have it...as a KEEPSAKE...
while I'm away.
I don't know what to say...

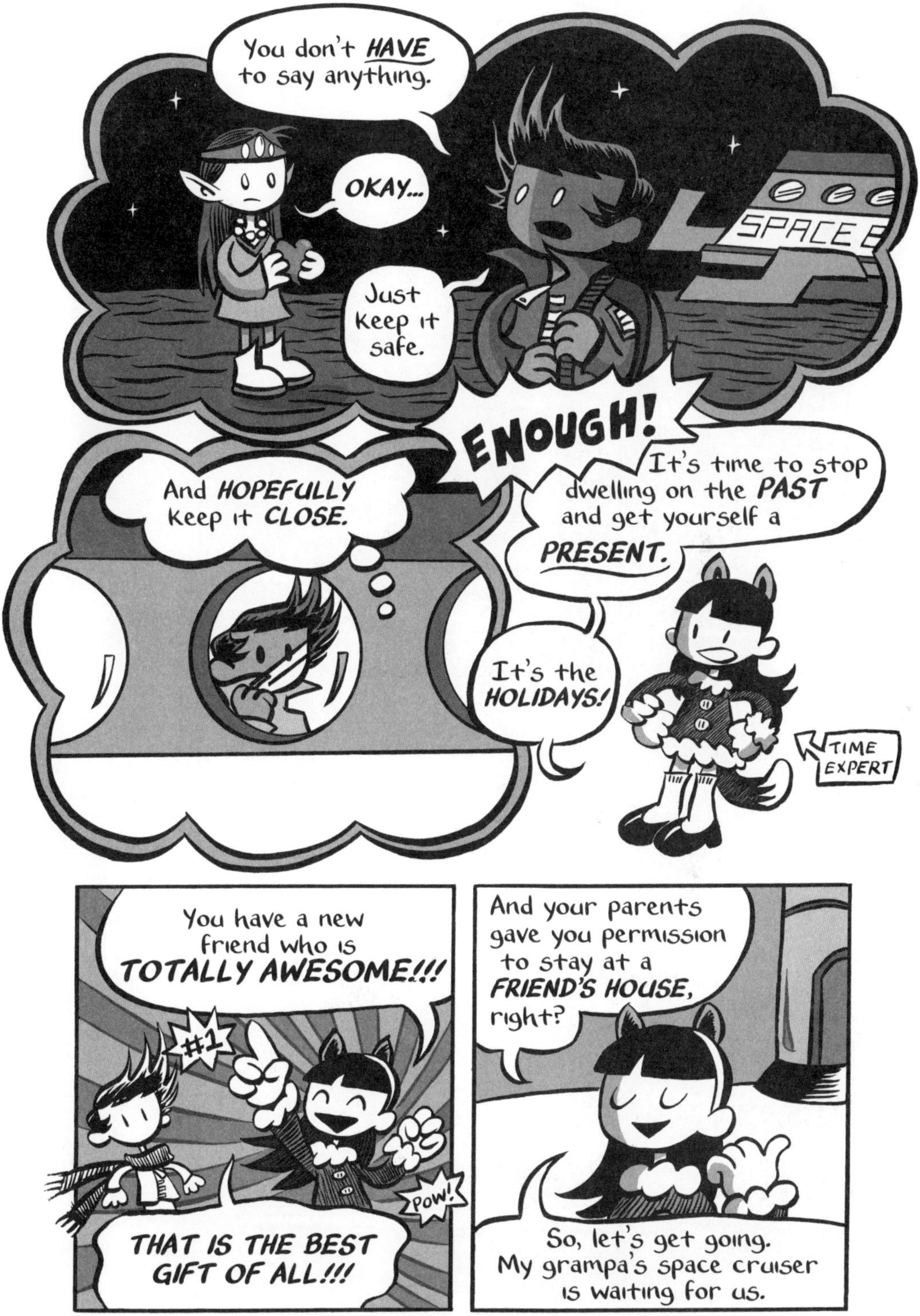
You don't HAVE to say anything.
OKAY...
Just keep it safe.
SPACE B
And HOPEFULLY keep it CLOSE.
ENOUGH!
It's time to stop dwelling on the PAST and get yourself a PRESENT.
It's the HOLIDAYS!
TIME EXPERT
You have a new friend who is TOTALLY AWESOME!!!
#1
POW!
THAT IS THE BEST GIFT OF ALL!!!
And your parents gave you permission to stay at a FRIEND'S HOUSE, right?
So, let's get going. My grampa's space cruiser is waiting for us.

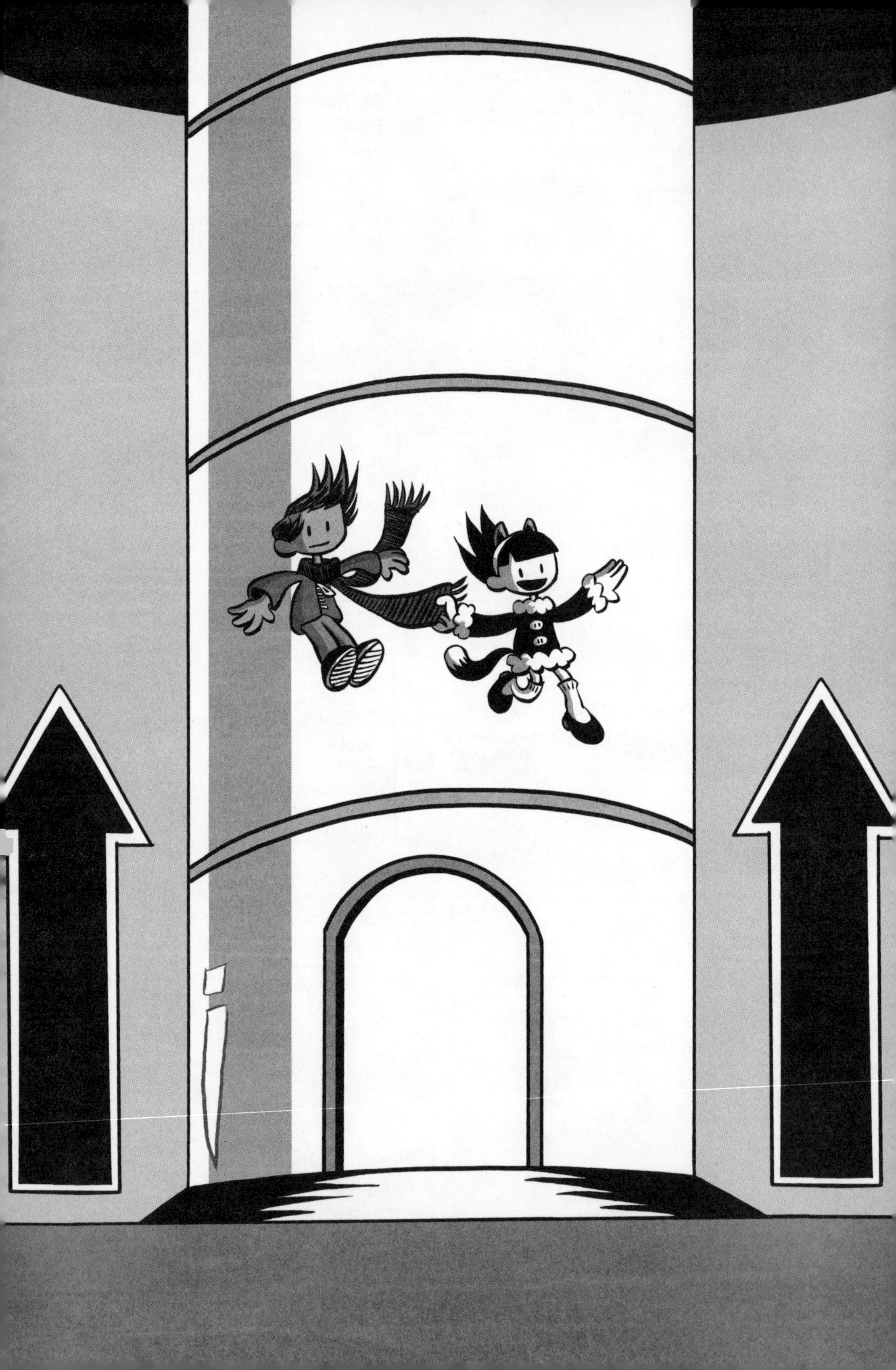

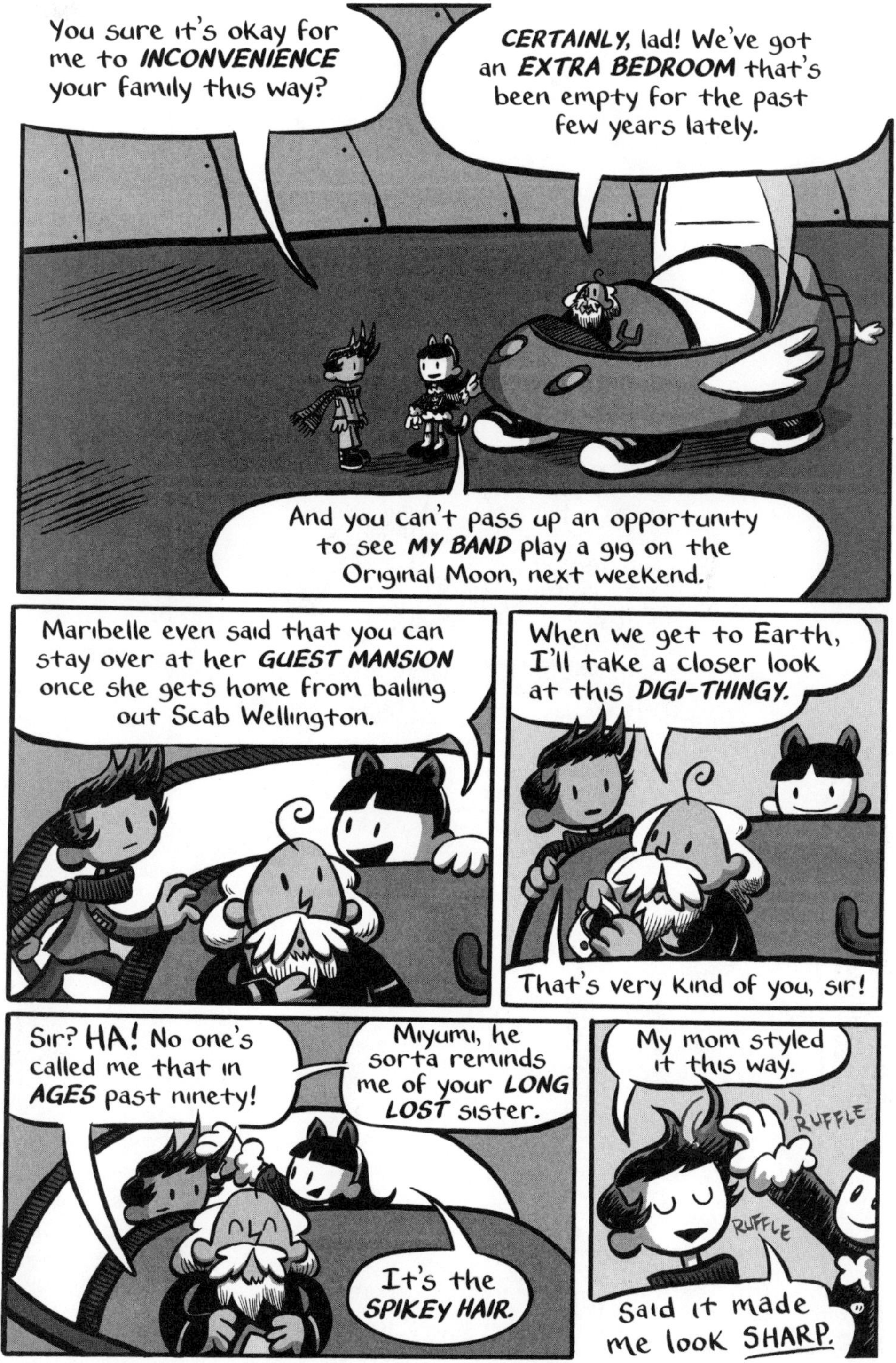
You sure it's okay for me to INCONVENIENCE your family this way?
CERTAINLY, lad! We've got an EXTRA BEDROOM that's been empty for the past few years lately.
And you can't pass up an opportunity to see MY BAND play a gig on the Original Moon, next weekend.
Maribelle even said that you can stay over at her GUEST MANSION once she gets home from bailing out Scab Wellington.
When we get to Earth, I'll take a closer look at this DIGI-THINGY.
That's very kind of you, sir!
Sir? HA! No one's called me that in AGES past ninety!
Miyumi, he sorta reminds me of your LONG LOST sister.
It's the SPIKEY HAIR.
My mom styled it this way.
RUFFLE
RUFFLE
Said it made me look SHARP.

184

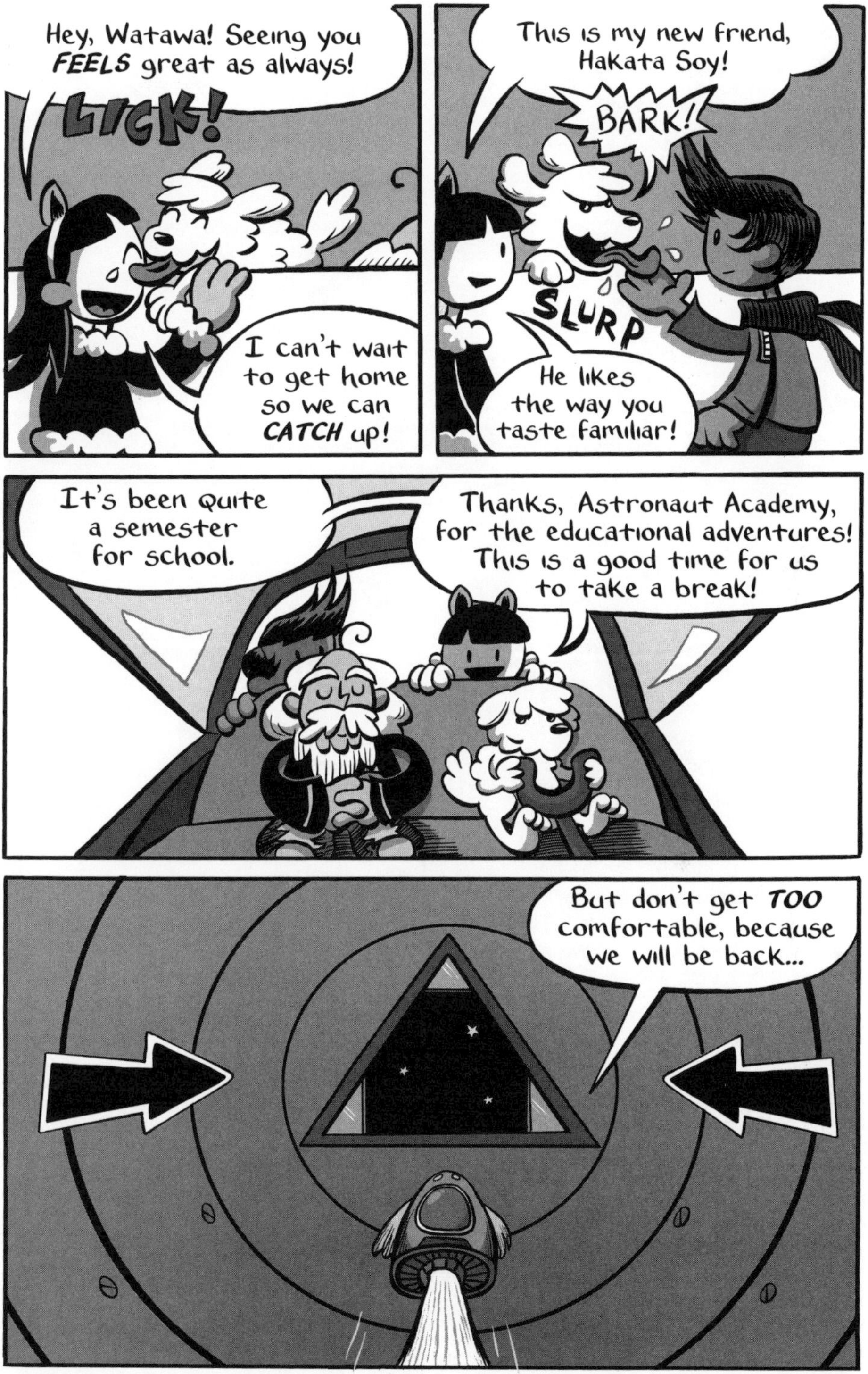

Hey, Watawa! Seeing you FEELS great as always!
LICK!
I can't wait to get home so we can CATCH up!
This is my new friend, Hakata Soy!
BARK!
SLURP
He likes the way you taste familiar!
It's been quite a semester for school.
Thanks, Astronaut Academy, for the educational adventures! This is a good time for us to take a break!
But don't get TOO comfortable, because we will be back...

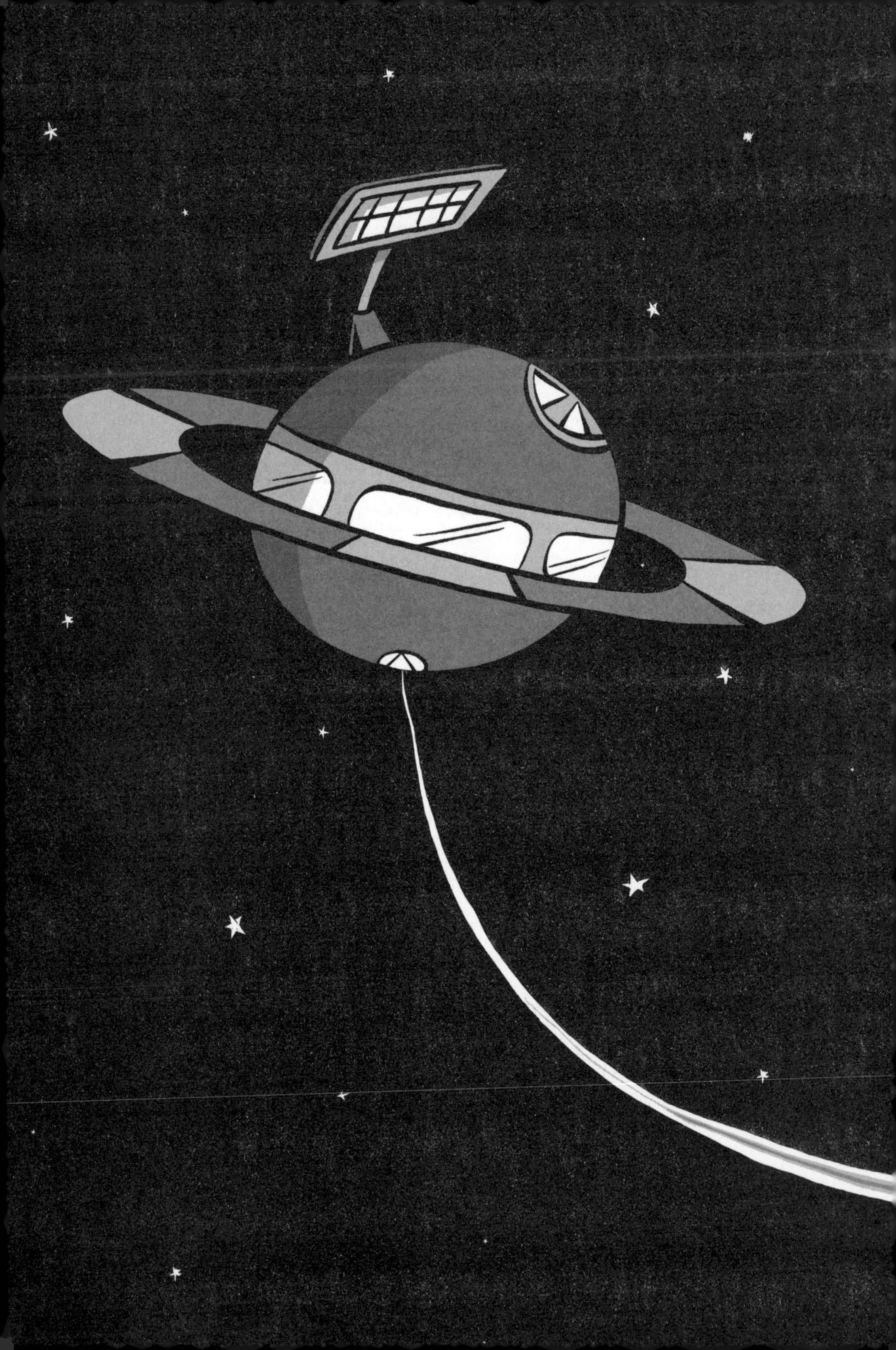

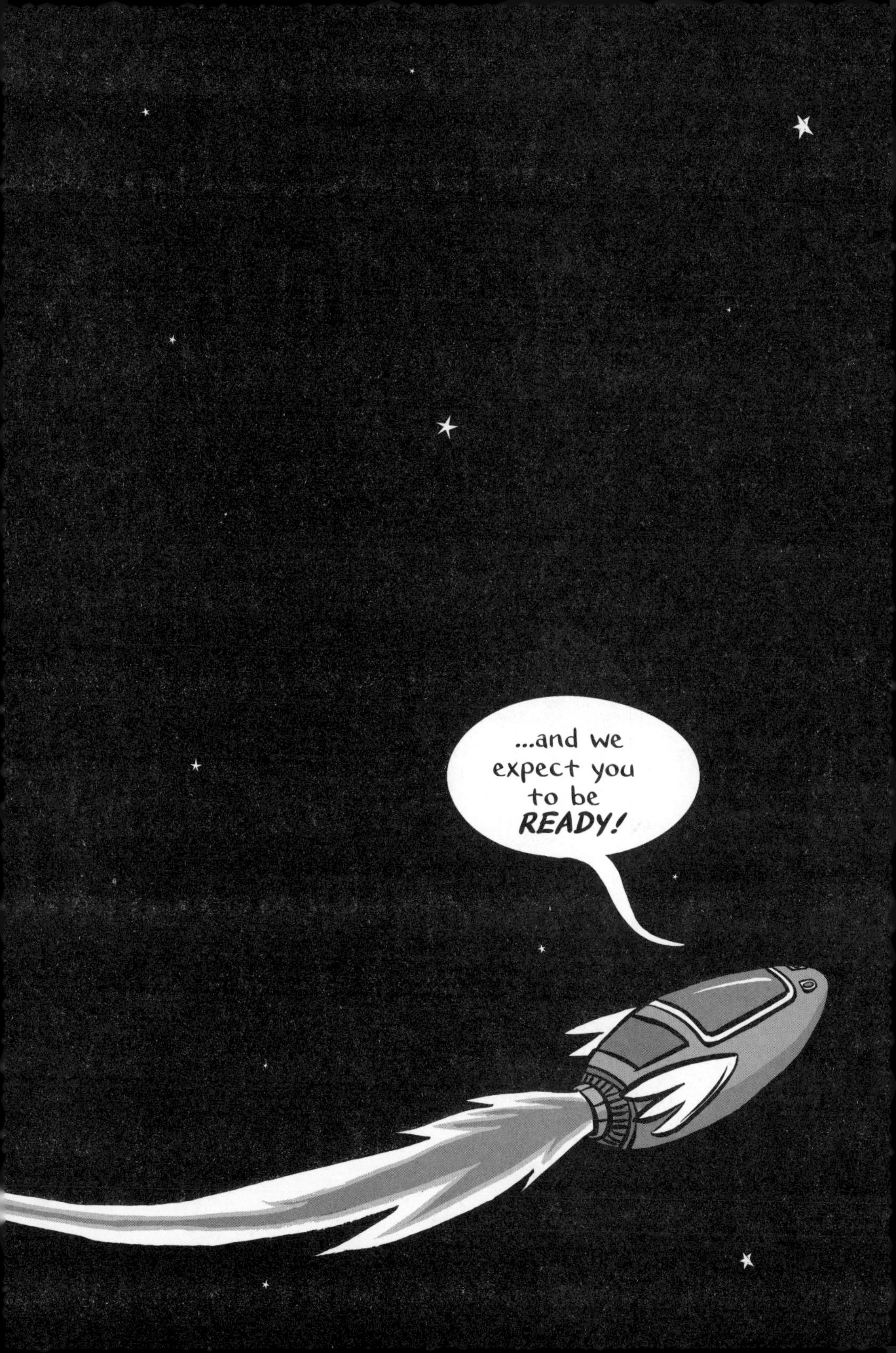
...and we expect you to be READY!

coming soon:

astronaut academy
Re-Entry

ROCK YOUR SOCKS OFF AT
The Sock Factory
(on the Original Moon)
GORDY PRESENTS...
A TRIPLE BILL OF HANGAR ROCK/ SYNTH/ TWEE-POP
FEATURING:
LEE OF THE STONE
PLAYING ALL HIS HITS!
Auto Gyro
Special holiday-themed set!
PLUS: Local Band
The SUPERCUTES!
ALL-AGES SHOW
$10 $8 W/FLYER
Doors open at 7PM
* Complimentary Apple Juice

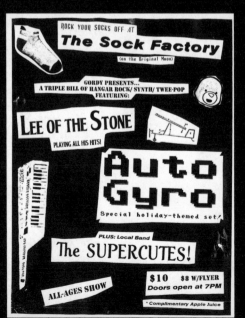

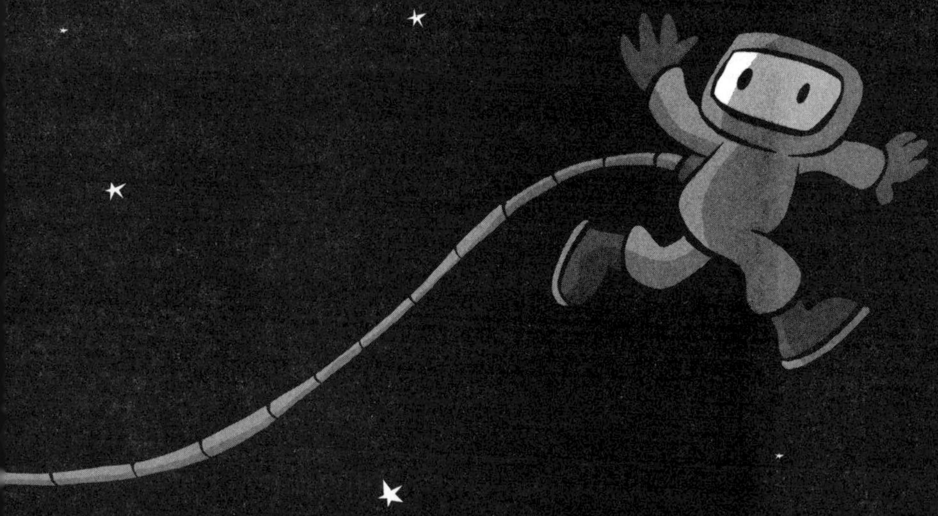

Gray color assists by Craig Arndt, Rosemary Travale, and Naseem Hrab. Additional crunch help from Jeremy Arambulo, Jordyn Bochon, John Green, Alisa Harris, Yuko Ota, Colleen MacIssac, Marion Vitus, and Dalton Webb.

Thanks to:

Raina Telgemeier, for making every day an awesome adventure. This book would not be possible without you.

My parents and family, for letting me get away with being a full-time cartoonist even when I was just a kid.

Chris Duffy, Laura Galen, and everyone at *Nickelodeon Magazine*, for eleven years of encouragement, inspiration, and camaraderie.

John Green, for being a great friend and comics-making teammate. Matt Hawkins, Zack Giallongo, Debbie Huey, and all my friends and fellow cartoonists who help make the world so much fun.

Everyone who was a fan and supporter of Astronaut Elementary! Tintin Pantoja, for asking me to contribute to her SVA manga anthology. Lea Hernandez and Joey Manley, for giving me an online home. Everyone at Lunchbox Funnies. Erin Houlihan, for designing the early mini-comics.

Judy Hansen, for taking even my silliest ideas so seriously.

Calista Brill, Mark Siegel, Colleen Venable, Gina Gagliano, and everyone else at First Second, for being amazing people to work with and welcoming me with such open arms.

First Second
New York & London

Text and illustrations copyright © 2011 by Dave Roman
Published by First Second
First Second is an imprint of Roaring Brook Press,
a division of Holtzbrinck Publishing Holdings Limited Partnership
175 Fifth Avenue, New York, New York 10010
All rights reserved

Distributed in the United Kingdom by Macmillan Children's Books,
a division of Pan Macmillan.

Cataloging-in-Publication Data is on file at the Library of Congress.
Paperback ISBN: 978-1-59643-620-6
Hardcover ISBN: 978-1-59643-756-2

First Second books are available for
special promotions and premiums.
For details, contact: Director of Special Markets,
Holtzbrinck Publishers.

Interior book design by
Colleen AF Venable and Lawrence Lee Derks III

FIRST
EDITION

First edition 2011

Printed in the United States of America
by LSC Communications, Harrisonburg, Virginia

Paperback 11 13 15 17 19 20 18 16 14 12
Hardcover 3 5 7 9 8 6 4 2

BY ART
WE LIVE